Hopeless

Hopeless

COLLEEN HOOVER

**SIMON &
SCHUSTER**

London · New York · Sydney · Toronto · New Delhi

First published in the USA by Colleen Hoover in 2012
This edition first published in the UK in 2013 by
Simon & Schuster UK Ltd

19

Simon & Schuster UK Ltd
1st Floor
222 Gray's Inn Road
London
WC1X 8HB

www.simonandschuster.co.uk

Simon & Schuster Australia, Sydney
Simon & Schuster India, New Delhi

A CIP catalogue copy for this book is available from the British Library.

Paperback ISBN: 978-1-47113-343-5
Ebook ISBN: 978-1-47113-266-7

For Vance.
Some fathers give you life. Some show you how to live it.
Thank you for showing me how.

I stand up and look down at the bed, holding my breath in fear of the sounds that are escalating from deep within my throat.

I will not cry.

I will not cry.

Slowly sinking to my knees, I place my hands on the edge of the bed and run my fingers over the yellow stars poured across the deep blue background of the comforter. I stare at the stars until they begin to blur from the tears that are clouding my vision.

I squeeze my eyes shut and bury my head into the bed, grabbing fistfuls of the blanket. My shoulders begin to shake as the sobs I've been trying to contain violently break out of me. With one swift movement, I stand up, scream, and rip the blanket off the bed, throwing it across the room.

I ball my fists and frantically look around for something else to throw. I grab the pillows off the bed and chuck them at the reflection in the mirror of the girl I no longer know. I watch as the girl in the mirror stares back at me, sobbing pathetically. The weakness in her tears infuriates me. We begin to run toward each other until our fists collide against the glass, smashing the mirror. I watch as she falls into a million shiny pieces onto the carpet.

I grip the edges of the dresser and push it sideways, let-

1

ting out another scream that has been pent up for way too long. When the dresser comes to rest on its back, I rip open the drawers and throw the contents across the room, spinning and throwing and kicking at everything in my path. I grab at the sheer blue curtain panels and yank them until the rod snaps and the curtains fall around me. I reach over to the boxes piled high in the corner, and without even knowing what's inside, I take the top one and throw it against the wall with as much force as my five-foot, three-inch frame can muster.

"I hate you!" I cry. "I hate you, I hate you, I hate you!"

I'm throwing whatever I can find in front of me at whatever else I can find in front of me. Every time I open my mouth to scream, I taste the salt from the tears that are streaming down my cheeks.

Holder's arms suddenly engulf me from behind and grip me so tightly I become immobile. I jerk and toss and scream some more until my actions are no longer thought out. They're just reactions.

"Stop," he says calmly against my ear, unwilling to release me. I hear him, but I pretend not to. Or I just don't care. I continue to struggle against his grasp but he only tightens his grip.

"Don't touch me!" I yell at the top of my lungs, clawing at his arms. Again, it doesn't faze him.

Don't touch me. Please, please, please.

The small voice echoes in my mind and I immediately become limp in his arms. I become weaker as my tears grow stronger, consuming me. I become nothing more than a vessel for the tears that won't stop shedding.

I am weak, and I'm letting *him* win.

Holder loosens his grip around me and places his hands on my shoulders, then turns me around to face him. I can't even look at him. I melt against his chest from exhaustion and defeat, taking in fistfuls of his shirt as I sob, my cheek pressed against his heart. He places his hand on the back of my head and lowers his mouth to my ear.

"Sky." His voice is steady and unaffected. "You need to leave. Now."

Saturday, August 25, 2012
11:50 p.m.

Two months earlier . . .

I'd like to think most of the decisions I've made throughout my seventeen years have been smart ones. Hopefully intelligence is measured by weight, and the few dumb decisions I've made will be outweighed by the intelligent ones. If that's the case, I'll need to make a shitload of smart decisions tomorrow because sneaking Grayson into my bedroom window for the third time this month weighs pretty heavily on the dumb side of the scale. However, the only accurate measurement of a decision's level of stupidity is time . . . so I guess I'll wait and see if I get caught before I break out the gavel.

Despite what this may look like, I am *not* a slut. Unless, of course, the definition of slut is based on the fact that I make out with lots of people, regardless of my lack of attraction to them. In that case, one might have grounds for debate.

"Hurry," Grayson mouths behind the closed window, obviously irritated at my lack of urgency.

I unlock the latch and slide the window up as quietly as possible. Karen may be an unconventional parent, but when it comes to boys sneaking through bedroom windows at midnight, she's your typical, disapproving mother.

4

"Quiet," I whisper. Grayson hoists himself up and throws one leg over the ledge, then climbs into my bedroom. It helps that the windows on this side of the house are barely three feet from the ground; it's almost like having my own door. In fact, Six and I have probably used our windows to go back and forth to each other's houses more than we've used actual doors. Karen has become so used to it, she doesn't even question my window being open the majority of the time.

Before I close the curtain, I glance to Six's bedroom window. She waves at me with one hand while pulling on Jaxon's arm with the other as he climbs into her bedroom. As soon as Jaxon is safely inside, he turns and sticks his head back out the window. "Meet me at your truck in an hour," he whispers loudly to Grayson. He closes Six's window and shuts her curtains.

Six and I have been joined at the hip since the day she moved in next door four years ago. Our bedroom windows are adjacent to each other, which has proven to be extremely convenient. Things started out innocently enough. When we were fourteen, I would sneak into her room at night and we would steal ice cream from the freezer and watch movies. When we were fifteen, we started sneaking boys in to eat ice cream and watch movies *with* us. By the time we were sixteen, the ice cream and movies took a backseat to the boys. Now, at seventeen, we don't even bother leaving our respective bedrooms until *after* the boys go home. That's when the ice cream and movies take precedence again.

Six goes through boyfriends like I go through flavors of ice cream. Right now her flavor of the month is Jaxon. Mine is Rocky Road. Grayson and Jaxon are best friends, which is how Grayson and I were initially thrown together. When Six's flavor of the month has a hot best friend, she eases him into my graces. Grayson is definitely hot. He's got an undeniably great body, perfectly sloppy hair, piercing dark eyes . . . the works. The majority of girls I know would feel privileged just to be in the same room as him.

It's too bad *I* don't.

I close the curtains and spin around to find Grayson inches from my face, ready to get the show started. He places his hands on my cheeks and flashes his panty-dropping grin. "Hey, beautiful." He doesn't give me a chance to respond before his lips greet mine in a sloppy introduction. He continues kissing me while slipping off his shoes. He slides them off effortlessly while we both walk toward my bed, mouths still meshed together. The ease with which he does both things simultaneously is impressive *and* disturbing. He slowly eases me back onto my bed. "Is your door locked?"

"Go double check," I say. He gives me a quick peck on the lips before he hops up to ensure the door is locked. I've made it thirteen years with Karen and have never been grounded; I don't want to give her any reason to start now. I'll be eighteen in a few weeks and even then, I doubt she'll change her parenting style as long as I'm under her roof.

Not that her parenting style is a negative one. It's just . . . very contradictory. She's been strict my whole life. We've never had access to the internet, cell phones, or even a television because she believes technology is the root of all evil in the world. Yet, she's extremely lenient in other regards. She allows me to go out with Six whenever I want, and as long as she knows where I am, I don't even really have a curfew. I've never pushed that one too far, though, so maybe I do have a curfew and I just don't realize it.

She doesn't care if I cuss, even though I rarely do. She even lets me have wine with dinner every now and then. She talks to me more like I'm her friend than her daughter (even though she adopted me thirteen years ago) and has somehow even warped me into being (almost) completely honest with her about everything that goes on in my life.

There is no middle ground with her. She's either extremely lenient or extremely strict. She's like a conservative liberal. Or a liberal conservative. Whatever she is, she's hard to figure out, which is why I stopped trying years ago.

The only thing we've ever really butted heads on was the issue of public school. She has homeschooled me my whole life (public school is another root of evil) and I've been begging to be enrolled since Six planted the idea in my head. I've been applying to colleges and feel like I'll have a better chance at getting into the schools that I want if I can add a few extracurricular activities to the applications. After months of incessant pleas from Six and me, Karen finally conceded and allowed me to enroll for my senior year. I could have enough credits to graduate from my home study program in just a couple of months, but a small part of me has always had a desire to experience life as a normal teenager.

Of course, if I had known then that Six would be leaving for a foreign exchange the same week as what was supposed to be our first day of senior year together, I never would have entertained the idea of public school. But I'm unforgivably stubborn and would rather stab myself in the meaty part of my hand with a fork than tell Karen I've changed my mind.

I've tried to avoid thinking about the fact that I won't have Six this year. I know how much she was hoping the exchange would work out, but the selfish part of me was really hoping it wouldn't. The idea of having to walk through those doors without her terrifies me. But I realize that our separation is inevitable and I can only go so long before I'm forced into the real world where other people besides Six and Karen live.

My lack of access to the real world has been replaced completely by books, and it can't be healthy to live in a land of happily-ever-afters. Reading has also introduced me to the (perhaps dramatized) horrors of high school and first days and cliques and mean girls. It doesn't help that, according to Six, I've already got a bit of a reputation just being associated with her. Six doesn't have the best track record for celibacy, and apparently some of the guys I've made out with don't have the best track record for secrecy. The combination should make for a pretty interesting first day of school.

Not that I care. I didn't enroll to make friends or impress anyone, so as long as my unwarranted reputation doesn't interfere with my ultimate goal, I'll get along just fine.

I hope.

Grayson walks back toward the bed after ensuring my door is locked, and he shoots me a seductive grin. "How about a little striptease?" He sways his hips and inches his shirt up, revealing his hard-earned set of abs. I'm beginning to notice he flashes them any chance he gets. He's pretty much your typical, self-absorbed bad boy.

I laugh when he twirls the shirt around his head and

throws it at me, then slides on top of me again. He slips his hand behind my neck, pulling my mouth back into position.

The first time Grayson snuck into my room was a little over a month ago, and he made it clear from the beginning that he wasn't looking for a relationship. I made it clear that I wasn't looking for *him*, so naturally we hit it off right away. Of course, he'll be one of the few people I know at school, so I'm worried it might mess up the good thing we've got going—which is absolutely nothing.

He's been here less than three minutes and he's already got his hand up my shirt. I think it's safe to say he's not here for my stimulating conversation. His lips move from my mouth in favor of my neck, so I use the moment of respite to inhale deeply and try again to feel something.

Anything.

I fix my eyes on the plastic glow-in-the-dark stars adhered to the ceiling above my bed, vaguely aware of the lips that have inched their way to my chest. There are seventy-six of them. Stars, that is. I know this because for the last few weeks I've had ample time to count them while I've been in this same predicament. Me, lying unnoticeably unresponsive, while Grayson explores my face and neck, and sometimes my chest, with his curious, overexcited lips.

Why, if I'm not into this, do I let him do it?

I've never had any emotional connection to the guys I make out with. Or rather, the guys that make out with *me*. It's unfortunately mostly one-sided. I've only had one guy come close to provoking a physical or emotional response from me once, and that turned out to be a self-induced delusion. His name was Matt and we ended up dating for less than a month before his idiosyncrasies got the best of me.

Like how he refused to drink bottled water unless it was through a straw. Or the way his nostrils flared right before he leaned in to kiss me. Or the way he said, "I love you," after only three weeks of declaring ourselves exclusive.

Yeah. That last one was the kicker. Buh-bye Matty boy.

Six and I have analyzed my lack of physical response to guys many times in the past. For a while she suspected I might be gay. After a very brief and awkward "theory-testing" kiss between us when we were sixteen, we both concluded that wasn't the case. It's not that I don't enjoy making out with guys. I do enjoy it—otherwise, I wouldn't do it. I just don't enjoy it for the same reasons as other girls. I've never been swept off my feet. I don't get butterflies. In fact, the whole idea of being swooned by anyone is foreign to me. The real reason I enjoy making out with guys is simply that it makes me feel completely and comfortably numb. It's situations like the one I'm in right now with Grayson when it's nice for my mind to shut down. It just completely stops, and I like that feeling.

My eyes are focused on the seventeen stars in the upper right quadrant of the cluster on my ceiling, when I suddenly snap back to reality. Grayson's hands have ventured further than I've allowed them to in the past and I quickly become aware of the fact that he has unbuttoned my jeans and his fingers are working their way around the cotton edge of my panties.

"No, Grayson," I whisper, pushing his hand away.

He pulls his hand back and groans, then presses his forehead into my pillow. "Come on, Sky." He's breathing heavily against my neck. He adjusts his weight to his right arm and looks down at me, attempting to play me with his smile.

Did I mention I'm immune to his panty-dropping grin?

"How much longer are you gonna keep this up?" He slides his hand over my stomach and inches his fingertips into my jeans again.

My skin crawls. "Keep *what* up?" I attempt to ease out from under him.

He pushes up on his hands and looks down at me like I'm clueless. "This 'good girl' act you've been trying to put on. I'm over it, Sky. Let's just do this already."

This brings me back to the fact that, contrary to popular belief, I am *not* a slut. I've never had sex with any of the boys I've made out with, including the currently pouting Grayson. I'm aware that my lack of sexual response would probably make it easier on an emotional level to have sex with random people. However, I'm also aware that it might be the very reason I *shouldn't* have sex. I know that once I cross that line, the rumors about me will no longer be rumors. They'll all be fact. The last thing I want is for the things people say about me to be validated. I guess I can chalk my almost eighteen years of virginity up to sheer stubbornness.

For the first time in the ten minutes he's been here, I notice the smell of alcohol reeking from him. "You're drunk." I push against his chest. "I told you not to come over here drunk again." He rolls off me and I stand up to button my pants and pull my shirt back into place. I'm relieved he's drunk. I'm beyond ready for him to leave.

He sits up on the edge of the bed and grabs my waist, pulling me toward him. He wraps his arms around me and rests his head against my stomach. "I'm sorry," he says. "It's just that I want you so bad I don't think I can take coming over here again if you don't let me have you." He lowers his hands and cups my butt, then presses his lips against the area of skin where my shirt meets my jeans.

"Then don't come over here." I roll my eyes and back away from him, then head to the window. When I pull the curtain back, Jaxon is already making his way out of Six's window. Somehow we both managed to condense this hour-long visit into ten minutes. I glance at Six and she gives me the all-knowing "time for a new flavor" look.

She follows Jaxon out of her window and walks over to me. "Is Grayson drunk, too?"

I nod. "Strike three." I turn and look at Grayson, who's lying back on the bed, ignorant of the fact that he's no longer welcome. I walk over to the bed and pick his shirt up, tossing it at his face. "Leave," I say. He looks up at me and cocks an eyebrow, then begrudgingly slides off the bed when he sees I'm not making a joke. He slips his shoes back on, pouting like a four-year-old. I step aside to let him out.

Six waits until Grayson has cleared the window, then she climbs inside when one of the guys mumbles the word "whores." Once inside, Six rolls her eyes and turns around to stick her head out.

"Funny how we're whores because you *didn't* get laid. Assholes." She shuts the window and walks over to the bed, plopping down on it and crossing her hands behind her head. "And another one bites the dust."

I laugh, but my laugh is cut short by a loud bang on my bedroom door. I immediately go unlock it, then step aside, preparing for Karen to barge in. Her motherly instincts don't let me down. She looks around the room frantically until she eyes Six on the bed.

"Dammit," she says, spinning around to face me. She puts her hands on her hips and frowns. "I could have sworn I heard boys in here."

I walk over to the bed and attempt to hide the sheer panic coursing throughout my body. "And you seem disappointed *because* . . ." I absolutely don't understand her reaction to things sometimes. Like I said before . . . *contradictory*.

"You turn eighteen in a month. I'm running out of time to ground you for the first time ever. You need to start screwing up a little more, kid."

I breathe a sigh of relief, seeing she's only kidding. I almost feel guilty that she doesn't actually suspect her daughter was being felt up five minutes earlier in this very room. My heart is pounding against my chest so incredibly loud, I'm afraid she might hear it.

"Karen?" Six says from behind us. "If it makes you feel better, two hotties just made out with us, but we kicked them out right before you walked in because they were drunk."

My jaw drops and I spin around to shoot Six a look that I'm hoping will let her know that sarcasm isn't at all funny when it's the *truth*.

Karen laughs. "Well, maybe tomorrow night you'll get some cute *sober* boys."

I don't think I have to worry about Karen hearing my heartbeat anymore, because it just completely stopped.

"Sober boys, huh? I think I can arrange that," Six says, winking at me.

"Are you staying the night?" Karen says to Six as she makes her way back to the bedroom door.

Six shrugs her shoulders. "I think we'll stay at my house

tonight. It's my last week in my own bed for six months. Plus, I've got Channing Tatum on the flat-screen."

I glance back at Karen and see it starting.

"Don't, Mom." I begin walking toward her, but I can see the mist forming in her eyes. "No, no, no." By the time I reach her, it's too late. She's bawling. If there's one thing I can't stand, it's crying. Not because it makes me emotional, but because it annoys the hell out of me. And it's awkward.

"Just one more," she says, rushing toward Six. She's already hugged her no less than ten times today. I almost think she's sadder than I am that Six is leaving in a few days. Six obliges her request for the eleventh hug and winks at me over Karen's shoulder. I practically have to pry them apart, just so Karen will get out of my room.

She walks back to the door and turns around one last time. "I hope you meet a hot Italian boy," she says to Six.

"I better meet more than just one," Six deadpans.

When the door closes behind Karen, I spin around and jump on the bed, then punch Six in the arm. "You're such a *bitch*," I say. "That wasn't funny. I thought I got caught."

She laughs and grabs my hand, then stands up. "Come. I've got Rocky Road."

She doesn't have to ask twice.

Monday, August 27, 2012
7:15 a.m.

I debated whether to run this morning but I ended up sleeping in, instead. I run every day except Sunday, but it seems wrong having to get up extra early today. Being the first day of school is enough torture in itself, so I decide to put off my run until after school.

Luckily, I've had my own car for about a year now, so I don't have to rely on anyone other than myself to get me to school on time. Not only do I get here on time, I get here forty-five minutes early. I'm the third car in the parking lot, so at least I get a good spot.

I use the extra time to check out the athletic facilities next to the parking lot. If I'm going to be trying out for the track team, I should at least know where to go. Besides, I can't just sit in my car for the next half hour and count down the minutes.

When I reach the track, there's a guy across the field running laps, so I cut right and walk up the bleachers. I take a seat at the very top and take in my new surroundings. From up here, I can see the whole school laid out in front of me. It doesn't look nearly as big or intimidating as I've been imagining. Six made me a hand-drawn map and even wrote a few pointers down, so I pull the paper out of my backpack and look at it for the first time. I think she's trying to over-compensate because she feels bad for abandoning me.

15

I look at the school grounds, then back at the map. It looks easy enough. Classrooms in the building to the right. Lunchroom on the left. Track and field behind the gym. There is a long list of her pointers, so I begin reading them.

—*Never use the restroom next to the science lab. Ever. Not ever.*

—*Only wear your backpack across one shoulder. Never double-arm it, it's lame.*

—*Always check the date on the milk.*

—*Befriend Stewart, the maintenance guy. It's good to have him on your side.*

—*The cafeteria. Avoid it at all costs, but if the weather is bad, just pretend you know what you're doing when you walk inside. They can smell fear.*

—*If you get Mr. Declare for math, sit in the back and don't make eye contact. He loves high school girls, if you know what I mean. Or, better yet, sit in the front. It'll be an easy A.*

The list goes on, but I can't read anymore right now. I'm still stuck on "*they can smell fear.*" It's times like these that I wish I had a cell phone, because I would call Six right now and demand an explanation. I fold the paper up and put it back in my bag, then focus my attention on the lone runner. He's seated on the track with his back turned to me, stretching. I don't know if he's a student or a coach, but if Grayson saw this guy without a shirt, he'd probably become a lot more modest about being so quick to flash his own abs.

The guy stands up and walks toward the bleachers,

never looking up at me. He exits the gate and walks to one of the cars in the parking lot. He opens his door and grabs a shirt off the front seat, then pulls it on over his head. He hops in the car and pulls away, just as the parking lot begins to fill up. And it's filling up fast.

Oh, God.

I grab my backpack and purposefully pull both arms through it, then descend the stairs that lead straight to Hell.

Did I say Hell? Because that was putting it mildly. Public school is everything I was afraid it would be and worse. The classes aren't so bad, but I had to (out of pure necessity and unfamiliarity) use the restroom next to the science lab, and although I survived, I'll be scarred for life. A simple side note from Six informing me that it's used as more of a brothel than an actual restroom would have sufficed.

It's fourth period now and I've heard the words "slut" and "whore" whispered not so subtly by almost every girl I've passed in the hallways. And speaking of not-so-subtle, the heap of dollar bills that just fell out of my locker, along with a note, were a good indicator that I may not be very welcome. The note was signed by the principal, but I find that hard to believe based on the fact that "your" was spelled "you're," and the note said, *"Sorry you're locker didn't come with a pole, slut."*

I stare at the note in my hands with a tight-lipped smile, shamefully accepting my self-inflicted fate that will be the next two semesters. I seriously thought people only acted this way in books, but I'm witnessing firsthand that idiots actually exist. I'm also hoping most of the pranks being played at my expense are going to be just like the stripper-cash prank I'm experiencing right now. What idiot gives away money as an insult? I'm guessing a rich one. Or rich *ones*.

I'm sure the clique of giggling girls behind me that are scantily, yet expensively clad, are expecting my reaction to be to drop my things and run to the nearest restroom crying. There are only three issues with their expectations.

1. *I don't cry. Ever.*
2. *I've been to that restroom and I'll never go back.*
3. *I like money. Who would run from that?*

I set my backpack on the floor of the hallway and pick the money up. There are at least twenty one-dollar bills scattered on the floor, and more than ten still in my locker. I scoop those up as well and shove it all into my backpack. I switch books and shut my locker, then slide my backpack on both shoulders and smile.

"Tell your daddies I said thank you." I walk past the clique of girls (that are no longer giggling) and ignore their glares.

It's lunchtime, and looking at the amount of rain flooding the courtyard, it's obvious that Karma has retaliated with shitty weather. Who she's retaliating against is still up in the air.

I can do this.

I place my hands on the doors to the cafeteria and open them, half-expecting to be greeted by fire and brimstone.

I step through the doorway and it's not fire and brimstone that I'm met with. It's a decibel level of noise unlike anything my ears have ever been subjected to. It's almost as if every single person in this entire cafeteria is trying to talk louder than every other person in this entire cafeteria. I've just enrolled in a school of nothing but one-uppers.

I do my best to feign confidence, not wanting to attract unwanted attention from anyone. Guys, cliques, outcasts, *or* Grayson. I make it halfway to the food line unscathed, when someone slips his arm through mine and pulls me along behind him.

"I've been waiting for you," he says. I don't even get a good look at his face before he's guiding me across the cafeteria, weaving in and out of tables. I would object to this sudden disruption, but it's the most exciting thing that's happened to me all day. He slips his arm from mine and grabs my hand, pulling me faster along behind him. I stop resisting and go with the flow.

From the looks of the back of him, he's got style, as strange as that style may be. He's wearing a flannel shirt that's edged with the exact same shade of hot pink as his shoes. His pants are black and tight and very figure flattering . . . if he were a girl. Instead, the pants just accentuate the frailty of his frame. His dark brown hair is cropped short on the sides and is a little longer on top. His eyes are . . . staring at me. I realize we've come to a stop and he's no longer holding my hand.

"If it isn't the whore of Babylon." He grins at me. Despite the words that just came out of his mouth, his expression is contrastingly endearing. He takes a seat at the table and flicks his hand like he wants me to do the same. There are two trays in front of him, but only one *him*. He scoots one of the trays of food toward the empty spot in front of me. "Sit. We have an alliance to discuss."

I don't sit. I don't do anything for several seconds as I contemplate the situation before me. I have no idea who this kid is, yet he acts like he was expecting me. Let's not overlook the fact that he just called me a whore. And from the looks of it, he bought me . . . lunch? I glance at him sideways, attempting to figure him out, when the backpack in the seat next to him catches my eye.

"You like to read?" I ask, pointing at the book peering out of the top of his backpack. It's not a textbook. It's an actual book-book. Something I thought was lost on this generation of internet fiends. I reach over and pull the book out of his backpack and take a seat across from him. "What genre is it? And please don't say sci-fi."

He leans back in his seat and grins like he just won something. Hell, maybe he did. I'm sitting here, aren't I?

"Should it matter what genre it is if the book is good?" he says.

I flip through the pages, unable to tell if it's a romance or not. I'm a sucker for romances, and based on the look of the guy across from me, he might be, too.

"Is it?" I ask, flipping through it. "Good?"

"Yes. Keep it. I just finished it during computer lab."

I look up at him and he's still basking in his glow of victory. I put the book in my backpack, then lean forward and inspect my tray. The first thing I do is check the date on the milk. It's good.

"What if I was a vegetarian?" I ask, looking at the chicken breast in the salad.

"So eat around it," he retorts.

I grab my fork and stab a piece of the chicken, then bring it to my mouth. "Well you're lucky, because I'm not."

He smiles, then picks up his own fork and begins eating.

"Whom are we forming an alliance against?" I'm curious as to why I've been singled out.

He glances around him and raises his hand in the air, twirling it in all directions. "Idiots. Jocks. Bigots. Bitches." He brings his hand down and I notice that his nails are all painted black. He sees me observing his nails and he looks down at them and pouts. "I went with black because it best depicts my mood today. Maybe after you agree to join me on my quest, I'll switch to something a bit more cheerful. Perhaps yellow."

I shake my head. "I hate yellow. Stick with black, it matches your heart."

He laughs. It's a genuine, pure laugh that makes me smile. I like . . . this kid whose name I don't even know.

"What's your name?" I ask.

"Breckin. And you're Sky. At least I'm hoping you are. I guess I could have confirmed your identity before I spilled to you the details of my evil, sadistic plan to take over the school with our two-person alliance."

"I am Sky. And you really have nothing to worry about, seeing as how you really haven't shared any details about your evil plan yet. I am curious though, how you know who I am. I know four or five guys at this school and I've made out with every one of them. You aren't one of them, so what gives?"

For a split second, I see a flash of what looks like pity in his eyes. He's lucky it was just a flash, though.

Breckin shrugs. "I'm new here. And if you haven't deduced from my impeccable fashion sense, I think it's safe to say that I'm . . ." he leans forward and cups his hand to his mouth in secrecy. "Mormon," he whispers.

I laugh. "And here I was thinking you were about to say *gay*."

"That, too," he says with a flick of his wrist. He folds his hands under his chin and leans forward a couple of inches. "In all seriousness, Sky. I noticed you in class today and it's obvious you're new here, too. And after seeing the stripper money fall out of your locker before fourth period, then witnessing your nonreaction to it, I knew we were meant to be. Also, I figured if we teamed up, we might prevent at least two unnecessary teenage suicides this year. So, what do you say? Want to be my very bestest friend ever in the whole wide world?"

I laugh. How could I not laugh at that? "Sure. But if the book sucks, we're re-evaluating the friendship."

Turns out, Breckin was my saving grace today . . . and he really *is* Mormon. We have a lot in common, and even more out of common, which makes him that much more appealing. He was adopted as well, but has a close relationship with his birth family. Breckin has two brothers who aren't adopted, and who also aren't gay, so his parents assume his gayness (his word, not mine) has to do with the fact that he doesn't share a bloodline with them. He says they're hoping it fades with more prayer and high school graduation, but he insists that it's only going to flourish.

His dream is to one day be a famous Broadway star, but he says he lacks the ability to sing or act, so he's scaling down his dream and applying to business school instead. I told him I wanted to major in creative writing and sit around in yoga pants and do nothing but write books and eat ice cream every day. He asked what genre I wanted to write and I replied, "It doesn't matter, so long as it's good, right?" I think that comment sealed our fate.

Now I'm on my way home, deciding whether or not to go fill Six in on the bittersweet happenings of day one, or go grocery shopping in order to get my caffeine fix before my daily run.

The caffeine wins, despite the fact that my affection for Six is slightly greater.

My minimal portion of familial contribution is the weekly grocery shopping. Everything in our house is sugar-free, carb-free, and *taste*-free, thanks to Karen's unconventional vegan way of life, so I actually prefer doing the grocery shopping. I grab a six-pack of soda and the biggest bag of bite-size Snickers I can find and throw them in the cart. I have a nice hiding spot for my secret stash in my bedroom. Most teenagers are stashing away cigarettes and weed—I stash away sugar.

When I reach the checkout, I recognize the girl ringing me up is in my second-period English class. I'm pretty sure her name is Shayna, but her nametag reads *Shayla*. Shayna/Shayla is everything I wish I were. Tall, voluptuous, and sun-kissed blonde. I can maybe pull off five-three on a good day and my flat brown hair could use a trim—maybe even some highlights. They would be a bitch to maintain considering the amount of hair that I have. It falls about six inches past my shoulders, but I keep it pulled up most of the time due to the southern humidity.

"Aren't you in my Science class?" Shayna/Shayla asks.

"English," I correct her.

She shoots me a condescending look. "I *did* speak English," she says defensively. "I said, 'aren't you in my Science class?'"

Oh, holy hell. Maybe I don't want to be *that* blonde.

"No," I say. "I meant English as in 'I'm not in your *Science* class, I'm in your *English* class.'"

She looks at me blankly for a second, then laughs. "Oh." Realization dawns on her face. She eyes the screen in front of her and reads out my total. I slip my hand in my back pocket and retrieve the credit card, hoping to hurry and excuse myself from what I fear is about to become a less than stellar conversation.

"Oh, dear *God*," she says quietly. "Look who's back."

I glance up at her and she's staring at someone behind me in the other checkout line.

No, let me correct that. She's *salivating* over someone behind me in the other checkout line.

"Hey, Holder," she says seductively toward him, flashing her full-lipped smile.

Did she just bat her eyelashes? Yep. I'm pretty sure she just batted her eyelashes. I honestly thought they only did that in cartoons.

I glance back to see who this *Holder* character is that has somehow managed to wash away any semblance of self-respect Shayna/Shayla might have had. The guy looks up at her and nods an acknowledgment, seemingly uninterested.

"Hey . . ." He squints his eyes at her nametag. "*Shayla*." He turns his attention back to his cashier.

Is he ignoring her? One of the prettiest girls in school practically gives him an open invitation and he acts like it's an inconvenience? Is he even *human*? This isn't how the guys I know are supposed to react.

She huffs. "It's *Shayna*," she says, annoyed that he didn't know her name. I turn back toward Shayna and swipe my credit card through the machine.

"Sorry," he says to her. "But you do realize your nametag says *Shayla*, right?"

She looks down at her chest and flips her nametag up so she can read it. "Huh," she says, narrowing her eyebrows as if she's deep in thought. I doubt it's that deep, though.

"When did you get back?" she asks Holder, ignoring me

completely. I just swiped my card and I'm almost positive she should be doing something on her end, but she's too busy planning her wedding with this guy to remember she has a customer.

"Last week." His response is curt.

"So are they gonna let you come back to school?" she asks.

I can hear him sigh from where I'm standing.

"Doesn't matter," he says flatly. "Not going back."

This last statement of his immediately gives Shayna/Shayla cold feet. She rolls her eyes and turns her attention back to me. "It's a shame when a body like that doesn't come with any brains," she whispers.

The irony in her statement isn't lost on me.

When she finally starts punching numbers on the register to complete the transaction, I use her distraction as an opportunity to glance behind me again. I'm curious to get another look at the guy who seemed to be irritated by the leggy blonde. He's looking down into his wallet, laughing at something his cashier said. As soon as I lay eyes on him, I immediately notice three things:

1. *His amazingly perfect white teeth hidden behind that seductively crooked grin.*

2. *The dimples that form in the crevices between the corners of his lips and cheeks when he smiles.*

3. *I'm pretty sure I'm having a hot flash.*

Or I have butterflies.

Or maybe I'm coming down with a stomach virus.

The feeling is so foreign; I'm not sure *what* it is. I can't say what is so different about him that would prompt my first-ever normal biological response to another person. However, I'm not sure I've ever seen anyone so incredibly like *him* before. He's beautiful. Not beautiful in the pretty-boy sense. Or even in the tough-guy sense. Just a perfect mixture of in-between. Not too big, but not at all small. Not too rough, not too perfect. He's wearing jeans and a white T-shirt, nothing special. His hair doesn't look like it's even been brushed today and could probably use a good trim, just like mine. It's just long enough in the front that he has to move it out of his eyes when he looks up and catches me full-on staring.

Shit.

I would normally pull my gaze away as soon as direct eye contact is made, but there's something odd about the way he reacts when he looks at me that keeps my focus glued to his. His smile immediately fades and he cocks his head. An inquisitive look enters his eyes and he slowly shakes his head, either in disbelief or . . . *disgust*? I can't put my finger on it, but it's certainly not a pleasant reaction. I glance around, hoping I'm not the recipient of his displeasure. When I turn back to look at him, he's still staring.

At *me*.

I'm disturbed, to say the least, so I quickly turn around and face Shayla again. Or Shayna. Whatever the hell her name is. I need to regain my bearings. Somehow, in the course of sixty seconds, this guy has managed to swoon me, then terrify the hell out of me. The mixed reaction is not good for my caffeine-deprived body. I'd much rather he regard me with the same indifference he showed toward

Shayna/Shayla, than to look at me like that again. I grab my receipt from what's-her-face and slip it into my pocket.

"Hey." His voice is deep and demanding and immediately causes my breathing to halt. I don't know if he's referring to what's-her-face or me, so I slip my hands through the handles of the grocery sacks, hoping to make it to my car before he finishes checking out.

"I think he's talking to you," she says. I grab the last of the sacks and ignore her, walking as fast as I can toward the exit.

Once I reach my car, I let out a huge breath as I open the back door to put the groceries inside. *What the hell is wrong with me?* A good-looking guy tries to get my attention and I *run*? I'm not uncomfortable around guys. I'm confident to a fault, even. The one time in my life I might actually feel what could possibly be an attraction for someone, and I run.

Six is going to kill me.

But that *look*. There was something so disturbing about the way he looked at me. It was uncomfortable, embarrassing, and somehow flattering all at once. I'm not used to having these sorts of reactions at all, much less more than one at a time.

"Hey."

I freeze. His voice is without a doubt directed at me now.

I still can't distinguish between butterflies or a stomach virus, but either way I'm not fond of the way that voice penetrates right to the pit of my stomach. I stiffen and slowly turn around, all of a sudden aware that I'm nowhere near as confident as my past would lead me to believe.

He's holding two sacks down at his side with one hand

while he rubs the back of his neck with his other hand. I'm really wishing the weather were still shitty and rainy so he wouldn't be standing here right now. He rests his eyes on mine and the look of contempt from inside the store is now replaced with a crooked grin that seems a bit forced in our current predicament. Now that I have a closer look at him, it's apparent the stomach virus isn't the root of the sudden stomach issues at all.

It's simply *him*.

Everything about him, from his tousled dark hair, to his stark blue eyes, to that . . . *dimple*, to his thick arms that I just want to reach out and touch.

Touch? Really, Sky? Get ahold of yourself!

Everything about him causes my lungs to fail and my heart to go into overdrive. I have a feeling if he smiles at me like Grayson tries to smile at me, my panties will be on the ground in record time.

As soon as my eyes leave his physique long enough for us to make eye contact again, he releases the tight grip he has on his neck and switches the sacks to his left hand.

"I'm Holder," he says, extending his hand out to me.

I look down at his hand, then take a step back without shaking it. This whole situation is entirely too awkward for me to trust him with this innocent introduction. Maybe if he hadn't pierced me with his intense glare in the store, I would be more susceptible to his physical perfection.

"What do you want?" I'm careful to look at him with suspicion rather than awe.

His dimple reappears with his hasty laugh and he shakes his head, then looks away again. "Um," he says with a nervous stutter that doesn't match his confident persona in the least. His eyes dart around the parking lot like he's looking for an escape, and he sighs before locking eyes with me again. His multitude of reactions confuses the hell out of me. He seems close to disgusted by my presence one minute, to practically running me down the next. I'm usually pretty good at reading people, but if I had to make an assumption about Holder based on the last two minutes alone, I'd have to say he suffers from split-personality disorder. His sudden shifts between flippant and intense are unnerving.

"This might sound lame," he says. "But you look really familiar. Do you mind if I ask what your name is?"

Disappointment sets in as soon as the pickup line escapes his lips. He's one of *those* guys. You know. The incredibly gorgeous guys who can have anyone, anytime, anywhere, and they know it? The guys that, all they have to do is flash a crooked smile or a dimple and ask a girl her name and she melts until she's on her knees in front of him? The guys who spend their Saturday nights climbing through windows?

I'm highly disappointed. I roll my eyes and reach behind me, pulling on the door handle to my car. "I've got a boyfriend," I lie. I spin around and open the door, then climb inside. When I reach to pull the door shut, I'm met with resistance when it refuses to budge. I look up to see his hand grasping the top of the car door, holding it open. There's a hard desperation in his eyes that sends chills down my arms.

He looks at me and I get *chills*? Who the hell *am* I?

"Your name. That's all I want."

I debate whether I should explain to him that my name isn't going to help him in his stalking endeavors. I'm more than likely the only seventeen-year-old left in America without an online presence. With my grip still on the door handle, I discharge a warning shot with my glare. "Do you mind?" I say sharply, my eyes darting to the hand that's preventing me from shutting my door. My eyes trail from his hand to the tattoo written in small script across his forearm.

Hopeless

I can't help but laugh internally. I am obviously the target of Karma's retaliation today. I'm finally introduced to the one guy that I find attractive, and he's a high school dropout with the word "hopeless" tattooed on himself.

Now I'm irritated. I pull on the door one more time, but he doesn't budge.

"Your name. *Please*."

The desperate look in his eyes when he says *please* prompts a surprisingly sympathetic reaction from me, way out of left field.

"Sky," I say abruptly, suddenly feeling compassion for the pain that is clearly masked behind those blue eyes of his. The ease with which I give in to his request based on one look leaves me disappointed in myself. I let go of the door and crank my car.

"Sky," he repeats to himself. He ponders this for a second, then shakes his head like I got the answer to his question wrong. "Are you sure?" He cocks his head at me.

Am I *sure*? Does he think I'm Shayna/Shayla and don't even know my own name? I roll my eyes and shift in my seat, pulling my ID from my pocket. I hold it up to his face.

"Pretty sure I know my own name." I begin to pull the

ID back when he releases my door and grabs the ID out of my hand, bringing it in closer for inspection. He eyes it for a few seconds, then flicks it over in his fingers and hands it back to me.

"Sorry." He takes a step away from my car. "My mistake."

His expression is glossed over with hardness now and he watches me as I put my ID back into my pocket. I stare at him for a second, waiting for something more, but he just works his jaw back and forth while I put my seatbelt on.

He's giving up on asking me out that easily? Seriously? I put my fingers on the door handle, expecting him to hold the door open again in order to spit out another lame pickup line. When that doesn't happen and he steps back even farther as I shut my door, eeriness consumes me. If he really didn't follow me out here to ask me out, what the hell was this all about?

He runs his hand through his hair and mutters to himself, but I can't hear what he says through the closed window. I throw the car in reverse and keep my eyes on him as I back out of the parking lot. He remains motionless, staring at me the entire time I pull away. When I'm heading in the opposite direction, I adjust the rearview mirror to get a last glance at him before exiting the parking lot. I watch as he turns to walk away, smashing his fist into the hood of a car.

Good call, Sky. He's got a temper.

Monday, August 27, 2012
4:47 p.m.

After the groceries are put away, I grab a handful of chocolate from my stash and shove it in my pocket, then crawl out my window. I push Six's window up and pull myself in. It's almost five o'clock in the afternoon and she's asleep, so I tiptoe to her side of the bed and kneel down. She's got her facemask on and her dirty blonde hair is matted to her cheek, thanks to the amount of drool she produces while she sleeps. I inch in as close as I can to her face and scream her name.

"SIX! WAKE UP!"

She jerks herself up with such force that I don't have time to move out of her way. Her flailing elbow crashes into my eye and I fall back. I immediately cover my throbbing eye with my hand and sprawl out on the floor of her bedroom. I look up at her out of my good eye, and she's sitting up in the bed holding on to her head, scowling at me. "You're such a bitch," she groans. She throws her covers off and gets out of bed, then heads straight for the bathroom.

"I think you gave me a black eye," I moan.

She leaves the bathroom door open and sits down on the toilet. "Good. You deserve it." She grabs the toilet paper and kicks the bathroom door shut with her foot. "You better have something good to tell me for waking me up. I was up all night packing."

Six has never been a morning person, and from the

looks of it, she's not an afternoon person, either. In all honesty, she's also not a night person. If I had to guess when her most pleasant time of day occurs, it's probably while she sleeps, which may be why she hates to wake up so much.

Six's sense of humor and straightforward personality are huge factors in why we get along so well. Peppy, fake girls annoy the hell out of me. I don't know that *pep* is even in Six's vocabulary. She's one black wardrobe away from being your typical, broody teenager. And fake? She's as straight shooting as they come, whether you want her to be or not. There isn't a fake thing about Six, other than her name.

When she was fourteen and her parents told her they were moving to Texas from Maine, she rebelled by refusing to respond to her name. Her real name is Seven Marie, so she would only answer to *Six* just to spite her parents for making her move. They still call her Seven, but everyone else calls her Six. Just goes to show she's as stubborn as I am, which is one of the many reasons we're best friends.

"I think you'll be happy I woke you up." I pull myself up from the floor and onto her bed. "Something monumental happened today."

Six opens the bathroom door and walks back to her bed. She lies down next to me and pulls the covers up over her head. She rolls away from me, fluffing her pillow with her hand until she gets comfortable. "Let me guess . . . Karen got cable?"

I roll onto my side and scoot closer to her, wrapping my arm around her. I put my head on her pillow and spoon her. "Guess again."

"You met someone at school today and now you're pregnant and getting married and I can't be a bridesmaid at your wedding because I'll be all the way across the damn world?"

"Close, but nope." I drum my fingers on her shoulder.

"Then *what*?" she says, irritated.

I roll over onto my back and let out a deep sigh. "I saw a guy at the store after school, and holy shit, Six. He was beautiful. Scary, but beautiful."

Six immediately rolls over, managing to send an elbow straight into the same eye that she assaulted a few minutes ago. "What?!" she says loudly, ignoring the fact that I'm holding my eye and groaning again. She sits up on the bed and pulls my hand away from my face. "What?!" she yells again. "Seriously?"

I stay on my back and attempt to force the pain from my throbbing eye into the back of my mind. "I know. As soon as I looked at him it was like my entire body just melted to the floor. He was . . . wow."

"Did you talk to him? Did you get his number? Did he ask you out?"

I've never seen Six so animated before. She's being a little too giddy, and I'm not sure that I like it.

"*Jesus*, Six. Simmer down."

She looks down at me and frowns. "Sky, I've been worried about you for four years, thinking this would never happen. I would be fine if you were gay. I would be fine if you only liked skinny, short, geeky guys. I would even be fine if you were only attracted to really old, wrinkly men with even wrinklier penises. What I haven't been fine with is the thought of you never being able to experience lust." She falls back onto the bed, smiling. "Lust is the best of all the deadly sins."

I laugh and shake my head. "I beg to differ. Lust sucks. I think you've played it up all these years. My vote is still with gluttony." With that, I pull a piece of chocolate out of my pocket and pop it into my mouth.

"I need details," she says.

I scoot up on the bed until my back meets the head-board. "I don't know how to describe it. When I looked at him, I never wanted to stop. I could have stared at him all day. But then when he looked back at me, it freaked me out. He looked at me like he was pissed off that I even noticed him. Then when he followed me to my car and demanded to know my name, it was like he was mad at me for it. Like I was inconveniencing him. I went from wanting to lick his dimples to wanting to get the hell *away* from him."

"He followed you? To your car?" she asks skeptically. I nod and give her every last detail of my trip to the grocery store, all the way up to the point where he smashed his fist into the car next to him.

"God, that's so bizarre," she says when I finish. She sits up and mirrors my position against her headboard. "Are you sure he wasn't flirting with you? Trying to get your number? I mean, I've seen you with guys, Sky. You put on a good act, even if you *don't* feel it with them. I know you know how to read guys, but I think maybe the fact that you were actually attracted to him might have muddied your intuition. You think?"

I shrug. She could be right. Maybe I just read him wrong and my own negative reaction prompted him to change his mind about asking me out. "Could be. But whatever it was, it was ruined just as fast. He's a dropout, he's moody, he's got a temper and . . . he's just . . . he's *hopeless*. I don't know what my type is, but I know I don't want it to be Holder."

Six grabs my cheeks, squeezing them together, and

turns my face to hers. "Did you just say *Holder*?" she asks, her exquisitely groomed eyebrow arched in curiosity.

My lips are squished together due to her hold on my cheeks, so I just nod rather than give her a verbal response.

"*Dean* Holder? Messy brown hair? Smoldering blue eyes? A temper straight out of Fight Club?"

I shrug. "Dowds sike dim," I say, my words barely audible thanks to the grip she still has on my face. She releases her hold and I repeat what I said. "Sounds like him." I bring my hand to my face and massage my cheeks. "You know him?"

She stands up and throws her hands up in the air. "*Why*, Sky? Of all the guys you could be attracted to, why the hell is it *Dean Holder*?"

She seems disappointed. Why does she seem so disappointed? I've never heard her mention Holder before, so it's not like she's ever dated him. Why the hell does it seem that this just went from sort of exciting . . . to very, very bad?

"I need details," I say.

She rolls her head and swings her legs off the bed. She walks to her closet and grabs a pair of jeans out of a box, then pulls them up over her underwear. "He's a jerk, Sky. He used to go to our school but he got sent to juvi right after school started last year. I don't know him that well, but I know enough about him to know he's not boyfriend material."

Her description of Holder doesn't surprise me. I wish I could say it didn't disappoint me, but I can't.

"Since when is *anyone* boyfriend material?" I don't think Six has ever had a boyfriend for more than one night in her life.

She looks at me, then shrugs. "Touché." She pulls a shirt on over her head and walks to her bathroom sink. She picks up a toothbrush and squeezes toothpaste onto it, then walks back into the bedroom brushing her teeth.

"Why was he sent to juvi?" I ask, not sure if I really want to know the answer.

Six pulls the toothbrush from her mouth. "They got him for a hate crime . . . beat up some gay kid from school. Pretty sure it was a strike three kind of thing." She puts the toothbrush back into her mouth and walks to the sink to spit.

A hate crime? Really? My stomach does a flip, but not in the good way this time.

Six walks back into the bedroom after pulling her hair into a ponytail. "This sucks," she says, perusing her jewelry. "What if this is the one time you get horny for a guy and you never feel it again?"

Her choice of words makes me grimace. "I wasn't horny for him, Six."

She waves her hand in the air. "Horny. Attracted. It's all the same," she says flippantly, walking back to the bed. She places an earring in her lap and brings the other one up to her ear. "I guess we should be relieved to know that you aren't completely broken." Six narrows her eyes and leans over me. She pinches my chin, turning my face to the left. "What in the hell happened to your eye?"

I laugh and roll off the bed, out of harm's way. "*You* happened." I make my way toward the window. "I need to clear my head. I'm gonna go for a run. Wanna come?"

Six crinkles up her nose. "Yeah . . . *no*. You have fun with that."

I have one leg over the windowsill when she calls back to me. "I want to know all about your first day at school later. And I have a present for you. I'm coming over tonight."

Monday, August 27, 2012
5:25 p.m.

My lungs are aching; my body went numb way back at
Aspen Road. My breath has moved from controlled inhaling and exhaling to uncontrolled gasps and spurts. This is
the point at which I usually love running the most. When
every single ounce of my body is poured into propelling me
forward, leaving me committedly focused on my next step
and nothing else.

My next step.

Nothing else.

I've never run this far before. I usually stop when I
know I hit my mile-and-a-half mark a few blocks back, but
I didn't this time. Despite the familiar despair that my body
is currently in, I still can't seem to shut my mind off. I keep
running in hopes that I'll get to that point, but it's taking a
lot longer than usual. The only thing that makes me decide
to stop going is the fact that I still have to cover as much
tread going home, and I'm almost out of water.

I stop at the edge of a driveway and lean against the mailbox, opening the lid to my water bottle. I wipe the sweat off
my forehead with the back of my arm and bring the bottle to
my lips, managing to get about four drops into my mouth before it runs dry. I've already downed an entire bottle of water
in this Texas heat. I silently scold myself for deciding to skip
my run this morning. I'm a wuss in the heat.

Fearing for my hydration, I decide to walk the rest of the way back, rather than run. I don't think pushing myself to the point of physical exertion would make Karen too happy. She gets nervous enough that I run by myself as it is.

I begin walking when I hear a familiar voice speak up from behind me.

"Hey, you."

As if my heart wasn't already beating fast enough, I slowly turn around and see Holder staring down at me, smiling, his dimples breaking out in the corners of his mouth. His hair is wet from sweat and it's obvious he's been running, too.

I blink twice, half believing this is a mirage brought on by my exhaustion. My instinct is telling me to run and scream, but my body wants to wrap itself around his glistening, sweaty arms.

My body is a damn traitor.

Luckily, I haven't recovered from the stretch I just completed, so he won't be able to tell that my erratic breathing pattern is mostly from just seeing him again.

"Hey," I say back, breathless. I do my best to keep looking at his face but I can't seem to stop my eyes from dipping below his neck. Instead, I just look down at my feet in order to avoid the fact that he isn't wearing anything but shorts and running shoes. The way his shorts are hanging off his hips is reason enough for me to forgive every single negative thing I've learned about him today. I have never, as long as I can remember, been the type of girl to swoon over a guy's looks. I feel shallow. Pathetic. Lame, even. And a little bit pissed at myself that I'm letting him get to me like this.

"You run?" he asks, leaning his elbow on the mailbox.

I nod. "Usually in the mornings. I forgot how hot it is in the afternoons." I attempt to look back up at him, lifting my hand over my eyes to shield the sun that's glowing over his head like a halo.

How ironic.

He reaches out and I flinch before I realize he's just handing me his bottle of water. The way his lips purse in an attempt not to smile makes it obvious he can see how nervous I am around him.

"Drink this." He nudges the half-empty bottle at me. "You look exhausted."

Normally I wouldn't take water from strangers. I would especially not take water from people I know are bad news, but I'm thirsty. *So* damn thirsty.

I grab the bottle out of his hands and tilt my head back, downing three huge gulps. I'm dying to drink the rest, but I can't deplete his supply, too. "Thanks," I say, handing it back to him. I wipe my hand over my mouth and look behind me at the sidewalk. "Well, I've got another mile and a half return, so I better get started."

"Closer to two and a half," he says, cutting his eyes to my stomach. He presses his lips to the bottle without wiping the rim off, keeping his eyes trained on me while he tilts his head back and gulps the rest of the water. I can't help but watch his lips as they cover the opening of the bottle that my lips were just touching. We're practically kissing.

I shake my head. "Huh?" I'm not sure if he said something out loud or not. I'm a little preoccupied watching the sweat drip down his chest.

"I said it's more like two and a half. You live over on

Conroe, that's over two miles away. That's almost a five-mile run round trip." He says it like he's impressed.

I eye him curiously. "You know what street I live on?"

"Yeah."

He doesn't elaborate. I keep my gaze fixed on his and remain silent, waiting for some sort of explanation.

He can see I'm not satisfied with his "yeah," so he sighs. "Linden Sky Davis, born September 29; 1455 Conroe Street. Five feet three inches. Donor."

I take a step back, suddenly seeing my near-future murder played out in front of my eyes at the hands of my dreamy stalker. I wonder if I should stop shielding my vision from the sun so I can get a better look at him in case I get away. I might need to recount his features to the sketch artist.

"Your ID," he explains when he sees the mixture of terror and confusion on my face. "You showed me your ID earlier. At the store."

Somehow, that explanation doesn't ease my apprehension. "You looked at it for two seconds."

He shrugs. "I have a good memory."

"You stalk," I deadpan.

He laughs. "*I* stalk? You're the one standing in front of my house." He points over his shoulder at the house behind him.

His house? What the hell are the chances?

He straightens up and taps his fingers against the letters on the front of the mailbox.

The Holders.

I can feel the blood rushing to my cheeks, but it doesn't matter. After a middle of the afternoon run in the Texas heat and a limited supply of water, I'm sure my entire body is flushed. I try not to glance back at his house, but curiosity is my weakness. It's a modest house, not too flashy. It fits in well with the midincome neighborhood we're in. As does the car that's in his driveway. I wonder if that's *his* car? I can deduce from his conversation with what's-her-face from the grocery store that he's my age, so I know he must live with his parents. But how have I not seen him before? How could I not know I lived less than three miles from the only boy in existence who can turn me into a ball of frustrated hot flashes?

I clear my throat. "Well, thanks for the water." I can think of nothing I want more than to escape this awkwardness. I give him a quick wave and break into a stride.

"Wait a sec," he yells from behind me. I don't slow down, so he passes me and turns around, jogging backward against the sun. "Let me refill your water." He reaches over and grabs my water bottle out of my left hand, brushing his hand against my stomach in the process. I freeze again.

"I'll be right back," he says, running off toward his house.

I'm stumped. That is a completely contradictory act of kindness. Another side effect of the split personality disorder, maybe? He's probably a mutation, like the Hulk. Or Jekyll and Hyde. I wonder if Dean is his nice persona and Holder is his scary one. Holder is definitely the one I saw at the grocery store earlier. I think I like Dean a lot better.

I feel awkward waiting, so I walk back toward his driveway, pausing every few seconds to look at the path that leads back to my home. I have no idea what to do. It feels like any decision I make at this point will be one for the dumb side of the scale.

Should I stay?

Should I run?

Should I hide in the bushes before he comes back outside with handcuffs and a knife?

Before I have a chance to run, his front door swings open and he comes back outside with a full bottle of water. This time the sun is behind me, so I don't have to struggle so hard to see him. That's not a good thing, either, since all I want to do is stare at him.

Ugh! I absolutely hate lust.

Hate. It.

Every fiber of my being knows he's not a good person, yet my body doesn't seem to give a shit at all.

He hands me the bottle and I quickly down another drink. I hate Texas heat as it is, but coupled with Dean Holder, it feels like I'm standing in the pits of Hell.

"So . . . earlier? At the store?" he says with a nervous pause. "If I made you uneasy, I'm sorry."

My lungs are begging me for air, but I somehow find a way to reply. "You didn't make me uneasy."

You sort of creeped me out.

Holder narrows his eyes at me for a few seconds, studying me. I've discovered today that I don't like being studied . . . I like going unnoticed. "I wasn't trying to hit on you, either," he says. "I just thought you were someone else."

"It's fine." I force a smile, but it's *not* fine. Why am I suddenly consumed with disappointment that he wasn't trying to hit on me? I should be happy.

"Not that I *wouldn't* hit on you," he adds with a grin. "I just wasn't doing it at that particular moment."

Oh, thank you, Jesus. His clarification makes me smile, despite all my efforts not to.

"Want me to run with you?" he asks, nudging his head toward the sidewalk behind me.

Yes, please.

"No, it's fine."

He nods. "Well, I was going that way anyway. I run twice a day and I've still got a couple . . ." He stops speaking midsentence and takes a quick step toward me. He grabs my chin and tilts my head back. "Who did this to you?" The same hardness I saw in his eyes at the grocery store returns behind his scowl. "Your eye wasn't like this earlier."

I pull my chin away and laugh it off. "It was an accident. Never interrupt a teenage girl's nap."

He doesn't smile. Instead, he takes a step closer and gives me a hard look, then brushes his thumb underneath my eye. "You would tell someone, right? If someone did this to you?"

I want to respond. Really, I do. I just *can't*. He's touching my face. His hand is on my cheek. I can't think, I can't speak, I can't *breathe*. The intensity that exudes from his whole existence sucks the air out of my lungs and the strength out of my knees. I nod unconvincingly and he frowns, then pulls his hand away.

"I'm running with you," he says, without question. He places his hands on my shoulders and turns me in the opposite direction, giving me a slight shove. He falls into stride next to me and we run in silence.

I want to talk to him. I want to ask him about his year in juvi, why he dropped out of school, why he has that tattoo . . . but I'm too scared to find out the answers. Not to mention I'm completely out of breath. So instead, we run in complete silence the entire way back to my house.

When we close in on my driveway, we both slow down to a walk. I have no idea how to end this. No one ever runs with me, so I'm not sure what the etiquette is when two runners part ways. I turn and give him a quick wave. "I guess I'll see you later?"

"Absolutely," he says, staring right at me.

I smile at him uncomfortably and turn away. *Absolutely?* I flip this word over in my mind as I head back up the driveway. What does he mean by that? He didn't try to get my number, despite not knowing I don't have one. He didn't ask if I wanted to run with him again. But he said *absolutely* like he was certain; and I sort of hope he *is*.

"Sky, wait." The way his voice wraps around my name makes me wish the only word in his entire vocabulary was *Sky.* I spin around and pray he's about to come up with another cheesy pickup line. I would totally fall for it now.

"Do me a favor?"

Anything. I'll do anything you ask me to, so long as you're shirtless.

"Yeah?"

He tosses me his bottle of water. I catch it and look down at the empty bottle, feeling guilty that I didn't think to offer him a refill myself. I shake it in the air and nod, then jog up the steps and into the house. Karen is loading the dishwasher when I run into the kitchen. As soon as the front door closes behind me, I gasp for the air my lungs have been begging for.

"My God, Sky. You look like you're about to pass out. Sit down." She takes the bottle from my hands and forces me into a chair. I let her refill it while I breathe in through my nose and out my mouth. She turns around and hands it to me and I put the lid on it, then stand up and run it back outside to him.

"Thanks," he says. I stand and watch as he presses those same full lips to the opening of the water bottle.

We're practically kissing again.

I can't distinguish between the effect my near-five-mile run has had on me and the effect Holder is having on me. Both of them make me feel like I'm about to pass out from lack of oxygen. Holder closes the lid on his water bottle and his eyes roam over my body, pausing at my bare midriff for a beat too long before he reaches my eyes. "Do you run track?"

I cover my stomach with my left arm and clasp my hands at my waist. "No. I'm thinking about trying out, though."

"You should. You're barely out of breath and you just ran close to five miles," he says. "Are you a senior?"

He has no idea how much effort it's taking on my part not to fall onto the pavement and wheeze from lack of air. I've never run this far in one shot before, and it's taking everything I have to come across like it's not a big deal. Apparently it's working.

"Shouldn't you already know if I'm a senior? You're slacking on your stalking skills."

When his dimples make a reappearance, I want to high-five myself.

"Well, you make it sort of difficult to stalk you," he says. "I couldn't even find you on Facebook."

He just admitted to looking me up on Facebook. I met him less than two hours ago, so the fact that he went straight home and looked me up on Facebook is a little bit flattering. An involuntary smile breaks out on my face, and

I want to punch this pathetic excuse for a girl that has taken over my normally indifferent self.

"I'm not on Facebook. I don't have internet access," I explain.

He cuts his eyes to me and smirks like he doesn't believe a thing I'm saying. He pushes the hair back from his forehead. "What about your phone? You can't get internet on your phone?"

"No phone. My mother isn't a fan of modern technology. No TV, either."

"Shit." He laughs. "You're serious? What do you do for fun?"

I smile back at him and shrug. "I run."

Holder studies me again, dropping his attention briefly to my stomach. I'll think twice from now on before I decide to wear a sports bra outside.

"Well in that case, you wouldn't happen to know what time a certain someone gets up for her morning runs, would you?" He looks back up at me and I don't see the person Six described to me in him at all. The only thing I see is a guy, flirting with a girl, with a seminervous, endearing gleam in his eye.

"I don't know if you'd want to get up that early," I say. The way he's looking at me coupled with the Texas heat is suddenly causing my vision to blur, so I inhale a deep breath, wanting to appear anything but exhausted and flustered right now.

He tilts his head toward mine and narrows his eyes. "You have no *idea* how bad I want to get up that early." He flashes me his dimple-laden grin, and I faint.

No . . . literally. I fainted.

And based on the ache in my shoulder and the dirt and gravel embedded in my cheek, it wasn't a beautiful, graceful fall. I blacked out and smacked the pavement before he even had a chance to catch me. *So* unlike the heroes in the books.

I'm flat on the couch, presumably where he laid me after carrying me inside. Karen is standing over me with a glass of water and Holder is behind her, watching the aftermath of the most embarrassing moment of my life.

"Sky, drink some water," Karen says, lifting the back of my neck, pressing me toward the cup. I take a sip, then lean back on the pillow and close my eyes, hoping more than anything that I black out again.

"I'll get you a cold rag," Karen says. I open my eyes, hoping Holder decided to sneak out once Karen left the room, but he's still here. And he's closer now. He kneels on the floor beside me and reaches his hand to my hair, pulling out what I assume is either dirt or gravel.

"You sure you're okay? That was a pretty nasty fall." His eyes are full of concern and he wipes something from my cheek with his thumb, then rests his hand on the couch beside me.

"Oh, God," I say, covering my eyes with my arm. "I'm so sorry. This is so embarrassing."

Holder grabs my wrist and pulls my arm away from my face. "Shh." The concern in his eyes eases and a playful grin takes over his features. "I'm sort of enjoying it."

Karen makes her way back into the living room. "Here's a rag, sweetie. Do you want something for the pain? Are you nauseous?" Rather than hand the rag to me, she hands it to Holder and walks back to the kitchen. "I might have some calendula or burdock root."

Great. If I wasn't already embarrassed enough, she's about to make it even worse by forcing me to down her homemade tinctures right in front of him.

"I'm fine, Mom. Nothing hurts."

Holder gently places the rag on my cheek and wipes at it. "You might not be sore now, but you will be," he says, too quiet for Karen to hear him. He looks away from examining my cheek and locks eyes with me. "You should take something, just in case."

I don't know why the suggestion sounds more appealing coming out of his mouth than Karen's, but I nod. And gulp. And hold my breath. And squeeze my thighs together. And attempt to sit up, because me lying on the couch with him hovering over me is about to make me faint again.

When he sees my effort to sit up, he takes my elbow and assists me. Karen walks back into the living room and hands me a small glass of orange juice. Her tinctures are so bitter, I have to down them with juice in order to avoid spitting them back out. I take this one from her hand and down it faster than I've ever downed one before, then immediately hand her back the glass. I just want her to go back to the kitchen.

"I'm sorry," she says, extending her hand to Holder. "I'm Karen Davis."

Holder stands up and shakes her hand in return. "Dean Holder. My friends call me Holder."

I'm jealous she's getting to touch his hand. I want to take a number and get in line. "How do you and Sky know each other?" she asks.

He looks down at me at the same time I look up at him. His lip barely curls up in a smile, but I notice. "We don't, actually," he says, looking back at her. "Just in the right place at the right time, I guess."

"Well, thank you for helping her. I don't know why she fainted. She's never fainted." She looks down at me. "Did you eat anything today?"

"A bite of chicken for lunch," I say, not admitting to the Snickers I had before my run. "Cafeteria food sucks ass."

She rolls her eyes and throws her hands up in the air. "Why were you running without eating first?"

I shrug. "I forgot. I don't usually run in the evenings."

She walks back to the kitchen with the glass and sighs heavily. "I don't want you running anymore, Sky. What would have happened if you had been by yourself? You run too much, anyway."

She's got to be kidding me. There is no way I can stop running.

"Listen," Holder says, watching as the rest of the color drains from my face. He looks back toward the kitchen at Karen. "I live right over on Ricker and I run by here every day on my afternoon runs." (He's lying. I would have noticed.) "If you'd feel more comfortable, I'd be happy to run with her for the next week or so in the mornings. I usually run the track at school, but it's not a big deal. You know, just to make sure this doesn't happen again."

Ah. Light bulb. No wonder those abs looked familiar.

Karen walks back to the living room and looks at me, then back at him. She knows how much I enjoy my solitary running breaks, but I can see in her eyes that she would feel more comfortable if I had a running partner.

"I'm okay with that," she says, looking back at me. "If Sky thinks it's a good idea."

Yes. Yes, I do. But only if my new running partner is shirtless.

"It's fine," I say. I stand up, and when I do, I get light-headed again. I guess my face goes pale, because Holder has his hand on my shoulder in less than a second, lowering me back to the couch.

"Easy," he says. He looks up at Karen. "Do you have any crackers she can eat? That might help."

Karen walks away to the kitchen and Holder looks back down at me, his eyes full of concern again. "You sure you're okay?" He brushes his thumb across my cheek.

I shiver.

A devilish grin creeps across his face when he sees me attempt to cover the chill bumps on my arms. He glances behind me at Karen in the kitchen, then refocuses his gaze to mine.

"What time should I come stalk you tomorrow?" he whispers.

"Six-thirty?" I breathe, looking up at him helplessly.

"Six-thirty sounds good."

"Holder, you don't have to do this."

His hypnotizing blue eyes study my face for several quiet seconds and I can't help but stare at his equally hypnotizing mouth while he speaks. "I know I don't have to do this, Sky. I do what I want." He leans in toward my ear and lowers his voice to a whisper. "And I want to run with you." He pulls back and studies me. Due to all the chaos parading through my head and stomach, I fail to muster a reply.

Karen is back with the crackers. "Eat," she says, placing them in my hand.

Holder stands up and says good-bye to Karen, then turns back to me. "Take care of yourself. I'll see you in the morning?"

I nod and watch him as he turns to leave. I can't tear my eyes away from the front door after it shuts behind him. I'm losing it. I've completely lost any form of self-control. So this is what Six loves? This is *lust*?

I hate it. I absolutely, positively *hate* this beautiful, magical feeling.

"He was so nice," Karen says. "And handsome." She turns to face me. "You don't know him?"

I shrug. "I know *of* him," I say. And that's *all* I say. If she only knew what kind of hopeless boy she just assigned as my "running partner," she'd have a conniption. The less she knows about Dean Holder, the better it'll be for both of us.

Monday, August 27, 2012
7:10 p.m.

"What the hell happened to your face?" Jack drops my chin and walks past me to the refrigerator.

Jack has been a fixture in Karen's life for about a year and a half now. He has dinner with us a few nights a week, and since tonight is Six's going away dinner, he's gracing us with his presence. As much as he likes to give Six a hard time, I know he'll miss her, too.

"I kicked the road's ass today," I reply.

He laughs. "So *that's* what happened to the road."

Six grabs a slice of bread and opens a jar of Nutella. I grab my plate and fill it with Karen's latest vegan concoction. Karen's cooking is an acquired taste, one that Six still hasn't acquired after four years. Jack, on the other hand, is Karen's twin incarnate, so he doesn't mind the cooking. Tonight's menu consists of something I can't even pronounce, but it's completely animal-product-free, like it always is. Karen doesn't force me to eat vegan, so unless I'm home, I usually eat what I want.

Everything Six eats is only eaten to complement her main course of Nutella. Tonight, she's having a cheese and Nutella sandwich. I don't know if I could ever acquire a taste for that.

"So, when are you moving in?" I ask Jack. He and Karen have been discussing the next step, but they can never seem to get past the hump of her strict antitechnology rule. Well, Jack can't get past it. It's not a hump that will ever be scaled by Karen.

"Whenever your mom caves and gets ESPN," Jack says.

They don't argue about it. I think their arrangement is fine with both of them, so neither of them is in a hurry to sacrifice their opposing views on modern technology.

"Sky passed out in the road today," Karen says, changing the subject. "Some adorable man-boy carried her inside."

I laugh. "*Guy*, Mom. Please just say guy."

Six glares at me from across the table and it occurs to me that I haven't filled her in on my afternoon run. I also haven't filled her in on my first day of school. It's been an active day today. I wonder who I'm going to fill in after she leaves tomorrow. Just the thought of her being on the other side of the world in two days fills me with dread. I hope Breckin can fill her shoes. Well, he would probably love to fill her shoes. Literally. But I'm hoping he does so in the figurative sense.

"You okay?" Jack asks. "It must have been a pretty good fall to get that shiner."

I reach up to my eye and grimace. I'd completely forgotten about the black eye. "That's not from fainting. Six elbowed me. Twice."

I expect one of them to at least ask Six why she attacked me, but they don't. This just goes to show how much they love her. They wouldn't even care if she beat me up, they'd tell me I probably deserved it.

"Doesn't that annoy you, having a number for a name?" Jack asks her. "I never understood that. It's like when a parent names their child after one of the days of the week." He pauses with his fork midair and looks at Karen. "When we have a baby, we aren't doing that to them. Anything you can find on a calendar is off-limits."

Karen stares at him with a stone-cold expression. If I had to guess by her reaction, this is the first time Jack has mentioned babies. If I had to guess based on the look on her face, babies aren't something she's anticipating in her future. Ever.

Jack refocuses his attention back to Six. "Isn't your real name like Seven or Thirteen or something like that? I don't get why you picked Six. It's possibly the worst number you could pick."

"I'm going to accept your insults for what they are," Six says. "Just your way of burying your devastation over my impending absence."

Jack laughs. "Bury my insults wherever you want. There'll be more to come when you get back in six months."

After Jack and Six leave, I help Karen in the kitchen with the dishes. Since the second Jack brought up babies, she's been unusually quiet.

"Why did that freak you out so bad?" I ask her, handing her the plate to rinse.

"What?"

"His comment about having a baby with you. You're in your thirties. People have babies at your age all the time."

"Was it that noticeable?"

"It was to me."

She grabs another plate from me to rinse, then lets out

a sigh. "I love Jack. I just love me and you, too. I like our arrangement and I don't know if I'm ready to change it, much less bring another baby into the picture. But Jack is so intent on moving forward."

I turn the water off and wipe my hands on the hand towel. "I'll be eighteen in a few weeks, Mom. As much as you want our arrangement to stay the same . . . it won't. I'll be off at college after next semester and you'll be living here alone. It might not hurt to entertain the idea of at least letting him move in."

She smiles at me, but it's a pained smile just like it always is when I bring up college. "I have been entertaining the idea, Sky. Believe me. It's just a huge step that can't be undone once it's taken."

"What if it's a step you don't *want* undone, though? What if it's a step that just makes you want to take another step, and another step, until you're full-on sprinting?"

She laughs. "That's exactly what I'm afraid of."

I wipe off the counter and rinse the rag in the sink. "I don't understand you, sometimes."

"And I don't understand you, either," she says, nudging my shoulder. "I'll never for the life of me understand why you wanted to go to public school so bad. I know you said it was fun, but tell me how you really feel."

I shrug. "It was good," I lie. My stubbornness wins every time. There's no way I'm telling her how much I hated school today, despite the fact that she would never say, "*I told you so.*"

She dries her hands and smiles at me. "Happy to hear it. Now maybe when I ask you again tomorrow, you'll tell me the truth."

I grab the book Breckin gave me out of my backpack and plop down on my bed. I get through all of two pages when Six crawls through my window.

"School first, then present," she says. She scoots in on the bed next to me and I put the book down on my nightstand.

"School sucked ass. Thanks to you and your inability to just say no to guys, I've inherited your terrible reputation. But by divine intervention, I was rescued by Breckin, the adopted gay Mormon who can't sing or act but loves to read and is my new very bestest friend ever in the whole wide world."

Six pouts. "I'm not even out the door yet and you've already replaced me? Vicious. And for the record, I don't have an inability to say no to guys. I have an inability to grasp the moral ramifications of premarital sex. Lots and lots of premarital sex."

She places a box in my lap. An unwrapped box.

"I know what you're thinking," she says. "And you should know by now that my lack of wrapping doesn't reflect how I feel about you. I'm just lazy."

I pick the box up and shake it. "You're the one leaving, you know. I should be the one getting *you* a gift."

"Yes, you should be. But you suck at gift giving and I don't expect you to change on my account."

She's right. I'm a horrible gift giver, but mostly because I hate receiving gifts so much. It's almost as awkward as people crying. I turn the box and find the flap, then untuck it and open it. I pull out the tissue paper and a cell phone drops into my hand.

"Six," I say. "You know I can't . . ."

"Shut up. There is no way I'm going halfway across the world without a way to communicate with you. You don't even have an email address."

"I know, but I can't . . . I don't have a job. I can't pay for this. And Karen . . ."

"Relax. It's a prepaid phone. I put just enough minutes on it to where we can text each other once a day while I'm gone. I can't afford international phone calls, so you're out of luck there. And just to keep with your mother's cruel, twisted parental values, there isn't even internet on the damn thing. Just texting."

She grabs the phone and turns it on, then enters her contact info. "If you end up getting a hot boyfriend while I'm away, you can always add extra minutes. But if he uses up any of mine I'm cutting his balls off."

She hands me back the phone and I press the Home button. Her contact information pulls up as *Your very, VERY bestest friend ever in the whole wide world.*

I suck at receiving gifts and I *really* suck at good-byes. I set the phone back in the box and bend over to pick my backpack up. I pull the books out and set them on the floor, then turn around and dump my backpack over her and watch all the dollar bills fall in her lap.

"There's thirty-seven dollars here," I say. "It should hold you over until you get back. Happy foreign exchange day."

She picks up a handful of dollars and throws them up in the air, then falls back on the bed. "Only one day at public school and the bitches already made your locker rain?" she laughs. "Impressive."

I lay the good-bye card that I wrote to her on her chest, then lean my head into her shoulder. "You think *that's* impressive? You should have seen me work the pole in the cafeteria."

She picks the card up and brushes her fingers over it, smiling. She doesn't open it because she knows I don't like it when things get uncomfortably emotional. She tucks the card back to her chest and leans her head on my shoulder.

"You're such a slut," she says quietly, attempting to hold back tears that we're both too stubborn to cry.

"So I've heard."

The alarm sounds and I instantly debate skipping today's run until I remember who's waiting for me outside. I get dressed faster than I've ever dressed since the first day I started getting dressed, then head to the window. There's a card taped to the inside of my window with the word "slut" written on it in Six's handwriting. I smile and pull the card off the window, then throw it on my bed before heading outside.

He's sitting on the curb stretching his legs. His back is to me, which is good. Otherwise he would have caught my frown as soon as I noticed he was wearing a shirt. He hears me approaching and spins around to face me.

"Hey, you." He smiles and stands up. I notice when he does that his shirt is already soaked. He ran here. He ran over two miles here, he's about to run three more miles with me, then he'll be running over two miles home. I seriously don't understand why he's going to all this trouble. Or why I'm allowing it. "You need to stretch first?" he asks.

"Already did."

He reaches out and touches my cheek with his thumb. "Doesn't look so bad," he says. "You sore?"

I shake my head. Does he really expect me to vocalize a response when his fingers are touching my face? It's pretty hard to speak and hold your breath at the same time.

He pulls his hand back and smiles. "Good. You ready?"

I let out a breath. "Yeah."

And we run. We run side by side for a while until the path narrows, then he falls into step behind me, which makes me incredibly self-conscious. I normally lose myself when I run, but this time I'm acutely aware of every single thing, from my hair, to the length of my shorts, to each drop of sweat that trails down my back. I'm relieved once the path widens and he falls back into step beside me.

"You better try out for track." His voice is steady and it doesn't sound anything like he's already run four miles this morning. "You've got more stamina than most of the guys from the team last year."

"I don't know if I want to," I say, unattractively breathless. "I don't really know anyone at school. I planned on trying out, but so far most of the people at school are sort of . . . mean. I don't really want to be subjected to them for longer periods of time under the guise of a team."

"You've only been in public school for a day. Give it time. You can't expect to be homeschooled your whole life, then walk in the first day with a ton of new friends."

I stop dead in my tracks. He takes a few more steps before he notices I'm no longer beside him. When he turns around and sees me standing still on the pavement, he rushes toward me and grabs my shoulders. "Are you okay? Are you dizzy?"

I shake my head and push his arms off my shoulders. "I'm fine," I say with a very audible amount of annoyance in my response.

He cocks his head. "Did I say something wrong?"

I start walking in the direction of my house, so he follows suit. "A little," I say, cutting my eyes toward him. "I was halfway joking about the stalking yesterday, but you admitted to looking me up on Facebook right after meeting me. Then you insist on running with me, even though it's out of your way. Now you somehow know how long I've been in public school? And that I was homeschooled? I'm not gonna lie, it's a little unnerving."

I wait for the explanation, but instead he just narrows his eyes and watches me. We're both still walking forward, but he just silently watches me until we round the next corner. When he does finally speak, his words are preempted with a heavy sigh. "I asked around," he finally says. "I've lived here since I was ten, so I have a lot of friends. I was curious about you."

I eye him for a few steps, then drop my gaze down to the sidewalk. I suddenly can't look at him, wondering what else his "friends" have told him about me. I know the rumors have been going around since Six and I became best friends, but this is the first time I've ever felt remotely defensive or embarrassed by them. The fact that he's going out of his way to run with me can only mean one thing. He's heard the rumors, and he's probably hoping they're true.

He can tell I'm uncomfortable, so he grabs my elbow and stops me. "Sky." We turn and face each other, but I keep my eyes trained on the concrete. I'm actually wearing more than just a sports bra today but I fold my arms across my T-shirt anyway and hug myself. There's nothing showing that needs covering up, but I somehow feel really naked right now.

"I think we got off on the wrong foot at the store yesterday," he says. "And the talk about stalking, I swear, it was a joke. I don't want you to feel uncomfortable around me.

Would it make you feel better if you knew more about me? Ask me something and I'll tell you. Anything."

I'm really hoping he's being genuine because I can already tell he isn't the kind of guy a girl gets a simple crush on. He's the kind of guy you fall hard for, and the thought of that terrifies me. I don't really want to fall hard for anyone at all, especially someone who's only making an effort because he thinks I'm easy. I also don't want to fall for someone who has already branded himself hopeless. But I'm curious. So curious.

"If I ask you something, will you be honest?"

He tilts his head toward me. "That's all I'll ever be."

The way he lowers his voice when he speaks makes my head spin and for a second, I'm afraid if he keeps talking like that, I'll pass out again. Luckily, he takes a step back and waits on my question. I want to ask him about his past. I want to know why he was sent away and why he did what he did and why Six doesn't trust him. But again, I'm not sure I want to know the truth yet.

"Why did you drop out of school?"

He sighs like that's one of the questions he was hoping to be able to dodge. He begins walking forward again and I'm the one following him this time.

"Technically, I haven't dropped out yet."

"Well you obviously haven't been in over a year. I'd say that's dropping out."

He turns back to me and looks torn, like he wants to tell me something. He opens his mouth, then shuts it again after hesitating. I hate that I can't read him. Most people are easy to read. They're simple. Holder is all kinds of confusing and complicated.

"I just moved back home a few days ago," he says. "My mother and I had a pretty shitty year last year, so I moved in with my dad in Austin for a while. I've been going to school there, but felt like it was time to come back home. So here I am."

The fact that he failed to mention his stint in juvi makes me question his ability to be forthcoming. I understand it's probably not something he wants to talk about, but he shouldn't claim that he'll only ever be honest when he's being anything but.

"None of that explains why you decided to drop out, rather than just transfer back."

He shrugs his shoulders. "I don't know. To be honest, I'm still trying to decide what I want to do. It's been a pretty fucked-up year. Not to mention I hate this school. I'm tired of the bullshit and sometimes I think it would be easier to just test out."

I stop walking and turn to face him. "That's a crap excuse."

He cocks an eyebrow at me. "It's crap that I hate high school?"

"No. It's crap that you're letting one bad year determine your fate for the rest of your life. You're nine months away from graduation, so you drop out? It's just . . . it's stupid."

He laughs. "Well, when you put it so eloquently."

"Laugh all you want. You quitting school is just giving in. You're proving everyone that's ever doubted you right." I look down and eye the tattoo on his arm. "You're gonna drop out and show the world just how hopeless you really are? Way to stick it to 'em."

He follows my gaze down to his tattoo and he stares at it

for a moment, working his jaw back and forth. I really didn't mean to go off on a tangent, but skimping on an education is a touchy subject with me. I blame Karen for all those years of drilling it in my head that I'm the only one who can be held accountable for the way my life turns out.

Holder shifts his eyes away from the tattoo that we're both staring at, and he looks back up and nudges his head toward my house. "You're here," he says matter-of-factly. He turns away from me without so much as a smile or a wave good-bye.

I stand on the sidewalk and watch him as he disappears around the corner without once looking back in my direction.

And here I was, thinking I would actually have a conversation with just *one* of his personalities today. So much for that.

I walk into first period and Breckin is seated in the back of the room in all of his hot pink glory. How I didn't notice those hot pink shoes and the boy they're attached to before lunch yesterday boggles my mind.

"Hey, gorgeous," I say as I slide into an empty seat next to him. I take the cup of coffee out of his hands and take a sip. He lets me, because he doesn't know me well enough yet to object. Or maybe he lets me because he knows the ramifications of intercepting a self-proclaimed caffeine addict.

"I learned a lot about you last night," he says. "It's too bad your mother won't let you have internet. It's an amazing place to discover facts about yourself that you never even knew."

I laugh. "Do I even want to know?" I tilt my head back and finish off his coffee, then hand him back the cup. He looks down at the empty cup and places it back on my desk.

"Well," he says. "According to some probing on Facebook, you had someone named Daniel Wesley over on Friday night and that resulted in a pregnancy scare. Saturday you had sex with someone named Grayson and then kicked him out. Yesterday . . ." he drums his fingers on his chin. "Yesterday you were seen running with a guy named Dean Holder after school. That concerns me a bit because, rumor has it . . . he doesn't like *Mormons*."

Sometimes I'm thankful I don't have access to the internet like everyone else.

"Let's see," I say, running through the list of rumors. "I don't even know who Daniel Wesley is. Saturday, Grayson *did* come over, but he barely got to cop a feel before I kicked his drunk ass out. And yes, I was running with a guy named Holder yesterday, but I have no idea who he is. We just happened to be running at the same time and he doesn't live far from me, so . . ."

I immediately feel guilty for downplaying the run with Holder. I just haven't figured him out and I'm not sure I'm ready for someone to infiltrate mine and Breckin's twenty-hour-old alliance just yet.

"If it makes you feel better, I found out from some chick named Shayna that I'm a product of old money and I'm filthy rich," he says.

I laugh. "Good. Then you won't have a problem bringing me coffee every morning."

The classroom door opens and we both look up, just as Holder walks in dressed in a casual white T-shirt and dark denim jeans, his hair freshly washed since our run this morning. As soon as I see him, the stomach virus/hot flashes/butterflies return.

"Shit," I mutter. Holder walks to Mr. Mulligan's desk and lays a form on it, then walks toward the back of the room fiddling with his phone the whole time. He takes a seat at the desk directly in front of Breckin and never even notices me. He turns the volume down on his phone, then puts it in his pocket.

I'm too in shock that he showed up to even speak to him. Did I somehow change his mind about reenrolling?

Am I happy about the fact that I may have changed his mind? Because I sort of feel nothing but regret.

Mr. Mulligan walks in and sets his things on the desk, then turns toward the blackboard and writes his name, followed by the date. I'm not sure if he honestly thinks we forgot who he was since yesterday, or if he just wants to remind us that he thinks we're ignorant.

"Dean," he says, still facing the blackboard. He spins around and eyes Holder. "Welcome back, albeit a day late. I take it you won't be giving us any trouble this semester?"

My mouth drops at his condescending remark right off the bat. If this is the kind of shit Holder has to put up with when he's here, no wonder he didn't want to come back. At least I just get shit from other students. I don't care who the student is, teachers should never be condescending. That should be the first rule in the teacher handbook. The second rule should be that teachers aren't allowed to write their names on blackboards beyond third grade.

Holder shifts in his seat and replies to Mr. Mulligan's comment with just as much bite. "I take it you won't be saying anything that will incite me to *give* you trouble this semester, Mr. Mulligan?"

Okay, the "shit giving" is obviously a two-way street. Maybe my next lesson, beyond talking him into coming back to school, should be to teach him the meaning of respecting authority.

Mr. Mulligan tucks his chin in and glares at Holder over the rims of his glasses.

"Dean. Why don't you come to the front of the room and introduce yourself to your classmates. I'm sure there are some new faces since you left us last year."

Holder doesn't object, which I'm sure is exactly what Mr. Mulligan expected him to do. Instead, he practically leaps from his chair and walks swiftly to the front of the room. His sudden burst of energy causes Mr. Mulligan to take a quick step back. Holder spins around to face the class, not an ounce of self-doubt or insecurity about him.

"Gladly," Holder says, cutting his eyes toward Mr. Mulligan. "I'm Dean Holder. People call me Holder." He looks away from Mr. Mulligan and back toward the class. "I've been a student here since freshmen year with the exception of a one-and-a-half-semester sabbatical. And according to Mr. Mulligan, I like to incite trouble, so this class should be fun."

Several of the students laugh at this comment, but I fail to find the humor in it. I've already been doubting him based on everything I've heard; now he's showing his true colors by the way he's acting. Holder opens his mouth to continue with his introduction, but breaks out into a smile as soon as he spots me in the back of the room. He winks at me and I immediately want to crawl under my desk and hide. I give him a quick, tight-lipped smile, then look down at my desk as soon as other students begin turning around in their seats to see whom he's staring at.

An hour and a half ago, he walked away from me in a pissy mood. Now he's smiling at me like he's just seen his best friend for the first time in years.

Yep. He's got issues.

Breckin leans across his desk. "What the hell was that?" he whispers.

"I'll tell you at lunch," I say.

"Is that all the wisdom you wish to impart to us today?" Mr. Mulligan asks Holder.

Holder nods, then walks back to his seat, never pulling his gaze from mine. He sits and cranes his neck, facing me. Mr. Mulligan begins his lecture and everyone's focus returns to the front of the room. Everyone's but Holder's. I glance down to my book and flip it open to the current chapter, hoping he'll do the same. When I glance back up, he's still staring at me.

"*What?*" I mouth, tossing my palms up in the air.

He narrows his eyes and watches me silently for a moment. "Nothing," he finally says. He turns around in his seat and opens the book in front of him.

Breckin taps his pencil on my knuckles and looks at me inquisitively, then returns his attention to his book. If he's expecting an explanation of what just happened, he'll be disappointed when I'm unable to give him one. *I* don't even know what just happened.

I steal several glances in Holder's direction during the lecture, but he doesn't turn around again for the entire period. When the bell rings, Breckin jumps out of his seat and drums his fingers on my desk.

"Me. You. Lunch," he says, raising his eyebrow at me. He walks out of the classroom and I turn my gaze to Holder. He's watching the classroom door that Breckin just walked out of with a hard look in his eyes.

I grab my things and head out the door before Holder has a chance to strike up a conversation. I really am glad he decided to reenroll, but I'm disturbed at the way he looked at me like we were best friends. I really don't want Breckin, or anyone else for that matter, thinking I'm okay with the things Holder does. I'd rather just not associate myself with him, but I have a feeling that's going to be an issue for him.

I go to my locker and switch books, grabbing my English text. I wonder if Shayna/Shayla will actually acknowledge me in class today. Probably not, that was twenty-four hours ago. I doubt she has enough brain cells to recall information from that long ago.

"Hey, you."

I squeeze my eyes shut apprehensively, not wanting to turn around to see him standing there in all his beautiful glory.

"You came." I adjust the books in my locker, then turn around and face him. He smiles, then leans up against the locker next to mine.

"You clean up nice," he says, eyeing me up and down. "Although, the sweaty version of you isn't so bad, either."

He cleans up nice, too, but I'm not about to tell him that.

"Are you here stalking me or did you actually reenroll?"

He grins mischievously and drums his fingers against the locker. "Both."

I really need to cut it out with the stalking jokes. It would be funnier if I didn't think he was actually capable.

I look around at the hallway clearing out. "Well, I need to get to class," I say. "Welcome back."

He narrows his eyes at me, almost as if he can sense my discomfort. "You're being weird."

I roll my eyes at his assessment. How can he know how I'm being? He doesn't even know me. I look back into my locker and try to mask the real thoughts on why I'm being "weird." Thoughts like, why does his past not scare me more than it does? Why does he have a temper so bad that he would do what he did to that poor kid last year? Why does he want to go out of his way to run with me? Why was

72

he asking around about me? Instead of verbally admitting to the questions inside my head, I just shrug and go with, "I'm just surprised to see you here."

He leans his shoulder against the locker next to mine and shakes his head. "Nope. It's something else. What's wrong?"

I sigh and lean against my locker. "You want me to be honest?"

"That's all I ever want you to be."

I pull my lips into a tight line and nod. "Fine," I say. I roll my shoulder against the locker and face him. "I don't want to give you the wrong idea. You flirt and say things like you have intentions with me that I'm not willing to reciprocate. And you're . . ." I pause, searching for the right word.

"I'm *what*?" he says, watching me intently.

"You're . . . *intense*. Too intense. And moody. And a little bit scary. And there's the other thing," I say, without saying it. "I just don't want you getting the wrong idea."

"What other thing?" He says it like he knows exactly what other thing I'm referring to, but he's daring me to say it.

I let out a breath and press my back against the locker, staring down at my feet. "You know," I say, not wanting to bring up his past any more than he probably does.

Holder steps in front of me and places his hand on the locker beside my head, then leans in toward me. I look up at him and he's staring down at me, less than six inches from my face.

"I *don't* know, because you're skirting around whatever issue it is you have with me like you're too afraid to say it. Just say it."

Looking up at him right now, feeling trapped like I'm

feeling, the same panic returns to my chest that he left there after our first encounter.

"I heard about what you did," I say abruptly. "I know about the guy you beat up. I know about you being sent to juvi. I know that in the two days I've known you, you've scared the shit out of me at least three times. And since we're being honest, I also know that if you've been asking around about me, then you've probably heard about my reputation, which is more than likely the only reason you're even making an effort with me. I hate to disappoint you, but I'm not screwing you. I don't want you thinking anything will happen between us besides what's already happening. We run together. That's it."

His jaw tightens, but his expression never changes. He lowers his arm and takes a step back, allowing me room to breathe again. I don't understand why anytime he steps within a foot of my personal space, it sucks the breath out of me. I especially don't understand why I like that feeling.

I tuck my books to my chest and begin to shove past him when an arm goes around my waist and I'm pulled away from Holder. I glance next to me to see Grayson eyeing Holder up and down, his grip tightening around my waist.

"Holder," Grayson says coldly. "Didn't know you were coming back."

Holder doesn't even acknowledge Grayson. He continues to stare at me for several seconds, only breaking his gaze from mine to look down at Grayson's hand that's gripping my waist. He nods slightly and smiles, as if he's come to some sort of realization, then brings his eyes back to mine.

"Well, I'm back," he says bluntly, without looking directly at Grayson.

What the hell is this? Where did Grayson come from, and why does he have his arm around me like he's staking claim?

Holder cuts his eyes away from mine and turns around to walk away, but stops abruptly. He spins back around and looks at me. "Track tryouts are Thursday after school," he says. "Go."

Then he's gone.

Too bad Grayson isn't.

"You busy this Saturday?" Grayson says in my ear, pulling me against him.

I push off his chest and pull my neck away from him. "Stop," I say, irritated. "I think I made myself pretty clear last weekend."

I slam my locker shut and walk away, wondering how in the hell I've escaped drama my entire life, yet I have enough for an entire book from the last two days alone.

Breckin takes his seat across from me and slides me a soda. "They didn't have coffee, but I found caffeine."

I smile. "Thank you, very bestest friend in the whole wide world."

"Don't thank me, I bought it with evil intentions. I'm using it to bribe you so I can get the dirt on your love life."

I laugh and open the soda. "Well, you'll be disappointed, because my love life is nonexistent."

He opens his own soda and grins. "Oh, I doubt that. Not from the way bad boy has been eyeing you from over there." He nudges his head to the right.

Holder is three tables down, staring at me. He's sitting with several guys from the football team who seem excited to have him back. They're patting him on the back and talking around him, never noticing that he's not even a part of their conversation. He takes a drink of his water, his eyes keeping their lock on mine. He sets his drink down on the table a little too forcefully, then nudges his head to the right as he stands up. I glance to the right and see the exit to the cafeteria. He's walking toward it, expecting me to follow him.

"Huh," I say, more to myself than to Breckin.

"Yeah. Huh. Go see what the hell he wants, then report back to me."

I take another drink of my soda, then set it on the table. "Yes, sir."

My body stands up to follow Holder, but I leave my heart at the table. I'm pretty sure it jumped out of my chest as soon as he indicated for me to follow him. I can put up a good front for Breckin all I want, but dammit if I can't have a little control over my own organs.

Holder is several feet in front of me and when he swings the doors open, they swing shut behind him. I place my hand on the swinging doors when I reach them and hesitate a moment before pushing out into the hallway. I think I'd rather be heading to detention right now than to talk to him. My stomach is tied up in so many knots it could make a Boy Scout envious.

I look both ways, but I don't see him. I take a few steps until I get to the edge of the lockers, then round the corner. His back is leaned up against one of them and his knee is bent, his foot propped against the locker behind him. His arms are folded across his chest and he's looking right at me. The baby-blue hue of his eyes isn't even kind enough to mask the anger behind them.

"Are you dating Grayson?"

I roll my eyes and walk to the lockers opposite him and lean against them. I'm really getting tired of his mood swings already, and I just met the guy. "Does it matter?" I'm curious how it's any of his business. He gives me that silent pause that I've noticed comes before almost everything he says.

"He's an asshole."

"Sometimes you are, too," I say quickly, not needing nearly as much time as he does to come up with a response.

"He's not good for you."

I let out an exasperated laugh. "And you *are*?" I ask, throwing his point right back at him. If we were keeping score, I'd say it's two and zero in my favor.

He drops his arms and turns around to face the lockers, hitting one of them with a flat palm. The sound of skin against metal reverberates in the hallway and straight into my stomach.

"Don't factor me into this," he says, turning back around. "I'm talking about Grayson, not me. You shouldn't be with him. You have no idea what kind of person he is."

I laugh. Not because he's funny . . . but because he's *serious*. This guy that I don't even know is seriously trying to tell me who I should and shouldn't date? I roll my head back against the locker in a wave of defeat.

"Two days, Holder. I've known you all of two days." I kick off the lockers behind me and walk toward him. "In those two days, I've seen five different sides of you, and only one of them has been appealing. The fact that you think you have any right to even voice an opinion about me or my decisions is absurd. It's ridiculous."

Holder works his jaw back and forth and stares down at me, arms tightly folded against his chest. He takes a challenging step toward me. His eyes are so hard and cold, I'm beginning to think this is a sixth side of him that I'm seeing. An even angrier, more possessive side.

"I don't like him. And when I see things like this?" He brings his hand to my face and gently runs his finger underneath the prominent bruise on my eye. "And then see him with his arm around you? Forgive me if I get a little *ridiculous.*"

His fingertips trailing across my cheekbone have left me breathless. It's a struggle to keep my eyes open and not lean in toward his palm, but I hold fast to my resolve. I'm building up an immunity to this boy. Or . . . at least I'm attempting to. That's my new goal, anyway.

I take a step away from him until his hand is no longer touching my face. He curls his fingers up into a fist and drops his hand to his side.

"You think I should stay away from Grayson because you're afraid he has a temper?" I tilt my head to the side and narrow my eyes at him. "A bit hypocritical, don't you think?"

After another few seconds of studying me, he lets out a short sigh with a barely noticeable roll of the eyes. He looks away and shakes his head, grabbing at the back of his neck. He stays in this position, facing opposite me for several seconds. When he slowly turns around, he doesn't look me in the eyes. He folds his arms across his chest once again and looks down at the floor.

"Did he hit you," he says without any inflection in his voice. He keeps his head trained to the floor, but looks up at me through his eyelashes. "Has he *ever* hit you?"

Here he goes again, inducing me into submission by a simple switch in demeanor. "No," I say, quietly. "And no. I told you . . . it was an accident."

We stare at each other in complete silence until the bell for second lunch rings and the hallway fills with students. I'm the first to break our gaze. I walk back to the cafeteria without looking back at him.

I've been running for almost three years. I don't remember what started it or what made it so enjoyable that I became so disciplined at it. I think a lot of it has to do with how frustratingly sheltered I am. I try to stay positive about it, but it's hard seeing the interactions and relationships the other students have at school that I'm not a part of. Not having internet access wouldn't have been a big deal in high school a few years ago, but now it's pretty much social suicide. Not that I care what anyone thinks.

I won't deny it, I've had an overwhelming urge to look Holder up online. In the past when I had these urges to find out more about people, Six and I would just look them up at her house. But Six is on a transatlantic flight over the Atlantic ocean right now, so I can't ask her. Instead, I just sit on my bed and wonder. I wonder if he's really as bad as his reputation makes him out to be. I wonder if he has the same effect on other girls that he has on me. I wonder who his parents are, if he has siblings, if he's dating anyone. I wonder why he seems so intent on being angry with me all the time when we just met. Is he always this angry? Is he always so charming when he isn't busy being angry? I hate that he's either one way or the other and never in between. It would be nice to see a laid-back, calm side to him. I wonder if he even *has* an in between. I wonder . . . because that's all I can do. Silently wonder about the hopeless boy who somehow burrowed himself into the forefront of my thoughts and won't go the hell away.

I snap out of my trance and finish pulling my running shoes on. At least our tiff in the hallway yesterday was left unresolved. He won't be running with me today because of it, and I'm pretty relieved about that. I need the quiet time to myself today, more than anything. I don't know why, though. It'll just be spent wondering.

About him.

I open my bedroom window and crawl outside. It's darker than usual for this time of morning. I look up and see that the sky is overcast, a perfect indicator of my mood. I take in the direction of the clouds, then glance at the sky to the left, curious if I have enough time to run before the bottom falls out.

"Do you always climb out your window or were you just hoping to avoid me?"

I spin around at the sound of his voice. He's standing at the edge of the sidewalk, decked out in shorts and running shoes. No shirt today.

Dammit.

"If I was trying to avoid you I would have just stayed in bed." I walk toward him with confidence, hoping to hide the fact that the sight of him is causing my entire body to go haywire. A small part of me is disappointed he showed up today, but most of me is stupidly, pathetically happy. I walk past him and drop onto the sidewalk to stretch. I extend my legs out in front of me and lean forward, grabbing my shoes and burying my head against my knees—partly for the muscle stretch, but mostly to avoid having to look at him.

"I wasn't sure if you'd show up." He drops down and claims a spot on the sidewalk in front of me.

I raise up and look at him. "Why wouldn't I? I'm not the one with the issues. Besides, neither of us owns the road." I practically snap at him. I'm not even sure why.

He does that staring and thinking thing again where his intense gaze somehow renders me unresponsive. It's becoming such a habit of his I almost want to give it a name. It's like he holds me with his eyes while he silently thinks, purposefully giving no tells in his expression. I've never met anyone who puts so much thought into his own responses. The way he lets things soak in while he prepares his own response—it's like words are limited and he only wants to use the ones that are absolutely necessary.

I stop stretching and face him, unwilling to back down from this visual standoff. I'm not going to let him perform his little Jedi mind tricks on me, no matter how much I wish I could perform them on him. He's completely unreadable and even more unpredictable. It pisses me off.

He stretches his legs out in front of me. "Give me your hands. I need to stretch, too."

He's sitting with his hands out in front of me like we're about to play patty-cake. If anyone was to drive by right now I can just imagine the rumors. Just the thought of it makes me laugh. I place my hands in his outstretched palms and he pulls me forward toward him for several seconds. When he eases the tension, I pull back while he stretches forward, only he doesn't look down. He keeps his gaze locked on mine in his debilitating eye-hold while he stretches.

"For the record," he says, "I wasn't the one with the issue yesterday."

I pull him harder, more out of malice than a desire to help him stretch.

"Are you insinuating *I'm* the one with the issue?"

"Aren't you?"

"Clarify," I say. "I don't like vague."

He laughs, but it's an irritable laugh. "Sky, if there's one thing you should know about me, it's that I don't do vague. I told you I'll only ever be honest with you, and to me, vague is the same thing as dishonesty." He pulls my hands forward and leans back.

"That's a pretty vague answer you just gave me," I point out.

"I was never asked a question. I've told you before, if you want to know something, just ask. You seem to think you know me, yet you've never actually asked me anything yourself."

"I *don't* know you."

He laughs again and shakes his head, then releases my hands. "Forget it." He stands up and starts walking away.

"Wait." I pull myself up from the concrete and follow him. If anyone has the right to be angry here, it's me. "What did I say? I *don't* know you. Why are you getting all pissy with me again?"

He stops walking and turns around, then takes a couple of steps toward me. "I guess after spending time with you over the last few days, I thought I'd get a slightly different reaction from you at school. I've given you plenty of opportunity to ask me whatever you want to ask me, but for some reason you want to believe everything you hear, despite the fact that you never heard any of it from *me*. And coming from someone with her own share of rumors, I figured you'd be a little less judgmental."

My own share of rumors? If he thinks he's going to win points by having something in common with me, he's dead wrong.

"So that's what this is about? You thought the slutty new girl would be sympathetic to the gay-bashing asshole?"

He groans and runs his hands through his hair, frustrated. "Don't do that, Sky."

"Don't do what? Call you a gay-bashing asshole? Okay. Let's practice this honesty policy of yours. Did you or did you not beat up that student last year so badly that you spent a year in juvenile detention?"

He puts his hands on his hips and shakes his head, then looks at me with what seems like disappointment in his expression.

"When I said *don't do that*, I wasn't referring to you insulting me. I was referring to you insulting *yourself*." He takes a step forward, closing the gap between us. "And yes. I beat his ass to within an inch of his life, and if the bastard was standing in front of me right now, I'd do it again."

His eyes are filled with pure anger and I'm too scared to even ask him why or what it's about. He may have said he'd be honest about it . . . but his answers terrify me more than asking the questions. I take a step back at the same time he does. We're both quiet and I'm wondering how we even got to this point.

"I don't want to run with you today," I say.

"I don't really feel like running with you, either."

With that, we both turn in opposite directions. He toward his house, me toward my window. I don't even feel like running alone today.

I climb back in my window just as the rain starts pouring from the sky, and for a second, I feel sorry for him that he still has to run home. But only for a second, because Karma's a bitch, and Holder is definitely who she's retaliating against right now. I close the window and walk to my bed. My heart is racing as fast as if I had just run the three miles. Except right now it's racing because I'm so incredibly pissed.

I met the guy a couple of days ago, yet I've never argued more with anyone in my entire life. I could add up all the arguments Six and I have had over the last four years, and it wouldn't begin to compare to the last forty-eight hours with Holder. I don't know why he even bothers. I guess after this morning, he more than likely won't.

I pick the envelope up from my nightstand and tear it open. I pull Six's letter out and lean back on my pillow and read it, just hoping to escape from the chaos in my head.

Sky,

Hopefully by the time you're reading this (because I know you won't read it right away) I'll be madly in love with a hot Italian boyfriend and not thinking about you at all.

But I know that isn't the case, because I'll be thinking about you all the time.

I'll be thinking about all the nights we stayed up with our ice cream and our movies and our boys. But mostly, I'll be thinking about you, and all the reasons why I love you.

Just to name a few: I love how you suck at good-byes and feelings and emotions, because I do, too. I love how you always scoop from the strawberry and vanilla side of the ice cream because you know how much I love the chocolate, even though you love it, too. I love how you aren't weird and awkward, despite the fact that you've been severely cut off from socialization to the point where you make the Amish look trendy.

But most of all, I love that you don't judge me. I love that in the past four years, you've never once questioned me about my choices (as poor as they may be) or the guys I've been with or the fact that I don't believe in commitment. I would say that it's simple for you not to judge me, because you're a dirty slut, too. But we both know you're not. So thank you for being a nonjudgmental friend. Thank you for never being condescending or treating me like you're better than me (even though we both know you are). As much as I can laugh about the things people say about us behind our backs, it kills me that they say these things about you, too. For that, I'm sorry. But not too sorry, because I know if you were given the choice to either be my slutty best friend or be the girl with the good reputation, you'd screw every guy in the world. Because you love me that much. And I'd let you, because I love you that much.

And one more thing I love about you, then I'll shut up because I'm only six feet away writing this letter right now and it's really hard to not climb out my window and come squeeze you.

I love your indifference. I love how you really just don't give a shit what people think. I love how you are focused on your future and everyone else can kiss your ass. I love how, when I told you I was leaving for Italy after talking you into enrolling at my school, you just smiled and shrugged your shoulders even though it would have torn most best friends apart. I left you hanging to follow my dream, and you didn't let it eat you up. You didn't even give me crap about it.

I love how (last one, I swear) when we watched The Forces of Nature and Sandra Bullock walked away in the end and I was screaming at the TV for such an ugly ending, you just shrugged your shoulders and said, "It's real, Six. You can't get mad at a real ending. Some of them are ugly. It's the fake happily-ever-afters that should piss you off."

I'll never forget that, because you were right. And I know you weren't trying to teach me a lesson, but you did. Not everything is going to go my way and not everyone gets a happily-ever-after. Life is real and sometimes it's ugly and you just have to learn how to cope. I'm going to accept it with a dose of your indifference, and move on.

So, anyway. Enough about that. I just want you to know that I'll miss you and this new very best friend ever in the whole wide world at school better back off when I get home in six months. I hope you realize how amazing you are, but in case you don't, I'm going to text you every single day to remind you. Prepare to be bombarded for the next six months with endless annoying texts of nothing but positive affirmations about Sky.

I love you,
6

I fold the letter up and smile, but I don't cry. She wouldn't expect me to cry over it, no matter how much she might have just made me want to. I reach over to the nightstand and take the cell phone she gave me out of the drawer. I already have two missed text messages.

> **Have I told you lately how awesome you are? Missing you.**

> **It's day two, you better text me back. I need to tell you about Lorenzo. Also, you're sickeningly smart.**

I smile and text her back. It takes me about five tries before I figure it out. I'm almost eighteen and this is the first text I've ever sent? This has to be one for Guinness.

> **I can get used to these daily positive affirmations. Make sure to remind me of how beautiful I am, and how I have the most impeccable taste in music, and how I'm the fastest runner in the world. (Just a few ideas to get you started.) I miss you, too. And I can't wait to hear about Lorenzo, you slut.**

The next few days at school are the same as the first two. Full of drama. My locker seems to have become the hub for sticky notes and nasty letters, none of which I ever see actually being placed on or in my locker. I really don't get what people gain out of doing things like this if they don't even own up to it. Like the note that was stuck to my locker this morning. All it said was "Whore."

Really? Where's the creativity in that? They couldn't back it up with an interesting story? Maybe a few details of my indiscretion? If I have to read this shit every day, the least they could do is make it interesting. If I were going to stoop so low as to leave an unfounded note on someone's locker, I'd at least have the courtesy to entertain whoever read it in the process. I'd write something interesting like, *"I saw you in bed with my boyfriend last night. I really don't appreciate you getting massage oil on my cucumbers. Whore."*

I laugh and it feels odd, laughing out loud at my own thoughts. I look around and no one is left in the hallway but me. Rather than rip the sticky notes off my locker like I probably should, I take out my pen and make them a little more creative. You're welcome, passersby.

Breckin sets his tray down across from mine. We've been getting our own trays now, since he seems to think I want nothing but salad. He smiles at me like he's got a secret that he knows I want. If it's another rumor, I'll pass.

"How were track tryouts yesterday?" he asks.

I shrug. "I didn't go."

"Yeah, I know."

"Then why'd you ask?"

He laughs. "Because I like to clarify things with you before I believe them. Why didn't you go?"

I shrug again.

"What's with the shoulder shrugs? You have a nervous tic?"

I shrug. "I just don't feel like being part of a team with anyone here. It's lost its appeal."

He frowns. "First of all, track is one of the most individual sports you can join. Second, I thought you said extracurricular activities were the reason you were here."

"I don't *know* why I'm here," I say. "Maybe I feel like I need to witness a good dose of human nature at its worst before I enter the real world. It'll be less of a shock."

He points a celery stick at me and cocks his eyebrow. "This is true. A gradual introduction to the perils of society will help cushion the blow. We can't release you alone into the wild when you've been pampered in a zoo your whole life."

"Nice analogy."

He winks at me and bites his stick of celery. "Speaking of analogies. What's up with your locker? It was covered in sexual analogies and metaphors today."

I laugh. "You like that? Took me a while, but I was feeling creative."

He nods. "I especially liked the one that said '*You're such a slut, you screwed Breckin the Mormon.*'"

I shake my head. "Now that one I can't lay claim to. That was an original. But they're fun, aren't they? Now that they've been dirtied up?"

"Well," he says. "They *were* fun. They aren't there anymore. I saw Holder ripping them off your locker just now."

I snap my gaze back up to his and he's grinning mischievously again. I guess this is the secret he was having trouble holding in.

"That's strange." I'm curious why Holder would bother to do such a thing. We haven't been running together since we spoke last. In fact, we don't even interact at all. He sits across the room now in first period and I don't see him at all the rest of the day, aside from lunch. Even then, he sits on the other side of the cafeteria with his friends. I thought after coming to an impasse, we'd successfully moved on to mutual avoidance, but I guess I was wrong.

"Can I ask you something?" Breckin says.

I shrug again, mostly just to irritate him.

"Are the rumors about him true? About his temper? And his sister?"

I try not to appear taken aback by his comment, but it's the first I've heard anything about a sister. "I don't know. All I know is that I've spent enough time with him to know he scares me enough to not want to spend more time with him."

I really want to ask him about the sister comment, but I can't help which situations my stubbornness rears its ugly head in. For some reason, probing for information about Dean Holder is one of those situations.

"Hey," a voice from behind me says. I immediately know it isn't Holder's, because I'm indifferent to the voice. About the time I turn around, Grayson swings his leg over the seat bench next to me and sits. "You busy after school?"

I dip my celery stick into a blob of ranch dressing and take a bite. "Probably."

Grayson shakes his head. "That's not a good enough answer. I'll meet you at your car after last period."

He's up and gone before I can object. Breckin smirks at me.

I just shrug.

I have no idea what Grayson wants to talk about, but if he's thinking he's coming over tomorrow night, he needs a lobotomy. I'm so ready to just swear off guys for the rest of the year. Especially if it means not having Six to eat ice cream with after they go home. Ice cream was the only appealing part to making out with the guys.

At least he's true to form. He's waiting at my car, leaning up against my driver's-side door when I reach the parking lot. "Hey, Princess," he says. I don't know if it's the sound of his voice or the fact that he just gave me a nickname, but his words make me cringe. I walk up to him and lean against the car next to him.

"Don't call me Princess again. Ever."

He laughs and slides in front of me, gripping my waist in his hands. "Fine. How about beautiful?"

"How about you just call me Sky?"

"Why do you have to be so angry all the time?" He reaches up to my face and holds my cheeks in his hands, then kisses me. Sadly, I let him. Mostly because I feel like he's earned it for putting up with me for an entire month. He doesn't deserve a whole lot of return favors, though, so I pull my face away after just a few seconds.

"What do you want?"

He snakes his arms around my waist and pulls me against him. "You." He starts kissing my neck, so I push against him and he backs away. *"What?"*

"Can you not take a hint? I told you I'm not sleeping with you, Grayson. I'm not trying to play games or get you to chase me like other sick, twisted girls do. You want more and I don't, so I think we just need to accept that we're at an impasse and move on."

He stares at me, then sighs and pulls me against him, hugging me. "I don't need more, Sky. It's fine the way it is. I won't push it again. I just like coming to your house and I want to come over tomorrow night." He tries to flash me that panty-dropping grin. "Now stop being mad at me and come here." He pulls my face to his and kisses me again.

As irritated and as angry as I am, I can't help but be relieved that as soon as his lips meet mine, my irritation subsides, thanks to the numbness that takes over. For that reason alone, I continue to let him kiss me. He backs me against the car and runs his hands in my hair, then kisses down my jaw and to my neck. I lean my head against the car and bring my wrist up behind him to check the time on my watch. Karen's going out of town for work, so I need to go to the grocery store to get enough sugar to last me all weekend. I don't know how long he plans on feeling me up, but ice cream is really starting to sound tempting right about now. I roll my eyes and drop my arm. All at once, my heart rate triples and my stomach flips and I get all of the feelings a girl is supposed to get when a hot guy's lips are all over her. Only I'm not having the reaction to the hot guy whose lips are all over me. I'm having the reaction to the hot guy glaring at me from across the parking lot.

Holder is standing next to his car with his elbow on the top of his doorframe, watching us. I immediately shove Grayson off me and turn around to get in my car.

"So we're on for tomorrow night?" he asks.

I climb into the car and crank it, then look up at him. "No. We're done."

I pull the door shut and back out of the parking lot, not sure if I'm angry, embarrassed, or infatuated. How does he do that? How the hell does he incite these kinds of feelings from me from clear across a parking lot? I think I'm in need of an intervention.

"Is Jack going with you?" I open the car door for Karen so she can throw the last of her luggage into the backseat.

"Yeah, he's coming. We'll be home . . . *I'll* be home on Sunday," she says, correcting herself. It pains her to count Jack as a "we." I hate that she feels that way because I really like Jack and I know he loves Karen, so I don't understand what her hang-up is at all. She's had a couple of boyfriends in the past twelve years, but as soon as it starts getting serious for the guy, she runs.

Karen shuts the back door and turns to me. "You know I trust you, but please . . ."

"Don't get pregnant," I interrupt. "I know, I know. You've been saying that every time you leave for the past two years. I'm not getting pregnant, Mom. Only terribly high and cracked out."

She laughs and hugs me. "Good girl. And wasted. Don't forget to get really wasted."

"I won't forget, I promise. And I'm renting a TV for the weekend so I can sit around and eat ice cream and watch trash on cable."

She pulls back and glares at me. "Now that's not funny."

I laugh and hug her again. "Have fun. I hope you sell lots of herbal thingies and soaps and tinctures and whatever else it is you do at these things."

"Love you. If you need me, you know you can use Six's house phone."

I roll my eyes at the same instructions she gives me every time she leaves. "See ya," I say. She gets in the car and pulls out of the driveway, leaving me parent-free for the weekend. To most teenagers, this would be the point at which they pull out their phones and post an invite to the most kick-ass party of the year. Not me. Nope. Instead, I go inside and decide to bake cookies, because that's the most rebellious thing I can come up with.

I love to bake, but I don't claim to be very good at it. I usually end up with more flour and chocolate on my face and hair than in the actual end product. Tonight's no exception. I've already made a batch of chocolate chip cookies, a batch of brownies, and something I'm not sure what it was supposed to be. I'm working on pouring the flour into the mixture for a homemade German chocolate cake when the doorbell rings.

I'm pretty sure I should know what to do in situations like this. Doorbells ring all the time, right? Not mine. I stare at the door, not sure what I'm expecting it to do. When it rings for a second time, I put down the measuring cup and wipe my hair out of my eyes, then walk to the front door. When I open it, I'm not even surprised to see Holder. Okay, I'm surprised. But not really.

"Hey," I say. I can't think of anything else to say. Even if I could think of something else to say, I probably wouldn't be able to say it since I can't freaking *breathe*! He's standing on the top step of my entryway, hands hanging loosely in the pockets of his jeans. His hair still needs a trim, but when he brings his hand up and pushes it out of his eyes, the thought of him trimming that hair is suddenly the worst idea in the world.

"Hi." He's smiling awkwardly and he looks nervous and it's terribly attractive. He's in a good mood. For now, anyway. Who knows when he'll get pissed off and feel like arguing again.

"Um," I say, uneasily. I know the next step is to invite him in, but that's only if I'm actually wanting him inside my house, and to be honest, the jury is still out on that one.

"You busy?" he asks.

I glance back into the kitchen at the inconceivable mess I've made. "Sort of." It's not a lie. I'm sort of incredibly busy.

He looks away and nods, then points behind him to his car. "Yeah. I guess I'll . . . go." He takes a step back off the top step.

"No," I say, much too quickly and a decibel too loudly. It's an almost desperate *no*, and I cringe from embarrassment. As much as I don't know why he's here or why he even keeps bothering, my curiosity gets the best of me. I step aside and open the door farther. "You can come in, but you might be put to work."

He hesitates, then ascends the step again. He walks inside and I shut the door behind us. Before it can get any more awkward, I walk into the kitchen and pick up the measuring cup and get right back to work like there isn't some random, temperamental, hot guy standing in my house.

"You prepping for a bake sale?" He makes his way around the bar and eyes the plethora of desserts covering my counter.

"My mom's out of town for the weekend. She's anti-sugar, so I kind of go crazy when she's not here."

He laughs and picks up a cookie, but looks at me first for permission.

"Help yourself," I say. "But be warned, just because I like to bake doesn't mean I'm good at it." I sift the last of the flour and pour it into the mixing bowl.

"So you get the house to yourself and you spend Friday night baking? Typical teenager," he says mockingly.

"What can I say?" I shrug. "I'm a rebel."

He turns around and opens a cabinet, eyeing the contents, then shuts it. He steps to the left and opens another cabinet, then takes out a glass. "Got any milk?" he asks while heading to the refrigerator. I pause from stirring and watch as he pulls the milk out and pours himself a glass like he's right at home. He takes a drink and turns around to catch me staring at him, then he grins. "You shouldn't offer cookies without milk, you know. You're a pretty pathetic hostess." He grabs another cookie and walks himself and the milk to the bar and takes a seat.

"I try to save my hospitality for *invited* guests," I say sarcastically, turning back to the counter.

"Ouch." He laughs.

I turn the mixer on, creating an excuse to not have to talk to him for three minutes on medium to high speed. I try to remember what I look like, without noticeably searching for a reflective surface. I'm pretty sure I've got flour everywhere. I know my hair is being held up with a pencil and my sweatpants are being worn for the fourth evening in a row. *Unwashed.* I try to nonchalantly wipe away any visible traces of flour, but I'm aware it's a lost cause. Oh, well, there's no way I could look any worse right now than when I was laid out on the couch with gravel embedded in my cheek.

I turn off the mixer and depress the button to free the mixing blades. I bring one to my mouth and lick it, and walk the other one to where he's seated. "Want one? It's German chocolate."

He takes it out of my hand and smiles. "How hospitable of you."

"Shut up and lick it or I'm keeping it for myself." I walk to the cabinet and grab my own cup, but pour myself a glass of water instead. "You want some water or do you want to continue pretending you can stomach that vegan shit?"

He laughs and crinkles up his nose, then pushes his cup across the bar toward me. "I was trying to be nice, but I can't take another sip of whatever the hell this is. Yes, water. *Please.*"

I laugh and rinse out his cup, then slide him the glass of water. I take a seat in the chair across from him and eye him while I bite into a brownie. I'm waiting for him to explain why he's here, but he doesn't. He just sits across from me and watches me eat. I don't ask him why he's here because I sort of like the quiet between us. It works better when we both shut up, since all of our conversations tend to end in arguments.

Holder stands up and walks into the living room without an explanation. He looks around curiously, his attention being stolen by the photographs on the walls. He walks closer to them and slowly scans each picture. I lean back in my chair and watch him be nosy.

He's never in much of a hurry and seems so assured in every movement he makes. It's like all of his thoughts and actions are meticulously planned out days in advance. I can just picture him in his bedroom, writing down the words he plans to use the following day, because he's so selective with them.

"Your mom seems really young," he says.

"She is young."

"You don't look like her. Do you look like your dad?" He turns and faces me.

I shrug. "I don't know. I don't remember what he looks like."

He turns back to the pictures and runs his finger across one of them.

"Is your dad dead?" He's so blunt about it, I'm almost certain he knows my dad isn't dead or he wouldn't have asked it like that. So carelessly.

"I don't know. Haven't seen him since I was three."

He walks back toward the kitchen and takes a seat in front of me again. "That's all I get? No story?"

"Oh, there's a story. I just don't want to tell it." I'm sure there is a story . . . I just don't *know* it. Karen doesn't know anything about my life before I was put into foster care and I've never seen the point of digging it up. What's a few forgotten years when I've had thirteen great ones?

He smiles at me again, but it's a wary smile when accompanied by the quizzical look in his eyes. "Your cookies were good," he says, skillfully changing the subject. "You shouldn't downplay your baking abilities."

Something beeps and I jump up from my seat and run to the oven. I open it, but the cake isn't even close to being done. When I turn around, Holder is holding up my cell phone. "You got a text." He laughs. "Your cake is fine."

100

I throw the oven mitt on the counter, then walk back to my seat. He's scrolling through the texts on my phone without a shred of respect for privacy. I really don't care, though, so I just let him.

"I thought you weren't allowed to have a phone," he says. "Or was that a really pathetic excuse to avoid giving me your number?"

"I'm *not* allowed. My best friend gave it to me the other day. It can't do anything but text."

He turns the screen around to face me. "What the hell kind of texts are these?" He turns the phone around and reads one.

"*Sky, you are beautiful. You are possibly the most exquisite creature in the universe and if anyone tells you otherwise, I'll cut the bitch.*" He arches an eyebrow and looks up at me, then back down to the phone. "Oh, God. They're all like this. Please tell me you don't text these to yourself for daily motivation."

I laugh and reach across the bar and snatch the phone out of his hand. "Stop. You're ruining the fun of it."

He leans his head back and laughs. "Oh, my God, you do? Those are all from you?"

"No!" I say, defensively. "They're from Six. She's my best friend and she's halfway around the world and she misses me. She wants me to not be sad, so she sends me nice texts every day. I think it's sweet."

"Oh, you do not. You think it's annoying and you probably don't even read them."

How does he know that?

I set the phone down and cross my arms over my chest. "She means well," I say, still not admitting that the texts are annoying the living hell out of me.

"They'll ruin you. Those texts will inflate your ego so much, you'll explode." He grabs the phone and pulls his own phone out of his pocket. He scrolls through the screens on both phones and punches some numbers on his phone. "We need to rectify this situation before you start suffering from delusions of grandeur." He hands me back my phone and types something into his own phone, then puts it in his pocket. My phone sounds off, indicating a new text message. I look down at the screen and laugh.

Your cookies suck ass. And you're really not that pretty.

"Better?" he says, teasingly. "Did the ego deflate enough?"

I laugh and set the phone down on the counter, then stand up. "You know just the right things to say to a girl." I walk to the living room and turn around. "Want a tour of the house?"

He stands up and follows me while I point out boring facts and knick-knacks and rooms and pictures, but of course he's slowly soaking it all in, never in a rush. He has to stop and inspect every tiny thing, never speaking a single word the whole time.

When we finally get to my bedroom, I swing open the door. "My room," I say, flashing my Vanna White pose. "Feel free to look around, but being as though there aren't any people eighteen or older here, stay off the bed. I'm not allowed to get pregnant this weekend."

He pauses as he's passing through the doorway and tilts his head toward me. "Only *this* weekend? You plan on getting knocked up next weekend, instead?"

I follow him into my bedroom. "Nah. I'll probably wait a few more weeks."

He inspects the room, slowly turning around until he's facing me again. "I'm eighteen."

I cock my head to the side, confused about why he pointed out that random fact. "Yay for you?"

He cuts his eyes to the bed, then back to me. "You said to stay off your bed because I'm not eighteen. I'm just pointing out that I am."

I don't like the way my lungs just constricted when he looked at my bed. "Oh. Well then, I meant nineteen."

He spins around, then walks slowly to the open window. He bends down and sticks his head out of it, then pulls back inside. "So this is the infamous window, huh?"

He doesn't look at me, which is probably a good thing because if looks could kill he'd be dead. Why the hell did he have to go and say something like that? I was actually enjoying his company for a change. He turns back to me and his playful expression is gone, replaced by a challenging one that I've seen too many times before.

I sigh. "What do you want, Holder?" He either needs to get his point across about why he's here, or he needs to leave. He folds his arms across his chest and narrows his eyes at me.

"Did I say something wrong, Sky? Or untrue? Unfounded, maybe?" It's obvious from his taunting remarks that he knows exactly what he was insinuating with the window comment. I'm not in the mood to play his games; I have cakes that need baking. And eating.

I walk to the door and hold it open. "You know exactly what you said and you got the reaction you wanted. Happy? You can go now."

He doesn't. He drops his arms and turns around, then walks to my nightstand. He picks up the book Breckin gave me and inspects it as though the last thirty seconds never even occurred.

"Holder, I'm asking you as nicely as I'm going to ask you. Please leave."

He lays the book down gently, then proceeds to lie down on the bed. He literally lies down on my bed. He's on my damn bed.

I roll my eyes and walk over to where he is, then reach down and pull his legs off my bed. If I have to physically remove him from the house, I'll do it. When I grab his wrists and lift upward, he pulls me to him in a move that happens faster than my mind can even comprehend. He flips me over until I'm on my back and he's holding my arms to the mattress. It happens so unexpectedly; I don't even have time to fight him. And looking up at him right now, half of me doesn't even *want* to fight him. I don't know if I should scream for help or rip off my clothes.

He releases my arms and brings one of his hands to my face. He brushes his thumb across my nose and laughs. "Flour," he says, wiping it away. "It's been bugging me." He sits up against my headboard and brings his feet back onto the bed. I'm still flat on the mattress, staring up at the stars, actually feeling something other than nothing for the first time ever while looking at them.

I can't even move, because I'm sort of afraid he's crazy. I mean literally, clinically insane. It's the only logical explanation for his personality. And the fact that I still find him so incredibly attractive can only mean one thing. I'm insane, too.

"I didn't know he was gay."

Yep, he's crazy.

I turn my head toward him, but say nothing. What the hell do you say to a crazy person who literally refuses to leave your house, then starts spouting off random shit?

"I beat him up because he was an asshole. I had no idea he was gay."

His elbows are resting on his knees and he's looking right at me, waiting for a reaction. Or a response. Neither of which he's getting for a few seconds, because I need to process this.

I look back up at the stars and give myself time to analyze the situation. If he's not crazy, then he's definitely trying to make a point. But what point? He comes over here, uninvited, to defend his reputation and insult mine? What would be the point of even making the effort? I'm just one person, what does my opinion matter?

Unless, of course, he likes me. The thought literally makes me smile and I feel dirty and wrong for hoping a lunatic likes me. I had it coming, though. I should have never let him in the house, knowing I'm alone. And now he knows I'll be home all weekend alone. If I had to weigh tonight's decisions, this would probably be so heavy it would break the dumb side of the scale. I foresee this ending in one of two ways. We'll either come to a mutual understanding of each other, or he's going to kill me and chop me up into tiny pieces and bake me into cookies. Either way, it makes me sad for all the dessert that isn't being eaten right now.

"Cake!" I yell, jumping up off the bed. I run to the kitchen just in time to smell my latest disaster. I grab the oven mitt and pull the cake out, then throw it on the counter in disappointment. It's not too badly burnt. I could probably salvage it by drowning it in icing.

I shut the oven and decide that I'm moving on to a new hobby. Maybe I'll make jewelry. How hard could that be? I grab two more cookies and walk back to my bedroom and hand one of the cookies to Holder, then lie down on the bed next to him.

"I guess the gay-bashing asshole remark was really judgmental on my part then, huh? You aren't really an ignorant homophobe who spent the last year in juvenile detention?"

He grins and scoots down on the bed next to me and looks up at the stars. "Nope. Not at all. I spent the entire last year living with my father in Austin. I don't even know where the story about me being sent to juvi came into the picture."

"Why don't you defend yourself against the rumors if they aren't true?"

He turns his head toward me on the pillow. "Why don't *you?*"

I purse my lips and nod. "Touché."

We both sit quietly on the bed eating our cookies. Some of the things he's said over the past few days are starting to make sense, and I begin to feel more and more like the people I despise. He told me outright that he would answer anything if I just asked, yet I chose to believe the rumors about him instead. No wonder he was so irritated with me. I was treating him just like everyone else treats me.

"The window comment from earlier?" I say. "You were just making a point about rumors? You really weren't trying to be mean?"

"I'm not mean, Sky."

"You're intense. I'm right about that, at least."

"I may be intense, but I'm not mean."

"Well, I'm not a slut."

"I'm not a gay-bashing asshole."

"So we're all clear?"

He laughs. "Yeah, I guess so."

I inhale a deep breath, then exhale, preparing to do something I don't do very often. Apologize. If I wasn't so stubborn, I might even admit that my judgmental behavior this week was completely mortifying and he had every right in the world to be angry with me for being so ignorant. Instead, I keep the apology short and sweet.

"I'm sorry, Holder," I say quietly.

He sighs heavily. "I know, Sky. I know."

And we sit like this in complete silence for what seems like forever but also doesn't feel like near long enough. It's getting late and I'm afraid he's about to say he needs to leave because there's nothing else to say, but I don't want him to. It feels right, being here with him now. I don't know why, but it just does.

"I need to ask you something," he says, finally breaking the silence. I don't respond, because it doesn't feel like his statement is waiting for a response. He's just taking one of his moments to prepare whatever it is he wants to ask me. He takes a breath, then rolls over onto his side to face me. He tucks his elbow under his head and I can feel him looking at me, but I keep staring at the stars. He's way too close for me to look at him right now, and by the way my heart is already pounding against my chest, I'm afraid moving any closer will physically kill me. It doesn't seem possible that lust can cause a heart to take this much of a beating. It's worse than running.

"Why were you letting Grayson do what he was doing to you in the parking lot?"

I want to crawl under my covers and hide. I was hoping this wouldn't come up. "I already told you. He's not my boyfriend and he's not the one who gave me the black eye."

"I'm not asking because of any of that. I'm asking because I saw how you reacted. You were irritated with him. You even looked a little bored. I just want to know why you allow him to do those things if you clearly don't want him touching you."

His words throw me for a loop and I'm suddenly feeling claustrophobic and sweaty. I don't feel comfortable talking about this. It makes me uneasy how he reads me so well, yet I can't read him for anything.

"My lack of interest was that obvious?" I ask.

"Yep. And from fifty yards away. I'm just surprised he didn't take the hint."

This time I turn to face him without thinking, and tuck my elbow under my head. "I know, right? I can't tell you how many times I've turned him down but he just doesn't stop. It's really pathetic. And unattractive."

"Then why do you let him do it?" he says, eyeing me sharply. We're in a compromising position right now, facing each other on the same bed. The way he's staring at me and dropping his eyes to my lips prompts me to roll onto my back again. I don't know if he feels the same, but he rolls onto his back, too.

"It's complicated."

"You don't have to explain," he says. "I was just curious. It's really not my business."

I tuck my hands behind my head and look up at the stars

that I've counted more times than I can count. I've been in this bed with Holder longer than I've probably been in this bed with *any* boy, and it occurs to me that I haven't felt the need to count a single star.

"Have you ever had a serious girlfriend?"

"Yep," he says. "But I hope you aren't about to ask for details, because I don't go there."

I shake my head. "That's not why I'm asking." I pause for a few seconds, wanting to word things the right way. "When you kissed her, what did you feel?"

He pauses for a moment, probably thinking this is a trick question. "You want honesty, right?" he asks.

"That's all I ever want."

I can see him smile out of the corner of my eyes. "All right then. I guess I felt . . . horny."

I try to appear unaffected, hearing that word come out of his mouth, but . . . *wow.* I cross my legs, hoping it'll help minimize the hot flashes racing through me. "So you get the butterflies and the sweaty palms and the rapid heartbeat and all that?"

He shrugs. "Yeah. Not with every girl I've been with, but most of them."

I angle my head in his direction, trying not to analyze the way that sentence came out. He turns his head toward me and grins.

"There weren't *that* many." He smiles and his dimple is even cuter close up. For a moment, I get lost in it. "What's your point?"

I bring my eyes back to his, briefly, then face the ceiling again. "My point is that I *don't.* I don't feel any of that. When I make out with guys, I don't feel anything at all.

Just numbness. So sometimes I let Grayson do what he does to me, not because I enjoy it, but because I like not feeling anything at all." He doesn't respond and his silence makes me uncomfortable. I can't help but wonder if he's mentally labeling *me* crazy. "I know it doesn't make sense, and no, I'm not a lesbian. I've just never been attracted to anyone before you and I don't know why."

As soon as I say it, he darts his head toward me at the same second I squeeze my eyes shut and throw my arm over my face. I can't believe I just admitted, out loud, that I'm attracted to him. I could die right now and it wouldn't be soon enough.

I feel the bed shift and he encompasses my wrist with his hand and removes my arm from over my eyes. I reluctantly open them and he's propped up on his hand, smiling at me. "You're attracted to me?"

"Oh, God," I groan. "That's the last thing you need for your ego."

"That's probably true." He laughs. "Better hurry up and insult me before my ego gets as big as yours."

"You need a haircut," I blurt out. "Really bad. It gets in your eyes and you squint and you're constantly moving it out of the way like you're Justin Bieber and it's really distracting."

He fingers his hair with his hand and frowns, then falls back onto the bed. "Man. That really hurt. It seems like you've thought that one out for a while."

"Just since Monday," I admit.

"You *met* me on Monday. So technically, you've been thinking about how much you hate my hair since the moment we met?"

"Not *every* moment."

He's quiet for a minute, then grins again. "I can't believe you think I'm hot."

"Shut up."

"You probably faked passing out the other day, just so you could be carried in my hot, sweaty, manly arms."

"Shut up."

"I'll bet you fantasize about me at night, right here in this bed."

"Shut up, Holder."

"You probably even . . ."

I reach over and clamp my hand over his mouth. "You're way hotter when you aren't speaking."

When he finally shuts his mouth, I remove my hand and put it back behind my head. Again, we both go a while without speaking. He's probably silently gloating at the fact that I admitted I'm attracted to him, while I'm silently cringing that he's now privy to that knowledge.

"I'm bored," he says.

"So go home."

"I don't want to. What do you do when you're bored? You don't have internet or TV. Do you just sit around all day and think about how hot I am?"

I roll my eyes. "I read," I say. "A lot. Sometimes I bake. Sometimes I run."

"Read, bake, and run. And fantasize about me. What a riveting life you lead."

"I like my life."

"I sort of like it, too," he says. He rolls over and grabs the book off my nightstand. "Here, read this."

I take the book out of his hands and open it to the

marker on page two. It's as far as I've gotten. "You want me to read it out loud? You're that bored?"

"Pretty damn bored."

"It's a romance," I warn.

"Like I said. Pretty damn bored. Read."

I scoot my pillow up toward the headboard and make myself comfortable, then start reading.

This morning if you had told me I'd be reading a romance novel to Dean Holder in my bed tonight, I'd tell you that you were crazy. But then again, I'm obviously not the best judge of crazy.

When I open my eyes, I immediately slide my hand to the other side of the bed, but it's empty. I sit up and look around. My light is off and my covers are on. The book is closed on the nightstand, so I pick it up. There's a bookmark almost three-quarters of the way through.

I read until I fell asleep? *Oh, no, I fell asleep.* I throw the covers off and walk to the kitchen, then flip on the light and look around in shock. The entire kitchen is clean and all the cookies and brownies are wrapped in Saran Wrap. I look down at my phone sitting on the counter and pick it up to find a new text message.

> **You fell asleep right when she was about to find out her mother's secret. How dare you. I'll be back tomorrow night so you can finish reading it to me. And by the way, you have really bad breath and you snore way too loud.**

I laugh. I'm also grinning like an idiot, but luckily no one is here to witness it. I glance at the clock on the stove and it's only just past two in the morning, so I go back to the bedroom and crawl into bed, hoping he really does show up tomorrow night. I don't know how this hopeless boy weaseled his way into my life this week, but I know I'm definitely not ready for him to leave.

Saturday, September 1, 2012
5:05 p.m.

I've learned an invaluable lesson about lust today. It causes double the work. I took two showers today, instead of just one. I changed clothes four times instead of the usual two. I've cleaned the house once (that's one more than I usually clean it) and I've checked the time on the clock no less than a thousand times. I may have checked my phone for incoming texts just as many.

Unfortunately, he didn't state in his text from last night what time he would be here, so by five o'clock I'm pretty much sitting and waiting. There isn't much else to do, since I've already baked enough sweets for an entire year and I've run no less than four miles today. I thought about cooking dinner for us, but I have no idea what time he's coming over, so I wouldn't know when to have it ready. I'm sitting on the couch, drumming my nails on the sofa, when I get a text from him.

What time can I come over? Not that I'm looking forward to it or anything. You're really, really boring.

He texted me. Why didn't I think of that? I should have texted him a few hours ago to ask what time he would be here. It would have saved me so much unnecessary, pathetic fretting.

Be here at seven. And bring me something to eat. I'm not cooking for you.

I set the phone down and stare at it. An hour and forty-five minutes to go. Now what? I look around at my empty living room and, for the first time ever, the boredom starts to have a negative effect on me. Up until this week, I was pretty content with my lackluster life. I wonder if being exposed to the temptations of technology has left me wanting more, or if it's being exposed to the temptations of Holder. Probably both.

I stretch my legs out on the coffee table in front of me. I'm wearing jeans and a T-shirt today after finally deciding to give my sweatpants a break. I also have my hair down, but only because Holder has never seen me in anything other than a ponytail. Not that I'm trying to impress him.

I'm totally trying to impress him.

I pick up a magazine and flip through it, but my leg is shaking and I'm fidgeting to the point that I can't focus. I read the same page three times in a row, so I throw the magazine back on the coffee table and lean my head back into the couch. I stare at the ceiling. Then I stare at the wall. Then I stare at my toes and wonder if I should repaint them.

I'm going crazy.

I finally groan and reach for my phone, then text him again.

Now. Come right now. I'm bored out of my freaking mind and if you don't come right now I'll finish the book before you get here.

I hold the phone in my hands and watch the screen as it bounces up and down against my knee. He texts back right away.

Lol. I'm getting you food, bossy pants. Be there in twenty.

Lol? What the hell does that mean? Lots of love? Oh, God, that better not be it. He'll be out the door faster than Matty-boy. But really, what the hell does it mean?

I stop thinking about it and focus on the last word. Twenty. Twenty minutes. Oh, shit, that suddenly seems way too soon. I run to the bathroom and check my hair, my clothes, my breath. I make a quick run through the house, cleaning it for the second time today. When the doorbell finally rings, I actually know what to do this time. Open it.

He's standing with two armfuls of groceries, looking very domesticated. I eye the groceries suspiciously. He holds the sacks up and shrugs. "One of us has to be the hospitable one." He eases past me and walks straight to the kitchen and sets the sacks on the counter. "I hope you like spaghetti and meatballs, because that's what you're getting." He begins removing items from the sacks and pulling cookware out of cabinets.

I shut the front door and walk to the bar. "You're cooking dinner for me?"

"Actually, I'm cooking for *me*, but you're welcome to eat some if you want." He glances at me over his shoulder and smiles.

"Are you always so sarcastic?" I ask.

He shrugs. "Are *you*?"

"Do you always answer questions with questions?"

"Do *you*?"

I pick up a hand towel off the bar and throw it at him. He dodges it, then walks to the refrigerator. "You want something to drink?" he asks.

I put my elbows on the bar and rest my chin in my hands, watching him. "You're offering to make me something to drink in my own house?"

He searches through the refrigerator shelves. "Do you want milk that tastes like ass or do you want soda?"

"Do we even have soda?" I'm almost positive I already drank up the stash I bought yesterday.

He leans back out of the refrigerator and arches an eyebrow. "Can either of us say anything that isn't a question?"

I laugh. "I don't know, can we?"

"How long do you think we can keep this up?" He finds a soda and grabs two glasses. "You want ice?"

"Are *you* having ice?" I'm not stopping with the questions until he does. I'm highly competitive.

He walks closer to me and places our glasses on the counter. "Do you *think* I should have ice?" he says with a challenging grin.

"Do you *like* ice?" I challenge back.

He nods his head, impressed that I've kept up to speed with him. "Is your ice any good?"

"Well, do you prefer crushed ice or cubed ice?"

He narrows his eyes at me, aware that I just trapped him. He can't answer that one with a question. He pops the lid open and begins pouring the soda into my cup. "No ice for you."

"Ha!" I say. "I win."

He laughs and walks back to the stove. "I let you win because I feel sorry for you. Anyone that snores as bad as you do deserves a break every now and then."

I smirk at him. "You know, the insults are really only funny when they're in text form." I pick my glass up and take a drink. It definitely needs ice. I walk to the freezer and pull out a few ice cubes and drop them into my cup.

When I turn around, he's standing right in front of me,

staring down at me. The look in his eyes is slightly mischievous, but just serious enough that it causes my heart to palpitate. He takes a step forward until my back meets the refrigerator behind me. He casually lifts his arm and places his hand on the refrigerator beside my head.

I don't know how I'm not sinking to the floor right now. My knees feel like they're about to give out.

"You know I'm kidding, right?" he says softly. His eyes are scrolling over my face and he's smiling just enough that his dimples are showing.

I nod and hope he backs the hell away from me, because I'm about to have an asthma attack and I don't even have asthma.

"Good," he says, moving in just a couple more inches. "Because you *don't* snore. In fact, you're pretty damn adorable when you sleep."

He really shouldn't say things like that. Especially when he's leaning in this close to me. His arm bends at the elbow and he's suddenly a whole lot closer. He leans in toward my ear and I inhale sharply.

"Sky," he whispers seductively into my ear. "I *need* you . . . to move. I need to get in the fridge." He slowly pulls back and keeps his eyes trained on mine, watching for my reaction. A smile pulls at the corners of his mouth and he tries to hold it in, but he breaks out in laughter.

I push against his chest and duck under his arm. "You're such an ass!"

He opens the refrigerator, still laughing. "I'm sorry, but damn. You're so blatantly attracted to me, it's hard not to tease you."

I know he's joking, but it still embarrasses the hell out

of me. I sit back down at the bar and drop my head into my hands. I'm beginning to hate the girl he's turning me into. It wouldn't be nearly as hard to be around him if I hadn't slipped and told him I was attracted to him. It also wouldn't be as hard if he weren't so funny. And sweet, when he wants to be. And hot. I guess that's what makes lust so bittersweet. The feeling is beautiful, but the effort it takes to deny it is way too hard.

"Want to know something?" he asks. I look up at him and he's looking down at the pan in front of him, stirring.

"Probably not."

He glances at me for a few seconds, then looks back down at the pan. "It might make you feel better."

"I doubt it."

He cuts his eyes to me again and the playful smile is gone from his lips. He reaches into a cabinet and pulls out a pan, then walks to the sink and fills it with water. He walks back to the stove and begins stirring again. "I might be a little bit attracted to you, too," he says.

I unnoticeably inhale, then let out a slow, controlled breath in an attempt not to appear blindsided by that comment.

"Just a little bit?" I ask, doing what I do best by infusing awkward moments with sarcasm.

He smiles again, but keeps his eyes trained on the pan in front of him. The room grows silent for several minutes. He's focused on cooking and I'm focused on him. I watch him as he moves effortlessly around the kitchen and I'm in awe at his level of comfort. This is my house and I'm more nervous than he is. I can't stop fidgeting and I wish he would start talking again. He doesn't seem as affected by the silence, but it's looming in the air around me and I need to get rid of it.

"What does *lol* mean?"

He laughs. "Seriously?"

"Yes, seriously. You typed it in your text earlier."

"It means laugh out loud. You use it when you think something is funny."

I can't deny the relief I feel that it wasn't *lots of love*.

"Huh," I say. "That's dumb."

"Yeah, it is pretty dumb. It's just habit, though, and the abbreviated texts make it a lot faster to type once you get the hang of it. Sort of like OMG and WTF and IDK and . . ."

"Oh, God, stop," I say, interrupting him before he spouts off more abbreviations. "You speaking in abbreviated text form is really unattractive."

He turns to me and winks, then walks to the oven. "I'll never do it again, then."

And it happens again . . . the silence. Yesterday the silence between us was fine, but for some reason, it's incredibly awkward tonight. It is for me, anyway. I'm beginning to think I'm just nervous for what the rest of the night holds. It's obvious with the chemistry between us that we'll end up kissing eventually. It's just really hard to focus on the here and now and be engaged in conversation when that's the only thing on my mind. I can't stand not knowing when he'll do it. Will he wait until after dinner when my breath smells like garlic and onions? Will he wait until it's time for him to leave? Will he just spring it on me when I'm least expecting it? I almost just want to get it over with right now. Cut to the chase so the inevitable can be put aside and we can get on with the night.

"You okay?" he asks. I snap my gaze back up to his and he's standing across the bar from me. "Where'd you go? You checked out for a while there."

I shake my head and pull myself back into the conversation. "I'm fine."

He picks up a knife and begins chopping a tomato. Even his tomato-chopping skills are effortless. Is there anything this boy is bad at? His knife stills on the cutting board and I look up at him. He's looking down at me with a serious expression.

"Where'd you go, Sky?" He watches me for a few seconds, waiting on my response. When I fail to give him one, he drops his eyes back to the cutting board.

"Promise you won't laugh?" I ask.

He squints and ponders my question, then shakes his head. "I told you that I'll only ever be honest with you, so no. I can't promise I won't laugh because you're kind of funny and that's only setting myself up for failure."

"Are you always so difficult?"

He grins at me, but doesn't respond. He keeps eyeing me like he's challenging me to say what's really on my mind. Unfortunately, I don't back down from challenges.

"Okay, fine." I sit up straight in my chair and take a deep breath, then let all my thoughts out at once. "I'm really not any good at this whole dating thing, and I don't even know if this *is* a date, but I know that whatever it is, it's a little more than just two friends hanging out, and knowing that makes me think about later tonight when it's time for you to leave and whether or not you plan to kiss me and I'm the type of person who hates surprises so I can't stop feeling awkward about it because I *do* want you to kiss me and this may be presumptuous of me, but I sort of think you want to kiss me, too, and so I was thinking how much easier it would be if we just went ahead and kissed already so you can go back to cooking dinner and I can stop trying to mentally map out how our night's about to play out." I inhale an incredibly huge breath, as though I have nothing left in my lungs.

He stopped chopping somewhere in the middle of that rant, but I'm not sure which part. He's looking at me with his mouth slightly agape. I take a deep breath and slowly exhale, thinking I may have just completely sent him out the front door. And sadly, I wouldn't blame him if he ran.

He lays the knife gently on the cutting board and places his palms on the counter in front of him, never breaking his gaze from mine. I fold my hands in my lap and wait for a reaction. It's all I can do.

"That," he says pointedly, "was the longest run-on sentence I've ever heard."

I roll my eyes and slouch back against my seat, then fold my arms across my chest. I just practically begged him to kiss me, and he's critiquing my grammar?

"Relax," he says with a grin. He slides the tomatoes off the cutting board and into the pan, then places it on the stove. He adjusts the temperature of one of the burners and pours the pasta into the boiling water. Once everything is set, he dries his hands on the hand towel, then walks around the bar to where I'm seated.

"Stand up," he directs.

I look up at him warily, but I do what he says. Slowly. When I'm standing up, facing him, he places his hands on my shoulders and looks around the room. "Hmm," he says, thinking audibly. He glances into the kitchen, then slides his hands down my shoulders and grabs my wrists. "I sort of liked the fridge backdrop." He pulls me into the kitchen, then positions me like a puppet with my back against the refrigerator. He places both of his hands against the refrigerator on either side of my head, and looks down at me.

It's not the most romantic way I've pictured him kissing me, but I guess it'll do. I just want to get it over with. Especially now that he's making such a big production out of it. He begins to lean in toward me, so I take a deep breath and close my eyes.

I wait.

And I wait.

Nothing happens.

I open my eyes and he's so close I actually flinch, which only makes him laugh. He doesn't back away, though, and his breath teases my lips like fingers. He smells like mint leaves and soda and I never thought the two would make a good combination, but they really do.

"Sky?" he says, quietly. "I'm not trying to torture you or anything, but I already made up my mind before I came over here. I'm not kissing you tonight."

His words cause my stomach to sink from the weight of my disappointment. My self-confidence has just gone out the window, and I really need an ego-building text from Six right now.

"Why not?"

He slowly drops one of his hands and brings it to my face, then traces down my cheek with his fingers. I try not to shudder under his touch, but it's taking every ounce of my willpower not to appear completely flustered right now.

His eyes follow his hand as it slowly moves down my jaw, then my neck, stopping at my shoulder. He brings his eyes back to mine and there's an undeniable amount of lust in them. Seeing the look in his eyes eases my disappointment by a tiny fraction.

"I want to kiss you," he says. "Believe me, I do." He drops his eyes to my lips and brings his hand back up to my cheek, cupping it. I willingly lean into his palm this time. I pretty much relinquished control to him the moment he walked through the front door. Now I'm nothing but putty in his hands.

"But if you really want to, then why don't you?" I'm terrified he's about to spout off an excuse that contains the word *girlfriend*.

He cases my face in both of his hands and tilts my face up toward his. He brushes his thumbs back and forth along my cheekbones and I can feel the rapid rise and fall of his chest against mine. "Because," he whispers. "I'm afraid you won't feel it."

I suck in a quick breath and hold it. The conversation we had on my bed last night replays in my head, and I realize that I never should have told him any of that. I never should have said I feel nothing but numbness when I kiss people, because he's the absolute exception to the rule. I bring my hand to his hand on my cheek, and I cover it with mine.

I'll feel it, Holder. I already do. I want to say those words out loud, but I can't. Instead, I just nod.

He closes his eyes and inhales, then pulls me away from the refrigerator and into his chest. He wraps one arm around my back and holds his other hand against my head.

My arms are still awkwardly at my sides, so I tentatively bring them up and wrap them around his waist. When I do this, I quietly gasp at the peacefulness that consumes me, being wrapped up in him like this. We both simultaneously pull each other closer and he kisses me on top of the head. It's not the kiss I was expecting, but I'm pretty sure I love it just as much.

We're standing in the same position when the timer on the oven dings. He doesn't immediately release me, though, which makes me smile. When he does begin to drop his arms, I look down to the floor, unable to look at him. Somehow, my trying to rectify the awkwardness about kissing him has just made things even more awkward for me.

As if he can sense my embarrassment, he takes both of my hands in his and interlocks our fingers. "Look at me." I lift my eyes to his, trying to hide the disappointment from realizing our mutual attraction is on two different levels. "Sky, I'm not kissing you tonight but believe me when I tell you, I've never wanted to kiss a girl more. So stop thinking I'm not attracted to you because you have no idea just how much I am. You can hold my hand, you can run your fingers through my hair, you can straddle me while I feed you spaghetti, but you are not getting kissed tonight. And probably not tomorrow, either. I need this. I need to know for sure that you're feeling every single thing that I'm feeling the moment my lips touch yours. Because I want your first kiss to be the best first kiss in the history of first kisses." He pulls my hand up to his mouth and kisses it. "Now stop sulking and help me finish the meatballs."

I grin, because that was seriously the best excuse ever for being turned down. He could turn me down every day for the rest of my life, so long as it's followed up by that excuse.

He swings our hands between us, peering down at me. "Okay?" he says. "Is that enough to get you through a couple more dates?"

I nod. "Yep. But you're wrong about one thing."

"What's that?"

"You said you want my first kiss to be the best first kiss, but this won't be my first kiss. You know that."

He narrows his eyes and pulls his hands from mine, then cups my face again. He pushes me back against the refrigerator and brings his lips dangerously close to mine. The smile is gone from his eyes and is replaced by a very serious expression. An expression so intense, I stop breathing.

He leans in excruciatingly slowly until his lips just barely reach mine, and the anticipation of them alone is enough to paralyze me. He doesn't close his eyes, so neither do I. He holds me in this position for a moment, allowing our breath to blend between us. I've never felt so helpless and out of control of myself, and if he doesn't do something within the next three seconds, I'm more than likely going to pounce on him.

He looks at my lips and when he does, it prompts me to pull my bottom lip between my teeth. Otherwise, I just might bite him.

"Let me inform you of something," he says in a low voice. "The moment my lips touch yours, it *will* be your first kiss. Because if you've never felt anything when someone's kissed you, then no one's ever really kissed you. Not the way *I* plan on kissing you."

He drops his hands and keeps his eyes locked on mine

while he backs up to the stove. He turns around to tend to the pasta like he didn't just ruin me for any other guy for the rest of my life.

I can't feel my legs, so I do the only thing I can. I slide down the refrigerator until my butt meets the floor, and I inhale.

"Your spaghetti sucks ass." I take another bite and close my eyes, savoring what is possibly the best pasta that's ever passed my lips.

"You love it and you know it," he says. He stands up from the table and grabs two napkins, then brings them back and hands me one. "Now wipe your chin, you've got sucky ass spaghetti sauce all over it."

After the incident against the refrigerator, the night pretty much went back to normal. He gave me a glass of water and helped me stand up, then slapped me on the ass and put me to work. It was all I needed to let go of the awkwardness. A good slap on the ass.

"Have you ever played Dinner Quest?" I ask him.

He slowly shakes his head. "Do I want to?"

I nod. "It's a good way to get to know each other. After our next date, we'll be spending most of our time making out, so we need to get all the questions out of the way now."

He laughs. "Fair enough. How do you play?"

"I ask you a really personal, uncomfortable question and you aren't allowed to take a drink or eat a bite of food until you answer it honestly. And vice versa."

"Sounds easy enough," he says. "What if I don't answer the question?"

"You starve to death."

128

He drums his fingers on the table, then lays his fork down. "I'm in."

I probably should have had questions prepared, but considering I just made this game up thirty seconds ago, that would have been sort of hard. I take a sip of what's left of my watered-down soda and think. I'm a little nervous about delving too deep, as it always seems to end badly with us.

"Okay, I have one." I set my cup down on the table and lean back in my chair. "Why did you follow me to my car at the grocery store?"

"Like I said, I thought you were someone else."

"I know, but who?"

He shifts uncomfortably in his seat and clears his throat. He naturally reaches for his glass, but I intercept it.

"No drinks. Answer the question first."

He sighs, but eventually relents. "I wasn't sure who you reminded me of, you just reminded me of someone. I didn't realize until later that you reminded me of my sister."

I crinkle my nose. "I remind you of your sister?" I wince. "That's kind of gross, Holder."

He laughs, then grimaces. "No, not like that. Not like that at all, you don't even look anything like she did. There was just something about seeing you that made me think of her. And I don't even know why I followed you. It was all so surreal. The whole situation was a little bizarre, and then running into you in front of my house later . . ." He stops midsentence and looks down at his hand as he traces the rim of his plate with his fingers. "It was like it was meant to happen," he says quietly.

I take a deep breath and absorb his answer, careful to tiptoe around that last sentence. He looks up at me with a nervous glance and I realize that he thinks his answer may have just scared me. I smile at him reassuringly and point to his drink. "You can drink now," I say. "Your turn to ask me a question."

"Oh, this one's easy," he says. "I want to know whose toes I'm stepping on. I received a mysterious inbox message from someone today. All it said was, 'If you're dating my girl, get your own prepaid minutes and quit wasting mine, jackass.'"

I laugh. "That would be Six. The bearer of my daily doses of positive affirmation."

He nods. "I was hoping you'd say that." He leans forward and narrows his eyes at me. "Because I'm pretty competitive, and if it came from a guy, my response would not have been as nice."

"You responded? What'd you say?"

"Is that your question? Because if it isn't, I'm taking another bite."

"Hold your horses and answer the question," I say.

"Yes, I responded to her text. I said, 'How do I buy more minutes?'"

My heart is a big puddle of mush right now, and I'm trying not to grin. It's really pathetic and sad. I shake my head. "I was only joking, that wasn't my question. It's still my turn."

He puts his fork back down and rolls his eyes. "My food's getting cold."

I place my elbows on the table and fold my hands under my chin. "I want to know about your sister. And why you referred to her in the past tense."

He tilts his head back and looks up, rubbing his hands down his face. "Ugh. You really ask the deep questions, huh?"

"That's how the game is played. I didn't make up the rules."

He sighs again and smiles at me, but there's a hint of sadness in his smile and it instantly makes me wish I could take the question back.

"Remember when I told you my family had a pretty fucked-up year last year?"

I nod.

He clears his throat and begins tracing the rim of his plate again. "She died thirteen months ago. She killed herself, even though my mother would rather we use the term, 'purposely overdosed.'"

He never stops looking at me when he speaks, so I show him the same respect, even though it's really difficult to look him in the eyes right now. I have no idea how to respond to that, but it's my own fault for bringing it up.

"What was her name?"

"Lesslie. I called her Les."

Hearing his nickname for her stirs up sadness within me and I suddenly don't feel like eating anymore. "Was she older than you?"

He leans forward and picks up his fork, then twirls it in his bowl. He brings the forkful of pasta to his mouth. "We were twins," he says flatly, right before taking the bite.

Jesus. I reach for my drink, but he takes it out of my hands and shakes his head. "My turn," he says with a mouthful. He finishes chewing and takes a sip, then wipes his mouth with a napkin. "I want to know the story about your dad."

I'm the one groaning this time. I fold my arms on the table in front of me and accept my payback. "Like I said, I haven't seen him since I was three. I don't have any memories of him. At least, I don't think I do. I don't even know what he looks like."

"Your mom doesn't have any pictures of him?"

It dawns on me when he asks this question that he doesn't even know I'm adopted. "You remember when you said my mom looked really young? Well, it's because she is. She adopted me."

Being adopted isn't really a stigma I've ever had to overcome. I've never been embarrassed by it, ashamed of it, or felt the need to hide the fact. But the way Holder is looking at me right now, you would think I just told him I was born with a penis. He's staring at me uncomfortably and it makes me fidget. "*What?* You've never met anyone who was adopted?"

It takes him a few more seconds to recover, but he puts away his puzzled expression and locks it up, replacing it with a smile. "You were adopted when you were three? By Karen?"

I nod my head. "I was put into foster care when I was three, after my biological mother died. My dad couldn't raise me on his own. Or he didn't *want* to raise me on his own. Either way, I'm fine with it. I lucked out with Karen and I have no urge whatsoever to go figure it all out. If he wanted to know where I was, he'd come find me."

I can tell he's not finished with the questions by the look in his eyes, but I really want to take a bite and get the ball back in my court.

I point to his arm with my fork. "What does your tattoo mean?"

He holds his arm out and traces his fingers over it. "It's a reminder. I got it after Les died."

"A reminder for what?"

He picks up his cup and diverts his eyes from mine. It's the only question he hasn't been able to answer with direct eye contact. "It's a reminder of the people I've let down in my life." He takes a drink and places his glass back on the table, still unable to make eye contact.

"This game's not very fun, is it?"

He laughs softly. "It's really not. It sort of sucks ass." He looks back up at me and smiles. "But we need to keep going because I still have questions. Do you remember anything from before you were adopted?"

I shake my head. "Not really. Bits and pieces, but it comes to a point that, when you don't have anyone to validate your memories, you just lose them all. The only thing I have from before Karen adopted me is some jewelry, and I have no idea who it came from. I can't distinguish now between what was reality, dreams, or what I saw on TV."

"Do you remember your mother?"

I pause for a moment and mull over his question. I don't remember my mother. At all. That's the only thing about my past that makes me sad. "Karen is my mother," I say point-blank. "My turn. Last question, then we eat dessert."

"Do you think we even have enough dessert?" he teases.

I glare at him, then ask my last question. "Why did you beat him up?"

I can tell by the shift in his expression that he doesn't need me to elaborate on the question. He shakes his head and pushes his bowl away from him. "You don't want to know the answer to that, Sky. I'll take the punishment."

"But I do want to know."

He tilts his head sideways and brings his hand to his

jaw, then pops his neck. He keeps his hand on his chin and rests his elbow on the table. "Like I told you before, I beat him up because he was an asshole."

I narrow my eyes at him. "That's vague. You don't do vague."

His expression doesn't change and he keeps his eyes locked on mine. "It was my first week back at school since Les died," he says. "She went to school there, too, so everyone knew what happened. I overheard the guy saying something about Les when I was passing him in the hallway. I disagreed with it, and I let him know. I took it too far and it came to a point when I was on top of him that I just didn't care. I was hitting him, over and over, and I didn't even care. The really fucked-up part is that the kid will more than likely be deaf out of his left ear for the rest of his life, and I *still* don't care."

He's staring at me, but not really looking at me. It's the hard, cold look that I've seen in his eyes before. I didn't like it then and I don't like it now . . . but at least now I can understand it more.

"What did he say about her?"

He slumps back in his chair and drops his eyes to an empty spot on the table between us. "I heard him laughing, telling his friend that Les took the selfish, easy way out. He said if she wasn't such a coward, she would have toughed it out."

"Toughed what out?"

He shrugs. "Life," he says indifferently.

"You don't think she took the easy way out," I say, dropping the end of the sentence as more of a statement than a question.

Holder leans forward and reaches across the table, taking my hand into both of his. He runs his thumbs across my palm and takes in a deep breath, then carefully releases it. "Les was the bravest fucking person I've ever known. It takes a lot of guts to do what she did. To just end it, not knowing what's next? Not knowing if there's *anything* next? It's easier to go on living a life without any life left in it than it is to just say 'fuck it' and leave. She was one of the few that just said, 'fuck it.' And I'll commend her every day I'm still alive, too scared to do the same thing."

He stills my hand between his, and it isn't until he does this that I realize I'm shaking. I look up at him and he's staring back at me. There are absolutely no words that can follow that up, so I don't even try. He stands up and leans over the table, then slides his hand behind my neck. He kisses me on top of the head, then releases his hold and walks to the kitchen. "You want brownies or cookies?" he asks over his shoulder, as if he didn't just absolutely stun me into silence.

He looks back at me and I'm still staring at him in shock. I don't even know what to say. Did he just admit that he's suicidal? Was he being metaphorical? Melodramatic? I have no idea what to do with the bomb he just placed in my lap.

He brings a plate of both cookies and brownies back to the table, then kneels down in front of me.

"Hey," he says soothingly, taking my face in his hands. His expression is serene. "I didn't mean to scare you. I'm not suicidal if that's what's freaking you out. I'm not fucked up in the head. I'm not deranged. I'm not suffering from post-traumatic stress disorder. I'm just a brother who loved his sister more than life itself, so I get a little intense when

I think about her. And if I cope better by telling myself that what she did was noble, even though it wasn't, then that's all I'm doing. I'm just coping." He's got a tight grip on my face and he's looking at me desperately, wanting me to understand where he's coming from. "I fucking loved that girl, Sky. I need to believe that what she did was the only answer she had left, because if I don't, then I'll never forgive myself for not helping her find a different one." He presses his forehead to mine. "Okay?"

I nod, then pull his hands from my face. I can't let him see me do this. "I need to use the bathroom." He backs up and I rush to the bathroom and shut the door behind me, then I do something I haven't done since I was five. I cry.

I don't ugly cry. I don't sob and I don't even make a noise. A single tear falls down my cheek and it's one tear too many, so I quickly wipe it away. I take a tissue and wipe at my eyes in an attempt to stop any other tears from forming.

I still don't know what to say to him, but I feel like he put a pretty tight lid on the subject, so I decide to let it go for now. I shake out my hands and take a deep breath, then open the door. He's standing across the hallway with his feet crossed at the ankles and his hands hanging loosely in his pockets. He straightens up and takes a step closer to me.

"We good?" he asks.

I smile my best smile and nod, then take a deep breath. "I told you I think you're intense. This just proves my point."

He smiles and nudges me toward the bedroom. He wraps his arms around me from behind and rests his chin on top of my head while we make our way toward my room. "Are you allowed to get pregnant yet?"

I laugh. "Nope. Not this weekend. Besides, you have to kiss a girl before you can knock her up."

"Did someone not have sex education when she was homeschooled?" he says. "Because I could totally knock you up without ever kissing you. Want me to show you?"

I hop on the bed and grab the book, opening it up to where we left off last night. "I'll take your word for it. Besides, I'm hoping we're about to get a hefty dose of sex education before we make it to the last page."

Holder drops down on the bed and I lie beside him. He puts his arm around me and pulls me toward him, so I rest my head on his chest and begin reading.

I know he's not doing it on purpose, but the entire time I'm reading I'm completely distracted by him. He's looking down at me, watching my mouth as I read, twirling my hair between his fingertips. Every time I flip a page, I glance up at him and he's got the same concentrated expression on his face each time. An expression so concentrated on my mouth, it tells me he's not paying a damn bit of attention to a single word I'm reading. I close the book and bring it to my stomach. I don't even think he notices I closed the book.

"Why'd you stop talking?" he says, never changing his expression or pulling his gaze from my mouth.

"Talking?" I ask curiously. "Holder, I'm *reading*. There's a difference. And from the looks of it, you haven't been paying a lick of attention."

He looks me in the eyes and grins. "Oh, I've been paying attention," he says. "To your mouth. Maybe not to the words coming out of it, but definitely to your mouth."

He scoots me off his chest and onto my back, then he slides down beside me and pulls me against him. Still, his expression hasn't changed and he's staring at me like he wants to eat me. I sort of wish he would.

He brings his fingers up to my lips and begins tracing them, slowly. It feels so incredible; I'm too scared to breathe for fear he might stop. I swear it's as though his fingers have a direct line to every sensitive spot on my entire body.

"You have a nice mouth," he says. "I can't stop looking at it."

"You should taste it," I say. "It's quite lovely."

He squeezes his eyes shut and groans, then leans in and presses his head into my neck. "Stop it, you evil wench."

I laugh and shake my head. "No way. This is your stupid rule, why should I be the one to enforce it?"

"Because you know I'm right. I can't kiss you tonight because kissing leads to the next thing, which leads to the next thing, and at the rate we're going we'll be all out of firsts by next weekend. Don't you want to drag our firsts out a little longer?" He pulls his head away from my neck and looks back down at me.

"Firsts?" I ask. "How many firsts are there?"

"There aren't that many, which is why we need to drag them out. We've already passed too many since we met."

I tilt my head sideways so I can look at him straight on. "What firsts have we already passed?"

"The easy ones. First hug, first date, first fight, first time we slept together, although I wasn't the one sleeping. Now we barely have any left. First kiss. First time to sleep together when we're both actually *awake*. First marriage. First kid. We're done after that. Our lives will become mundane and boring and I'll have to divorce you and marry a wife who's twenty years younger than me so I can have a lot more firsts and you'll be stuck raising the kids." He cups my cheek in his hand and smiles at me. "So you see, babe? I'm only doing this for your benefit. The longer I wait to kiss you, the longer it'll be before I'm forced to leave you high and dry."

I laugh. "Your logic terrifies me. I sort of don't find you attractive anymore."

He slides on top of me, holding up his weight on his hands. "You *sort of* don't find me attractive? That can also mean you sort of *do* find me attractive."

I shake my head. "I don't find you attractive at all. You repulse me. In fact, you better not kiss me because I'm pretty sure I just threw up in my mouth."

He laughs, then drops his weight onto one arm, still hovering over me. He lowers his mouth to the side of my head and presses his lips to my ear. "You're a liar," he whispers. "You're a whole *lot* attracted to me and I'm about to prove it."

I close my eyes and gasp the second his lips meet my neck. He kisses me lightly, right below the ear, and it feels like the whole room just turned into a Tilt-a-Whirl. He slowly moves his lips back to my ear and whispers, "Did you feel that?"

I shake my head no, but barely.

"You want me to do it again?"

I'm shaking my head no out of stubbornness, but I'm hoping he's telepathic and can hear what I'm really screaming inside my head, because hell yes, I liked it. Hell yes, I want him to do it again.

He laughs when I shake my head no, so he brings his lips closer to my mouth. He kisses me on the cheek, then continues trailing soft pecks down to my ear, where he stops and whispers again. "How about that?"

Oh, God, I've never been so *not* bored in my life. He's not even kissing me and it's already the best kiss I've ever had. I shake my head again and keep my eyes closed, because I like not knowing what's coming next. Like the hand that just planted itself on my outer thigh and is working its way up to my waist. He slides his hand under my T-shirt until his fingers barely graze the edge of my pants, and he leaves his hand there, slowly moving his thumb back and forth across my stomach. I'm so acutely aware of everything about him in this moment that I'm almost positive I could pick his thumbprint out of a lineup.

He runs his nose along my jawline and the fact that he's breathing just as heavily as I am assures me there's no way he can wait until after tonight to kiss me. At least that's what I'm desperately hoping.

When he reaches my ear again, he doesn't speak this time. Instead, he kisses it and there isn't a nerve ending in my body that doesn't feel it. From my head all the way down to my toes, my entire body is screaming for his mouth.

I place my hand on his neck and when I do, chills break out on his skin. Apparently, that one simple move momentarily melts his resolve and for a second, his tongue meets my neck. I moan and the sound completely sends him into a frenzy.

He moves his hand from my waist to the side of my head and he pulls my neck against his mouth, holding nothing back. I open my eyes, shocked at how quickly his demeanor changed. He kisses and licks and teases every inch of my neck, only gasping for air when it's absolutely necessary. As soon as I see the stars above my head, there isn't even enough time to count one of them before my eyes roll back in my head and I'm holding back sounds that I'm too embarrassed to utter.

He moves his lips farther from my neck and closer to my chest. If we didn't have such a limited supply of firsts, I'd tear my shirt off and make him keep going. Instead, he doesn't even give me this option. He kisses his way back up my neck, up my chin, and trails soft kisses around my entire mouth, careful not to once touch my lips. My eyes are closed, but I can feel his breath against my mouth, and I know he's struggling not to kiss me. I open my eyes and look at him and he's staring at my lips again.

"They're so perfect," he says, breathlessly. "Like hearts. I could literally stare at your lips for days and never get bored."

"No. Don't do that. If all you do is stare, then *I'll* be the bored one."

He grimaces, and it's obvious that he's having a really, really hard time not kissing me. I don't know what it is about him staring at my lips like he is, but it's definitely the hottest thing about this whole situation right now. I do something I probably shouldn't do. I lick them. Slowly.

He groans again and presses his forehead against mine. His arm gives way beneath him and he drops his weight on me, pressing himself against me. Everywhere. All of him. We moan simultaneously once our bodies find that perfect connection, and suddenly it's game on. I'm tearing off his shirt and he's on his knees, helping me pull it over his head. After it's completely off, I wrap my legs around his waist and lock him against me, because there could be nothing more detrimental than if he were to pull away right now.

He brings his forehead back to mine and our bodies reunite and fuse together like the last two pieces of a puzzle. He's slowly rocking against me and every time he does it, his lips come closer and closer, until they brush lightly against mine. He doesn't close the gap between our mouths, even though I absolutely need him to. Our lips are simply resting together, not kissing. Every time he moves against me, he lets out a breath that seeps into my mouth and I try to take them all in, because it feels like I need them if I want to survive this moment.

We remain in this rhythm for several minutes, neither of us wanting to be the first to initiate the kiss. It's obvious we both want to, but it's also obvious that I may have just met my match when it comes to stubbornness.

He holds the side of my head in place and keeps his forehead pressed against mine, but pulls his lips back far enough so he can lick them. When he lets them fall back into place, the wetness of his lips sliding against mine drags me completely under, and I doubt I'll ever be able to come up for air.

He shifts his weight, and I don't know what happens when he does this, but somehow it causes my head to roll back and the words, "*Oh, God,*" to come out of my mouth. I didn't mean to pull away from his mouth when I tilted my head back, because I really liked it being there, but I like where I'm going even more. I wrap my arms around his back and tuck my head against his neck for some semblance of stability, because it feels like the entire earth has been shifted off its axis and Holder is the core.

I realize what's about to happen and I begin to internally panic. Other than his shirt, we're completely clothed, not even kissing . . . yet the room is beginning to spin from the effect his rhythmic movements are having on my body. If he doesn't stop what he's doing, I'll fall apart and melt right here beneath him, and that would quite possibly mark the most embarrassing moment of my life. But if I ask him to stop, then he'll stop, and that would quite possibly mark the most *disappointing* moment of my life.

I try to calm my breaths and minimize the sounds escaping my lips, but I've lost any form of self-control. It's obvious my body is enjoying this nonkissing friction a little too much and I can't find it in me to stop. I'll try the next best thing. I'll ask *him* to stop.

"Holder," I say breathlessly, not really wanting him to stop, but hoping he'll get the hint and stop anyway. I need him to stop. Like two minutes ago.

He doesn't. He continues kissing my neck and moving his body against mine in a way that boys have done to me before, but this time it's different. It's so incredibly different and wonderful and it absolutely petrifies me.

"Holder." I attempt to say his name louder, but there isn't enough effort left in my body.

He kisses the side of my head and slows down, but he doesn't stop. "Sky, if you're asking me to stop, I will. But I'm hoping you're not, because I really don't want to stop, so please." He pulls back and looks down into my eyes, still barely moving his body against mine. His eyes are full of ache and worry and he's breathless when he speaks. "We won't go any further than this, I promise. But please don't ask me to stop where we already are. I need to watch you and I need to hear you because the fact that I know you're actually feeling this right now is so fucking amazing. You feel incredible and this feels incredible and *please*. Just . . . *please*."

He lowers his mouth to mine and gives me the softest peck imaginable. It's enough of a preview of what his real kiss will feel like and just the thought of it makes me shudder. He stops moving against me and pushes himself up on his hands, waiting for me to decide.

The moment he separates from me, my chest grows heavy with disappointment and I almost feel like crying. Not because he stopped or because I'm torn about what to do next . . . but because I never imagined that two people could connect on this sort of intimate level, and that it could feel so overwhelmingly right. Like the purpose of the entire human race revolves around this moment; around the two of us. Everything that's ever happened or will happen in this world is simply just a backdrop for what's occurring between us right now, and I don't want it to stop. I don't. I'm shaking my head, looking into his pleading eyes, and all I can do is whisper, "Don't. Whatever you do, don't stop."

He slides his hand behind my neck and lowers his head, pressing his forehead to mine. "*Thank* you," he breathes, gently easing himself onto me again, recreating the connection between us. He kisses the edges of my mouth several times, trailing close to my lips and down my chin and across my neck. The faster he breathes, the faster *I* breathe. The faster *I* breathe, the faster he plants kisses all over my neck. The faster he plants kisses all over my neck, the faster we move together—creating a tantalizing rhythm between us that, according to my pulse, isn't going to last much longer.

I dig my heels into the bed and my nails into his back.

He stops kissing my neck and looks down at me with heated eyes, watching me. He focuses on my mouth again, and as much as I want to watch him stare at me like he does, I can't keep my eyes open. They close involuntarily as soon as the first wave of chills washes over my body like a warning shot of what's about to come.

"Open your eyes," he says firmly.

I would if I could, but I'm completely helpless.

"Please."

That one word is all I need to hear and my eyes flick open beneath him. He's staring down at me with such an intense need, it's almost more intimate than if he were actually kissing me right now. As hard as it is to do in this moment, I keep my eyes locked on his as I drop my arms, clench the sheets with both fists and thank Karma for bringing this hopeless boy into my life. Because until this moment— until the first waves of pure and utter enlightenment wash over me—I had no idea that he was even missing.

I begin to shudder beneath him and he never once breaks our stare. I can no longer keep my eyes open no matter how hard I try, so I let them fall shut. I feel his lips slide delicately back to mine, but he still doesn't kiss me. Our mouths are stubbornly resting together as he holds his rhythm, allowing the last of my moans and a rush of my breaths and maybe even part of my heart to slip out of me and into him. I slowly and blissfully slide back down to earth and he eventually holds still, allowing me to recover from an experience that he somehow made not at all embarrassing for me.

When I'm completely spent and emotionally drained and my whole body is shaking, he continues to kiss my neck and shoulders and everywhere else in the vicinity of the one place I want kissed the most—my mouth.

But he would obviously rather hold his resolve than give in to his stubbornness, because he pulls his lips from my shoulder and brings his face closer to mine, but still refuses to make the connection. He reaches up and runs his hand along my hairline, smoothing away a stray strand from my forehead.

"You're incredible," he whispers, looking only at my eyes this time and not at all at my mouth. His words make up for his stubbornness and I can't help but smile back. He collapses to the bed beside me, still panting, while he makes a cognizant effort to contain the desire that I know is still coursing through him.

I close my eyes and listen to the silence that builds between us as our gasps for breath subside into soft, gentle rhythms. It's quiet and calm and quite possibly the most peaceful moment my mind has ever experienced.

Holder moves his hand closer to me on the bed between us and he wraps his pinky around mine as if he doesn't have the strength to hold my entire hand. But it's nice, because we've held hands before, but never pinkies . . . and I realize that this is another first we passed. And realizing this doesn't disappoint me, because I know that firsts don't matter with him. He could kiss me for the first time, or the twentieth time, or the millionth time and I wouldn't care if it was a first or not, because I'm pretty sure we just broke the record for the best first kiss in the history of first kisses—without even kissing.

After a long stretch of perfect silence, he takes a deep breath, then sits up on the bed and looks down at me. "I have to go. I can't be on this bed with you for another second."

I tilt my head toward his and look at him dejectedly as he stands up and pulls his shirt back on. He grins at me when he sees me pouting, then he bends forward until his face is hovering over mine, dangerously close. "When I said you weren't getting kissed tonight, I meant it. But *dammit*, Sky. I had no idea how fucking difficult you would make it." He slips his hand behind my neck and I gasp quietly, willing my heart to remain within the walls of my chest. He kisses my cheek and I can feel his hesitation when he reluctantly pulls away.

He walks backward toward the window, watching me the whole time. Before he slips outside, he pulls his phone out and runs his fingers swiftly over the screen for a few seconds, then slips it back into his pocket. He smiles at me, then climbs out the window and pulls it shut behind him.

I somehow find the strength to jump up and run to the kitchen. I grab my phone and, sure enough, there's a missed text from him. It's only one word, though.

Incredible.

I smile, because it was. It absolutely was.

Thirteen years earlier

"Hey."

I keep my head buried in my arms. I don't want him to see me crying again. I know he won't laugh at me—neither of them would ever laugh at me. But I really don't even know why I'm crying and I wish it would just stop but it won't and I can't and I hate it, hate it, hate it.

He sits down on the sidewalk next to me and she sits down on the other side of me. I still don't look up and I'm still sad, but I don't want them to leave because it feels nice with them here.

"This might make you feel better," she says. "I made us both one at school today." She doesn't ask me to look up so I don't, but I can feel her put something on my knee.

I don't move. I don't like getting presents and I don't want her to see me look at it.

I keep my head down and keep crying and wish that I knew what was wrong with me. Something's wrong with me or I wouldn't feel like this every time it happens. Because it's supposed to happen. That's what Daddy tells me, anyway. It's supposed to happen and I have to stop crying because it makes him so, so sad when I cry.

They sit by me for a long, long time but I don't know how long because I don't know if hours are longer than minutes. He leans over and whispers in my ear. "Don't forget what I told you. Remember what you need to do when you're sad?"

I nod into my arm, but I don't look up at him. I have been doing what he said I should do when I get sad, but sometimes I'm still sad, anyway.

They stay for a few more hours or minutes, but then she stands up. I wish they would stay for one more minute or two more hours. They never ask me what's wrong and that's why I like them so much and wish they would stay.

I lift my elbow and peek out from underneath it and see her feet walking away from me. I grab her present off my knee and run it through my fingers. She made me a bracelet. It's stretchy and purple and has half of a heart on it. I slide it on my wrist and smile, even though I'm still crying. I lift up my head and he's still here, looking at me. He looks sad and I feel bad because I feel like I'm making him sad.

He stands up and faces my house. He looks at it for a long time without saying anything. He always thinks a lot and it makes me wonder what he's always thinking about. He stops looking at the house and looks back down at me. "Don't worry," he says, trying to smile for me. "He won't live forever." He turns around and walks back to his house, so I close my eyes and lay my head on my arms again.

I don't know why he would say that. I don't want my daddy to die . . . I just want him to stop calling me Princess.

I don't pull it out very often, but for some reason I want to look at it today. I guess talking about the past with Holder Saturday has left me feeling a little nostalgic. I know I told Holder I'd never look for my father, but sometimes I'm still curious. I can't help but wonder how a parent can raise a child for several years, then just give that child away. I'll never understand it, and maybe I don't need to. That's why I never push it. I never ask Karen questions. I never try to separate the memories from the dreams and I don't like bringing it up . . . because I just don't need to.

I take the bracelet out of the box and slide it onto my wrist. I don't know who gave it to me, and I don't even really care. I'm sure with two years in foster care, I received lots of things from friends. What's different about this gift, though, is that it's attached to the only memory I have of that life. The bracelet validates that my memory is a real one. And knowing that the memory is real somehow validates that I was someone else before I was me. A girl I don't remember. A girl who cried a lot. A girl that isn't anything like who I am today.

Someday I'll throw the bracelet away because I need to. But today, I just feel like wearing it.

Holder and I decided to take a breather from each other yesterday. And I say breather, because after Saturday night, we went quite a while on my bed without breathing at all. Besides, Karen was coming home and the last thing I wanted to do was reintroduce her to my new . . . whatever he is. We never got far enough to label what's going on between us. It feels like I haven't known him near long enough to refer to him as my boyfriend, considering we haven't even kissed yet. But dammit if it doesn't piss me off to think of his lips being on anyone else. So whether or not we're dating, I'm declaring us exclusive. Can you even be exclusive without actually kissing first? Are exclusive and dating mutually exclusive?

I make myself laugh out loud. Or *lol*.

When I woke up yesterday morning, I had two texts. I'm really getting into this whole texting thing. I get really giddy when I have one and I can't imagine how addictive email and Facebook and everything else technology-related must be. One of the texts was from Six, going on and on about my impeccable baking abilities, followed up with strict instructions to call her Sunday night from her house phone to catch her up on everything. I did. We talked for an hour and she's just as floored as I am that Holder isn't at all how we expected him to be. I asked her about Lorenzo and she didn't even know who I was referring to, so I laughed and dropped it. I miss her and hate that she's gone, but she's loving it and that makes me happy.

The second text I had was from Holder. All it said was, *"I'm dreading seeing you at school on Monday. So bad."*

Running used to be the highlight of my day, but now it's receiving insulting texts from Holder. And speaking of running and Holder, we aren't doing that anymore. To-gether, anyway. After texting back and forth yesterday, we decided it was probably best if we didn't run together on a daily basis because that might be too much, too soon. I told him I didn't want things to get weird between us. Besides, I'm really self-conscious when I'm sweaty and snotty and wheezing and smelly and I would just rather run alone.

Now I'm staring into my locker in a daze, sort of stall-ing because I really don't want to go to class. It's first period and the only class I have with Holder, so I'm really nervous about how it'll play out. I take Breckin's book out of my backpack and the other two books I brought him, then put the rest of my things in my locker. I walk into the classroom and to my seat, but Breckin isn't here yet, and neither is Holder. I sit down and stare at the door, not really sure why I'm so nervous. It's just different, seeing him here rather than on home turf. Public school is just way too . . . *public*.

The door opens and Holder walks in, followed closely by Breckin. They both start toward the back of the room. Holder smiles at me, walking down one aisle. Breckin smiles at me, walking down the other aisle, holding two cups of coffee. Holder reaches the seat next to me and starts to lay his backpack on it at the same time Breckin reaches it and begins to set the coffee cups down. They look up at each other, then they both look back at me.

Awkward.

I do the only thing I know how to do in awkward situa-tions—infuse them with sarcasm.

"Looks like we have quite the predicament here, boys." I smile at both of them, then eye the coffee in Breckin's hands. "I see the Mormon brought the queen her offering of coffee. Very impressive." I look at Holder and cock my eyebrow. "Do you wish to reveal your offering, hopeless boy, so that I may decide who shall accompany me at the classroom throne today?"

Breckin looks at me like I've lost my mind. Holder laughs and picks his backpack up off the desk. "Looks like someone's in need of an ego-shattering text today." He moves his backpack to the empty seat in front of Breckin and claims his spot.

Breckin is still standing, holding both coffees with an incredibly confused look on his face. I reach out and grab one of the cups. "Congratulations, squire. You are the queen's chosen one today. Sit. It's been quite the weekend."

Breckin slowly takes his seat and sets his coffee on his desk, then pulls his backpack off his shoulder, eyeing me suspiciously the whole time. Holder is seated sideways at his desk, staring at me. I gesture with my hand toward Holder. "Breckin, this is Holder. Holder is not my boyfriend, but if I catch him trying to break the record for best first kiss with another girl, then he'll soon be my *not breathing* non-boyfriend."

Holder arches an eyebrow at me and a hint of a smile plays in the corner of his mouth. "Likewise." His dimples are taunting me and I have to force myself to look directly into his eyes or I might be compelled to do something that would be grounds for suspension.

I gesture toward Breckin. "Holder, this is Breckin. Breckin is my new very bestest friend ever in the whole wide world."

Breckin eyes Holder and Holder smiles at him, then reaches out to shake his hand. Breckin tentatively shakes

Holder's hand in return, then pulls it back and turns to me, narrowing his eyes. "Does *not-your-boyfriend* realize I'm Mormon?"

I nod. "It turns out, Holder doesn't have an issue with Mormons at all. He just has an issue with assholes."

Breckin laughs and turns back to Holder. "Well, in that case, welcome to the alliance."

Holder gives him a half smile, but he's staring at the coffee cup on Breckin's desk. "I thought Mormons weren't allowed to have caffeine."

Breckin shrugs. "I decided to break that rule the morning I woke up gay."

Holder laughs and Breckin smiles and everything is right with the world. Or at least in the world of first period. I lean back in my chair and smile. This won't be hard at all. In fact, I think I just started loving public school.

Holder follows me to my locker after class. We don't speak. I switch my books while he rips more insults off my locker. There were only two sticky notes after class today, which makes me a little sad. They're giving up so easily and it's only the second week of school.

He wads the notes up and flicks them on the floor and I shut my locker, then turn toward him. We're both leaning against the lockers, facing each other.

"You trimmed your hair," I say, noticing it for the first time.

He runs his hand through it and grins. "Yeah. This chick I know couldn't stop whining about it. It was really annoying."

"I like it."

He smiles. "Good."

I purse my lips and rock back and forth on my heels. He's grinning at me and he looks adorable. If we weren't in a hallway right now full of people, I'd grab his shirt and pull him to me so I could show him just how adorable I think he looks. Instead, I push the images away and smile back at him. "I guess we should get to class."

He nods slowly. "Yep," he says, without walking away.

We stand there for another thirty seconds or so before I laugh and kick off the locker, then start to walk away. He grabs my arm and pulls me back so quickly, I gasp. Before I know it, my back is against the locker and he's standing in front of me, blocking me in with his arms. He shoots me a devilish grin, then tilts my face up to his. He brings his right hand to my cheek and slides it under my jaw, cupping my face. He delicately strokes both of my lips with his thumb and I have to remind myself again that we're in public and I can't act on my impulses right now. I press myself against the lockers behind me, trying to use the sturdiness of them to make up for the support my knees are no longer providing.

"I wish I had kissed you Saturday night," he says. He drops his eyes to my lips where his thumb is still stroking them. "I can't stop imagining what you taste like." He presses his thumb firmly against the center of my lips, then very briefly connects his mouth to mine without moving his thumb out of the way. His lips are gone and his thumb is gone and it happens so fast, I don't even realize *he's* gone until the hallway stops spinning and I'm able to stand up straight.

I don't know how much longer I can take this. I'm

reminded of my nervous rant on Saturday night, when I wanted him to just get it over with and kiss me in the kitchen. I had absolutely no idea what I would be in for.

"How?"

It's just one word, but as soon as I lay my tray down across from Breckin, I know exactly what all that word encompasses. I laugh and decide to spill all the details before Holder shows up at our table. *If* he shows up at our table. Not only have we not discussed relationship labels, we also haven't discussed lunchroom seating arrangements.

"He showed up at my house on Friday and after quite a few misunderstandings, we finally came to an understanding that we just misunderstood each other. Then we baked, I read him some smut, and he went home. He came back over Saturday night and cooked for me. Then we went to my room and . . ."

I stop talking when Holder takes a seat beside me.

"Keep going," Holder says. "I'd love to hear what we did next."

I roll my eyes and turn back to Breckin. "Then we broke the record for best first kiss in the history of first kisses without even kissing."

Breckin nods carefully, still looking at me with eyes full of skepticism. Or curiosity. "Impressive."

"It was an excruciatingly boring weekend," Holder says to Breckin.

I laugh, but Breckin looks at me like I'm crazy again. "Holder loves boring," I assure him. "He means that in a nice way."

Breckin looks back and forth between the two of us, then shakes his head and leans forward, picking up his fork. "Not much confuses me," he says, pointing his fork at us. "But you two are an exception."

I nod in complete agreement.

We continue with lunch and have somewhat normal, decent interaction among the three of us. Holder and Breckin start talking about the book he let me borrow and the fact that Holder is even discussing a romance novel at all is entertaining in itself, but the fact that he's arguing about the plot with Breckin is sickeningly adorable. Every now and then he places his hand on my leg or rubs my back or kisses the side of my head, and he's going through these motions like they're second nature, but to me not a single one of them goes unnoticed.

I'm trying to process the shift from last week to this week and I can't get past the notion that we might just be too good. Whatever this is and whatever we're doing seems too good and too right and too perfect and it makes me think of all the books I've read and how, when things get too good and too right and too perfect, it's only because the ugly twist hasn't yet infiltrated the goodness of it all and I suddenly—

"Sky," Holder says, snapping his fingers in front of my face. I look at him and he's eyeing me cautiously. "Where'd you go?"

I shake my head and smile, not knowing what just set off that mini internal panic attack. He slides his hand just below my ear and runs his thumb across my cheekbone. "You have to quit checking out like that. It freaks me out a little bit."

"Sorry," I say with a shrug. "I'm easily distracted." I bring my hand up and pull his hand away from my neck, squeezing his fingers reassuringly. "Really, I'm fine."

His gaze drops to my hand. He flips it over and slides my sleeve up, then twists my wrist back and forth.

"Where'd you get that?" he says, looking down at my wrist.

I look down to see what he's referring to and realize I'm still wearing the bracelet I put on this morning. He looks back up at me and I shrug. I'm not really in the mood to explain it. It's complicated and he'll ask questions and lunch is almost over.

"Where'd you get it?" he says again, this time a little more demanding. His grip tightens around my wrist and he's staring at me coldly, expecting an explanation. I pull my wrist away, not liking where this is going.

"You think I got it from a guy?" I ask, puzzled by his reaction. I hadn't really pegged him for the jealous type, but this doesn't really seem like jealousy. It seems like crazy.

He doesn't answer my question. He keeps glaring at me like I've got some sort of huge confession that I'm refusing to reveal. I don't know what he expects, but his attitude right now is more than likely going to end up with him getting slapped, rather than with me giving an explanation.

Breckin shifts uncomfortably in his seat and clears his throat. "Holder. Ease up, man."

Holder's expression doesn't change. If anything, it grows even colder. He leans forward a few inches and lowers his voice when he speaks. "Who gave you the damn bracelet, Sky?"

His words transform into an unbearable weight in my

chest and all the same warning signs that flashed in my head when I first met him are flashing again, only this time they're in big neon letters. I know my mouth is agape and my eyes are wide, but I'm relieved that hope isn't a tangible thing, because everyone around me would see mine crumbling.

He closes his eyes and faces forward, setting his elbows on the table. His palms press against his forehead and he inhales a long, deep breath. I'm not sure if the breath is more for a calming effect, or a distraction to keep him from yelling. He runs his hand through his hair and grips the back of his neck.

"Shit!" he says. His voice is harsh and it causes me to flinch. He stands up and walks away unexpectedly, leaving his tray on the table. My eyes follow him as he continues across the cafeteria without once looking back at me. He slaps the cafeteria doors with both palms and disappears through them. I don't even blink or breathe again until the doors finish swinging, coming to a complete standstill.

I turn back to Breckin and I can only imagine the shock on my face right now. I blink and shake my head, replaying the last two minutes of the scene in my head. Breckin reaches across the table and takes my hand in his, but doesn't say anything. There's nothing to say. We both lost all of our words the second Holder disappeared through those doors.

The bell rings and the cafeteria becomes a whirlwind of commotion, but I can't move. Everyone is moving around and emptying trays and clearing tables, but the world of our table is a stilled one. Breckin finally lets go of my hand and grabs our trays, then comes back for Holder's tray and clears off the table. He picks up my backpack and takes my hand again, pulling me up. He puts my backpack over his shoulder, then walks me out of the cafeteria. He doesn't walk me to my locker or walk me to my classroom. He holds my hand and pulls me along behind him until we're out the doors and across the parking lot and he's opening a door and pushing me inside an unfamiliar car. He slides into his seat and cranks the car, then turns in his seat and faces me.

"I'm not even going to tell you what I think about what just happened in there. But I know it sucked and I have no idea why you aren't crying right now, but I know your heart hurts, and maybe even your pride. So fuck school. We're going for ice cream." He puts his car in reverse, then pulls out of the parking spot.

I don't know how he does it because I was just about to burst into tears and sob and snot all over his car, but after those words come out of his mouth, I actually smile.

"I love ice cream."

The ice cream helped, but I don't think it helped that much because Breckin just dropped me off at my car and I'm sitting in my driver's seat, unable to move. I'm sad and I'm scared and I'm mad and I'm feeling all the things that I'm warranted to feel after what just happened, but I'm not crying.

And I won't cry.

When I get home I do the only thing that I know will help. I run. Only when I get back and climb in the shower I realize that, like the ice cream, the run really didn't help that much, either.

I go through the same motions that I go through any other night of the week. I help Karen with dinner, I eat with her and Jack, I work on schoolwork, I read a book. I try to act like it doesn't upset me at all, because I really wish it didn't, but the second I climb into bed and turn off my light, my mind begins wandering. Only this time it doesn't wander very far, because I'm stuck on just one thing and one thing only. Why the hell hasn't he apologized?

I half expected him to be waiting at my car when Breckin and I got back from ice cream, but he wasn't. When I pulled into my driveway, I expected him to be there, ready to grovel and beg and provide me with even the smallest bit of an explanation, but he wasn't here. I kept my phone hidden in my pocket (because Karen still doesn't know I have it) and I checked it every chance I got, but the only text I received was from Six and I still haven't even read it yet.

So now I'm in my bed, hugging my pillow, feeling incredibly guilty for not having the urge to egg his house and slash his tires and kick him in the balls. Because I know that's what I wish I was feeling. I wish I was pissed and angry and unforgiving, because it would feel so much better than feeling disappointed over the realization that the Holder I had this weekend . . . wasn't even Holder at all.

I open my eyes and don't climb out of bed until the seventy-sixth star on my ceiling is counted. I throw the covers off and change into my running clothes. When I climb out of my bedroom window, I pause.

He's standing on the sidewalk with his back to me. His hands are clasped on top of his head and I can see the muscles in his back contracting from labored breaths. He's in the middle of a run and I'm not sure if he's waiting on me or just happens to be taking a breather, so I remain stilled outside my window and wait, hoping he keeps running.

But he doesn't.

After a couple of minutes, I finally work up the nerve to walk into the front yard. When he hears my footsteps, he turns around. I stop walking when we make eye contact and I stare back at him. I'm not glaring or frowning and I'm sure as hell not smiling. I'm just staring.

The look in his eyes is a new one and the only word I can use to describe it is regret. But he doesn't speak, which means he doesn't apologize, which means I don't have time to try to figure him out right now. I just need to run.

I walk past him and step onto the sidewalk, then start running. After a few steps, I hear him begin running behind me, but I keep my eyes focused forward. He never falls into step beside me and I make it a point not to slow down because I want him to stay behind me. At some point I begin running faster and faster until I'm sprinting, but he keeps in pace with me, always just a few steps behind. When we get to the marker that I use as a guide to turn around, I make it a point not to look at him. I turn around and pass him and head back toward my house, and the entire second half of the run is the exact same as the first. Quiet.

We're less than two blocks from reaching my house and I'm angry that he showed up at all today and even angrier that he still hasn't apologized. I begin running faster and faster, more than likely faster than I've ever run before, and he continues to match my speed step for step. This pisses me off even more, so when we turn on my street I somehow increase my speed and I'm running toward my house as fast as I possibly can and it's still not fast enough, because he's still there. My knees are buckling and I'm exerting myself so hard that I can't even catch a breath, but I only have twenty more feet until I reach my window.

I only make it ten.

As soon as my shoes meet the grass, I collapse onto my hands and knees and take several deep breaths. Never once, even in my four-mile runs, have I ever felt this drained. I roll onto my back on the grass and it's still wet with dew, but it feels good against my skin. My eyes are closed and I'm gasping so loud that I can barely hear Holder's breaths over my own. But I do hear them and they're close and I know he's on the grass next to me. We both lie still, panting for breath, and it reminds me of just a few nights ago when we were in the same position on my bed recovering from what he did to me. I think he's also reminded of this, because I barely feel his pinky when he reaches between us and wraps it around mine. Only this time when he does it, I don't smile. I wince.

I pull my hand away and roll over, then stand up. I walk the ten feet back to my house and I climb into my room, then close the window behind me.

It's been almost four weeks now. He never showed up to run with me again and he never apologized. He doesn't sit by me in class or in the cafeteria. He doesn't send me insulting texts and he doesn't show up on weekends as a different person. The only thing he does, at least I think he's the one that does it, is remove the sticky notes from my locker. They're always crumpled in a wad on the hallway floor at my feet.

I continue to exist, and he continues to exist, but we don't exist together. Days continue to pass no matter who I exist with, though. And each additional day that plants itself between the present and that weekend with him just leaves me with more and more questions that I'm too stubborn to ask.

I want to know what set him off that day. I want to know why he didn't just let it go instead of storming off like he did. I want to know why he never apologized, because I'm almost positive I would have given him at least one more chance. What he did was crazy and strange and a little possessive, but if I weighed it on a scale against all the wonderful things about him, I know it wouldn't have weighed nearly as much.

Breckin doesn't even try to analyze it anymore so I pretend not to, either. But I do, and the thing that eats at me the most is the fact that everything that happened between us is starting to seem surreal, like it was all just a dream. I catch myself questioning whether that weekend even happened at all, or if it was just another invalidated memory of mine that may not even be real.

For this entire month, the one thing in the forefront of my mind more than anything (and I know this is really pathetic) is the fact that I never did get to kiss him. I wanted to kiss him so incredibly badly that knowing I won't get to experience it leaves me feeling like there's this huge gaping hole in my chest. The ease with which we interacted, the way he would touch me like it was what he was supposed to do, the kisses he would plant in my hair—they were all small pieces of something so much bigger. Something big enough that, even though we never kissed, deserves some sort of recognition from him. Some sort of respect. He treats whatever was about to develop between us like it was wrong, and it hurts. Because I know he felt it. I *know* he did. And if he felt it in the same way that I felt it, then I know he *still* feels it.

I'm not heartbroken and I still haven't shed a single tear over the entire situation. I can't be heartbroken because luckily, I had yet to give him that part of me. But I'm not too proud to admit that I am a little sad about it all, and I know it'll take time because I really, really liked him. So, I'm fine. I'm a little sad, and a whole lot confused, but I'm fine.

"What's this?" I ask Breckin, looking down at the table. He just placed a box in front of me. A very nicely wrapped box.

"Just a little reminder."

I look up at him questioningly. "For what?"

He laughs and pushes the box closer to me. "It's a reminder that tomorrow's your birthday. Now open it."

I sigh and roll my eyes, then push it to the side. "I was hoping you'd forget."

He grabs the gift and pushes it back in front of me. "Open the damn present, Sky. I know you hate getting gifts, but I love giving them, so stop being a depressing bitch and open it and love it and hug me and thank me."

I slump my shoulders and push my empty tray aside, then pull the box back in front of me. "You're a good gift wrapper," I say. I untie the bow and tear open one end of the box, then slide open the paper. I look down at the picture on the box and cock my eyebrow. "You got me a TV?"

Breckin laughs and shakes his head, then picks the box up. "It's not a TV, dummy. It's an e-reader."

"Oh," I say. I have no idea what an e-reader is, but I'm pretty sure I'm not supposed to have one. I would just accept it like I accepted Six's cell phone, but this thing is too big for me to hide in my pocket.

"You're kidding, right?" He leans toward me. "You don't know what an e-reader is?"

I shrug. "It still looks like a tiny TV to me."

He laughs even louder and opens the box, pulling the e-reader out. He turns it on and hands it back to me. "It's an electronic device that holds more books than you'll ever be able to read." He pushes a button and the screen lights up, then he runs his finger across the front, pressing it in places until the whole screen is lit up with dozens of small pictures of books. I touch one of the pictures and the screen changes, then the book cover fills the entire screen. He slides his finger across it and the page virtually turns and I'm staring at chapter one.

I immediately start scrolling my finger across the screen and watch as each page turns effortlessly, one right after the other. It's absolutely the most amazing thing I've ever seen. I hit more buttons and click on more books and scroll through more chapters and I honestly don't think I've ever seen a more magnificent, practical invention.

"Wow," I whisper. I keep staring at the e-reader, hoping he's not playing some cruel joke on me, because if he tries to pry this out of my hands I'll run.

"You like it?" he asks proudly. "I loaded about two hundred free books on there so you should be good for a while."

I look up at him and he's grinning from ear to ear. I set the e-reader down on the table, then lunge forward over the table and squeeze his neck. It's the best present I've ever received and I'm smiling and squeezing him so tight, I completely don't care that I'm supposed to be horrible at receiving gifts. Breckin returns my hug and kisses me on the cheek. When I let go of his neck and open my eyes, I involuntarily glance at the table that I've been trying to avoid glancing at for almost four weeks now.

Holder is turned around in his seat, watching us. He's smiling. It's not a crazy or seductive or creepy smile. It's an endearing smile, and as soon as I see it and the waves of sadness crash against my core, I look away from him and back to Breckin.

I take my seat and pick the e-reader back up. "You know, Breckin. You really are pretty damn great."

He smiles and winks at me. "It's the Mormon in me. We're a pretty awesome people."

It's the last day I'll ever be seventeen. Karen is working out of town at her flea market again this weekend. She tried to cancel her trip because she felt bad for leaving during my birthday, but I wouldn't let her. Instead, we celebrated my birthday last night. Her gifts were good, but they're nothing like the e-reader. I've never been more excited to spend a weekend alone.

I didn't bake near as many things as the last time Karen was out of town. Not because I don't feel like eating them, but because I'm pretty sure my addiction to reading has just reached a whole new level. It's almost midnight and my eyes won't stay open, but I've read nearly two entire books and I absolutely need to get to the end of this one. I doze off, then awaken with a jerk, only to attempt to read another paragraph. Breckin has really great taste in books, and I'm sort of upset that it took him a whole month to tell me about this one. I know I'm not a big fan of happily-ever-afters, but if these two characters don't get theirs, I'll climb inside this e-reader and lock them inside that damn garage forever.

My eyelids slowly close and I keep trying to will them to stay open but the words are beginning to swim together on the screen and nothing is even making sense. I finally power off the e-reader and turn out my light and think about how my last day of being seventeen should have been so much better than it actually was.

My eyes flick open, but I don't move. It's still dark and I'm still in the same position I was in earlier, so I know I just fell asleep. I silence my breaths and listen for the same sound that pulled me out of my sleep—the sound of my window sliding open.

I can hear the curtains scraping against the rod and someone climbing inside. I know I should scream, or run for my door, or look around for some sort of object that can be used as a weapon. Instead, I remain frozen because whoever it is isn't trying to be at all quiet about the fact that he's climbing into my room, so I can only assume it's Holder. But still, my heart is racing and every muscle in my body stiffens when the bed shifts as he lowers himself onto it. The closer he gets, the more certain I am that it's him, because no one else can cause my body to react the way it's reacting right now. I squeeze my eyes shut and bring my hands to my face when I feel the covers lift up behind me. I'm absolutely terrified. I'm terrified, because I don't know *which* Holder is crawling into my bed right now.

His arm slides under my pillow and his other arm wraps tightly around my body when he finds my hands. He pulls me against his chest and laces his fingers into mine, then buries his head in my neck. I'm very conscious about the fact that I'm not wearing anything but a tank top and underwear, but I'm confident he's not here for that part of me. I'm still not positive *why* he's here, because he's not even talking, but he knows I'm awake. I know he knows I'm awake because the second his arms went around me, I gasped. He holds me as tight as he can and every now and then, he plants his lips into my hair and kisses me.

I'm angry with him for being here, but even angrier with myself for wanting him here. No matter how much I want to scream at him and make him leave, I find myself wishing he could squeeze me just a little bit tighter. I want him to lock his arms around me and throw away the key, because this is where he belongs and I'm scared he'll just let me go again.

I hate that there are so many sides to him that I don't understand, and I don't know if I even want to keep trying to understand them. There are parts of him I love, parts of him I hate, parts that terrify me, and parts that amaze me. But there's a part of him that does nothing but disappoint me . . . and that's the absolute hardest part of him to accept.

We lie here in complete silence for what could be half an hour, but I'm not sure. All I know is that he hasn't released his grip at all, nor has he made any attempt at explaining himself. But what's new? There isn't anything I'll ever get from him unless I ask the questions first. And right now, I just don't feel like asking any.

He releases my fingers from his and brings his hand to the top of my head. He presses his lips into my hair and he folds the arm up that's underneath my pillow and he's cradling me, burying his face in my hair. His arms begin to shake and he's holding me with such intensity and desperation that it becomes heartbreaking. My chest heaves and my cheeks burn and the only thing stopping the tears from flowing is the fact that my eyes are closed so tight, they can't escape.

I can't take the silence anymore, and if I don't get off my chest what I absolutely need to say, I might scream. I know my voice will be layered with heartbreak and sadness and I'll barely be able to speak while attempting to contain my tears, but I take a deep breath anyway and say the most honest thing I can say.

"I'm so mad at you."

As if it's possible, he somehow squeezes me even tighter. He moves his mouth to my ear and kisses it. "I know, Sky," he whispers. His hand slips underneath my shirt and he presses an open palm against my stomach, pulling me tighter against him. "I know."

It's amazing what the sound of a voice you've been longing to hear can do to your heart. He spoke five words just now, but in the time it took him to speak those five words, my heart was shredded and minced, then placed back inside my chest with the expectation that it should somehow know how to beat again.

I slip my fingers through the hand that's resting tightly against me and I squeeze it, not even knowing what it means, but every part of me wants to touch him and hold him and make sure he's really here. I need to know he's here and that this isn't just another vivid dream.

His mouth meets my shoulder and he parts his lips, kissing me softly. The feel of his tongue against my skin immediately sends a surge of heat through me and I can feel the flush rise from my stomach, straight up to my cheeks.

"I know," he whispers again, slowly exploring my collarbone and neck with his lips. I keep my eyes shut because the distress in his voice and the tenderness in his touch is making my head spin. I reach up behind me and run my hand through his hair, pressing him deeper into my neck. His warm breath against my skin becomes increasingly more frantic, along with his kisses. Our breathing picks up pace as he covers every inch of my neck twice over.

He lifts up on his arm and urges me flat onto my back, then brings his hand to my face and brushes the hair away from my eyes. Seeing him this close to me brings back every single feeling I've ever felt for this boy . . . the good *and* the bad. I don't understand how he can put me through what he's put me through when the sorrow in his eyes is so prominent. I don't know if it's the fact that I can't read him at all or if I read him too well, but looking up at him right now I know he feels what I'm feeling . . . which makes his actions that much more confusing.

"I know you're mad at me," he says, looking down at me. His eyes and his words are full of remorse, but the apology still doesn't come. "I need you to be mad at me, Sky. But I think I need you to still want me here with you even more."

My chest grows heavy with his words and it takes an extreme amount of effort to continue pulling breath into my lungs. I nod my head slightly, because I can completely agree to that. I'm pissed at him, but I want him here with me so much more than I *don't*. He drops his forehead to mine and we grab hold of each other's face, looking desperately into each other's eyes. I'm not sure if he's about to kiss me. I'm not even sure if he's about to get up and leave. The only thing I'm certain about right now is that after this moment, I will never be the same. I know, by the way his existence is like a magnetic pull on my heart, that if he ever hurts me again, I'll be far from just *fine*. I'll be broken.

Our chests are rising and falling as one as the silence and tension grow thicker. The firm grip he has on my face can be felt in every part of me, almost as if he's gripping me from the inside out. The intensity of the moment causes tears to sting at my eyes, and I'm completely taken aback by my unexpected emotions.

"I *am* mad at you, Holder," I say with an unsteady, but sure voice. "But no matter how mad I've been, I never for one second stopped wanting you here with me."

He somehow smiles and frowns in the same moment. "*Jesus*, Sky." His face contorts into an incredible amount of relief. "I've missed you so bad." He immediately drops his mouth and presses his lips to mine. The sensation has been so long overdue; neither of us has any patience left. I immediately respond by parting my lips and allowing him to fill me with the sweet taste of his mint leaves and soda. He's everything I've been imagining he would be and more. Gentle, rough, caring, selfish. In this one kiss I feel more of his emotions than in any words he's ever spoken. Our lips are finally intertwining for the first time, or the twentieth time, or the millionth time. It doesn't really matter because whichever time this is—it's absolutely perfect. It's incredible and flawless and almost worth everything we've been through in order to get to this moment.

Our lips move passionately together as we struggle to pull ourselves closer, wanting to find that perfect connection with our bodies that we've just found with our mouths. He works his mouth against mine delicately, yet fiercely, and I match him movement for movement. I release several moans and even more breaths and he drinks each one of them in with his mouth.

We kiss and kiss in every position possible, attempting to remain as restrained as our want will allow us. We kiss until I can no longer feel my lips and until I'm so exhausted and spent that I'm not even sure if we're still kissing when he presses his head to mine.

And that's exactly how we fall asleep—forehead to forehead, wrapped silently together. Because nothing else is spoken between us. Not even an apology.

I turn over to inspect the bed, half thinking what happened last night was a dream. Holder isn't here, but in his place is a small gift-wrapped box. I push myself up against my headboard and pick up the gift. I stare at it for a long time before I finally lift the lid and look inside. It's something that looks like a credit card, so I pick it up and read it.

He bought me a phone card with texting minutes. Lots of them.

I smile, because I know the significance of this card. It all lies within the message that Six sent him. He plans on stealing her girl, and he also plans on using a lot of her minutes. The gift makes me smile and I immediately reach to the nightstand and grab my phone. I have one missed text and it's from Holder.

You hungry?

The text is short and simple but it's his way of letting me know he's still here. Somewhere. Is he making me breakfast? I go to the bathroom before heading to the kitchen and brush my teeth. I change out of my tank top and pull on a simple sundress, then gather my hair up in a ponytail. I look at my reflection in the mirror and I see a girl who desperately wants to forgive a boy, but not without a hell of a lot of groveling first.

When I open the door to my bedroom, I'm met with the smell of bacon and the sound of grease sizzling from the kitchen. I walk down the hallway and around the corner, then pause. I stare at him for a while. His back is to me and he's working his way around the stove, humming to himself. He's shoeless, wearing jeans topped with a plain white sleeveless T-shirt. He already feels at home again, and I'm not sure how I feel about that.

"I left early this morning," he says, talking with his back still to me, "because I was afraid your mom would walk in and think I was trying to get you pregnant. Then when I went for my run, I passed by your house again and realized her car wasn't even home and remembered you said she does those weekend trade days every month. So I decided to pick up some groceries because I wanted to cook you breakfast. I also almost bought groceries for lunch and dinner, but maybe we should take it one meal at a time today." He turns around and faces me, slowly eyeing me up and down. "Happy birthday. I really like that dress. I bought real milk, you want some?"

I walk to the bar and keep my eyes trained on him, trying to process the plethora of words that just came out of his mouth. I scoot out a chair and take a seat. He pours me a glass of milk, even though I never said I wanted one, then slides it to me with a huge grin on his face. Before I can take a sip of the milk, he closes the gap between us and takes my chin in his hand.

"I need to kiss you. Your mouth was so damn perfect last night, I'm scared I dreamt that whole thing." He brings his mouth to mine and as soon as his tongue caresses mine, I can already tell this is going to be an issue.

His lips and his tongue and his hands are so incredibly perfect, I'll never be able to stay mad at him as long as he's able to use them against me like this. I grab his shirt and force my mouth against his even harder. He groans and fists his hands into my hair, then abruptly lets go and backs away. "Nope," he says, smiling. "Didn't dream it."

He walks back to the stove and turns off the burners, then transfers the bacon to a plate lined with eggs and toast. He walks it to the bar and begins filling the plate in front of me with food. He takes a seat and begins eating. He's smiling at me the whole time, and it suddenly hits me.

I *know*. I know what's wrong with him. I know why he's happy and angry and temperamental and all over the place and it finally makes so much sense.

"Are we allowed to play Dinner Quest, even though it's breakfast time?" he asks.

I take a sip of my milk and nod. "If I get the first question."

He lays his fork down on his plate and smiles. "I was thinking about just letting you have *all* the questions."

"I only need the answer to one."

He sighs and leans back against his seat, then looks down at his hands. I can tell by the way he's avoiding my gaze that he already knows I know. His reaction is one of guilt. I lean forward in my chair and glare at him.

"How long have you been using drugs, Holder?"

He shoots his eyes up to meet mine and his expression is stoic. He stares at me for a moment and I keep my stance, wanting him to know I'm not letting up until he tells me the truth. He purses his lips in a tight line, then looks down at his hands again. For a second I'm thinking he might be preparing to bolt out the front door in order to avoid talking about it, but then I see something on his face I wasn't expecting to see at all. A dimple.

He's grimacing, attempting to hold on to his expression, but the corners of his mouth give way and his smile breaks out into laughter.

He's laughing and he's laughing really hard and it's really pissing me off.

"*Drugs?*" he says between fits of laughter. "You think I'm on *drugs?*" He continues laughing until he realizes that I don't think it's the least bit funny at all. He eventually stops and sucks in a deep breath, then reaches across the table and takes my hand in his. "I'm not on drugs, Sky. I promise. I don't know why you would think that, but I swear."

"Then what the hell is wrong with you?"

His expression drops with that question, and he releases my hand from his. "Can you be a little less vague?" He falls back into his chair and folds his arms over his chest.

I shrug. "Sure. What happened to us and why are you acting like it never happened?"

His elbow is resting on the table and he looks down at his arm. He slowly traces each letter of his tattoo with his fingers, deep in thought. I know silence isn't considered a sound, but right now the silence between us is the loudest sound in the world. He pulls his arm off the table and looks up at me.

"I didn't want to let you down, Sky. I've let everyone down in my life that's ever loved me, and after that day at lunch I knew I let you down, too. So . . . I left you before you could start loving me. Otherwise, any effort to try not to disappoint you would be hopeless."

His words are full of apology and sadness and regret,

but he still can't just say them. He overreacted and jealousy got the best of him, but if he had just said those two words we would have been spared an entire month of emotional agony. I'm shaking my head, because I just don't get it. I don't understand why he couldn't just say *I'm sorry*.

"Why couldn't you just say it, Holder? Why couldn't you just apologize?"

He leans forward across the table and takes my hand, looking me hard in the eyes. "I'm not apologizing to you . . . because I don't want you to forgive me."

The sadness in his eyes must mirror mine and I don't want him seeing it. I don't want him seeing me sad, so I squeeze my eyes shut. He lets go of my hand and I hear him walk around the table until his arms are around me and he's picking me up. He sets me down on the bar so that we're at eye level and he brushes the hair from my face and makes me open my eyes again. His eyebrows are pulled together and the pain on his face is raw and real and heartbreaking.

"Babe, I screwed up. I've screwed up more than once with you, I know that. But believe me, what happened at lunch that day wasn't jealousy or anger or anything that should ever scare you. I wish I could tell you what happened, but I can't. Someday I will, but I can't right now and I need you to accept that. Please. And I'm not apologizing to you, because I don't want you to forget what happened and you should never forgive me for it. *Ever.* Never make excuses for me, Sky."

He leans in and kisses me briefly, then pulls back and continues. "I told myself to just stay away from you and let you be mad at me, because I do have so many issues that I'm not ready to share with you yet. And I tried so hard to

stay away, but I can't. I'm not strong enough to keep deny-
ing whatever this is we could have. And yesterday in the
lunchroom when you were hugging Breckin and laughing
with him? It felt so good to see you happy, Sky. But I wanted
so bad to be the one who was making you laugh like that.
It was tearing me up inside that you were thinking that I
didn't care about us, or that spending that weekend with
you wasn't the best weekend I've ever had in my life. Because I *do* care and it *was* the best. It was the best fucking
weekend in the history of all weekends."

My heart is beating wildly, almost as fast as the words
are pouring out of him. He releases his firm hold on my face
and strokes his hands over my hair, dropping them to the
nape of my neck. He keeps them there and calms himself
with a deep breath, then continues.

"It's killing me, Sky," he says, his voice much more calm
and quiet. "It's killing me because I don't want you to go
another day without knowing how I feel about you. And
I'm not ready to tell you I'm in love with you, because I'm
not. Not yet. But whatever this is I'm feeling—it's so much
more than just *like*. It's *so* much more. And for the past few
weeks I've been trying to figure it out. I've been trying to
figure out why there isn't some other word to describe it.
I want to tell you exactly how I feel but there isn't a single
goddamned word in the entire dictionary that can describe
this point between *liking* you and *loving* you, but I need that
word. I need it because I need you to hear me say it."

He pulls my face to his and he kisses me. They're short
kisses, mostly pecks, but he kisses me over and over, pulling
back after each kiss, waiting for me to respond.

"Say something," he pleads.

I'm looking into his terrified eyes and for the first time since we met . . . I think I actually understand him. *All* of him. He doesn't react the way he does because there are five different sides to his personality. He reacts the way he does because there's only *one* side to Dean Holder.

Passionate.

He's passionate about life, about love, about his words, about Les. And I'll be damned if I wasn't just added to his list. The intensity he conveys isn't unnerving . . . it's *beautiful.* I've gone so long trying to find ways to feel numb any chance I get, but seeing the enthusiasm behind his eyes right now . . . it makes me want to feel every single thing about life. The good, the bad, the beautiful, the ugly, the pleasure, the pain. I *want* that. I want to start feeling life the same way he does. And my first step to doing so starts with this hopeless boy in front of me who's pouring his heart out, searching for that perfect word, wanting desperately to help me add feeling back into living.

Back into living.

The word comes to me like it's always been there, tucked away between like and love in the dictionary, right where it belongs. "Living," I say.

The desperation in his eyes eases slightly, and he lets out a short, confused laugh. *"What?"* He shakes his head, trying to understand my response.

"Live. If you mix the letters up in the words like and love, you get live. You can use that word."

He laughs again, but this time it's a laugh of relief. He wraps his arms around me and he kisses me with nothing but a hell of a lot of relief. "I live you, Sky," he says against my lips. "I live you so much."

I have no idea how he does it, but I've completely forgiven him, have become infatuated with him, and now I can't stop kissing him, all in the span of fifteen minutes. He definitely has a way with words. I'm starting to not mind that it takes him so long to think of them. He pulls away from my mouth and smiles, grabbing my waist with his hands.

"So what do you want to do for your birthday?" he asks, pulling me down off the bar. He gives me another quick peck on the mouth and walks to the living room where his wallet and keys are on the end table.

"We don't have to do anything. I don't expect you to entertain me just because it's my birthday."

He slips his keys into the pocket of his pants and looks up at me. His mouth hints at a wicked smile and he won't stop staring at me.

"What?" I ask. "You look guilty."

He laughs and shrugs. "I was just thinking of all the ways I could entertain you if we stayed here today. Which is exactly why we need to leave."

Which is exactly why I want to stay here.

"We could go see my mom," I suggest.

"Your mom?" He looks at me warily.

"Yeah. She runs an herbal booth at the flea market. It's the place she goes some weekends. I never go because she's there fourteen hours a day and I get bored. But it's one of the biggest flea markets in the world and I've always wanted to go walk around. It's only an hour-and-a-half drive. They have funnel cake," I add, trying to make it sound enticing.

Holder walks back to me and wraps his arms around me. "If you want to go to the flea market, then we're going to the flea market. I'm gonna run home and change and I have something I need to do. Pick you up in an hour?"

I nod. I know it's just a flea market, but I'm excited. I don't know how Karen will feel with me showing up unannounced with Holder. I haven't really told her anything about him, so I feel bad sort of springing him on her like this. It's her own fault, though. If she didn't ban technology I could call her and give her a heads up.

Holder gives me another quick peck and walks to the front door.

"Hey," I say, just as he's about to walk out. He spins around and looks at me. "It's my birthday and the last two kisses you've given me have been pretty damn pathetic. If you expect me to spend the day with you, I suggest you start kissing me like a boyfriend kisses his—"

The word slips from my mouth and I immediately cut the rest of the sentence off. We still haven't discussed labels yet and the fact that we just made up within the past half hour makes my lackadaisical use of the word *boyfriend* feel like something Matty-boy would have said to me. "I mean . . ." I stutter, then I just give up and clamp my mouth shut. I can't recover from that.

He's turned around facing me, still standing by the front door. He's not smiling. He's looking at me with that look again, holding my gaze with his, not speaking. He tilts his head toward me and raises both of his eyebrows curiously. "Did you just refer to me as your boyfriend?"

He's not smiling about the fact that I just referred to him as my boyfriend and that realization makes me wince. God, this seems so childish.

"No," I say stubbornly, folding my arms across my chest. "Only cheesy fourteen-year-olds do that."

He takes a few steps toward me, never changing his expression. He stops two feet in front of me and mirrors my stance. "That's too bad. Because when I thought you referred to me as your boyfriend just now, it made me want to kiss the living hell out of you." He narrows his eyes and there's a playful look about him that immediately relieves the knot in my stomach. He turns around and heads back to the door. "I'll see you in an hour." He opens the door and turns around before he leaves, slowly easing his way outside, teasing me with his playful grin and lickable dimples.

I sigh and roll my eyes. "Holder, wait."

He pauses and proudly leans against the doorframe.

"You better come kiss your girlfriend good-bye," I say, feeling every bit as cheesy as I sound. His face washes with victory and he walks back into the living room. He slips his hand to the small of my back and pulls me against him. It's our first freestanding kiss and I love the way he's securing me protectively with his arm around my lower back. He traces his fingers along my cheek and runs them through my hair, bringing his lips closer to mine. He's not staring at my lips, though. He's looking straight into my eyes and his are full of something I can't place. It's not lust this time; it's more like a look of appreciation.

He continues to stare at me without closing the gap

between our lips. He's not teasing me or trying to get me to kiss him first. He's just looking at me with appreciation and affection, and it turns my heart to butter. My hands are on his shoulders, so I slowly run them up his neck and through his hair, enjoying whatever this silent moment is that's occurring between us. His chest rises and falls against the rhythm of mine and his eyes begin searching my face, scrolling over every feature. The way he's looking at me is causing my entire body to grow weak, and I'm thankful his arm is still locked around my waist.

He lowers his forehead to mine and lets out a long sigh, looking at me with a look that's quickly turned into something resembling pain. It prompts me to slide my hands down to his cheeks and softly stroke them with my fingers, wanting to take away whatever it is that's behind those eyes right now.

"Sky," he says, focusing on me intently. He says it like he's about to follow it up with something profound, but instead, my name is the only thing he says. He slowly brings his mouth to mine and our lips meet. He inhales a deep breath as he presses his closed lips against mine, breathing me into him. He pulls away and looks back down into my eyes for several more seconds, stroking my cheek. I've never been savored like this before, and it's absolutely beautiful.

He dips his head again and rests his lips against mine, my top lip between both of his. He kisses me as softly as possible, treating my mouth as though it's breakable. I part my lips and allow him to deepen his kiss, which he does, but even then it's still soft. It's appreciative and gentle and he keeps one hand on the back of my head and one on my hip as he slowly tastes and teases every part of my mouth. This kiss is just like he is—studied and never in a hurry.

Just when my mind has succumbed to every part of being wrapped up in him, his lips come to a standstill and he slowly pulls back. My eyes flutter open and I let out a breath that may have been mixed with the words, "*Oh, my.*"

Seeing my breathless reaction causes him to break out with a smug grin. "That was our first official kiss as a couple."

I wait for the panic to set in, but it doesn't. "A couple," I repeat, quietly.

"Damn straight." He still has his hand on my lower back and I'm pressed against him, looking up at his eyes as they focus down on me. "And don't worry," he adds. "I'll be informing Grayson myself. I ever see him trying to touch you like he does and he'll be reintroduced to my fist."

His hand moves from my lower back and up to my cheek. "I'm really leaving now. I'll see you in an hour. I live you." He gives me a quick peck on the lips and backs away, then turns toward the door.

"Holder?" I say as soon as I suck enough breath back into my lungs to speak. "What do you mean by *reintro-duced*? Have you and Grayson been in a fight before?"

Holder's expression turns into a tight-lipped blank one and he nods, but barely. "I told you before. He's not a good person." The door closes behind him and he leaves me with even more questions. But what's new?

I decide to forgo my own shower and call Six, instead. I've got a lot to catch her up on. I run to my room and crawl out the window, then slide hers up and pull myself inside. I pick up the phone by her bed and take out my cell phone to find the text that she sent with her international number. When I start dialing, my cell phone receives an incoming message from Holder.

I'm really dreading spending all day with you. This doesn't sound like fun at all. Also, your sundress is really unflattering and way too summery, but you should definitely keep it on.

I grin. Dammit, I really do live this hopeless boy.

I dial the number to reach Six and lie back on her bed. She answers groggily on the third ring.

"Hey," I say. "You sleeping?"

I can hear her yawn. "Obviously not. But you really need to start taking time differences into consideration."

I laugh. "Six? It's afternoon there. Even if I *did* take time differences into consideration, it wouldn't matter with you."

"I had a rough morning," she says defensively. "I miss your face. What's up?"

"Not much."

"You lie. You sound annoyingly happy. I'm guessing you and Holder finally worked out whatever the hell happened at school that day?"

"Yep. And you are the first to know that I, Linden Sky Davis, am now a taken woman."

She groans. "Why anyone would subject themselves to that sort of misery is beyond me. But I'm happy for you."

"Tha—" I was about to say thanks, but my words are cut off by a very loud "*Oh, my God!*" from Six's end.

"*What?*"

"I forgot. It's your freaking birthday and I forgot! Happy birthday Sky and holy crap I'm the worst best friend ever."

"It's okay," I laugh. "I'm sort of glad you forgot. You know how I hate presents and surprises and everything else that comes with birthdays."

"Oh, wait. I just remembered how incredibly awesome I am. Check behind your dresser today."

I roll my eyes. "Figures."

"And tell your new boyfriend to get him some damn minutes."

"Will do. I gotta go, your mom's gonna shit when she sees this phone bill."

"Yeah, well . . . she should be more in tune with the earth like your mom."

I laugh. "Love you, Six. Be safe, okay?"

"Love you, too. And Sky?"

"Yeah?"

"You sound happy. I'm happy you're happy."

I smile and the line disconnects. I head back to my room and, as much as I hate presents, I'm still human and naturally curious. I immediately walk to my dresser and look behind it. On the floor is a wrapped box, so I bend down and pick it up. I walk to my bed and sit, then slide the lid off it. It's a box full of Snickers.

Dammit, I love her.

I'm standing at my window impatiently waiting when Holder finally pulls up into the driveway. I walk out my front door and lock it behind me, then turn toward the car and freeze. He's not alone. The passenger door opens and a guy steps out. When he turns around, I'm positive my facial expression is stuck between an OMG and a WTF. *I'm learning.*

Breckin is holding the passenger door open with a huge grin on his face. "Hope you don't mind a third wheel today. My second best friend in the whole wide world invited me to come."

I reach the passenger door, confused as hell. Breckin waits until I climb inside, then he opens the back door and climbs into the backseat. I lean forward and tilt my head toward Holder, who's laughing like he just revealed the punch line to a really funny joke. A joke I'm not a part of.

"Would one of you like to explain what the hell is going on?" I say.

Holder grabs my hand and pulls it to his mouth, giving my knuckles a kiss. "I'll let Breckin explain. He talks faster, anyway."

I spin around in my seat as Holder begins backing out of the driveway. I arch an eyebrow at Breckin.

He shoots me a clear look of guilt. "I've sort of had a

double alliance going on for about two weeks now," he says sheepishly.

I shake my head, attempting to wrap this confession around my mind. I glance back and forth between them. "Two weeks? You guys have been talking for *two weeks*? Without me? Why didn't you tell me?"

"I was sworn to secrecy," Breckin says.

"But . . ."

"Turn around and put your seatbelt on," Holder says to me.

I glare at him. "In a minute. I'm trying to figure out why you made up with Breckin two weeks ago, but it took you until today to make up with me."

He glances at me, then looks back at the road in front of him. "Breckin deserved an apology. I acted like an asshole that day."

"And I *didn't* deserve one?"

He looks at me dead on this time. "No," he says firmly, turning his gaze back to the road. "You don't deserve words, Sky. You deserve actions."

I stare at him, wondering how long he stayed up at night forming that perfect sentence. He glances back at me and lets go of my hand, then tickles the top of my thigh. "Quit being so serious. Your boyfriend and your very best friend in the whole wide world are taking you to a flea market."

I laugh and slap his hand away. "How can I feel happy when my alliance has been infiltrated? You two have a hell of a lot of kissing up to do today."

Breckin rests his chin on the top of my headrest and looks down at me. "I think I've been the one that suffered the most out of this ordeal. Your boyfriend has ruined my last two Friday nights in a row, moping and whining about how much he wants you but how he doesn't want to let you down and blah, blah, blah. It's been rough not complaining to you about him at lunch every day."

Holder darts his head back toward Breckin. "Well, now you two can complain about me all you want. Life is back to how it should be." He slides his fingers through mine and squeezes my hand. My skin tingles and I'm not sure if it's from his touch or his words.

"I still think I deserve an ass kissing today," I say to both of them. "I want you to buy me whatever I want at the flea market. I don't care how much it costs or how big and heavy it is."

"Damn straight," Breckin says.

I groan. "Oh, God, Holder's already rubbing off on you."

Breckin laughs and reaches over the seat to grab my hands, then pulls me toward him. "He must be, because I really want to cuddle you in the backseat right now," Breckin says.

"I'm not rubbing off on you that much if you think I'd only be *cuddling* her in a backseat," Holder says. He slaps me on the ass right before I fall into the back with Breckin.

"You can't be serious," Holder says, holding the saltshaker I just placed in his hands. We've been walking around the flea market for over an hour now and I'm sticking to my plan. They're buying me whatever the hell I want. I have a betrayal to overcome and it's going to take a lot of random purchases before I feel better.

I look at the figurine in his hands and nod. "You're right. I should get the matching set." I pick up the peppershaker and hand it to him. They aren't anything I would ever want. I'm not sure how they could be anything *anyone* would ever want. Who makes ceramic salt and peppershakers fashioned out of small and large intestines?

"I bet they belonged to a doctor," Breckin says, admiring them with me. I reach into Holder's pocket and pull out his wallet, then turn to the man behind the table. "How much?"

He shrugs. "I don't know," he says unenthusiastically. "A dollar each?"

"How about a dollar for both?" I ask. He takes the dollar out of my hands and nods us away.

"Way to bargain," Holder says, shaking his head. "These better be on your kitchen table next time I come over."

"Gross, no," I say. "Who'd want to stare at guts while they eat?"

We browse a few more pavilions until we reach the pavilion Karen and Jack are set up in. When we reach their booth, Karen does a double take, eyeing Breckin and Holder.

"Hey," I say, holding out my hands. "Surprise!"

Jack jumps up and walks around the booth, giving me a quick hug. Karen follows him and is eyeing me guardedly the entire time.

"Relax," I say, after seeing her eye both Holder and Breckin with concern. "Neither one of them is getting me pregnant this weekend."

She laughs and finally wraps her arms around me. "Happy birthday." She pulls back and her motherly instincts kick in about fifteen seconds too late. "Wait. Why are you here? Is everything okay? Are you okay? Is the house okay?"

"It's fine. I'm fine. I was just bored so I asked Holder to come shopping with me."

Holder is behind me introducing himself to Jack. Breckin slips past me and gives Karen a hug. "I'm Breckin," he says. "I'm in an alliance to take over the public school system and all its minions with your daughter."

"Was," I clarify, glaring at Breckin. "He *was* in an alliance with me."

"I like you already," Karen says, smiling at Breckin. She looks past me at Holder and shakes his hand. "Holder," she says politely. "How are you?"

"Good," he says, his response guarded. I look at him and he appears extremely uncomfortable. I don't know if it's the salt and peppershakers he's holding, or the fact that seeing Karen this time garners a different reaction from him now that he's dating her daughter. I try to deflect the mood by turning around and asking Karen if she has a sack we can use for our things. She reaches under the table and holds it out to Holder. He places the shakers inside and she looks down into the sack and back up at me questioningly.

"Don't ask," I say. I take the sack from her and open it up so Breckin can place the other purchase inside. It's a small, wood-framed picture of the word "melt," written in black ink on white paper. It was twenty-five cents and made absolutely no sense, so of course I had to have it.

A couple of customers walk to the table so both Jack and Karen walk around the booth and begin helping them. I turn around and Holder is eyeing both of them with a hard look in his eyes. I haven't seen him with an expression like this since that day in the cafeteria. It unnerves me a little, so I walk up to him and slide my arm around his back, desperately wanting that look to go away.

"Hey," I say, pulling his focus down to me. "You okay?"

He nods and kisses me on the forehead. "I'm good," he says. He wraps his arm around my waist and smiles down at me reassuringly. "You promised me funnel cake," he says, brushing my cheek with his hand.

I nod, relieved to see he's okay. I don't really want Holder having one of his intense moments right now in front of Karen. I don't know that she'll quite understand his passionate approach to life like I'm starting to.

"Funnel cake?" Breckin says. "Did you say funnel cake?"

I turn back around and Karen's customer is gone. She's standing frozen behind the table, eyeing the arm that's wrapped around my waist. She looks pale.

What's the deal with everyone and their weird looks today?

"You okay?" I ask her. It's not like she's never seen me with a boyfriend before. Matt practically lived at our house the entire month I dated him.

She looks up at me, then glances at Holder briefly. "I just didn't realize you two were dating."

"Yeah. About that," I say. "I would have told you, but we sort of just started dating about four hours ago."

"Oh," she says. "Well . . . you look cute together. Can I talk to you?" She nudges her head behind her, indicating she wants privacy. I slip my arm out of Holder's and follow her to a safe speaking distance. She spins around and shakes her head.

"I don't know how I feel about this," she says, talking in a low whisper.

"About what? I'm eighteen and I have a boyfriend. Big deal."

She sighs. "I know, it's just . . . what happens tonight? When I'm not there? How do I know he won't hang around all night?"

I shrug. "You don't. You just have to trust me," I say, instantly feeling guilty for the lie. If she knew he already spent last night with me, I think it's safe to say Holder would no longer be my *breathing* boyfriend.

"It's just weird, Sky. We've never really discussed guy rules for when I'm not home." She looks extremely nervous, so I do what I can to ease her mind.

"Mom? Trust me. We literally just agreed to start dating a few hours ago. There's no way anything will happen between us that you fear might happen. He'll be gone by midnight, I promise."

She nods unconvincingly. "It's just . . . I don't know. Seeing the two of you just now with your arms around each other? The way both of you were interacting? It's not the way new couples look at each other, Sky. It just threw me off because I thought maybe you've been seeing him for a while but you've been keeping it from me. I want you to be able to talk to me about anything."

I grab her hand and squeeze it. "I know, Mom. And believe me, if we hadn't come here together today I would have told you all about him tomorrow. I'd probably have talked your ear off. I'm not keeping anything hidden from you, okay?"

She smiles and gives me a quick squeeze. "I still expect you to talk my ear off about him tomorrow."

Saturday, September 29, 2012
10:15 p.m.

"Sky, wake up."

I lift my head off Breckin's arm and wipe drool off the side of my cheek. He looks down at his wet shirt and grimaces.

"Sorry." I laugh. "You shouldn't be so comfortable."

We've arrived back at his house after spending eight hours walking and perusing junk. Holder and Breckin finally gave in and we all got a little competitive, seeing who could find the most random object. I think I still won with the gut shakers, but Breckin came in a close second with a velvet painting of a puppy riding on the back of a unicorn.

"Don't forget your painting," I say when he steps out of the car. He leans in and grabs the painting from the floorboard, then kisses my cheek.

"See you Monday," he says to me. He looks up at Holder. "Don't think you're getting my seat first period now just because she's your girlfriend."

Holder laughs. "I'm not the one bringing her coffee every morning. I doubt she'd let me overthrow you."

Breckin shuts the door and Holder waits until he's inside his house before he leaves. "What do you think you're doing back there?" he says, smiling at me in the rearview mirror. "Get up here."

I shake my head and remain put. "I sort of like having a chauffeur."

He puts the car in park and unbuckles his seatbelt, then turns around in his seat. "Come here," he says, reaching for my arms. He grabs my wrists and pulls me forward until our faces are just inches apart. He lifts his hands to my face and smashes my cheeks together like I'm a little kid. He gives me a loud peck on my squished-together lips. "I had fun today," he says. "You're kind of weird."

I cock my eyebrow, not sure if he just complimented me or not. "*Thanks?*"

"I like weird. Now get your ass in the front seat with me before I climb in the backseat and not cuddle you." He pulls my arm forward and I climb into the front seat, then put my seatbelt on.

"What are we doing now? Your house?" I ask.

He shakes his head. "Nope. One more stop."

"My house?"

He shakes his head again. "You'll see."

We drive until we're on the outskirts of town. I recognize we're at the local airport when he pulls the car over to the side of the road. He gets out without saying anything and comes around to open my door. "We're here," he says, waving his hand at the runway spread out in a field across from us.

"Holder, this is the smallest airport within a two-hundred-mile radius. If you're expecting to watch a plane land, we'll be here for two days."

He pulls on my hand and leads me down a small hill. "We're not here to watch the planes." He continues walking until he gets to a fence that edges the airport grounds. He shakes it to test for sturdiness, then takes my hand in his again. "Take off your shoes, it'll be easier," he says. I look at the fence, then look back at him.

"You expect me to climb that thing?"

"Well," he says, looking at it. "I could pick you up and throw you over, but it might hurt a little more."

"I'm in a dress! You didn't tell me we were climbing fences tonight. Besides, it's illegal."

He rolls his head and pushes me toward the fence. "It's not illegal when my stepdad manages the airport. And no, I didn't tell you we'd be climbing fences because I was scared you would change out of this dress."

I grab the fence and begin to test it when, in one swift movement, his hands are on my waist and I'm up in the air, already scaling over it.

"Jesus, Holder!" I yell, jumping down the other side.

"I know. That went a little too fast. I forgot to cop a feel." He pulls up on the fence and swings his leg over, then jumps down. "Come on," he says, grabbing my hand and pulling me forward.

We walk until we reach the runway. I pause and peer out over the massive length of it. I've never been on an airplane before and the thought of it sort of terrifies me. Especially seeing that there's a huge lake edging the far end of the runway.

"Have any planes ever landed in that lake?"

"Just one," he says, pulling me down with him. "But it was a small Cessna and the pilot was lit. He was okay, but the plane is still at the bottom of the lake." He lowers himself onto the runway and tugs at my hand, wanting me to do the same.

"What are we doing?" I ask, adjusting my dress and slipping off my shoes.

"Shush," he says. "Lie down and look up."

I lay my head back and look up, then suck in a sharp breath. Laid out before me in every direction is a blanket of stars brighter than I've ever seen them.

"Wow," I whisper. "They don't look like this from my backyard."

"I know. That's why I brought you." He reaches down between us and wraps his pinky around mine.

We sit for a long time without speaking, but it's a peaceful silence. Every now and then he lifts his pinky and grazes the side of my hand, but that's all he does. We're side by side and I'm in a dress with fairly easy access, but he never even so much as tries to kiss me. It's evident he didn't bring me out here in the middle of nowhere just to make out with me. He brought me out here to share this experience with me. Something else he's passionate about.

There is so much about Holder that surprises me, especially within the last twenty-four hours. I'm still not clear on what made him so upset in the cafeteria that day, but he seems confident that he knows exactly what it was and that it'll never happen again. And right now, all I can do is take his word. All I can do is take my trust and place it back into his hands. I just hope he knows that it's all the trust I have left to give him. I know for a fact that if he hurts me like he's hurt me before, it'll be the last time he ever hurts me.

I tilt my head toward his and watch him as he stares up to the sky. His brows are furrowed together and he's clearly got something on his mind. It seems like he always has something on his mind and I'm curious if I'll ever break through that. There are so many things I still want to know about his past and his sister and his family. But bringing it all up, when he's so deep in thought, would take him out of wherever his mind is right now. I don't want to do that. I know exactly where he is and what he's doing, staring off into space like he is. I know, because it's exactly what I do when I stare at the stars on my ceiling.

I watch him for a long time, then turn my gaze back up to the sky and begin to escape my own thoughts, when he breaks the silence with a question that comes out of nowhere.

"Have you had a good life?" he asks quietly.

I ponder his question, but mostly because I want to know what he was thinking about that made him ask it. Was he really thinking about my life or was he thinking about his own?

"Yeah," I reply honestly. "Yeah, I have."

He sighs heavily, then takes my hand completely in his. "Good."

Nothing else is spoken until half an hour later when he says he's ready to leave.

We pull up to my house at a few minutes before midnight. We both get out of the car and he grabs my sacks of random stuff and follows me to the front door. He stands in the doorway and sets them down. "I'm not coming in any further," he says, putting his hands in his pockets.

"Why not? Are you a vampire? Do you need permission to enter?"

He smiles. "I just don't think I should stay."

I walk to him and put my arms around him, then kiss him on the chin. "Why not? Are you tired? We can lie down, I know you barely got any sleep last night." I really don't want him to leave. I slept better last night in his arms than any other night before it.

He responds to my embrace by wrapping his arms around my shoulders and pulling me against his chest. "I can't," he says. "It's a combination of things, really. The fact that my mom will inundate me with questions about where I've been since last night. The fact that I heard you promise your mom I would leave by midnight. The fact that the entire time you were walking around today I couldn't stop thinking about what's underneath this dress."

He brings his hands to my face and stares down at my mouth. His eyelids become heavy and he drops his voice to a whisper. "Not to mention these lips," he says. "You have no idea how difficult it was trying to listen to a single word you said today when all I could think about was how soft they are. How incredible they taste. How perfect they fit between mine." He leans in and kisses me softly, then pulls away just as I begin to melt into him. "And this dress," he says, running his hand down my back and gently gliding it over my hip and to the top of my thigh. I shiver under his fingertips. "This dress is the main reason I'm not walking any further into this house."

With the way my body is responding to him, I quickly agree with his decision to leave. As much as I love being with him and love kissing him, I can already tell that I would have absolutely zero restraint, and I don't think I'm ready to pass that first yet.

I sigh, but I feel like groaning. As much as I can agree

with what he's saying, my body is still completely pissed off that I'm not begging him to stay. It's odd how just being around him today has somehow deepened the need I have to constantly want to be around him.

"Is this normal?" I ask, looking up into his eyes, which hold more desire than I've ever seen in them before. I know why he's leaving now, because it's clear that he wants to pass this first, too.

"Is *what* normal?"

I press my head into his chest to avoid having to look at him while I speak. Sometimes I say things that are embarrassing, but I just have to say them regardless. "Is the way we feel about each other normal? We haven't really known each other for very long. Most of that time was spent avoiding each other. But I don't know, it just seems different with you. I assume when most people date, the first few months are spent trying to build a connection." I lift my head off his chest and look up at him. "I feel like I had that with you the moment we met. Everything about us is so natural. It feels like we're already there, and we're trying to go backward now. Like we're trying to *re*-get to know each other by slowing it down. Is that weird?"

He brushes the hair out of my face and looks down at me with a completely different look in his eyes this time. The lust and desire has been replaced by anguish, and it makes my heart heavy seeing it in his eyes.

"Whatever this is, I don't want to analyze it. I don't want you analyzing it either, okay? Let's just be grateful I finally found you."

I laugh at his last sentence. "You say that like you've been looking for me."

He furrows his brows and places his hands on the sides of my head, tilting my face up to his. "I've been looking for you my whole damn life." His expression is solid and determined and he meshes our mouths together as soon as the sentence leaves his lips. He kisses me hard and with more passion than he's kissed me all day. I'm about to pull him inside with me but he lets go and backs away as soon as my hands fist in his hair.

"I live you," he says, forcing himself off the steps. "I'll see you on Monday."

"I live you, too."

I don't ask him why I'm not seeing him tomorrow, because I think the time will be good for us in order to process the last twenty-four hours. It'll be good for Karen as well, since I really need to fill her in on my new love life. Or, my new *live* life, rather.

It's been almost a month since Holder and I declared ourselves a couple. So far, I haven't found any idiosyncrasies of
his that drive me crazy. If anything, the small habits he has
just make me adore him even more. Like the way he still
stares at me like he's studying me, and the way he pops his
jaw when he's irritated, and the way he licks his lips every
time he laughs. It's actually sort of hot. And don't get me
started on the dimples.

Luckily, I've had the same Holder since the night he
crawled through my window and into my bed. I haven't seen
any snippets of the moody and temperamental Holder at all
since then. In fact, we somehow become more and more in
tune with each other the more time we spend together, and
I feel like I can read him now almost as well as he reads me.

With Karen being home every weekend, we haven't had a
lot of alone time. Most of our time together is spent at school
or on dates over the weekends. For some reason, he doesn't
feel right coming to my bedroom when Karen is home and
he always makes excuses when I suggest we go to his house.
So instead, we've seen a lot of movies. We've also been out a
few times with Breckin and his new boyfriend, Max.

Holder and I have been having a lot of fun together, but
we haven't had a lot of *fun* together. We're both beginning
to get a little frustrated at our lack of a decent place to make

out. His car is kind of small, but we've made do. I think we're both counting down the hours until Karen is out of town again next weekend.

I sit down at the table with Breckin and Max, waiting for Holder to bring both our trays. Max and Breckin met at a local art gallery about two weeks ago, not even realizing they attended the same school. I'm happy for Breckin, because I started to get the feeling he felt like a third wheel, when it wasn't like that at all. I love his company, but seeing him pour his attention into his own relationship has made things a lot easier.

"Are you and Holder busy this Saturday?" Max asks when I take a seat.

"I don't think so. Why?"

"There's an art gallery downtown that's displaying one of my pieces in their local art show. I want you guys there."

"Sounds cool," Holder says, taking his seat next to me. "Which piece are you displaying?"

Max shrugs. "I don't know yet. I'm still trying to decide between two."

Breckin rolls his eyes. "You know which one you need to enter and it isn't either of those two."

Max cuts his eyes to Breckin. "We live in East Texas. I doubt the gay-themed painting will go over very well around here."

Holder looks back and forth between them. "Who gives a shit what people around here think?"

Max's smile fades and he picks up his fork. "My parents," he says.

"Do your parents know you're gay?" I ask.

He nods. "Yeah. They're pretty supportive for the most part, but they're still hoping none of their friends at church find out. They don't want to be pitied for having the child who's damned to Hell."

I shake my head. "If God's the type of guy that would damn you to Hell just for loving someone, then I wouldn't want to spend eternity with Him, anyway."

Breckin laughs. "I bet they have funnel cake in Hell."

"What time is it over Saturday?" Holder asks. "We'll be there, but Sky and I have plans later that night."

"It's over at nine," Breckin says.

I glance at Holder. "We have plans? What are we doing?"

He grins at me and wraps his arm around my shoulder, then whispers in my ear. "My mom will be gone Saturday night. I want to show you my bedroom."

My arms break out in chills and I suddenly have visions that are entirely too inappropriate for a high school cafeteria.

"I don't even want to know what he said to make you blush like that," Breckin says, laughing.

Holder pulls his arm away and rests his hand on my leg. I take a bite, then look back up at Max. "What's the dress code for this showing on Saturday? I have a sundress I was thinking about wearing that night, but it's not very formal." Holder squeezes my thigh and I grin, knowing exactly what kind of thoughts I just put into his head.

Max begins to answer me when a guy from the table behind us says something to Holder that I fail to catch. Whatever he said, it immediately gets Holder's attention and he turns completely around, facing the guy. "Could you repeat that?" Holder says, glaring at him.

I don't turn around. I don't even want to see who the guy is that's responsible for bringing back the temperamental Holder in less than two seconds flat.

"Maybe I need to speak more clearly," the guy says, raising his voice. "I said if you can't beat them *completely* to death, you might as well join them."

Holder doesn't move right away, which is good. It gives me time to grab his face and pull his focus to mine. "Holder," I say firmly. "Ignore it. *Please.*"

"Yeah, ignore it," Breckin says. "He's just trying to piss you off. Max and I get that shit all the time, we're used to it."

Holder works his jaw back and forth, breathing in slowly through his nose. The expression in his eyes slowly softens and he takes my hand, then slowly turns back around without looking at the guy again. "I'm good," he says, convincing himself more than the rest of us. "I'm good."

As soon as Holder faces forward, the laughter at the table behind us bellows throughout the lunchroom. Holder's shoulders tense, so I place my hand on his leg and squeeze, willing him to stay calm.

"That's nice," the guy says from behind us. "Let the slut talk you down from defending your new friends. I guess they don't mean as much to you as Lesslie did, otherwise I'd be in as bad a shape as Jake was last year after you laid into him."

It takes all I have not to jump up and kick the guy's ass myself, so I know Holder has absolutely no restraint left in him. He begins to turn around and his face is expressionless. I've never seen him so rigid—it's terrifying. I know something terrible is about to happen and I have no clue how to prevent it. Before he can leap across the table and beat the shit out of the guy, I do something that shocks even myself. I slap Holder as hard as I can across the face. He immediately pulls his hand to his cheek and looks at me, completely taken aback. But he's looking at me, which is good.

"Hallway," I say determinedly as soon as I have his attention. I push him until he's off the bench and I keep my hands on his back, then push him until he's walking toward the exit to the cafeteria. When we walk out into the hallway, he slams his fist into the nearest locker, causing a loud gasp to escape from my lips. The force behind his fist leaves a huge dent, and I'm relieved the guy in the cafeteria wasn't the recipient of that force.

He's seething. His face is red and I've never seen him this upset before. He begins pacing the hallway, pausing to stare at the cafeteria doors. I'm not convinced he isn't about to walk back through them, so I decide to get him even farther away.

"Let's go to your car." I push him toward the exit and he lets me. We walk all the way to the car and he's silently fuming the entire time. He climbs into the driver's seat and I climb into the passenger seat and we both shut our doors. I don't know if he's still on the verge of running back into the school and finishing the fight that asshole was trying to start, but I'll do everything I can to keep him out of there until he isn't angry anymore.

What happens next isn't what I'm expecting to happen at all. He reaches across the seat and pulls me tightly against him and begins to shake uncontrollably. His shoulders are trembling and he's squeezing me, burying his head in my neck.

He's crying.

I wrap my arms around him and let him hold on to me while he lets out whatever it is that's been pent up inside him. He slides me onto his lap and squeezes me tightly against him. I adjust my legs until they're on either side of him and I kiss him lightly on the side of his head over and over. He's barely making any sound and what little sound he is making is muffled into my shoulder. I have no idea what made him break just now, but it's the absolute most heartbreaking thing I've ever seen. I continue to kiss the side of his head and run my hands up and down his back. I do this for several minutes until he's finally quiet, but he still has a death grip around me.

"You want to talk about it?" I whisper, stroking his hair. I pull back and he leans his head into the headrest and looks at me. His eyes are red and full of so much hurt, I have to kiss them. I kiss each eyelid softly, then pull back again and wait for him to speak.

"I lied," he says. His words stab at my heart and I'm terrified of what he's about to say. "I told you I'd do it again. I told you I'd beat Jake's ass again if I had the chance." He takes my cheeks in his palms and looks at me desperately. "I wouldn't. He didn't deserve what I did to him, Sky. And that kid in there just now? He's Jake's little brother. He hates me for what I did and he has every right to hate me. He has every right to say whatever the fuck he wants to say to me, because I deserve it. I do. That's the only reason I didn't want to come back to this school, because I knew whatever anyone was going to say to me was deserved. But I can't let him talk about you and Breckin like that. He can say whatever the fuck he wants to say about me or Les because we deserve it, but you don't." His eyes are glossing over again and he's in absolute agony, holding my face in his hands.

"It's okay, Holder. You don't have to defend everyone. And you *don't* deserve it. Jake shouldn't have said what he did about your sister last year and his brother shouldn't have said what he did today."

He shakes his head in disagreement. "Jake was right. I know he shouldn't have said it and I definitely know I shouldn't have laid a finger on him, but he was right. What Les did wasn't brave or noble or courageous. What she did was selfish. She didn't even *try* to tough it out. She wasn't thinking about me, she wasn't thinking about my parents. She was thinking about herself and she didn't give a shit about the rest of us. And I hate her for it. I fucking hate her for it and I'm tired of hating her, Sky. I'm so tired of hating her because it's tearing me down and making me this person I don't want to be. She doesn't deserve to be hated. It's my fault she did what she did. I should have helped her, but I didn't. I didn't know. I loved that girl more than I've ever loved anyone and I had no idea how bad it was for her."

I wipe away his tear with my thumb and I do the only thing I can think to do because I have no idea what to say. I kiss him. I kiss him desperately and try to take away his pain the only way I know how to do. I've never experienced death like this, so I don't even try to understand where he's coming from. He wraps his hands in my hair and kisses me back with such strength, it's almost painful. We kiss for several minutes until the tension in him slowly begins to subside.

I pull my lips from his and look directly into his eyes. "Holder, you have every right to hate her for what she did. But you also have every right to still love her in spite of it. The only thing you don't have a right to do is to keep blaming yourself. You'll never understand why she did it, so you need to stop beating yourself up for not having all the answers. She made the choice she thought was best for her, even though it was the wrong one. But that's what you have to remember . . . *she* made that choice. Not you. And you can't blame yourself for not knowing what she failed to tell you." I kiss him on the forehead, then bring my eyes back to his. "You have to let it go. You can hold on to the hate and the love and even the bitterness, but you *have* to let go of the blame. The blame is what's tearing you down."

He closes his eyes and pulls my head to his shoulder, breathing out a shaky breath. I can feel him nodding and I can sense his whole demeanor coming to a quiet calm. He kisses me on the side of the head and we hold each other in silence. Whatever connection we thought we had before this . . . it doesn't compare to this moment. No matter what happens between us in this life, this moment has just merged pieces of our souls together. We'll always have that, and in a way it's comforting to know.

Holder looks at me and cocks his eyebrow. "Why the hell did you slap me?"

I laugh and kiss the cheek that I slapped. My fingerprints are barely visible now, but they're still there. "Sorry. I just needed to get you out of there and I couldn't think of any other way to do it."

He smiles. "It worked. I don't know if anyone else could have said or done anything that would have pulled me out of that. Thank you for knowing exactly how to handle me, because sometimes I'm not even sure how to handle myself."

I kiss him softly. "Believe me. I have no idea how to handle you, Holder. I just take you one scene at a time."

Friday, October 26, 2012
3:40 p.m.

"What time do you think you'll get back?" I ask. Holder has his arms around me and we're leaning up against my car. We haven't been able to spend much time together since what happened in his car at lunch on Monday. Fortunately, the guy who tried to start shit with Holder hasn't said anything else. It's been a rather peaceful week considering the dramatic start of it.

"We won't be back until pretty late. Their company Halloween parties usually last a few hours. But you'll see me tomorrow. I can pick you up for lunch if you want and we'll just stay together all day until the gallery showing."

I shake my head. "Can't. It's Jack's birthday and we're taking him out to lunch because he has to work tomorrow night. Just come pick me up at six."

"Yes, ma'am," he says. He kisses me, then opens my door so I can climb inside. I wave good-bye to him as he walks away, then I pull my phone out of my backpack. There's a text from Six, which makes me happy. I haven't been receiving my daily promised texts like she said I would. I didn't think I'd miss them, but now that I only get one every third day or so, it bums me out a little.

Tell your boyfriend thank you for finally adding minutes to your phone. Have you had sex with him yet? Miss you.

213

I laugh at her candidness and text her back.

**No, we haven't had sex yet. We've done almost every-
thing else, though, so I'm sure his patience will wear
out soon. Ask me again after tomorrow night, I might
have a different answer. Miss you more.**

I hit Send and stare at the phone. I haven't really thought
about whether I'm ready to pass that first yet, but I guess I
just admitted to myself that I am. I wonder if inviting me to
his house is his way of finding out if I'm ready, too.

I put the car into reverse and my phone sounds off. I
pick it up and it's a text from Holder.

Don't leave. I'm walking back to your car.

I put the car in park again and roll down my window, just
as he approaches. "Hey," he says, leaning into my window. He
darts his eyes away from mine and he looks around the car
nervously. I hate this uncomfortable look about him, it always
means he's about to say something I might not want to hear.

"Um . . ." He looks back at me and the sun is shining
straight on him, highlighting every beautiful feature about
him. His eyes are bright and they're looking into mine like
they would never want to look anywhere else. "You uh . . .
you just sent me a text that I'm pretty sure you meant to
send to Six."

Oh, God, no. I immediately grab my phone and check
to see if he's telling the truth. Unfortunately, he is. I throw
the phone on the passenger seat and fold my arms across
the steering wheel, burying my face into my elbow. "Oh,
my, God," I groan.

"Look at me, Sky," he directs. I ignore him and wait for

a magic wormhole to come and suck me away from all the embarrassing situations I get myself into. I feel his hand touch my cheek and he pulls my face in his direction. He's looking at me, full of sincerity.

"Whether it's tomorrow night or next year, I can promise you it'll be the best damn night of my life. You just make sure you're making that decision for yourself and no one else, okay? I'll always want you, but I'm not going to let myself have you until you're one hundred percent sure you want me just as much. And don't say anything right now. I'm turning around and walking back to my car and we can pretend this conversation never happened. Otherwise, you may never stop blushing." He leans in the window and gives me a quick kiss. "You're cute as hell, you know that? But you really need to figure out how to work your phone." He winks at me and walks away. I lean my head against the headrest and silently curse myself.

I hate technology.

I spend the rest of the night doing my best to push the embarrassing text out of my head. I help Karen package things up for her next flea market, then eventually crawl into bed with my e-reader. As soon as I power it on, my cell phone lights up on the nightstand.

> **I'm walking to your house right now. I know it's late and your mom is home, but I can't wait until tomorrow night to kiss you again. Make sure your window is unlocked.**

After I read the text I jump out of bed and lock my bedroom door, thankful Karen called it an early night two hours ago. I immediately go to the bathroom and brush my teeth and hair, then turn out the lights and crawl back into bed. It's after midnight and he's never snuck in while Karen was home before. I'm nervous, but it's an exciting nervous. The fact that I don't feel the least bit guilty that he's on his way over is proof that I'm going to Hell. I'm the worst daughter ever.

Several minutes later, my window slides up and I hear him making his way inside. I'm so excited to see him that I run to meet him at the window and wrap my arms around his neck, then jump up and make him hold me while I kiss him. His hands have a firm grip on my ass and he walks to the bed, dropping me down gently.

"Well, hello to you, too," he says, smiling widely. He stumbles slightly, then falls on top of me and brings his lips to mine again. He's trying to kick off his shoes but he struggles, then starts laughing.

"Are you drunk?" I ask.

He presses his fingers to my lips and tries to stop laughing, but he can't. "No. Yes."

"How drunk?"

He moves his head to my neck and runs his mouth lightly along my collarbone, sending a surge of heat through me. "Drunk enough to want to do bad things to you, but not drunk enough that I would do them drunk," he says. "But just drunk enough to still remember them tomorrow if I *did* do them."

I laugh, completely confused by his answer, yet completely turned on by it at the same time. "Is that why you walked here? Because you've been drinking?"

He shakes his head. "I walked here because I wanted

a good-night kiss and fortunately, I couldn't find my keys. But I wanted one so bad, babe. I missed you so bad tonight." He kisses me and his mouth tastes like lemonade.

"Why do you taste like lemonade?"

He laughs. "All they had were these fruity froufrou drinks. I'm drunk off fruity froufrou girl drinks. It's really sad and unattractive, I know."

"Well, you taste really good," I say, pulling his mouth back to mine. He moans and presses himself against me, dipping his tongue farther into my mouth. As soon as our bodies connect on the bed, he pulls away and stands up, leaving me breathless and alone on the mattress.

"Time to go," he says. "I already see this heading somewhere I'm too drunk to go right now. I'll see you tomorrow night."

I jump up and run and block the window before he can leave. He stops in front of me and folds his arms over his chest. "Stay," I say. "Please. Just lie in bed with me. We can put pillows between us and I promise not to seduce you since you're drunk. Just stay for an hour, I don't want you to go yet."

He immediately turns and heads back to the bed. "Okay," he says simply. He throws himself onto my bed and pulls the covers out from beneath him.

That was easy.

I walk back to the bed and lie down beside him. Neither of us places a pillow between us. Instead, I throw my arm over his chest and entwine my legs with his.

"Good night," he says, brushing my hair back. He kisses my forehead and closes his eyes. I tuck my head against his chest and listen to the rhythm of his heart. After several minutes, his breathing and heart rate have both regulated and he's sound asleep. I can't feel my arm anymore, so I gently lift it off him and quietly roll over. As soon as I get situated on my pillow, he slides his arm over my waist and his legs over mine. "I love you, Hope," he mutters.

Um . . .

Breathe, Sky.

Just breathe.

It's not that hard.

Take a breath.

I squeeze my eyes shut and try to tell myself I did not just hear what I thought I heard. But he said it clear as day. And I honestly don't know what breaks my heart more—the fact that he called me by someone else's name, or the fact that he actually said *love* this time instead of *live*.

I attempt to talk myself down from rolling over and punching him in his damn face. He's been drinking and he was half asleep when he said it. I can't assume she really means something to him when it could have just been a dream. But . . . who the hell is Hope? And why does he love her?

Thirteen years earlier

I'm sweating because it's hot under these covers, but I don't want to take them off my head. I know if the door opens, it won't matter if I have covers on or not, but I feel safer with them on anyway. I poke my fingers out and lift the piece of cover up that's in front of my eyes. I look at the doorknob like I do every night.

Don't turn. Don't turn. Please, don't turn.

It's always so quiet in my room and I hate it. Sometimes I hear things that I think might be the doorknob turning and it makes my heart beat really hard and really fast. Right now, just staring at the doorknob is making my heart beat really hard and really fast, but I can't stop staring at it. I don't want it to turn. I don't want that door to open, I don't.

Everything is so quiet.

So quiet.

The doorknob doesn't turn.

My heart stops beating so fast, because the doorknob never turns.

My eyes get really heavy and I finally close them.

I'm so glad that tonight's not one of the nights that the doorknob turns.

It's so quiet.

So quiet.

And then it's not, because the doorknob turns.

"Sky."

I'm so heavy. Everything is so heavy. I don't like this feeling. There isn't anything physically on my chest, but I feel a pressure unlike anything I've ever felt. And sadness. An overwhelming sadness is consuming me, and I have no idea why. My shoulders are shaking and there are sobs coming from somewhere in the room. Who's crying?

Am *I* crying?

"Sky, wake up."

I feel his arm around me. His cheek is pressed against mine and he's behind me, holding me tightly against his chest. I grab his wrist and lift his arm off me. I sit up on the bed and look around. It's dark outside. I don't get it. I'm crying.

He sits up beside me and turns me toward him, brushing at my eyes with his thumbs.

"You're scaring me, babe." He's looking at me and he's worried. I squeeze my eyes shut and try to regain control, because I have no idea what the hell is happening and I can't breathe. I can hear myself crying and I can't inhale a breath because of it.

I look at the clock on the nightstand and it says three. Things are starting to come back into focus now, but . . . why am I crying?

"Why are you crying?" Holder asks. He pulls me to him and I let him. He feels safe. He feels like home when I'm wrapped up in him. He holds me and rubs my back, kissing the side of my head every now and then. He keeps saying, "Don't worry," over and over and he holds me for what feels like forever.

The weight gradually lifts off my chest, the sadness dissipates, and I'm eventually no longer crying.

I'm scared, though, because nothing like this has ever happened to me before. Never in my life have I felt sadness this unbearable, so how could it feel so real from a dream?

"You okay?" he whispers.

I nod against his chest.

"What happened?"

I shake my head. "I don't know. I guess it was a bad dream."

"Want to talk about it?" He soothes my hair with his hands.

I shake my head. "No. I don't want to remember it."

He hugs me for a long time, then kisses me on the forehead. "I don't want to leave you, but I need to go. I don't want you to get in trouble."

I nod, but I don't release my grip. I want to beg him not to leave me alone, but I don't want to sound desperate and terrified. People have bad dreams all the time; I don't understand why I'm responding like this.

"Go back to sleep, Sky. Everything's okay, you just had a bad dream."

I lie back down on the bed and close my eyes. I feel his lips brush against my forehead, and then he's gone.

Saturday, October 27, 2012
8:20 p.m.

I give both Breckin and Max a hug in the parking lot of the gallery. The gallery showing has ended and Holder and I are going back to his place. I know I should be nervous about what might happen between us tonight, but I'm not nervous at all. Everything with him feels right. Well, everything except the phrase that keeps repeating over and over in my head.

I love you, Hope.

I want to ask him about it, but I can't find the right moment. The gallery showing certainly wasn't the place to bring it up. Now seems like a good time, but every time I open my mouth to do it, I clamp it shut again. I think I'm more afraid of who she is and what she means to him than I am of actually working up the nerve to bring it up. The longer I put off asking him about it, the longer I have before I'm forced to learn the truth.

"You want to grab something to eat?" he asks, pulling out of the parking lot.

"Yeah," I say quickly, relieved that he interrupted my thoughts. "A cheeseburger sounds good. And cheese fries. And I want a chocolate milkshake."

He laughs and takes my hand in his. "A little demanding are we, Princess?"

I let go of his hand and turn to face him. "Don't call me that," I snap.

He glances at me and can more than likely see the anger on my face, even in the dark.

"Hey," he says soothingly, picking up my hand again. "I don't think you're demanding, Sky. It was a joke."

I shake my head. "Not demanding. Don't call me Princess. I hate that word."

He gives me a sidelong glance, then shifts his eyes back to the road. "Okay."

I turn my gaze out the window, trying to get the word out of my head. I don't know why I hate nicknames so much, but I do. And I know I overreacted just now, but he can never call me that again. He also shouldn't call me by the name of any of his ex-girlfriends either. He should just stick to Sky . . . it's much safer.

We drive in complete silence and I become increasingly more regretful for reacting like I did. If anything, I should be more upset by the fact that he called me by another girl's name than by his referring to me as Princess. It's almost like I'm displacing my anger because I'm too afraid to bring up what's really bothering me. Honestly, I just want a drama-free night with him tonight. There'll be plenty of time to ask him about Hope another day.

"I'm sorry, Holder."

He squeezes my hand and pulls it onto his lap, but doesn't say anything else.

When we pull into his driveway, I get out of the car. We never did stop for food, but I don't even feel like bringing it up now. He meets me at the passenger door and wraps his arms around me and I hug him back. He walks me until my back is against the car and I press my head to his shoulder, breathing in the scent of him. The awkwardness from the drive here still lingers, so I attempt to ease myself against him in a relaxing way to let him know I'm not thinking about it. He's lightly stroking his fingers up and down my arms, covering me in chills.

"Can I ask you something?" he says.

"Always."

He sighs, then pulls back and looks at me. "Did I freak you out Monday? In my car? If I did, I'm sorry. I don't know what got into me. I'm not a pussy, I swear. I haven't cried since Les died, and I sure as hell didn't mean to do it in front of you."

I lean my head into his chest again and hug him tighter. "You know last night when I woke up after that dream?"

"Yeah."

"That's the second time I've cried since I was five. The only other time I cried was when you told me about what happened to your sister. I cried when I was in the bathroom. It was just one tear, but it counts. I think when we're together, maybe our emotions become a little overwhelming and it turns us *both* into pussies."

He laughs and kisses me on top of the head. "I have a feeling I won't be living you for much longer." He gives me another quick kiss, then takes my hand. "Ready for the grand tour?"

I follow him toward his house, but I'm still stuck on the fact that he just told me he's about to stop living me. If he stops living me, that means he'll be loving me. He just confessed that he's falling in love with me without actually saying it. The most shocking thing about his confession is that I really liked it.

We walk inside and the house is nothing like I expected.

It doesn't seem very big from the outside, but there's a foyer. Normal houses don't have foyers. There's an archway to the right that leads to a living room. The walls are covered in nothing but books, and I feel like I've just died and gone to heaven. "Wow," I say, eyeing the bookshelves in the living room. Books are stacked on shelves from floor to ceiling on every single wall.

"Yeah," he says. "Mom was pretty pissed when they invented the e-reader."

I laugh. "I think I already like your mom. When do I get to meet her?"

He shakes his head. "I don't introduce girls to my mother." His voice is as detached as his words, and as soon as he says it, his expression drops and he knows he's just hurt my feelings. He walks swiftly to me and takes my face in his hands. "No, no. That's not what I meant. I'm not saying you're anything like the other girls I've dated. I didn't mean for it to come out like that."

I hear what he's saying, but we've been dating as long as we have and he still isn't convinced it's real enough for me to meet his mother? I wonder if we'll *ever* be real enough to him for me to meet his mother.

"Did Hope get to meet her?" I know I shouldn't have said it, but I couldn't keep it in any longer. Especially now, hearing him say "other girls." I'm not delusional; I know he dated other people before he met me. I just don't like hearing him say it. Much less calling me by their names.

"What?" he asks, dropping his hands. He's backing away from me. "Why did you say that?" The color is draining from his face and I immediately regret saying it.

"Never mind. It's nothing. I don't have to meet your

mom." I just want whatever this is to pass. I knew I wouldn't feel like talking about it tonight. I want to get back to the house tour and forget this conversation ever happened.

He grabs my hands and says it again. "Why would you say that, Sky? Why did you say that name?"

I shake my head. "It's not that big of a deal. You were drunk."

He narrows his eyes at me and it's clear I'm not escaping this conversation. I sigh and reluctantly give in, clearing my throat before I speak.

"Last night when you were falling asleep . . . you told me you loved me. But you called me Hope, so you weren't really talking to *me*. You'd been drinking and you were half asleep, so I don't need an explanation. I don't know if I really even want to know why you said it."

He brings his hands to his hair and groans. "Sky." He steps forward, taking me in his arms. "I'm so sorry. It must have been a stupid dream. I don't even know anyone named Hope and I've definitely never had an ex-girlfriend by that name if that's what you were thinking. I'm so sorry that happened. I should have never gone to your house drunk." He looks down at me and as much as my instincts are telling me he's lying, his eyes are completely sincere. "You have to believe me. It'll kill me if you think for a second that I feel anything at all for someone else. I've never felt this way about anyone."

Every word coming from his mouth is dripping with sincerity and honesty. Considering I can't even remember why I woke up crying, it's possible his sleep talking really was the result of a random dream. And hearing everything he just said to me puts into perspective just how serious things are becoming between us.

I look up at him, attempting to prepare some sort of response to everything he just said. I part my lips and wait for the words to come, but they don't. I'm suddenly the one needing more time to process my thoughts.

He's cupping my cheeks, waiting for me to break the silence between us. The proximity of his mouth to mine weathers his patience. "I need to kiss you," he says apologetically, pulling my face to his. We're still standing in the foyer, but he somehow picks me up effortlessly and sets me down on the stairs leading to the upstairs bedrooms. I lean back and he returns his lips to mine, his hands gripping the wooden steps on either side of my head.

Due to our position, he's forced to lower a knee between my thighs. It isn't that big a deal unless you take into consideration the dress that I have on. It would be so easy for him to take me right here on the stairs, but I'm hoping we at least make it to his room first before he tries. I wonder if he's expecting anything, especially after the text I accidentally sent him. He's a guy, of course he's expecting something. I wonder if he knows I'm a virgin. Should I even tell him I'm a virgin? I should. He'll probably be able to tell.

"I'm a virgin," I blurt against his mouth. I immediately wonder what the hell I'm doing even speaking aloud right now. I shouldn't be allowed to speak ever again. Someone should strip me of my voice, because I obviously have no filter when my sexual guard is down.

He immediately stops kissing me. He slowly backs his face away from mine and looks down into my eyes. "Sky," he says directly. "I'm kissing you because sometimes I can't *not* kiss you. You know what your mouth does to me. I'm not expecting anything else, okay? As long as I get to kiss you, the other stuff can wait." He's tucking my hair behind my ears now and looking down at me genuinely.

"I just thought you should know. I probably should have picked a better time to state that fact, but sometimes I just blurt things out without thinking. It's a really bad trait and I hate it because I do it at the most inopportune moments and it's embarrassing. Like right now."

He laughs and shakes his head. "No, don't stop doing that. I love it when you blurt things out without thinking. And I love it when you spout off long, nervous, ridiculous rants. It's kind of hot."

I blush. Being called hot is seriously . . . hot.

"You know what else is hot?" he says, leaning back in to me again.

The playfulness in his expression chips away at my embarrassment. "What?"

He grins. "Trying to keep our hands off each other while we watch a movie." He stands up and pulls me to my feet, then leads me up the stairs to his room.

He opens the door and walks in first, then turns around and tells me to close my eyes. I roll them, instead.

"I don't like surprises," I say.

"You also don't like presents and certain common terms of endearment. I'm learning. But this is just something cool I want to show you—it's not anything I bought you. So deal with it and shut your eyes."

I do what he says and he pulls me forward into the room. I already love it in here because it smells just like him. He walks me a few steps, then places his hands on my shoulders. "Sit," he says, pushing me down. I take a seat on what feels like a bed, then I'm suddenly flat on my back and he's lifting up my feet. "Keep your eyes closed."

I feel him pulling my feet onto the bed and propping me up against a pillow. His hand grabs the hem of my sundress and he pulls it down, making sure it stays in place. "Gotta keep you covered up. Can't be flashing me thigh when you're on your back like that."

I laugh, but I keep my eyes closed. He's suddenly crawling over me, careful not to knee me. I can feel him positioning himself next to me on his pillow. "Okay. Open your eyes and prepare to be wowed."

I'm scared. I slowly pry my eyes open. I hesitate to guess what I'm looking at, because I almost think it's a TV. But TVs don't usually take up eighty inches of wall space. This thing is ginormous. He points a remote at it and the screen lights up.

"Wow," I say, impressed. "It's huge."

"That's what *she* said."

I elbow him in the side and he laughs. He points the remote back up to the TV. "What's your favorite movie ever? I have Netflix."

I tilt my head in his direction. "Net *what*?"

He laughs and shakes his head in disappointment. "I keep forgetting you're technologically challenged. It's similar to an e-reader, only with movies and television shows instead of books. You can watch pretty much anything at the push of a button."

"Are there commercials?"

"Nope," he says proudly. "So what'll it be?"

"Do you have *The Jerk*? I love that movie."

His arm falls to his chest and he clicks the power button

and turns off the TV. He's silent for several long seconds, then he sighs forcefully. He leans over and sets the remote down on his nightstand, then rolls over and faces me. "I don't want to watch TV anymore."

He's pouting? What the hell did I say?

"Fine. We don't have to watch *The Jerk*. Pick something else out, you big baby." I laugh.

He doesn't respond for a few moments while he continues staring at me inexpressively. He lifts his hand and runs it across my stomach and around to my waist, then grips me tightly and pulls me against him. "You know," he says, narrowing his eyes as he meticulously rakes them down my body. He traces the pattern of my dress with a finger, delicately stroking over my stomach. "I can handle what this dress does to me." He lifts his eyes from my stomach, back up to my mouth. "I can even handle having to constantly stare at your lips, even when I don't get to kiss them. I can handle the sound of your laughter and how it makes me want to cover your mouth with mine and drink it all in."

His mouth is closing in on mine, and the way his voice has dropped into some sort of lyrical, godlike octave makes my heart pummel within my chest. He lowers his lips to my cheek and lightly kisses it, his warm breath colliding with my skin when he speaks. "I can even handle the millions of times I've replayed our first kiss over and over in my head this past month. The way you felt. The way you *sounded*. The way you looked up at me right before my lips met yours."

He rolls himself on top of me and brings my arms above my head, clasping them in his hands. I'm hanging on to every single word he's saying, not wanting to miss a single second of whatever it is he's doing right now. He straddles me, holding his weight up with his knees. "But what I can't handle, Sky? What drives me crazy and makes me want to put my hands and my mouth all over every single inch of you? It's the fact that you just said *The Jerk* is your favorite movie ever. Now *that*?" He drops his mouth to mine until our lips are touching. "That's incredibly fucking hot and I'm pretty sure we need to make out now."

His playfulness makes me laugh and I whisper seductively against his lips. "He hates these cans."

He groans and kisses me, then pulls away. "Do it again. Please. Hearing you talk in movie quotes is so much hotter than kissing you."

I laugh and give him another quote. "Stay away from the cans!"

He groans playfully in my ear. "That's my girl. One more. Do one more."

"That's all I need," I say teasingly. "The ashtray, this paddle game, and the remote control, and the lamp . . . and that's *all* I need. I don't need one other thing, not one."

He's laughing loudly now. As many times as Six and I stayed up watching this movie, he'll be surprised to know there's a lot more where those came from.

"That's *all* you need?" Holder quips. "Are you sure about that, Sky?" His voice is smooth and seductive and if I was standing up right now, my panties would without a doubt be on the floor.

I shake my head and my smile fades. "You," I whisper. "I need the lamp and the ashtray and the paddle game and the remote control . . . and *you*. That's all I need."

He laughs, but his laugh quickly fades once his eyes

drop to my mouth again. He scrutinizes it, more than likely mapping out just what he's about to do with it for the next hour. "I need to kiss you now." His mouth collides with mine and for this moment, he really *is* all I need.

He's propped up on his hands and knees, kissing me fiercely, but I need him to drop himself on top of me. My hands are still locked above my head and my mouth is useless to form words when he's teasing it like he is. The only thing I can do is lift my foot up and kick his knee out from under him, so that's what I do.

The second his body falls against mine, I gasp. Loudly. I hadn't taken into consideration that when I lifted my leg, it would also push the hem of my dress up. Way up. Couple that with the hard denim of his jeans and you have a pretty gasp-worthy combination.

"Holy shit, Sky," he says between breathless moments of completely ravishing my mouth with his. He's winded already and we haven't even been at it more than a minute. "God, you feel incredible. Thank you for wearing this dress." He's kissing me, sporadically muttering into my mouth. "I really . . ." He kisses my mouth, then runs his lips down my chin and halfway down my neck. "I really like it. Your dress." He's breathing so heavily now, I can barely make out the mumbling coming from him. He scoots slightly farther down on the bed until his lips are kissing the base of my throat. I tilt my head back to give him plenty of access, because his lips are more than welcome anywhere on me right now. He releases his grip on my hands so he can lower his mouth closer to my chest. One of his hands drops to my thigh, and he slowly runs it upward, pushing away what's left of the dress covering my legs. When he reaches the top of my thigh, he stills his hand and squeezes tightly, as if he's silently demanding his fingers not venture any further.

I twist my body beneath his, hoping he'll get the hint that I'm attempting to direct his hand to keep going wherever it wants to go. I don't want him to second-guess himself or think for a second that I'm hesitant to go any further. I just want him to do whatever it is he wants to do, because I need him to. I need him to conquer as many firsts as he can tonight, because I'm suddenly feeling greedy and I want us to pass them all.

He takes my physical cues and inches his hand closer to my inner thigh. The anticipation of him touching me alone is enough to cause every muscle from the waist down to clench. His lips have finally made their way past the base of my throat and down to the rise in my chest. I feel like the next step is for him to remove the dress completely so he can get to what's underneath it, but that would require his other hand, and I really like it where it is. I'd like it a little more if it were a few inches farther, but I absolutely don't want it farther away.

I bring my hands to his face and force him to kiss me harder, then drop my hands to his back.

He's still wearing a shirt.

This isn't good.

I reach around to his stomach and pull his shirt up over his head, but I don't realize that when I do, it also causes him to move his hand off my thigh. I may have whimpered a little, because he grins and kisses the corner of my mouth.

We keep our gaze locked and he gently strokes my face with his fingertips, trailing over every part of it. He never looks away and he keeps his eyes locked on mine, even when he dips his head to plant kisses around the edges of my lips. The way he looks at me makes me feel . . . I try to search for an adjective to follow up that thought, but I can't find one. He just makes me *feel*. He's the only boy that's ever cared whether I'm feeling anything at all, and for that alone, I let him steal another small piece of my heart. But it doesn't feel like enough, because I suddenly want to give it *all* to him.

"Holder," I breathe. He slides his hands up my waist and moves closer to me.

"Sky," he says, mimicking my tone. His mouth reaches my lips and he slips his tongue inside. It's sweet and warm and I know it hasn't been very long since I last tasted it, but I've missed it. His hands are on either side of my head and he's being careful not to touch me with any part of his hands or his body now. Only his mouth.

"Holder," I mumble, pulling away. I bring my hand to his cheek. "I want to. Tonight. Right now."

His expression doesn't change. He stares at me like he didn't hear me. Maybe he *didn't* hear me, because he certainly isn't taking me up on the offer.

"Sky . . ." His voice is full of hesitation. "We don't have to. I want you to be absolutely positive it's what you want. Okay?" He's caressing my cheek now. "I don't want to rush you into anything."

"I know that. But I'm telling you I want this. I've never wanted it with anyone before, but I want it with you."

His eyes are trained on mine and he's soaking in every single word I've said. He's either in denial or in shock, neither of which are helping my cause. I take both of my hands and place them on his cheeks, then pull his lips in close to mine. "This isn't me saying *yes*, Holder. This is me saying *please*."

With that, his lips crash to mine and he groans. Hearing that sound come from deep within his chest further solidifies my decision. I need him and I need him now.

"We're really doing this?" he says into my mouth, still kissing me frantically.

"Yes. We're really doing this. I've never been more positive of anything in my life."

His hand slides up my thigh and he slips his hand between my hip and my panties, then begins to slide them down.

"I just need you to promise me one thing first," I say.

He kisses me softly, then pulls his hand away from my underwear (dammit) and nods. "Anything."

I grab his hand and put it right back where it was on my hip. "I want to do this, but only if you promise we'll break the record for the best first time in the history of first times."

He grins down at me. "When it's you and me, Sky . . . it'll never be anything less."

He snakes his arm underneath my back and pulls me up with him. His hands move to my arms and he hooks his fingers underneath the thin straps of my dress, sliding them off my shoulders. I close my eyes tightly and press my cheek to his, fisting my hands in his hair. I can feel his breath meet my shoulder before his lips do. He barely kisses it, but it's as if he touches and ignites every part of me from the inside out with that one kiss.

"I'm taking it off," he says.

My eyes are still closed and I'm not sure if he's telling

me or asking my permission to remove the dress, but I nod anyway. He lifts my dress up and over my head—my bare skin prickling beneath his touch. He gently lays me back against my pillow and I open my eyes, looking up at him, admiring just how incredibly beautiful he really is. After regarding me intensely for several seconds, he drops his gaze to his hand that's curved around my waist.

He slowly moves his eyes up and down my body. "Holy shit, Sky." He runs his hand over my stomach, then leans down and kisses it softly. "You're incredible."

I've never been this exposed in front of someone before, but the way he's admiring me only makes me *want* to be this exposed. He slides his hand up to my bra and grazes his thumb just underneath it—causing my lips to part and my eyes to close again.

Oh, my God, I want him. Really, really bad.

I grab his face and pull it to mine, locking my legs around his hips. He groans and slips his hand away from my bra and down to my waist again. He slides my panties down my thighs, forcing me to unlock my legs and let him take them off completely. My bra is quick to follow and once all of my clothes have been removed, he scoots his legs off the bed and halfway stands up, leaning over me. I've still got hold of his face and we're still frantically kissing while he removes his pants, then climbs back onto the bed with me, lowering himself on top of me. We're skin to skin now for the first time, so close that air couldn't even pass between us, yet it still feels like we aren't near close enough. He reaches across the mattress and his hand fumbles over the nightstand. He removes a condom from the drawer, then lays it down on the bed, lowering himself on top of me again. The hardness and weight of him forces my legs farther apart. I wince when I realize the anticipation in my stomach is suddenly turning into dread.

And nausea.

And fear.

My heart is racing and my breaths begin to come in short gasps. Tears sting at my eyes as his hand moves around beside us on the bed, searching for the condom. He finds it and I hear him open it, but I'm squeezing my eyes shut. I can feel him pull back and lift up onto his knees. I know he's putting it on and I know what comes next. I know how it feels and I know how much it hurts and I know how it'll make me cry when it's over.

But how do I know? How do I know if I've never done this before?

My lips begin to tremble when he positions himself between my legs again. I try to think of something to take away the fear, so I visualize the sky and the stars and how beautiful it all is, attempting to ease my panic. If I remind myself that the sky is beautiful no matter what, I can think about that and forget how ugly *this* is. I don't want to open my eyes, so I just count silently inside my head. I visualize the stars above my bed and I start from the bottom of the cluster, working my way up.

One, two, three . . .

I count and I count and I count.

Twenty-two, twenty-three, twenty-four . . .

I hold my breath and focus, focus, focus on the stars.

Fifty-seven, fifty-eight, fifty-nine . . .

I want him to be done already. I just want him off me.

Seventy-one, seventy-two, seventy—

"Dammit, Sky!" Holder yells. He's pulling my arm away from my eyes. I don't want him to make me look, so I hold my arm tighter against my face so everything will stay dark and I can keep silently counting.

All of a sudden, my back is being lifted up in the air and I'm not against the pillow anymore. My arms are limp and his are wrapped tightly around me, but I can't move. My arms are too weak and I'm sobbing too hard. I'm crying so hard and he's moving me and I don't know why so I open my eyes. I'm going back and forth and back and forth and for a second, I panic and squeeze my eyes shut, thinking he's not finished. But I can feel the covers around me and his arm is squeezing my back and he's soothing my hair with his hand, whispering in my ear.

"Baby, it's okay." He's pressing his lips into my hair, rocking me back and forth with him. I open my eyes again and tears are clouding my vision. "I'm sorry, Sky. I'm so sorry."

He's kissing the side of my head over and over while he rocks me, telling me he's sorry. He's apologizing for something. Something he wants me to forgive him for this time.

He pulls back and sees that my eyes are open. His eyes are red but I don't see any tears. He's shaking, though. Or maybe it's me who's shaking. I think we're both shaking.

He's looking into my eyes, searching for something. Searching for *me*. I begin to relax in his arms, because when his arms are wrapped around me, I don't feel like I'm falling off the edge of the earth. "What happened?" I ask him. I don't understand where this is coming from.

He shakes his head, his eyes full of sorrow and fear and regret. "I don't know. You just started counting and crying and shaking and I kept trying to get you to stop, Sky. You wouldn't stop. You were terrified. What did I do? Tell me, because I'm so sorry. I am so, so sorry. What the fuck did I do?"

I just shake my head because I don't have an answer.

He grimaces and drops his forehead to mine. "I'm so sorry. I never should have let it go that far. I don't know what the hell just happened, but you're not ready yet, okay?"

I'm not ready yet?

"So we didn't . . . we didn't have sex?"

His hands loosen around me and I can feel his whole demeanor shift. The look in his eyes is nothing but loss and defeat. His eyebrows draw apart and he frowns, cupping my cheeks. "Where'd you go, Sky?"

I shake my head, confused. "I'm right here. I'm listening."

"No, I mean earlier. Where'd you go? You weren't here with me because no, nothing happened. I could see on your face that something was wrong, so I didn't do it. But now you need to think long and hard about where you were inside that head of yours, because you were panicked. You were hysterical and I need to know what it was that took you there so I can make sure you never go back."

He kisses me on the forehead and releases his hold from around my back. He stands up and pulls his jeans on, then picks up my dress. He shakes it out, then flips it over until it slides down his hands, then he walks toward me and puts it on over my head. He lifts my arms and helps me slide them into the dress, then he pulls it down over my waist, covering me. "I'll go get you some water. I'll be right back." He kisses me tentatively on the lips, almost as if he's scared to touch me again. After he walks out of the room, I lean my head against the wall and close my eyes.

I have no idea what just happened, but the fear of losing him because of it is a valid one. I just took one of the most intimate things imaginable, and I turned it into a disaster. I made him feel worthless, like he did something wrong, and now he feels bad for me because of it. He probably wants me to leave, and I don't blame him. I don't blame him a bit. I want to run away from me, too.

I throw the covers off and stand up, then pull my dress down. I don't even bother looking for my underwear. I need to find the bathroom and get myself together so he can take me home. This is twice this weekend that I've been reduced to tears and I don't even know why—and twice that he's had to save me. I'm not doing it to him again.

When I pass the stairs looking for the restroom, I glance down over the railing into the kitchen. He's leaning forward with his elbows on the bar and his face buried in his hands. He's just standing there, looking miserable and upset. I can't watch him anymore, so I open the first door to my right, assuming it's the bathroom.

It's not.

It's Lesslie's bedroom. I start to pull the door shut, but I don't. Instead, I open it wider and slip inside, then shut it behind me. I don't care if I'm in a bathroom, a bedroom, or a closet . . . I just need peace and quiet. Time to regroup from whatever the hell is going on with me. I'm beginning to think that maybe I *am* crazy. I've never spaced out that severely before and it terrifies me. My hands are still shaking, so I clasp them together in front of me and try to focus on something else in order to calm myself down.

I take in my surroundings and find the bedroom to be somewhat disturbing. The bed isn't made, which strikes me as odd. Holder's entire house is spotless, but Lesslie's bed isn't made. There's a pair of jeans in the middle of the floor and it looks like she just stepped out of them. I look around at the room and it seems typical of a teenage girl. Makeup on the dresser, an iPod on the nightstand. It looks like she still lives here. From the look of her room, it doesn't look like she's gone at all. It's obvious no one has touched this room since she died. Her pictures are all still hanging on the walls and stuck to her vanity mirror. All of her clothes are still in her closet, some piled on the closet floor. It's been over a year since he said she passed away, and I'm willing to bet that no one in his family has accepted it yet.

It feels eerie being in here, but it's keeping my mind off what's happening right now. I walk to the bed and look at the pictures hanging on the wall. Most of them are of Lesslie and her friends, with just a few of Holder and her together. She looks a lot like Holder with his intense, crystal-blue eyes and dark brown hair. What surprises me the most is how happy she looks. She looks so content and full of life in every single picture, it's hard to imagine what was really going on inside her head. No wonder Holder didn't have a clue about how desolate she really felt. She more than likely never let anyone know.

I pick up a picture from her nightstand that's turned facedown. When I flip it over and look at it, I gasp. It's a picture of her kissing Grayson on the cheek and they have their arms around each other. The picture stuns me and I have to take a seat on the bed to regain my bearings. This is why Holder hates him so much? This is why he didn't want him touching me? I wonder if he blames Grayson for what she did.

I'm holding the picture, still sitting on the bed, when the bedroom door opens. Holder peers around the door. "What are you doing?" He doesn't seem angry that I'm in here. He does seem uncomfortable, though, which is probably just a reaction from how I made him feel earlier.

"I was looking for the bathroom," I say, quietly. "I'm sorry. I just needed a second."

He leans against the doorway and crosses his arms over his chest while his eyes work their way around the room. He's taking in everything like I am. Like it's all new to him.

"Has no one been in here? Since she . . ."

"No," he says quickly. "What would be the point of it? She's gone."

I nod, then place the picture of Lesslie and Grayson back on the nightstand, facedown like she had left it. "Was she dating him?"

He takes a hesitant step into the bedroom, then walks over to the bed. He sits down beside me and rests his elbows on his knees, clasping his hands in front of him. He looks around the room slowly, not answering my question right away. He glances at me, then wraps his arm around my shoulders, pulling me to him. The fact that he's sitting here with me right now, still wanting to hold me, makes me want to burst into tears.

"He broke up with her the night before she did it," he says quietly.

I try not to gasp, but his words shock me. "Do you think he's the reason why she did it? Is that why you hate him so much?"

He shakes his head. "I hated him before he broke up with her. He put her through a lot of shit, Sky. And no, I don't think he's why she did it. I think maybe it was the deciding factor in a decision she had wanted to make for a long time. She had issues way before Grayson ever came into the picture. So no, I don't blame him. I never have." He stands up and takes my hand. "Come on. I don't want to be in here anymore."

I take one last glance around the room, then stand up to follow him. I stop before we reach the door, though. He turns around and watches me observe the pictures on her dresser. There's a framed picture of Holder and Lesslie when they were kids. I pick it up and bring it in closer for inspection. Something about seeing him that young makes me smile. Seeing both of them that young . . . it's refreshing. Like there's innocence about them before the ugly realities of life hit. They're standing in front of a white-framed house and Holder has his arm around her neck and he's squeezing her. She's got her arms wrapped around his waist and they're smiling at the camera.

My eyes move from their faces to the house behind them in the photo. It's a white-framed house with yellow trim, and if you were to see the inside of the house, the living room is painted two different shades of green.

I immediately close my eyes. *How do I know that? How do I know what color the living room is?*

My hands start shaking and I try to suck in a breath, but I can't. How do I know that house? I know that house like I somehow suddenly know the kids in the picture. How do I know there's a green-and-white swing set behind that house? And ten feet from the swing set is a dry well that has to stay covered because Lesslie's cat fell down it once.

"You okay?" Holder says. He tries to take the picture out of my hands, but I snatch it from him and look up at him. His eyes are concerned and he takes a step toward me. I take a step back.

How do I know him?

How do I know Lesslie?

Why do I feel like I *miss* them? I shake my head, looking down at the picture and back up at Holder, then down to the picture again. This time, Lesslie's wrist catches my eye. She's wearing a bracelet. A bracelet identical to mine.

I want to ask him about it but I can't. I try, but nothing comes out, so I just hold up the picture instead. He shakes his head and his face drops like his heart is breaking. "Sky, no," he says pleadingly.

"How?" My voice cracks and is barely audible. I look back down to the picture in my hands. "There's a swing set. And a well. And . . . your cat. It got stuck in the well." I dart my eyes up to his and the thoughts keep pouring out. "Holder, I know that living room. The living room is green and the kitchen had a countertop that was way too tall for us and . . . your mother. Your mother's name is Beth." I pause and try to take a breath, because the memories won't stop. They won't stop coming and I can't breathe. "Holder . . . is Beth your mother's name?"

Holder grimaces and runs his hands through his hair. "Sky . . ." he says. He can't even look at me. His expression is torn and confused and he's . . . he's been *lying* to me. He's holding something back and he's scared to tell me.

He *knows* me. How the hell does he know me and why hasn't he told me?

I suddenly feel sick. I rush past him and open the door across the hall, which happens to be a bathroom, thank God. I lock the door behind me and throw the framed picture on the counter, then fall straight to the floor.

The images and memories start inundating my mind like the floodgates have just been lifted. Memories of him, of her, of the three of us together. Memories of us playing, me eating dinner at their house, me and Les being inseparable. I loved her. I was so young and so small and I don't even know how I knew them, but I loved them. Both of them. The memory is coupled with the grief of now knowing the Lesslie I knew and loved as a little girl is gone. I suddenly feel sad and depressed that she's gone, but not for me. Not for Sky. I'm sad for the little girl I used to be, and somehow her grief over the loss of Lesslie is emerging through me.

How have I not known? How did I not remember him the first time I saw him?

"Sky, open the door. Please."

I fall back against the wall. It's too much. The memories and the emotions and the grief . . . it's too much to absorb all at once.

"Baby, please. We need to talk and I can't do it from out here. Please, open the door."

He *knew*. The first time he saw me at the grocery store, he knew. And when he saw my bracelet . . . he knew I got it from Lesslie. He saw me wearing it and he knew.

My grief and confusion soon turn to anger and I push myself up off the floor and walk swiftly to the bathroom door. I unlock it and swing it open. His hands are on either side of the doorframe and he's looking directly at me, but I feel like I don't even know who he is. I don't know what's real between us and what's fake anymore. I don't know what feelings of his are from his life with me or the life with that little girl I used to be.

I need to know. I need to know who she was. Who *I* was. I swallow my fear and release the question that I'm afraid I already know the answer to. "Who's Hope?"

His hardened expression doesn't change, so I ask him again, but louder this time.

"Who the hell is Hope?"

He keeps his eyes locked on mine and his hands placed firmly on the doorframe, but he can't answer me. For some reason he doesn't want me to know. He doesn't want me to remember who I was. I take a deep breath and try to fight back the tears. I'm too scared to say it, because I don't want to know the answer.

"Is it me?" I ask, my voice shaking and full of trepidation. "Holder . . . am I Hope?"

He lets out a quick breath at the same time he looks up at the ceiling, almost as if he's struggling not to cry. He closes his eyes and lays his forehead against his arm, then takes a long, deep breath before looking back at me. "Yes."

The air around me grows thick. Too thick to take in. I stand still, directly in front of him, unable to move. Everything grows quiet except for what's inside my head. There are so many thoughts and questions and memories and they're all trying to take over and I don't know if I need to cry or scream or sleep or run.

I need to go outside. I feel like Holder and the bathroom and the whole damn house are closing in on me and I need to go outside so there's room to get everything out of my head. I just want it all out.

I shove past him and he tries to grab my arm, but I yank it out of his grasp.

"Sky, wait," he yells after me. I keep running until I reach the stairs and I descend them as fast as I can, taking two at a time. I can hear him following me, so I speed up and my foot lands farther than I intend for it to. I lose my grip on the rail and fall forward, landing on the floor at the base of the stairs.

"Sky!" he yells. I try to pull myself up but he's on his knees with his arms around me before I even have the chance. I push against him, wanting him to let go of me so I can just go outside. He doesn't budge.

"Outside," I say, breathless and weak. "I just need outside. Please, Holder."

I can feel him struggling from within, not wanting to release me. He reluctantly pulls me away from his chest and looks down at me, searching my eyes. "Don't run, Sky. Go outside, but please don't leave. We need to talk."

I nod and he releases me, then helps me stand up. When I walk out the front door and onto the lawn, I clasp my hands together behind my head and inhale a huge, cold breath of air. I tilt my head back and look up at the stars, wishing more than anything that I was up there and not down here. I don't want the memories to keep coming, because with each confusing memory comes an even more confusing question. I don't understand how I know him. I don't understand why he kept it from me. I don't understand how my name could have been Hope, when all I've ever remembered being called was Sky. I don't understand why Karen would tell me that Sky was my birth name if it isn't. Everything I thought I understood after all these years is unraveling, revealing things that I don't want to know. I'm being lied to, and I'm terrified to know what it is that everyone's trying to keep from me.

I stand outside for what feels like forever, attempting to sort through this alone when I have no idea what it is I'm even trying to sort through. I need to talk to Holder and I need to know what he knows, but I'm hurt. I don't want to face him, knowing he's been hiding this secret all along. It makes everything that I thought was happening between us nothing but a façade.

I'm emotionally spent and have had all the revelations I can take for one night. I just want to go home and go to bed. I need to sleep on this before we go into the fact of why he didn't just tell me he knew me as a child. I don't understand why it was something he even thought he should keep from me.

I turn around and walk back toward the house. He's standing in the doorway, watching me. He steps aside to let me back in and I walk straight to the kitchen and open the refrigerator. I grab a bottle of water and open it, then take several gulps. My mouth is dry, as I never did get the water he said he was getting for me earlier.

I set the bottle down on the bar and look at him. "Take me home."

He doesn't object. He turns around and grabs his keys off the entryway table, then motions for me to follow him. I leave the water on the bar and silently follow him to the car. When I climb inside, he backs out of the driveway and pulls onto the road without speaking a word.

We pass my turnoff and it's apparent that he has no intention of taking me home. I glance over at him and his eyes are focused hard on the road in front of him. "Take me home," I say again.

He looks at me with a determined expression. "We need to talk, Sky. You have questions, I know you do."

I do. I have a million questions I need to ask, but I was hoping he would let me sleep on it so I could sort them out and try to answer as many of them as I could myself. But it's obvious he doesn't care what I prefer at this point. I reluctantly take off my seatbelt and turn in my seat, leaning with my back against the door to face him. If he doesn't want to give me time to let this soak in, I'll just lay all of my questions on him at once. But I'm making it fast because I want him to take me home.

"Fine," I say stubbornly. "Let's get this over with. Why have you been lying to me for two months? Why did my bracelet piss you off so much that you couldn't speak to me for weeks? Or why you didn't just say who you really thought I was the day we met at the grocery store? Because you knew, Holder. You knew who I was and for some reason you thought it would be funny to string me along until I figured it all out. Do you even *like* me? Was this game you've been playing worth hurting me more than I've ever been hurt in my life? Because that's what happened," I say, furious to the point that I'm shaking.

I finally give in to the tears because they're just one more thing that's trying to get out and I'm tired of fighting them. I wipe them away from my cheeks with the back of my hand and lower my voice. "You hurt me, Holder. So bad. You promised you would only ever be honest with me." I'm not raising my voice anymore. In fact, I'm talking so quietly that I'm not even sure he can hear me. He keeps staring at the road like the asshole that he is. I squeeze my eyes shut and fold my arms across my chest, then fall back into my seat. I stare out the passenger window and curse Karma. I curse Karma for bringing this hopeless boy into my life just so he could ruin it.

When he continues to drive without responding to a single word I've said, I can do nothing but let out a small, pathetic laugh. "You really are hopeless," I mutter.

Thirteen years earlier

"I need to pee," she giggles. We're crouched down under their porch, waiting for Dean to come find us. I like playing hide and seek, but I like to be the one hiding. I don't want them to know that I can't do the counting thing yet like they always ask me to do. Dean always tells me to count to twenty when they go hide, but I don't know how. So I just stand with my eyes closed and pretend I'm counting. Both of them are already in school and I can't go until next year, so I don't know how to count as good as they do.

"He's coming," she says, crawling backward a few feet. The dirt under the porch is cold, so I'm trying not to touch it with my hands like she is, but my legs are hurting.

"Les!" he yells. He walks closer to the porch and heads straight for the steps. We've been hiding a long time and he looks like he's tired of looking for us. He sits down on the steps, which are almost right in front of us. When I tilt my head, I can look right up at his face. "I'm tired of looking!"

I turn around and look at Lesslie to see if she's ready to run to base. She shakes her head no and holds her finger to her lips.

"Hope!" he yells, still sitting on the steps. "I give up!" He looks around the yard, then sighs quietly. He mumbles and kicks at the gravel under his foot and it makes me laugh. Lesslie punches me on the arm and tells me to be quiet.

He starts laughing, and at first I think it's because he hears us, but then I realize he's just talking to himself.

"Hope and Les," he says quietly. "Hopeless." He laughs again and stands up. "You hear that?" he yells, cupping his hands around his mouth. "The two of you are hopeless!"

Hearing him turn our names into a word makes Lesslie laugh and she crawls out from under the porch. I follow her and stand up as soon as Dean turns around and sees her. He smiles and looks at both of us, our knees covered in dirt, with cobwebs in our hair. He shakes his head and says it again. "Hopeless."

The memory is so vivid; I have no idea how it's just now coming to me. How I could see his tattoo day after day and hear him say Hope and how he talks about Les, yet still not remember. I reach over the seat and grab his arm, then pull his sleeve up. I know it's there. I know what it says. But this is the first time I'm looking at it, knowing what it actually means.

"Why did you get it?" He's told me before, but I want to know the real reason now. He pulls his gaze from the road and glances at me.

"I told you. It's a reminder of the people I've let down in my life."

I close my eyes and fall back into my seat, shaking my head. He said he doesn't do vague, but I can't think of an explanation more vague than the one he keeps giving me about his tattoo. How could he have let me down? The fact that he thinks he somehow let me down at that young an age doesn't even make sense. And the fact that he feels enough regret about it to turn it into some cryptic tattoo is really beyond any guesses I could fathom at this point. I don't know what else I can say or do to get him to take me back home. He didn't answer any of my questions and now he's playing his mind games again by giving me cryptic nonanswers. I just want to go home.

He pulls the car over and I'm hoping he's turning it around. Instead, he kills the ignition and opens his door. I look out the window and recognize that we're at the airport again. I'm annoyed. I don't want to come here and watch him stare at the stars again while he thinks. I want answers or I want to go home.

I swing open the door and reluctantly follow him to the fence, hoping if I appease him this one last time that I'll get a quick explanation from him. He helps me scale the fence again and we both walk back to our spots on the runway and lie down.

I look up in hopes of spotting a shooting star. I could really use a wish or two right now. I would wish I could go back to two months ago and never set foot in the grocery store that day.

"Are you ready for answers?" he says.

I turn my head toward his. "I'm ready if you're actually planning on being honest this time."

He faces me, then pulls up on his arm and rolls onto his side, looking down at me. He does his thing again, silently staring at me. It's darker than it was when we were out here the last time, so it's hard to make out the expression on his face. I can tell he's sad, though. His eyes have never been able to hide the sadness. He leans forward and lifts his hand, bringing it to my cheek. "I need to kiss you."

I almost break out into laughter, but I'm afraid if I do it will be the maniacal kind and that terrifies me, because I already assume I'm going crazy. I shake my head, shocked that he would even think I would let him kiss me right now. Not after finding out he's been lying to me for two solid months.

"No," I say forcefully. He keeps his face close to mine and his hand on my cheek. I hate that even though every ounce of anger in me is a result of his deceit, my body still responds to his touch. It's an odd internal battle when you can't decide if you want to punch the mouth sitting three inches in front of your face, or taste it.

"I need to kiss you," he says again, this time a desperate plea. "Please, Sky. I'm scared that after I tell you what I'm about to tell you . . . I'll never get to kiss you again." He pulls himself closer to me and strokes my cheek with his thumb, never taking his eyes off mine. *"Please."*

I nod slightly, unsure why my weakness is getting the best of me. He lowers his mouth to mine and kisses me. I close my eyes and allow him in, because a huge part of me is just as scared that this is the last time I'll feel his mouth against mine. I'm scared it's the last time I'll ever feel *anything*, because he's the only one I've ever wanted to feel anything with.

He adjusts himself until he's on his knees, holding on to my face with one hand and bracing his other hand on the concrete beside my head. I lift my hand and run it through his hair, pulling him to my mouth more urgently. Tasting him and feeling his breath as it mixes with mine momentarily takes everything about tonight and locks it away. In this moment, I'm focused on him and my heart and how it's swelling and breaking all at the same time. The thought that what I feel for him isn't even warranted or true is making me hurt. I hurt everywhere. In my head, in my gut, in my chest, in my heart, in my soul. Before, I felt like his kiss could cure me. Now his kiss feels like it's creating a terminal heartache deep within me.

He can sense my defeat taking over as the sobs start coming from my throat. He moves his lips to my cheek, then my ear. "I'm so sorry," he says, holding on to me. "I'm so sorry. I didn't want you to know."

I close my eyes and push him away from me, then sit up and take a deep breath. I wipe the tears away with the back of my hand and I pull my legs up, hugging them tightly. I bury my face in my knees so I don't have to look at him again.

"I just want you to talk, Holder. I asked you everything I could ever ask you on the way here. I need you to answer me now so I can just go home." My voice is defeated and done.

His hand moves to the back of my head and he drags his fingers through my hair, over and over again, while he works up a response. He clears his throat. "I wasn't sure if you were Hope the first time I saw you. I was so used to seeing her in every single stranger our age, I had given up trying to find her a few years ago. But when I saw you at the store and looked into your eyes . . . I had a feeling you really were her. When you showed me your ID and I realized you weren't, I felt ridiculous. It was like the wake-up call I needed to finally just let the memory of her go."

He stops talking and runs his hand slowly down my hair, resting it on my back, but tracing light circles with his finger. I want to push his hand away, but I want it right where it is even more.

"We lived next door to you and your dad for a year. You and me and Les . . . we were all best friends. It's so hard to remember faces from that long ago, though. I thought you were Hope, but I also thought that if you really were her, I wouldn't be doubting it. I thought if I ever saw her again, I'd know for sure.

"When I left the grocery store that day, I immediately looked up the name you gave me online. I couldn't find anything about you, not even on Facebook. I searched for an hour straight and became so frustrated that I went for a run to cool down. When I rounded the corner and saw you standing in front of my house, I couldn't breathe. You were just standing there, worn out and exhausted from running and . . . *Jesus*, Sky. You were so beautiful. I still wasn't sure if you were Hope or not, but at that point it wasn't even going through my mind. I didn't care *who* you were; I just needed to know you.

"After spending time with you that week, I couldn't stop myself from going to your house that Friday night. I didn't show up with the intention of digging up your past or even in the hope that something would happen between us. I went to your house because I wanted you to know the real me, not the me you had heard about from everyone else. After spending more time with you that night, I couldn't think of anything else besides figuring out how I could spend more time with you. I had never met anyone who got me the way you did. I still wondered if it was possible . . . if you were her. I was especially curious after you told me you were adopted, but again, I thought maybe it was a coincidence.

"But then when I saw the bracelet . . ." He stops talking and takes his hand off of my back. His fingers slide under my chin and he pulls my face away from my knees and makes me look him in the eyes. "My heart broke, Sky. I didn't want you to be her. I wanted you to tell me you got the bracelet from your friend or that you found it or you bought it. After all the years I spent searching for you in every single face I ever looked at, I finally found you . . . and I was devastated. I didn't want you to be Hope. I just wanted you to be you."

I shake my head, still just as confused as before. "But why didn't you just tell me? How hard would it have been to admit that we used to know each other? I don't understand why you've been lying about it."

He eyes me for a moment while he searches for a good enough response, then brushes hair away from my face. "What do you remember about your adoption?"

I shake my head. "Not a lot. I know I was in foster care after my father gave me up. I know Karen adopted me and we moved here from out of state when I was five. Other than that and a few odd memories, I don't know anything."

He squares his body up with mine and places both of his hands on my shoulders firmly, like he's getting frustrated. "That's all stuff Karen told you. I want to know what *you* remember. What do *you* remember, Sky?"

This time I shake my head slowly. "Nothing. The earliest memories I have are with Karen. The only thing I remember from before Karen was getting the bracelet, but that's only because I still have it and the memory stuck with me. I wasn't even sure who gave it to me."

Holder takes my face in his hands and lowers his lips to my forehead. He keeps his lips there, holding me against his mouth like he's afraid to pull away because he doesn't want to have to talk. He doesn't want to have to tell me whatever it is he knows.

"Just say it," I whisper. "Tell me what you're wishing you didn't have to tell me."

He pulls his mouth away and presses his forehead against

mine. His eyes are closed and he's got a firm grip on my face. He looks so sad and it makes me want to hold him despite my frustration with him. I reach my arms around him and I hug him. He hugs me back and pulls me onto his lap in the process. I wrap my legs around his waist and our foreheads are still meshed together. He's holding on to me, but this time it feels like he's holding on to me because his earth has been shifted off its axis, and I'm *his* core.

"Just tell me, Holder."

He runs his hand down to my lower back and he opens his eyes, pulling his forehead away from mine so he can look at me when he speaks.

"The day Les gave you that bracelet, you were crying. I remember every single detail like it happened yesterday. You were sitting in your yard against your house. Les and I sat with you for a long time, but you never stopped crying. After she gave you your bracelet she walked back to our house but I couldn't. I felt bad leaving you there, because I thought you might be mad at your dad again. You were always crying because of him and it made me hate him. I don't remember anything about the guy, other than I hated his guts for making you feel like you did. I was only six years old, so I never knew what to say to you when you cried. I think that day I said something like, 'Don't worry . . . '"

"He won't live forever," I say, finishing his sentence. "I remember that day. Les giving me the bracelet and you saying he won't live forever. Those are the two things I've remembered all this time. I just didn't know it was you."

"Yeah, that's what I said to you." He brings his hands to my cheeks and continues. "And then I did something I've regretted every single day of my life since."

I shake my head. "Holder, you didn't do anything. You just walked away."

"Exactly," he says. "I walked to my front yard even though I knew I should have sat back down in the grass beside you. I stood in my front yard and I watched you cry into your arms, when you should have been crying into mine. I just stood there . . . and I watched the car pull up to the curb. I watched the passenger window roll down and I heard someone call your name. I watched you look up at the car and wipe your eyes. You stood up and you dusted off your shorts, then you walked to the car. I watched you climb inside and I knew whatever was happening I shouldn't have just been standing there. But all I did was watch, when I should have been with you. It never would have happened if I had stayed right there with you."

The fear and regret in his voice is causing my heart to race against my chest. I somehow find strength to speak, despite the fear consuming me. "*What* never would have happened?"

He kisses me on the forehead again and his thumbs brush delicately over my cheekbones. He looks at me like he's scared he's about to break my heart.

"They took you. Whoever was in that car, they took you from your dad, from me, from Les. You've been missing for thirteen years, Hope."

Saturday, October 27, 2012
11:57 p.m.

One of the things I love about books is being able to define and condense certain portions of a character's life into
chapters. It's intriguing, because you can't do this with real
life. You can't just end a chapter, then skip the things you
don't want to live through, only to open it up to a chapter that better suits your mood. Life can't be divided into
chapters . . . only minutes. The events of your life are all
crammed together one minute right after the other without
any time lapses or blank pages or chapter breaks because
no matter what happens life just keeps going and moving
forward and words keep flowing and truths keep spewing
whether you like it or not and life never lets you pause and
just catch your fucking breath.

I need one of those chapter breaks. I just want to catch
my breath, but I have no idea how.

"Say something," he says. I'm still sitting in his lap,
wrapped around him. My head is pressed against his shoulder and my eyes are shut. He places his hand on the back
of my head and lowers his mouth to my ear, holding me
tighter. "*Please*. Say something."

I don't know what he wants me to say. Does he want me
to act surprised? Shocked? Does he want me to cry? Does he
want me to scream? I can't do any of those things because I'm
still trying to wrap my mind around what he's saying.

"You've been missing for thirteen years, Hope."

His words repeat over and over in my mind like a broken record.

"Missing."

I'm hoping he means missing in a figurative sense, like maybe he's just missed me all these years. I doubt that's the case, though. I could see the look in his eyes when he said those words, and he didn't want to say them at all. He knew what it would do to me.

Maybe he really does mean missing in the literal sense, but he's just confused. We were both so young; he probably doesn't remember the sequence of events correctly. But the last two months flash before my eyes, and everything about him . . . all of his personalities and mood swings and cryptic words come into clear focus. Like the night he was standing in my doorway and said he'd been looking for me his whole damn life. He was being literal about that.

Or our first night sitting right here on this runway when he asked if I'd had a good life. He's worried for thirteen years about what happened to me. He was being very literal then, wanting to know if I was happy with where I ended up.

Or the day he refused to apologize for the way he acted in the cafeteria, explaining that he knew why it upset him but he just couldn't tell me yet. I didn't question it then, because he seemed sincere that he wanted to explain himself one day. Never in a million years could I have guessed why it upset him so much to see that bracelet on me. He didn't want me to be Hope because he knew the truth would break my heart.

He was right.

"You've been missing for thirteen years, Hope."

The last word of his sentence sends a shiver down my spine. I slowly lift my face away from his shoulder and look at him. "You called me Hope. Don't call me that. It's not my name."

He nods. "I'm sorry, Sky."

The last word of *that* sentence sends a shiver down my spine as well. I slide off of him and stand up. "Don't call me that, either," I say resolutely. I don't want to be called *Hope* or *Sky* or *Princess* or anything else that separates me from any other part of myself. I'm suddenly feeling like I'm completely different people, wrapped up into one. Someone who doesn't know who she is or where she belongs, and it's disturbing. I've never felt so isolated in my life; like there isn't a single person in this entire world I can trust. Not even myself. I can't even trust my own memories.

Holder stands up and takes my hands, looking down at me. He's watching me, waiting for me to react. He'll be disappointed because I'm not going to react. Not right here. Not right now. Part of me wants to cry while he wraps his arms around me and whispers, "Don't worry," into my ear. Part of me wants to scream and yell and hit him for deceiving me. Part of me wants to allow him to continue to blame himself for not stopping what he says happened thirteen years ago. Most of me just wants it all to go away, though. I want to go back to feeling nothing again. I miss the numbness.

I pull my hands from his and begin to walk toward the car. "I need a chapter break," I say, more to myself than to him.

He follows a step behind me. "I don't even know what that means." His voice sounds defeated and overwhelmed.

He grabs my arm to stop me, more than likely to ask how I'm feeling, but I jerk it away and spin around to face him again. I don't want him to ask me how I'm feeling, because I have no idea. I'm running through an entire gamut of feelings right now, some I've never even experienced before. Rage and fear and sadness and disbelief are building up inside me and I want it to stop. I just want to stop feeling everything that I'm feeling, so I reach up and grab his face and press my lips to his. I kiss him hard and fast, wanting him to react, but he doesn't. He doesn't kiss me back. He refuses to help make the pain go away like this, so my anger takes over and I separate my lips from his, then slap him.

He barely flinches and it infuriates me. I want him to hurt like I'm hurting. I want him to feel what his words just did to me. I slap him again and he allows it. When he still doesn't react, I push against his chest. I push him and shove him over and over—trying to give him back every ounce of pain he's just immersed into my soul. I ball my fists up and hit him in the chest and when that doesn't work, I start screaming and hitting him and trying to get out of his arms because they're wrapped around me now. He spins me around so that my back is against his chest and our arms are locked together, folded tightly across my stomach.

"Breathe," he whispers into my ear. "Calm down, Sky. I know you're confused and scared, but I'm here. I'm right here. Just breathe."

His voice is calm and comforting and I close my eyes and soak it in. He simulates a deep breath, moving his chest in rhythm with mine, forcing me to take a breath and follow his lead. I take several slow, deep breaths in time with his. When I've stopped struggling in his arms, he slowly turns me around and pulls me into his chest.

"I didn't want you to hurt like this," he whispers, cradling my head in his hands. "That's why I haven't told you."

I realize in this moment that I'm not even crying. I haven't cried at all since the truth passed his lips and I make it a point to refuse the tears that are demanding to be set free. Tears won't help me right now. They'll just make me weaker.

I place my palms on his chest and lightly push against him. I feel like I'm vulnerable to more tears when he holds me because he feels so comforting. I don't need anyone's comfort. I need to learn how to rely on myself to stay strong because I'm the only one I can trust—and I'm even skeptical about *my own* trustworthiness. Everything I thought I knew has been a lie. I don't know who's in on it or who knows the truth and I find myself without an ounce of trust left in my heart. Not for Holder, not for Karen . . . not even for myself, really.

I back a step away from him and look him in the eyes. "Were you ever going to tell me who I was?" I ask, glaring at him. "What if I never remembered? Would you have *ever* told me? Were you scared I would leave you and you'd never get your chance to screw me? Is that why you've been lying to me this whole time?"

His eyes are awash with offense the moment the words flow from my lips. "No. That's not how it was. That's not how it *is*. I haven't told you because I'm scared of what will happen to you. If I report it, they'll take you from Karen. They'll more than likely arrest her and send you back to live with your father until you turn eighteen. Do you want that to happen? You love Karen and you're happy here. I didn't want to mess that up for you."

I release a quick laugh and shake my head. His reasoning makes no sense. None of this makes any sense. "First of all," I say. "They wouldn't put Karen in jail because I can guarantee you she knows nothing about this. Second, I've been eighteen since September. If my age was the reason you weren't being honest, you would have told me by now."

He squeezes the back of his neck and looks down at the ground. I don't like the nervousness seeping from him right now. I can tell by the way he's reacting that he isn't finished with the confessions.

"Sky, there's so much I still need to explain to you." He brings his eyes back up to meet mine. "Your birthday wasn't in September. Your birthday is May 7. You don't even turn eighteen for six more months. And Karen?" He takes a step toward me, grabbing both of my hands. "She has to know, Sky. She *has* to. Think about it. Who else could have done this?"

I immediately pull my hands from his and back away. I know this has more than likely been torture for him, keeping this secret to himself. I can see in his eyes that it's agonizing for him having to tell me all of this. But I've been giving him the benefit of the doubt since the moment I met him, and any sorrow I felt for him has just been negated by the fact that he's now attempting to tell me that my own mother was somehow involved.

"Take me home," I demand. "I don't want to hear anything else. I don't want to know anything else tonight."

He tries to take my hands again, but I slap them away. "TAKE ME HOME!" I scream. I begin walking back to the car. I've heard enough. I need my mom. I just need to see her and hug her and know that I'm not completely alone in this, because that's exactly how I feel right now.

I reach the fence before Holder does and I try to pull myself up, but I can't. My hands and arms are trembling and weak. I'm still attempting it on my own when he quietly comes up behind me and hoists me up. I jump down over the other side and walk to the car.

He sits in the driver's seat and pulls his door shut, but doesn't start the car. He's staring at the steering wheel with his hand paused on the ignition. I watch his hands with mixed emotions, because I want them around me so bad. I want them holding me and rubbing my back and my hair while he tells me it'll all be okay. But I also look at his hands in disgust, thinking about all the intimate ways he's touched me and held me, knowing all along that he was deceiving me. How could he be with me, knowing what he knows, yet still allow me to believe the lies? I don't know how I can forgive him for that.

"I know it's a lot to take in," he says quietly. "I *know* it is. I'll take you home, but we need to talk about this tomorrow." He turns toward me, looking at me with hardened eyes. "Sky, you *cannot* talk to Karen about this. Do you understand? Not until the two of us figure it out."

I nod, just to appease him. He can't honestly expect me not to talk to her about this.

He turns his whole body toward mine in the seat and leans in, placing his hand on my headrest. "I'm serious, babe. I know you don't think she's capable of doing something like this, but until we find out more, you need to keep this to yourself. If you tell anyone, your entire life will change. Give yourself time to process everything. *Please*. Please promise me you'll wait until after tomorrow. After we talk again."

The terrified undertone in his words pierces my heart, and I nod again, but this time I actually mean it.

He watches me for several seconds, then slowly turns around and cranks the car, pulling onto the road. He drives me the four miles back to my home and nothing is spoken until he pulls into my driveway. My hand is on the door handle and I'm stepping out of the car when he takes my other hand.

"Wait," he says. I wait, but I don't turn back around. I keep one foot on the floorboard and one foot on the driveway, facing the door. He moves his hand to the side of my head and brushes a strand of hair behind my ear. "Will you be okay tonight?"

I sigh at the simplicity of his question. *"How?"* I ease back against my seat and turn and face him. "How can I possibly be okay after tonight?"

He stares at me and continues to stroke the hair on the side of my head with his fingers. "It's killing me . . . letting you go like this. I don't want to leave you alone. Can I come back in an hour?"

I know he's asking if he can come through my window and lie with me, but I immediately shake my head no. "I can't," I say, my voice cracking. "It's too hard being around you right now. I just need to think. I'll see you tomorrow, okay?"

He nods and pulls his hand away from my cheek, then places it back on the steering wheel. He watches me as I step out of the car and walk away from him.

Sunday, October 28, 2012
12:37 a.m.

Stepping through the front door and into the living room, I'm hoping to be engulfed with a sense of comfort that I'm desperately in need of. The familiarity and sense of belonging in this house is something I need to calm me down so that I no longer feel like bursting into tears. This is my home where I live with Karen . . . a woman who loves me and would do anything for me, no matter what Holder may think.

I stand in the dark living room and wait for the feeling to envelop me, but it never does. I'm looking around with suspicion and doubt, and I hate that I'm observing my life from a completely different viewpoint right now.

I walk through the living room, pausing just outside Karen's bedroom door. I contemplate crawling into bed with her, but her light is out. I've never needed to be in her presence as much as I do in this moment, but I can't bring myself to open her bedroom door. Maybe I'm not ready to face her yet. Instead, I walk down the hallway to my bedroom.

The light in my room is peering out from the crack under the door. I put my hand on the doorknob and turn it, then slowly open the door. Karen is sitting on my bed. She looks up at me when she hears the door open and she immediately stands up.

269

"Where have you been?" She looks worried, but her voice has an edge of anger to it. Or maybe disappointment.

"With Holder. You never said what time I needed to be home."

She points to the bed. "Sit down. We need to talk."

Everything about her feels different now. I watch her guardedly. I feel like I'm going through false motions of being an obedient daughter while I nod. It's like I'm in a scene from a dramatic *Lifetime* movie. I walk over to the bed and sit, not sure what has her so riled up. I'm sort of hoping she found out everything that *I* found out tonight. It'll make it a hell of a lot easier when I tell her about it.

She takes a seat next to me and turns toward me. "You're not allowed to see him again," she says firmly.

I blink twice, mostly from shock at the subject matter. I wasn't expecting it to be about Holder. "What?" I say, confused. "Why?"

She reaches into her pocket and pulls out my cell phone. "What is this?" she says through gritted teeth.

I look at my phone being held tightly in her hands. She hits a button and holds up the screen to face me. "And what the hell kind of texts are these, Sky? They're awful. He says awful, vile things to you." She drops the phone onto the bed and reaches for my hands, grasping them. "Why would you allow yourself to be with someone who treats you this way? I raised you better than this."

She's no longer raising her voice. Now she's just playing the part of concerned mother.

I squeeze her hands in reassurance. I know I'll more than likely be in trouble for having the phone, but I need her to know that the texts aren't at all what she thinks they are. I actually feel a little silly that we're even having this conversation. When I compare this issue to the new issues I'm facing, it seems a little juvenile.

"Mom, he's not being serious. He sends me those texts as a joke."

She lets out a disheartened laugh and shakes her head in disagreement. "There's something off about him, Sky. I don't like how he looks at you. I don't like how he looks at *me*. And the fact that he bought you a phone without having any respect for my rules just goes to show you what kind of respect he holds for other people. Regardless of whether the texts are a joke, I don't trust him. I don't think you should trust him, either."

I stare at her. She's still talking, but the thoughts inside my head are becoming louder and louder, blocking out whatever words she's trying to drill into my brain. My palms instantly begin sweating and I can feel my heart pounding in my eardrums. All of her beliefs and choices and rules are flashing in my mind and I'm trying to separate them and put them into their own chapters, but they're all running together. I pull the first thought out of the pile of questions and just flat out ask her.

"Why can't I have a phone?" I whisper. I'm not even sure that I ask the question loud enough for her to hear me, but she stops moving her mouth so I'm pretty sure she heard me.

"And internet," I add. "Why don't you want me accessing the internet?"

The questions are becoming poison in my head and I feel like I have to get them out. It's all beginning to piece together and I'm hoping it's all coincidence. I'm hoping she's sheltered me my whole life because she loves me and wants to protect me. But deep down, it's quickly becoming apparent that I've been sheltered my whole life because she was *hiding* me.

"Why did you homeschool me?" I ask, my voice much louder this time.

Her eyes are wide and it's obvious she has no idea what is spurring these questions right now. She stands up and looks down at me. "You aren't turning this around on me, Sky. You live under my roof and you'll follow my rules." She grabs my phone off the bed and walks toward the door. "You're grounded. No more cell phones. No more boyfriend. We'll talk about this tomorrow."

She slams my door shut behind her and I immediately fall back onto the bed, feeling even more hopeless than before I walked through my front door.

I can't be right. It's just a coincidence, I *can't* be right. She wouldn't do something like this. I squeeze the tears back and refuse to believe it. There has to be some other explanation. Maybe Holder is confused. Maybe *Karen* is confused.

I know I'm confused.

I take off my dress and throw on a T-shirt, then turn out the light and crawl under the covers. I'm hoping I wake up tomorrow to realize this whole night was just a bad dream. If it's not, I don't know how much more I can take before my strength is completely diminished. I stare up at the stars, glowing above my head, and I begin counting them. I push everyone and everything else away and focus, focus, focus on the stars.

Thirteen years earlier

Dean walks back to his yard and he turns around and looks at me. I bury my head back into my arm and try to stop crying. I know they probably want to play hide and seek again before I have to go back inside, so I need to stop being sad so we can play.

"Hope!"

I look up at Dean and he isn't looking at me anymore. I thought he called my name, but he's looking at a car. It's parked in front of my house and the window is rolled down.

"Come here, Hope," the lady says. She's smiling and asking me to come to her window. I feel like I know her, but I can't remember her name. I stand up so I can go see what she wants. I wipe the dirt off my shorts and walk to the car. She's still smiling and she looks really nice. When I walk up to the car, she hits the button that unlocks the doors.

"Are you ready to go, sweetie? Your daddy wants us to hurry."

I didn't know I was supposed to go anywhere. Daddy didn't say we were going anywhere today.

"Where are we going?" I ask her.

She smiles and reaches over to the handle, then opens the door for me. "I'll tell you when we're on our way. Get in and put your seatbelt on, we can't be late."

She really doesn't want to be late to where we're going. I don't want her to be late, so I climb into the front seat and shut my door. She rolls up the window and starts driving away from my house.

She looks at me and smiles, then reaches into the backseat. She hands me a juice box, so I take it out of her hand and open the straw.

"I'm Karen," she says. "And you get to stay with me for a little while. I'll tell you all about it when we get there."

I take a sip from my juice. It's apple juice. I love apple juice.

"But what about my daddy? Is he coming, too?"

Karen shakes her head. "No, sweetie. It'll just be you and me when we get there."

I put the straw back in my mouth because I don't want her to see me smile. I don't want her to know that I'm happy my daddy isn't coming with us.

I sit up.

It was a dream.

It was just a dream.

I can feel my heart beating wildly in every facet of my body. It's beating so hard I can hear it. I'm panting for breath and covered in sweat.

It was just a dream.

I attempt to convince myself of just that. I want to believe with all my heart that the memory I just had wasn't a real one. It *can't* be.

But it was. I remember it clearly, like it happened yesterday. With every single memory I've recalled over the last few days, a new one pops up after it. Things I've either been repressing or was just too young to recall are coming back to me full force. Things I don't want to remember. Things I wish I never knew.

I throw the covers off me and reach over to the lamp, flipping the switch. The room fills with light and I scream at the realization that someone else is in my bed. As soon as the scream escapes my mouth, he wakes up and shoots straight up on the bed.

"What the hell are you doing here?" I whisper loudly.

Holder glances at his watch, then rubs his eyes with his palms. When he wakes up enough to respond, he places

275

his hand on my knee. "I couldn't leave you. I just needed to make sure you were okay." He puts his hand on my neck, right below my ear, and brushes along my jaw with his thumb. "Your heart," he says, feeling my pulse beating against his fingertips. "You're scared."

Seeing him in my bed, caring for me like he is . . . I can't be mad at him. I can't blame him. Despite the fact that I want to be mad at him, I just can't. If he wasn't here right now to comfort me after the realization I just had, I don't know what I would do. He's done nothing but place blame on himself for every single thing that's ever happened to me. I'm beginning to accept the fact that maybe he needs comforting just as much as I do. For that, I allow him to steal another piece of my heart. I grab his hand that's touching my neck and I squeeze it.

"Holder . . . I remember." My voice shakes when I speak and I feel the tears wanting to come out. I swallow and push them back with everything that I have. He scoots closer to me on the bed and turns me to face him completely. He places both of his hands on my face and looks into my eyes.

"What do you remember?"

I shake my head, not wanting to say it. He doesn't let go of me. He coaxes me with his eyes, nodding his head slightly, assuring me that it's okay to say it. I whisper as quietly as possible, afraid to say it out loud. "It was Karen in that car. She did it. She's the one who took me."

Pain and recognition consume his features and he pulls me to his chest, wrapping his arms around me. "I know, babe," he says into my hair. "I know."

I cling to his shirt and hold on to him, wanting to swim in the comfort that his arms provide. I close my eyes, but only for a second. He's pushing me away as soon as Karen opens the door to my bedroom.

"Sky?"

I spin around on the bed and she's standing in the doorway, glaring at Holder. She cuts her eyes to me. "Sky? What . . . what are you doing?" Confusion and disappointment cloud her face.

I snap my gaze back to Holder. "Get me out of here," I say under my breath. "Please."

He nods, then walks to my closet. He opens the door as I stand up and grab a pair of jeans from my dresser and pull them on.

"Sky?" Karen says, watching both of us from the doorway. I don't look at her. I *can't* look at her. She takes a few steps into the bedroom just as Holder opens a duffel bag and lays it on the bed.

"Throw some clothes in here. I'll get what you need out of the bathroom." His tone of voice is calm and collected, which slightly eases the panic coursing through me. I walk to my closet and begin pulling shirts off of hangers.

"You aren't going anywhere with him. Are you insane?" Karen's voice is near panic, but I still don't look at her. I continue throwing clothes into my bag. I walk to the dresser and pull open the top drawer, taking a handful of socks and underwear. I walk to the bed and Karen cuts me off, placing her hands on my shoulders and forcing me to look at her.

"Sky," she says, dumbfounded. "What are you doing? What's wrong with you? You're not leaving with him."

Holder walks back into the bedroom with a handful

of toiletries and walks directly around Karen, piling them into the bag. "Karen, I suggest you let go of her," he says as calmly as a threat can possibly sound.

Karen scoffs and spins around to face him. "You are *not* taking her. If you so much as walk out of this house with her, I'm calling the police."

Holder doesn't respond. He looks at me and reaches out for the items in my hands, then turns and places them into the duffel bag, zipping it shut. "You ready?" he says, taking my hand.

I nod.

"This isn't a joke!" Karen yells. Tears are beginning to roll down her cheeks and she's frantic, looking back and forth between us. Seeing the pain on her face breaks my heart because she's my mother and I love her, but I can't ignore the anger and betrayal I feel over the last thirteen years of my life.

"I'll call the police," she yells. "You have no right to take her!"

I reach into Holder's pocket, then pull out his cell phone and take a step toward Karen. I look directly at her and as calmly as I can, I hold the phone out to her. "Here," I say. "Call them."

She looks down at the phone in my hands, then back up to me. "Why are you doing this, Sky?" She's overcome with tears now.

I grab her hand and shove the phone into it, but she refuses to grasp it. "Call them! Call the police, Mom! *Please*." I'm begging now. I'm begging her to call them—to prove me wrong. To prove that she has nothing to hide. To prove that *I'm* not what she's hiding. "Please," I say again quietly. Everything in my heart and soul wants her to take the phone and call them so I'll know I'm wrong.

She takes a step back at the same time she sucks in a breath. She begins to shake her head, and I'm almost positive she knows I know, but I don't stick around to find out. Holder grabs my hand and leads me to the open window. He lets me climb out first, then he climbs out behind me. I hear Karen crying my name, but I don't stop walking until I reach his car. We both climb inside and he drives away. Away from the only family I've ever really known.

"We can't stay here," he says, pulling up to his house. "Karen might come here looking for you. Let me run in and grab a few things and I'll be right back."

He leans across the seat and pulls my face toward his. He kisses me, then gets out of the car. The entire time he's inside his house, I'm leaning my head against the headrest, staring out the window. There isn't a single star in the sky to count tonight. Only lightning. It seems fitting for the night I've had.

Holder returns to the car several minutes later and throws his own bag into the backseat. His mother is standing in the entryway, watching him. He walks back to her and takes her face in his hands, just like he does mine. He says something to her, but I don't know what he's saying. She nods and hugs him. He walks back to the car and climbs inside.

"What did you tell her?"

He grabs my hand. "I told her you and your mother got into a fight, so I was taking you to one of your relatives' houses in Austin. I told her I'd stay with my dad for a few days and that I'd be back soon." He looks at me and smiles. "It's okay, she's used to me leaving, unfortunately. She's not worried."

I turn and look out my window when he pulls out of the

driveway, just as the rain begins to slap the windshield. "Are we really going to stay with your dad?"

"We'll go wherever you want to go. I doubt you want to go to Austin, though."

I look over at him. "Why wouldn't I want to go to Austin?"

He purses his lips and flips on the windshield wipers. He places his hand on my knee and brushes it with his thumb. "That's where you're from," he says quietly.

I look back out the window and sigh. There is so much I don't know. So much. I press my forehead against the cool glass and close my eyes, allowing the questions I've been suppressing all night to re-emerge.

"Is my dad still alive?" I ask.

"Yes, he is."

"What about my mom? Did she really die when I was three?"

He clears his throat. "Yes. She died in a car wreck a few months before we moved in next door to you."

"Does he still live in the same house?"

"Yes."

"I want to see it. I want to go there."

He doesn't immediately respond to this statement. Instead, he slowly inhales a breath and releases it. "I don't think that's a good idea."

I turn to him. "Why not? I probably belong there more than I do anywhere else. He needs to know I'm okay."

Holder pulls off to the side of the road and throws the car into park. He turns in his seat and looks at me dead-on. "Babe, it's not a good idea because you just found out about this a few hours ago. It's a lot to take in before you

281

make any hasty decisions. If your dad sees you and recognizes you, Karen will go to prison. You need to think long and hard about that. Think about the media. Think about the reporters. Believe me, Sky. When you disappeared they camped out on our front lawn for months. The police interviewed me no less than twenty times over a two-month period. Your entire life is about to change, no matter what decision you make. But I want you to make the best decision for yourself. I'll answer any questions you have. I'll take you anywhere you want to go in a couple of days. If you want to see your dad, that's where we'll go. If you want to go to the police, that's where we'll go. If you want to just run away from everything, that's what we'll do. But for now, I just want you to let this soak in. This is your life. The rest of your *life*."

His words have tightened my chest like a vise. I don't know what I'm thinking. I don't know *if* I'm thinking. He's thought this through from so many angles and I have no clue what to do. I have no fucking clue.

I swing open the door and step out onto the shoulder of the highway, out into the rain. I pace back and forth, attempting to focus on something in order to hold the hyperventilating at bay. It's cold and the rain is no longer just falling; it's *pummeling*. Huge raindrops are stinging my skin and I can't keep my eyes open due to the force of them. As soon as Holder rounds the front of the car, I swiftly walk toward him and throw my arms around his neck, burying my face in his already soaked shirt. "I can't do this!" I yell over the sound of rain pounding the pavement. "I don't want this to be my life!"

He kisses the top of my head and bends down to talk

against my ear. "I don't want this to be your life, either," he says. "I'm so sorry. I'm so sorry I let this happen to you."

He slides a finger under my chin and pulls my gaze up to his. His height is shielding the rain from stinging my eyes, but the drops are sliding down his face, over his lips, and down his neck. His hair is soaked and matted to his forehead, so I wipe a strand out of his eyes. He already needs a trim again.

"Let's not let this be your life tonight," he says. "Let's get back in the car and pretend we're driving away because we *want* to . . . not because we *need* to. We can pretend I'm taking you somewhere amazing . . . somewhere you've always wanted to go. You can snuggle up to me and we can talk about how excited we are and we'll talk about everything we'll do when we get there. We can talk about the important stuff later. But tonight . . . let's not let this be your life."

I pull his mouth to mine and I kiss him. I kiss him for always having the perfect thing to say. I kiss him for always being there for me. I kiss him for supporting whatever decision I think I might need to make. I kiss him for being so patient with me while I figure everything out. I kiss him because I can't think of anything better than climbing back inside that car with him and talking about everything we'll do when we get to Hawaii.

I separate my mouth from his and somehow, in the midst of the worst day of my life, I find the strength to smile. "Thank you, Holder. *So* much. I couldn't do this without you."

He kisses me softly on the mouth again and smiles back at me. "Yes. You *could*."

His fingers have been slowly lacing through my hair. My head is resting in his lap and we've been driving for over four hours. He turned his phone off back in Waco after receiving pleading texts from Karen, using my phone, wanting him to bring me back home. The problem with that is, I don't even know where home is anymore.

As much as I love Karen I have no idea how to grasp what she did. There isn't a situation in the world that could ever make stealing a child okay, so I don't know that I'll ever want to go back to her. I plan on finding out as much information as I can about what happened before I make any decisions about how I need to handle this. I know the right thing to do would be to immediately call the police, but sometimes the right thing to do isn't always the best answer.

"I don't think we should stay at my father's house," Holder says. I assumed he thought I was sleeping, but it's obvious he knows I'm wide awake since he's talking to me. "We'll get a hotel for tonight and figure out what we need to do tomorrow. I didn't move out of his house on the best terms this summer, and we've got enough drama to deal with as it is."

I nod my head against his lap. "Whatever you want to do. I just know I need a bed, I'm exhausted. I have no idea

284

how you're still awake." I sit up and stretch my arms out in front of me, just as Holder pulls his car into the parking lot of a hotel.

After he checks us in, he gives me the key to the room and leaves to go park the car and get our things. I slide the key card into the door and open it, then walk into the hotel room. There's only one bed, which I assumed he would request. We've slept in the same bed several times before so it would have been a lot more awkward had he requested separate beds.

He returns to the room several minutes later and sets our bags down. I rifle through mine, looking for something to sleep in. Unfortunately, I didn't bring any pajamas, so I grab a long T-shirt and some underwear.

"I need to take a shower." I grab the few toiletries I brought and carry them into the bathroom with me and take an extremely long shower. When I'm finished, I attempt to blow dry my hair but I'm too exhausted. I pull my hair up in a wet ponytail instead and brush my teeth. When I walk out of the bathroom, Holder is unpacking both of our bags and hanging our shirts in the closet. He glances at me and does a double take when he sees I'm only wearing a T-shirt and underwear. He eyes me, but only for a second before he glances away uncomfortably. He's trying to be respectful, considering the day I've had. I don't want him treating me like I'm fragile. If this were any other day, he'd be commenting on what I was wearing and his hands would be on my ass in two seconds flat. Instead, he turns his back to me and takes the last of his items out of his duffel bag.

"I'm going to take a quick shower," he says. "I filled up the ice bucket and grabbed a few drinks. I wasn't sure if you wanted soda or water, so I got both." He grabs a pair of boxer shorts and walks around me toward the bathroom, careful not to look at me. As he passes me, I grab his wrist. He stops and turns around, carefully looking me in the eyes and nowhere else.

"Can you do me a favor?"

"Of course, babe," he says sincerely.

I slide my hand through his, then bring it up to my mouth. I lightly kiss his palm, then rest it against my cheek. "I know you're worried about me. But if what's happening in my life is causing you to feel uncomfortable about being attracted to me to the point that you can't even look at me when I'm half-naked, it'll break my heart. You're the only person I have left, Holder. Please don't treat me differently."

He looks at me knowingly, then pulls his hand away from my cheek. His eyes drop to my lips, and a small grin plays at the corner of his mouth. "You're giving me the go-ahead to admit that I still want you, even though your life has turned to shit?"

I nod. "Knowing you still want me is more of a necessity now than it was *before* my life turned to shit."

He smiles, then drops his lips to mine, sweeping his hand across my waist and around to my lower back. His other hand is planted firmly on the back of my head, guiding it as he kisses me deeply. His kiss is exactly what I need right now. It's the only thing that could possibly feel good in a world full of nothing but bad.

"I really need to shower," he says between kisses. "But now that I have the go-ahead to still treat you the same?"

He grabs my ass and pulls me against him. "Don't fall asleep while I'm in there, because when I get out, I want to show you just how incredible I think you look right now."

"Good," I whisper against his mouth. He releases me, then walks to the bathroom. I lie down on the bed just as the water kicks on.

I attempt to watch TV for a while since I never have the opportunity, but nothing can hold my attention. It's been such a grueling twenty-four hours, the sun is already up and we haven't even gone to bed yet. I shut the blinds and curtains, then crawl back into bed and throw a pillow over my eyes. As soon as I begin to welcome sleep, I feel Holder crawl into bed behind me. He slides one arm under my pillow and one over my side. I can feel his warm chest pressed against my back and the strength of his arms around me. He slides his hands through mine and kisses me lightly on the back of the head.

"I live you," I whisper to him.

He kisses my head again and sighs into my hair. "I don't think I live you back anymore. I'm pretty sure I've moved beyond that. Actually, I'm positive I've moved beyond that, but I'm still not ready to say it to you. When I say it, I want it to be separate from this day. I don't want you to remember it like this."

I pull his hand to my mouth and kiss it softly. "Me, too."

And once again in my new world full of heartache and lies, this hopeless boy somehow finds a way to make me smile.

We sleep through breakfast and lunch. By the time afternoon hits and Holder walks in with food, I'm starving. It's been over twenty-four hours since I've eaten anything. He pulls two chairs up to the desk and takes the items and drinks out of the sacks. He brought me the same thing I requested after the art showing last night, but that we never actually got around to ordering. I remove the lid from the chocolate shake and down a huge drink, then take the wrapper off my burger. When I do, a small square piece of paper falls out and lands on the table. I pick it up and read it.

> *Just because you don't have a phone anymore and your life is crazy dramatic, I still don't want your ego exploding. You looked really homely in your T-shirt and panties. I really hope you buy yourself some footed pajamas today so I don't have to look at your chicken legs again all night.*

When I set the note down and look at him, he's grinning at me. His dimples are so adorable; I actually lean over and lick one this time.

"What was that?" he asks, laughing.

I take a bite of my burger and shrug. "I've been wanting to do that since the day I saw you in the grocery store."

His smile turns smug and he leans back in his chair. "You wanted to lick my face the first time you saw me? Is that usually what you do when you're attracted to guys?"

I shake my head. "Not your face, your dimple. And no. You're the only guy I've ever had the urge to lick."

He smiles at me confidently. "Good. Because you're the only girl I've ever had the urge to love."

Holy shit. He didn't directly say he loves me, but hearing that word come out of his mouth makes my heart swell in my chest. I take a bite of my burger to hide my smile and let his sentence linger in the air. I'm not ready for it to leave just yet.

We both quietly finish our food. I stand up and clear off the table, then walk to the bed and slip my shoes on.

"Where you headed?" He's watching me tighten the laces on my shoes. I don't answer him right away because I'm not sure where it is I'm going. I just want to get out of this hotel room. When my shoelaces are tied, I stand up and walk to him, then wrap my arms around him.

"I want to go for a walk," I say. "And I want you to go with me. I'm ready to start asking questions."

He kisses my forehead, then reaches to the table and grabs the room key. "Then let's go." He reaches down and laces my fingers through his.

Our hotel isn't near any parks or walking trails, so instead we just head to the courtyard. There are several cabanas lining the pool, all of them empty. He leads me to one of them. We sit and I lean my head against his shoulder, looking out over the pool. It's October, but the weather is pretty mild. I pull my arms through the sleeves of my shirt and hug myself, snuggling against him.

"You want me to tell you what I remember?" he asks. "Or do you have specific questions?"

"Both. But I want to hear your story first."

His arm is draped over my shoulders. His fingers are stroking my upper arm and he kisses the side of my head. I don't care how many times he kisses me on the head; it always feels like a first.

"You have to understand how surreal this feels for me, Sky. I've thought about what happened to you every single day for the past thirteen years. And to think I've been living two miles away from you for seven of those years? I'm still having a hard time processing it myself. And now, finally having you here, telling you everything that happened . . ."

He sighs and I feel his head lean against the back of the chair. He pauses briefly, then continues. "After the car pulled away, I went into the house and told Les that you left with someone. She kept asking me who, but I didn't know. My mother was in the kitchen, so I went and told her. She didn't really pay any attention to me. She was cooking supper and we were just kids. She had learned to tune us out. Besides, I still wasn't sure anything had happened that wasn't supposed to happen, so I didn't sound panicked or anything. She told me to just go outside and play with Les. The way she was so nonchalant about it made me think everything was okay. Being six years old, I was positive adults knew everything, so I didn't say anything else about it. Les and I went outside to play and another couple of hours had passed by when your dad came outside, calling your name. As soon as I heard him call your name, I froze. I stopped in the middle of my yard and watched him standing on his porch, calling for you. It was that moment that I knew he had no idea you had left with someone. I knew I did something wrong."

"Holder," I interrupt. "You were just a little boy."

He ignores my comment and continues. "Your dad walked over to our yard and asked me if I knew where you were." He pauses and clears his throat. I wait patiently for him to continue, but it seems like he needs to gather his thoughts. Hearing him tell me what happened that day feels like he's telling me a story. It feels nothing like what he's saying is directly related to my life or to me.

"Sky, you have to understand something. I was scared of your father. I was barely six years old and knew I had just done something terribly wrong by leaving you alone. Now your police chief father is standing over me, his gun visible on his uniform. I panicked. I ran back into my house and ran straight to my bedroom and locked the door. He and my mother beat on the door for half an hour, but I was too scared to open it and admit to them that I knew what happened. My reaction worried both of them, so he immediately radioed for backup. When I heard the police cars pull up outside, I thought they were there for me. I still didn't understand what had happened to you. By the time my mother coaxed me out of the room, three hours had already passed since you left in the car."

He's still rubbing my shoulder, but his grip is tighter on me now. I push my arms through the sleeves of my shirt so I can take his hand and hold it.

"I was taken to the station and questioned for hours. They wanted to know if I knew the license plate number, what kind of car took you, what the person looked like, what they said to you. Sky, I didn't know *anything*. I couldn't even remember the color of the car. All I could tell them was exactly what you were wearing, because you were the only thing I could picture in my head. Your dad was furious with me. I could hear him yelling in the hallway of the station that if I had just told someone right when it happened, they would have been able to find you. He blamed me. When a police officer blames you for losing his daughter, you tend to believe he knows what he's talking about. Les heard him yelling, too, so she thought it was all my fault. For days, she wouldn't even talk to me. Both of us were trying to understand what had happened. For six years we lived in this perfect world where adults are always right and bad things don't happen to good people. Then, in the span of a minute, you were taken and everything we thought we knew turned out to be this false image of life that our parents had built for us. We realized that day that even adults do horrible things. Children disappear. Best friends get taken from you and you have no idea if they're even alive anymore.

"We watched the news constantly, waiting for reports. For weeks they would show your picture on TV, asking for leads. The most recent picture they had of you was from right before your mother died, when you were only three. I remember that pissing me off, wondering how almost two years could have gone by without someone having taken a more recent picture. They would show pictures of your house and would sometimes show our house, too. Every now and then, they would mention the boy next door who saw it happen, but couldn't remember any details. I remember one night . . . the last night my mother allowed us to watch the coverage on TV . . . one of the reporters showed a panned-out image of both our houses. They mentioned the only witness, but referred to me as '*The boy who lost Hope.*' It infuriated my mother so bad; she ran outside and began screaming at the reporters, yelling at them to leave us alone. To leave *me* alone. My dad had to drag her back into the house.

"My parents did their best to try to make our life as normal as possible. After a couple of months, the reporters stopped showing up. The endless trips to the police station for more questioning finally stopped. Things began to slowly return to normal for everyone in the neighborhood. Everyone but Les and me. It was like all of our hope was taken right along with our Hope."

Hearing his words and the desolation in his voice causes me nothing but guilt. One would think what happened to me would have been so traumatic that it would have affected me more than the people around me. However, I can barely even remember it. It was such an uneventful occurrence in my life, yet it practically ruined him and Lesslie. Karen was so calm and pleasant, and filled my head with lies about a life of adoption and foster care, that I never thought to even question it. Like Holder said, at such a young age you believe that adults are all so honest and truthful, you never even think to question them.

"I've spent so many years hating my father for giving up on me," I say quietly. "I can't believe she just took me from him. How could she do that? How could *anyone* do that?"

"I don't know, babe."

I sit up straight, then turn around to look him in the eyes. "I need to see the house," I say. "I want more memories, but I don't have any and right now it's hard. I can barely remember anything, much less him. I just want to drive by. I need to see it."

He rubs my arm and nods. "Right now?"

"Yes. I want to go before it gets dark."

The entire drive, I'm absolutely silent. My throat is dry and my stomach is in knots. I'm scared. I'm scared to see the house. I'm scared he might be home and I'm scared I might see him. I don't really want to see him yet; I just want to see the place that was my first home. I don't know if it will help me remember but I know it's something I have to do.

He slows the car down and pulls over to the curb. I'm looking at the row of houses across the street, scared to pull my gaze from my window because it's so hard to turn and look.

"We're here," he says quietly. "It doesn't look like anyone's home."

I slowly turn my head and look out his window at the first home I ever lived in. It's late and the day is being swallowed by night, but the sky is still bright enough that I can clearly make out the house. It looks familiar, but seeing it doesn't immediately bring back any memories. The house is tan with a dark brown trim, but the colors don't look familiar at all. As if Holder can read my mind, he says, "It used to be white."

I turn in my seat and face the house, trying to remember something. I try to visualize walking through the front door and seeing the living room, but I can't. It's like everything about that house and that life has been erased from my mind somehow.

"How can I remember what your living room and kitchen look like, but I can't remember my own?"

He doesn't answer me, because he more than likely knows I'm not really looking for an answer. He just places his hand on top of mine and holds it there while we stare at the houses that changed the paths of our lives forever.

Thirteen years earlier

"Is your daddy giving you a birthday party?" Lesslie asks.

I shake my head. "I don't have birthday parties."

Lesslie frowns, then sits down on my bed and picks up the unwrapped box lying on my pillow. "Is this your birthday present?" she asks.

I take the box out of her hands and set it back on my pillow. "No. My daddy buys me presents all the time."

"Are you going to open it?" she asks.

I shake my head again. "No. I don't want to."

She folds her hands in her lap and sighs, then looks around the room. "You have a lot of toys. Why don't we ever come here and play? We always go to my house and it's boring there."

I sit on the floor and grab my shoes to put them on. I don't tell her I hate my room. I don't tell her I hate my house. I don't tell her we always go to her house because I feel safer over there. I take my shoelaces between my fingers and scoot closer to her on the bed. "Can you tie these?"

She grabs my foot and puts it on her knee. "Hope, you need to learn how to tie your own shoes. Me and Dean knew how to tie our shoes when we were five." She scoots down on the floor and sits in front of me.

"Watch me," she says. "You see this string? Hold it out like this." She puts the strings in my hands and shows me how to wrap it and pull it until it ties like it's supposed to.

When she helps me tie both of them two times, she unties them and tells me to do it again by myself. I try to remember how she showed me to tie them. She stands up and walks to my dresser while I do my very best to loop the shoestring.

"Was this your mom?" she says, holding up a picture. I look at the picture in her hands, then look down at my shoes again.

"Yeah."

"Do you miss her?" she asks.

I nod and keep trying to tie my shoelaces and not think about how much I miss her. I miss her so much.

"Hope, you did it!" Lesslie squeals. She sits back down on the floor in front of me and hugs me. "You did it all by yourself. You know how to tie your shoes now."

I look down at my shoes and smile.

"Lesslie taught me how to tie my shoelaces," I say quietly, still staring at the house.

Holder looks at me and smiles. "You remember her teaching you that?"

"Yeah."

"She was so proud of that," he says, turning his gaze back across the street.

I place my hand on the door handle and open it, then step out. The air is growing colder now, so I reach back into the front seat and grab my hoodie, then slip it on over my head.

"What are you doing?" Holder says.

I know he won't understand and I really don't want him to try to talk me out of it, so I shut the door and cross the street without answering him. He's right behind me, calling my name when I step onto the grass. "I need to see my room, Holder." I continue walking, somehow knowing exactly which side of the house to walk to without having any actual concrete memories of the layout of the house.

"Sky, you can't. No one's here. It's too risky."

I speed up until I'm running. I'm doing this whether he gives me his approval or not. When I reach the window that I'm somehow certain leads to what used to be my bedroom, I turn and look at him. "I need to do this. There are things

298

of my mother's that I want in there, Holder. I know you don't want me to do this, but I need to."

He places his hands on my shoulders and his eyes are concerned. "You can't just break in, Sky. He's a cop. What are you gonna do, bust out the damn window?"

"This house is technically still my home. It's not really breaking in," I reply. He does raise a good point, though. How am I supposed to get inside? I purse my lips and think, then snap my fingers. "The birdhouse! There's a birdhouse on the back porch with a key in it."

I turn and run to the backyard; shocked when I see there actually is a birdhouse. I reach my fingers inside and sure enough, there's a key. The mind is a crazy thing.

"Sky, don't." He's practically begging me not to go through with this.

"I'm going in alone," I say. "You know where my bedroom is. Wait outside the window and let me know if you see anyone pull up."

He sighs heavily, then grabs my arm as soon as I insert the key into the back door. "Please don't make it obvious you were here. And hurry," he says. He pulls me in for a hug, then waits for me to walk inside. I turn the key and check to see if it unlocks the door.

The doorknob turns.

I walk inside and shut the door behind me. The house is dark and sort of eerie. I turn left and walk through the kitchen, somehow knowing exactly where the door to my bedroom is. I'm holding my breath and trying not to think about the seriousness or implications of what I'm doing. The thought of getting caught is terrifying, because I'm still not sure if I even want to be found. I do what Holder says and walk carefully, not wanting to leave any evidence behind that I was here. When I reach my door, I take a deep breath and place my hand on the doorknob, then slowly turn it. When the door opens and the room becomes visible, I flip on the light to get a better look at it.

Other than a few boxes piled into the corner, everything looks familiar. It still looks like a small child's room, untouched for thirteen years. It makes me think of seeing Lesslie's room and how no one has touched it since she died. It must be hard to move past the physical reminders of people you love.

I run my fingers across the dresser and leave a line in the dust. Seeing the trace of my finger quickly reminds me that I'm not wanting to leave evidence of my being here, so I lift my hand and bring it down to my side, then wipe away the trail with my shirt.

The picture of my biological mother isn't on the dresser where I remember it being. I look around the room, hoping to find something of hers that I can take with me. I have no memories of her, so a picture is more than I could ever ask for. I just want something to tie me to her. I need to see what she looks like and hope it will give me any memories at all that I can hold on to.

I walk over to the bed and sit down. The theme in the room is the sky, which is ironic, considering the name Karen gave me. There are clouds and moons on the curtains and walls, and the comforter is covered in stars. There are stars everywhere. The big plastic kind that stick to walls and ceilings and glow in the dark. The room is covered in them, just like the stars that are on my ceiling back at Karen's house. I remember begging Karen for them when I saw them at the store a few years ago. She thought they were childish, but I had to have them. I wasn't even sure why I wanted them so bad, but now it's becoming clear. I must have loved stars when I was Hope.

The nervousness already planted in my stomach intensifies when I lie back on the pillow and look up at the ceiling. A familiar wave of fear washes over me, and I turn to look at the bedroom door. It's the exact same doorknob I was praying wouldn't turn in the nightmare I had the other night.

I suck in a breath and squeeze my eyes shut, wanting the memory to go away. I've somehow locked it away for thirteen years, but being here on this bed . . . I can't lock it away anymore. The memory grabs hold of me like a web, and I can't break out of it. A warm tear trickles down my face and I wish I had listened to Holder. I should never have come back here. If I had never come back, I never would have remembered.

Thirteen years earlier

I used to hold my breath and hope he would think I was sleeping. It doesn't work, because he doesn't care if I'm sleeping or not. One time I tried to hold my breath and hoped he would think I was dead. That didn't work either, because he never even noticed I was holding my breath.

The doorknob turns and I'm all out of tricks right now and I try to think of another one really fast but I can't. He closes the door behind him and I hear his footsteps coming closer. He sits down beside me on my bed and I hold my breath anyway. Not because I think it'll work this time, but because it helps me not feel how scared I am.

"Hey, Princess," he says, tucking my hair behind my ear. "I got you a present."

I squeeze my eyes shut because I do want a present. I love presents and he always buys me the best presents because he loves me. But I hate it when he brings the presents to me at nighttime, because I never get them right away. He always makes me tell him thank you first.

I don't want this present. I don't.

"Princess?"

My daddy's voice always makes my tummy hurt. He always talks to me so sweet and it makes me miss my mommy. I don't remember what her voice sounded like, but daddy said it sounded like mine. Daddy also says that mommy would be sad if I stopped taking his presents because she's

302

not here to take his presents anymore. This makes me sad and I feel really bad, so I roll over and look up at him.

"Can I have my present tomorrow, Daddy?" I don't want to make him sad, but I don't want that box tonight. I don't.

Daddy smiles at me and brushes my hair back. "Sure you can have it tomorrow. But don't you want to thank Daddy for buying it for you?"

My heart starts to beat really loud and I hate it when my heart does that. I don't like the way my heart feels and I don't like the scary feeling in my stomach. I stop looking at my daddy and I look up at the stars instead, hoping I can think about how pretty they are. If I keep thinking about the stars and the sky, maybe it will help my heart to stop beating so fast and my tummy to stop hurting so much.

I try to count them, but I keep stopping at number five. I can't remember what number comes after five, so I have to start over. I have to count the stars over and over and only five at a time because I don't want to feel my daddy right now. I don't want to feel him or smell him or hear him and I have to count them and count them and count them and count them until I don't feel him or hear him or smell him anymore.

Then when my daddy finally stops making me thank him, he pulls my nightgown back down and whispers, "Goodnight, Princess." I roll over and pull the covers over my head and squeeze my eyes shut and I try not to cry again but I do. I cry like I do every time Daddy brings me a present at night.

I hate getting presents.

303

I stand up and look down at the bed, holding my breath in fear of the sounds that are escalating from deep within my throat.

I will not cry.

I will not cry.

Slowly sinking to my knees, I place my hands on the edge of the bed and run my fingers over the yellow stars poured across the deep blue background of the comforter. I stare at the stars until they begin to blur from the tears that are clouding my vision.

I squeeze my eyes shut and bury my head into the bed, grabbing fistfuls of the blanket. My shoulders begin to shake as the sobs I've been trying to contain violently break out of me. With one swift movement, I stand up, scream, and rip the blanket off the bed, throwing it across the room.

I ball my fists and frantically look around for something else to throw. I grab the pillows off the bed and chuck them at the reflection in the mirror of the girl I no longer know. I watch as the girl in the mirror stares back at me, sobbing pathetically. The weakness in her tears infuriates me. We begin to run toward each other until our fists collide against the glass, smashing the mirror. I watch as she falls into a million shiny pieces onto the carpet.

I grip the edges of the dresser and push it sideways, letting out another scream that has been pent up for way too long. When the dresser comes to rest on its back, I rip open the drawers and throw the contents across the room, spinning and throwing and kicking at everything in my path. I grab at the sheer blue curtain panels and yank them until the rod snaps and the curtains fall around me. I reach over to the boxes piled high in the corner and, without even knowing what's inside, I take the top one and throw it against the wall with as much force as my five-foot, three-inch frame can muster.

"I hate you!" I cry. "I hate you, I hate you, I hate you!"

I'm throwing whatever I can find in front of me at whatever else I can find in front of me. Every time I open my mouth to scream, I taste the salt from the tears that are streaming down my cheeks.

Holder's arms suddenly engulf me from behind and grip me so tightly I become immobile. I jerk and toss and scream some more until my actions are no longer thought out. They're just reactions.

"Stop," he says calmly against my ear, unwilling to release me. I hear him, but I pretend not to. Or I just don't care. I continue to struggle against his grasp but he only tightens his grip.

"Don't touch me!" I yell at the top of my lungs, clawing at his arms. Again, it doesn't faze him.

Don't touch me. Please, please, please.

The small voice echoes in my mind, and I immediately become limp in his arms. I become weaker, as my tears grow stronger, consuming me. I become nothing more than a vessel for the tears that won't stop shedding.

I am weak, and I'm letting *him* win.

Holder loosens his grip around me and places his hands on my shoulders, then turns me around to face him. I can't even look at him. I melt against his chest from exhaustion and defeat, taking in fistfuls of his shirt as I sob, my cheek pressed against his heart. He places his hand on the back of my head and lowers his mouth to my ear.

"Sky." His voice is steady and unaffected. "You need to leave. Now."

I can't move. My body is shaking so hard, I'm afraid my legs won't move, even if I will them to. As if he knows this, he scoops me up in his arms and walks me out of the bedroom. He carries me across the street and places me in the passenger seat. He takes my hand and looks at it, then grabs his jacket out of the backseat. "Here, use that to wipe off the blood. I'm going back inside to straighten up what I can." The door shuts and he sprints back across the street. I look down at my hand, surprised that I'm cut. I can't even feel it. I wrap my hand up in the sleeve of his jacket, then pull my knees up into the seat and hug them while I cry.

I don't look at him when he gets back into the car. My whole body is shaking from the sobs that are still pouring out of me. He cranks the car and pulls away, then reaches across the seat and places his hand on the back of my head, stroking my hair in silence the entire way back to the hotel.

He helps me out of the car and walks me back to the hotel room, never once asking me if I'm okay. He knows I'm not; there's really no point in even asking. When the hotel room door closes behind us, he walks me to the bed and I sit. He pushes my shoulders back until I'm flat on the bed and he slips off my shoes. He walks to the bathroom, then comes back with a wet rag and picks up my hand, wiping it clean. He checks it for shards of glass, then gently lifts my hand to his mouth and kisses it.

"It's just a few scratches," he says. "Nothing too deep." He adjusts me onto the pillow and slips his own shoes off, then climbs onto the bed beside me. He pulls the blanket over us and pulls me to him, tucking my head against his chest. He holds me and never once asks me why I'm crying. Just like he used to do when we were kids.

I try to get the images out of my head of what I remember happening to me at night in my room, but they won't go away. How any father could do that to his little girl . . . it's beyond my comprehension. I tell myself that it never happened, that I'm imagining it, but every part of me knows it did happen. Every part of me that remembers why I was happy to get into that car with Karen. Every part of me that remembers all the nights I've made out with guys in my bed, never feeling a single thing while looking up at the stars. Every part of me that broke out into a full-blown panic attack the night Holder and I almost had sex. Every single part of me remembers, and I would do anything just to forget. I don't want to remember how my father sounded or felt at night, but with each passing second the memories become more and more vivid, only making it harder for me to stop crying.

Holder is kissing me on the side of my head, telling me again how it'll be okay, that I shouldn't worry. But he has no idea. He has no idea how much I remember and what it's doing to my heart and my soul and my mind and to my faith in humanity as a whole.

To know that those things were done to me at the hands of the only adult I had in my life—it's no wonder I've blocked everything out. I hold barely any memories of the day I was taken by Karen, and now I know why. It didn't feel like I was in the middle of a calamitous event the moment she stole me away from my life. To a little girl who was terrified of her life, I'm sure it felt more like Karen was rescuing me.

I lift my gaze to Holder's and he's looking down at me. He's hurting for me; I can see it in his eyes. He wipes away my tears with his finger and kisses me softly on the lips. "I'm sorry. I should have never let you go inside."

He's blaming himself again. He always feels like he's done something terrible, when I feel like he's been nothing short of my hero. He's been with me through all of this, steadily carrying me through my panic attacks and freakouts until I'm calm. He's done nothing but be there for me, yet he still feels like this is somehow his fault.

"Holder, you didn't do anything wrong. Stop apologizing," I say through my tears. He shakes his head and tucks a loose strand of hair behind my ear.

"I shouldn't have taken you there. It's too much for you to deal with after just finding everything out."

I lift up on my elbow and look at him. "It wasn't just being there that was too much. It was what I remembered that was too much. You have no control over the things my father did to me. Stop placing blame on yourself for everything bad that happens to the people around you."

He slides his hand up and through my hair with a worried look on his face. "What are you talking about? What things did he do to you?" The words are so hesitant to come out of his mouth because he more than likely knows. I think we've both known what happened to me as a child, we've just been in denial.

I drop my arm and rest my head on his chest and don't answer him. My tears come back full force and he wraps one arm tightly around my back and grips the back of my head with his other. He presses his cheek to the top of my head. "No, Sky," he whispers. "No," he says again, not wanting to believe what I'm not even saying. I grab fistfuls of his shirt and just cry while he holds me with such conviction that it makes me love him for hating my father just as much as I do.

He kisses the top of my head and continues to hold me. He doesn't tell me he's sorry or ask how he can fix it because we both know we're at a loss. Neither of us knows what to do next. All I know at this point is that I have nowhere to go. I can't go back to the father who has rightful custody over me. I can't go back to the woman who wrongfully took me. And with light shed on my past it turns out I'm still underage, so I can't even rely on myself. Holder is the only thing about my life that hasn't left me completely hopeless.

And even though I feel protected wrapped up in his arms, the images and memories won't escape my head and no matter what I do or how hard I try, I can't stop crying. He's quietly holding me and I can't stop thinking about the fact that I need it to stop. I need Holder to take all of these emotions and feelings away for a little while because I can't take it. I don't like remembering what happened all those nights my father came into my room. I hate him. With every ounce of my being, I hate that man for stealing that first away from me.

I lift up and scoot my face closer to Holder, leaning over him. He places his hand on the side of my head and his eyes search mine, wanting to know if I'm okay.

I'm not.

I slide my body on top of his and kiss him, wanting him to take away the feelings. I'd rather feel nothing at all than the hatred and sadness consuming me right now. I grab Holder's shirt and try to lift it over his head, but he pushes me off him and onto my back. He lifts up on his arm and looks down at me.

"What are you doing?" he asks.

I slide my hand behind his neck and pull his face to mine, pressing my lips back to his. If I just kiss him enough, he'll relent and kiss me back. Then it'll all go away.

He places his hand on my cheek and kisses me back momentarily. I let go of his head and start to pull off my shirt, but he pulls my hands away and brings my shirt back down. "Stop it. Why are you doing this?"

His eyes are full of confusion and concern. I can't answer his question about why I'm doing this, because I'm not even sure. I know I just want the feeling to go away, but it's more than that. It's so much more than that, because I know if he doesn't take away what that man did to me right now, I feel like I'll never be able to laugh or smile or breathe again.

I just need Holder to take it away.

I inhale a deep breath and look him directly in the eyes. "Have sex with me."

His expression is unyielding and he's staring at me hard now. He pushes up from the bed and stands up, then paces the floor. He runs his hands through his hair nervously and walks back toward the bed, standing at the edge of it.

"Sky, I can't do this. I don't know why you're even asking for this right now."

I sit up in the bed, suddenly scared that he won't go through with it. I scoot to the edge of the bed where he's standing and I sit up on my knees, grasping his shirt. "Please," I beg. "Please, Holder. I need this."

He pulls my hands from his shirt and takes two steps back. He shakes his head, still completely confused. "I'm not doing this, Sky. *We're* not doing this. You're in shock or something . . . I don't know. I don't even know what to say right now."

I sink back down onto the bed in defeat. The tears start flowing again and I look up at him in complete desperation.

"*Please.*" I drop my gaze to my hands and fold them together in my lap, unable to look him in the eyes when I speak. "Holder . . . he's the only one that's ever done that to me." I slowly raise my eyes back up to meet his. "I need you to take that away from him. *Please.*"

If words could break souls, my words just broke his in two. His face drops and tears fill his eyes. I know what I'm asking him to do and I hate that I'm asking him for this, but I need it. I need to do whatever I can to minimize the pain and the hatred in me. "*Please*, Holder."

He doesn't want our first time to be this way. I wish it wasn't, but sometimes factors other than love make these decisions *for* you. Factors like hate. Sometimes in order to get rid of the hate, you become desperate. He knows hate and he knows pain and right now he knows how much I need this, whether he agrees with it or not.

He walks back to the bed and sinks to his knees on the floor in front of me, bringing himself to my eye level. He grabs my waist and scoots me to the edge of the bed, then slides his hands behind my knees and wraps my legs around him. He pulls my shirt over my head, never once looking away from my eyes. When my shirt is off, he pulls his own shirt off. He wraps his arms around me and stands up, picking me up with him and walking to the side of the bed. He lays me down gently and lowers himself on top of me, then places his palms against the mattress on either side of my head, looking down at me with uncertainty. His finger brushes a tear away that's sliding down my temple. "Okay," he says assuredly, despite his contrasting eyes.

He lifts up onto his knees and reaches to his wallet on the nightstand. He takes a condom out, then removes his pants, never once taking his eyes off mine. He's watching me like he's waiting for any signs that I've changed my mind. Or maybe he's watching me like he is because he's afraid I'm about to have another panic attack. I'm not even sure that I won't, but I have to do this. I can't let my father own this part of me for one more second.

Holder's fingers grasp the button on my jeans and he unbuttons them, then slides them off me. I shift my gaze to the ceiling, feeling myself slip further and further away with every step closer he gets.

I wonder if I'm ruined. I wonder if I'll ever be able to find pleasure in being with him in this way.

He doesn't ask if I'm sure this is what I want. He knows I'm sure, so the question remains unspoken. He lowers his lips to mine and kisses me while he removes my bra and underwear. I'm glad he's kissing me, because it gives me an excuse to close my eyes. I don't like the way he's looking at me . . . like he wishes he were anywhere else right now than here with me. I keep my eyes closed when his lips separate from mine in order for him to put on the condom. When he's back on top of me, I pull him against me, wanting him to do this before he changes his mind.

"Sky."

I open my eyes and see doubt in his expression, so I shake my head. "No, don't think about it. Just do it, Holder."

He closes his eyes and buries his head in my neck, unable to look at me. "I just don't know how to deal with all of this. I don't know if this is wrong or if it's what you really need. I'm scared if I do this, I'll make it even harder for you."

His words cut to my heart, because I know exactly what he means. I don't know if this is what I need. I don't know if it'll ruin things between us. But right now I'm so desperate to take this one thing away from my father—I'd risk it all. My arms that are wrapped tightly around him begin to shake, and I cry. He keeps his head buried in my neck and cradles my face in his hand, but as soon as he hears my tears, I can feel him attempting to hold back his own. The fact that this is causing him just as much distress lets me know that he understands. I tuck my head into his neck and lift myself against him, silently pleading with him to just do what I'm asking.

He does. He positions himself against me, kisses me on the side of the head, then slowly enters me.

I don't make a sound, despite the pain.

I don't even breathe, despite my need for air.

I don't even think about what's going on between us right now, because I'm not thinking at all. I'm picturing the stars on my ceiling and I'm wondering if I just tear the damn things off the ceiling if I'll never have to count them again.

I'm successfully able to keep myself separated from what he's doing until he abruptly stills himself on top of me, his head still buried tightly against my neck. He's breathing heavily and, after a moment, he sighs and separates himself from me completely. He looks down at me and closes his eyes, then rolls away from me, sitting up on the edge of the bed with his back to me.

"I can't do it," he says. "It feels wrong, Sky. It feels wrong because you feel so good but I'm regretting every single fucking second of it." He stands up and pulls his pants on, then grabs his shirt and the room key from the dresser. He never looks back at me as he exits the hotel room without another word.

I immediately crawl off the bed and get in the shower because I feel dirty. I feel guilty for having him do what he just did and I'm hoping the shower will somehow wash away that guilt. I scrub every inch of my body with soap until my skin hurts, but it doesn't help. I've successfully taken another intimate moment and ruined it for him. I could see the shame in his face when he left. When he walked out the door, refusing to look at me.

I turn off the water and step out of the shower. After I dry off, I grab the robe from the back of the bathroom door and put it on. I brush out my hair and place my toiletries back into my cosmetic bag. I don't want to leave without telling Holder, but I can't stay here. I also don't want him to feel like he has to face me again after what just happened. I can call a cab to take me to the bus station and be gone before he comes back.

If he's planning on even coming back.

I open the bathroom door and step out into the hotel

room, not expecting him to be sitting on the bed with his hands clasped between his knees. He darts his eyes up to mine as soon as he sees the bathroom door open. I pause midstep and stare back at him. His eyes are red and he's got a makeshift bandage made out of his T-shirt wrapped around his hand and covered in blood. I rush to him and take his hand, unwrapping the shirt to inspect it.

"Holder, what'd you do?" I twist his hand back and forth and take in the gash across his knuckles. He pulls his hand away and rewraps it with the piece of T-shirt.

"I'm fine," he says, brushing it off. He stands up and I take a step back, expecting him to walk out the door again. Instead, he stays directly in front of me, looking down at me.

"I'm so sorry," I whisper, looking up at him. "I shouldn't have asked you to do that. I just needed—"

He grabs my face and presses his lips to mine, cutting me off midapology. "Shut up," he says, looking into my eyes. "You have absolutely nothing to apologize for. I didn't leave earlier because I was mad at you. I left because I was mad at myself."

I back out of his grasp and turn to the bed, not wanting to watch as he places even more blame on himself. "It's okay." I walk back to the bed and lift the covers. "I can't expect you to want me in that way right now. It was wrong and selfish and way out of line for me to ask you to do that and I'm really sorry." I lie down on the bed and roll away from him so he can't see my tears. "Let's just go to sleep, okay?"

My voice is much calmer than I expected it to be. I really don't want him to feel bad. He's done nothing but be here for me throughout all of this, and I've done nothing for him in return. The best thing I could do for him at this point is to just break it off so he doesn't feel obligated to stand by me through this. He doesn't owe me a thing.

"You think I'm having a hard time with this because I don't *want* you?" He walks around to the side of the bed that I'm facing and he kneels down. "Sky, I'm having a hard time with this because everything that's happened to you is breaking my fucking heart and I have no idea how to help you. I want to be there for you and help you through this but every word that comes out of my mouth feels like the wrong one. Every time I touch you or kiss you, I'm afraid you don't want me to. Now you're asking me to have sex with you because you want to take that from him, and I get it. I absolutely get where you're coming from, but it doesn't make it easier to make love to you when you can't even look me in the eyes. It hurts so much because you don't deserve for it to be like this. You don't deserve this life and there isn't a fucking thing I can do to make it better for you. I want to make it better but I can't and I feel so helpless."

He has somehow sat up on the bed and pulled me to him during all of that, but I was so caught up in his words I didn't even notice. He wraps his arms around me and pulls me onto his lap, then wraps my legs around him. He takes my face in his hands and looks me directly in the eyes.

"And even though I stopped, I should have never even started without telling you first how much I love you. I love you so much. I don't deserve to touch you until you know for a fact that I'm touching you because I love you and for no other reason."

He presses his lips to mine and doesn't even give me a chance to tell him I love him in return. I love him so much it physically hurts. I'm not thinking about anything else right now but how much I love this boy and how much he loves me and how despite what's going on in my life, I wouldn't want to be anywhere else than in this moment with him.

I try to convey everything I'm feeling through my kiss, but it's not enough. I pull away and kiss his chin, then his nose, then his forehead, then I kiss the tear that's rolling down his cheek. "I love you, too. I don't know what I'd do right now if I didn't have you, Holder. I love you so much and I'm so sorry. I wanted you to be my first, and I'm sorry he took that from you."

Holder adamantly shakes his head and shushes me with a quick kiss. "Don't you ever say that again. Don't you ever *think* that again. Your father took that first from you in an unthinkable way, but I can guarantee you that's all he took. Because you are so strong, Sky. You're amazing and funny and smart and beautiful and so full of strength and courage. What he did to you doesn't take away from any of the best parts of you. You survived him once and you'll survive him again. I know you will."

He places his palm over my heart, then pulls my hand to his chest over his own heart. He lowers his eyes to my level, ensuring I'm here with him, giving him my complete attention. "Fuck all the firsts, Sky. The only thing that matters to me with you are the forevers."

I kiss him. Holy *shit*, do I kiss him. I kiss him with every ounce of emotion that's coursing through me. He cradles my head with his hand and lowers me back to the bed, climbing on top of me. "I love you," he says. "I've loved you for so long but I just couldn't tell you. It didn't feel right letting you love me back when I was keeping so much from you."

Tears are streaming down my cheeks again, and even though they're the exact same tears that come from the exact same eyes, they're completely new to me. They aren't tears from heartache or anger . . . they're tears from the incredible feeling overcoming me right now, hearing him say how much he loves me.

"I don't think you could have picked a better time to tell me you loved me than tonight. I'm happy you waited."

He smiles, looking down at me with fascination. He dips his head and kisses me, infusing my mouth with the taste of him. He kisses me softly and gently, delicately sliding his mouth over mine as he unties my robe. I gasp when his hand eases inside, stroking my stomach with his fingertips. The feel of his touch on me right now is a completely different sensation than just fifteen minutes ago. It's a sensation I *want* to feel.

"*God*, I love you," he says, moving his hand from my stomach and across my waist. He slowly trails his fingers down to my thigh and I moan into his mouth, resulting in an even more determined kiss. He places a flat palm on the inside of my leg and puts slight pressure against it, wanting to ease himself against me, but I flinch and become tense. He can feel my involuntary moment of hesitation, so he pulls his lips from mine and looks down at me. "Remember . . . I'm touching you because I love you. No other reason."

I nod and close my eyes, still afraid that the same numbness and fear is about to wash over me again. Holder kisses my cheek and pulls my robe closed.

"Open your eyes," he says gently. When I do, he reaches up and traces a tear with his finger. "You're crying."

I smile up at him reassuringly. "It's okay. They're the good kind of tears."

He nods, but doesn't smile. He studies me for a moment, then takes my hand in his and laces our fingers together. "I want to make love to you, Sky. And I think you want it, too. But I need you to understand something first." He squeezes my hand and bends down, kissing another escaping tear. "I know it's hard for you to allow yourself to feel this. You've gone so long training yourself to block the feelings and emotions out anytime someone touches you. But I want you to know that what your father physically did to you isn't what hurt you as a little girl. It's what he did to your faith in him that broke your heart. You suffered through one of the worst things a child can go through at the hands of your hero . . . the person you idolized . . . and I can't even begin to imagine what that must have felt like. But remember that the things he did to you are in *no way* related to the two of us when we're together like this. When I touch you, I'm touching you because I want to make you happy. When I kiss you, I'm kissing you because you have the most incredible mouth I've ever seen and you know I can't not kiss it. And when I make love to you—I'm doing exactly that. I'm making love to you because I'm in love with you. The negative feeling you've been associating with physical touch your whole life doesn't apply to me. It doesn't apply to *us*. I'm touching you because I'm in love with you and for no other reason."

His gentle words flood my heart and ease my nerves. He kisses me softly and I relax beneath his hand—a hand that's touching me out of nothing but love. I respond by completely dissolving into him, allowing my lips to follow his, my hands to intertwine with his, my rhythm to match his. I quickly become invested, ready to experience him because I *want* to and for no other reason.

"I love you," he whispers.

The entire time he's touching me, exploring me with his hands and his lips and his eyes, he continues to tell me over and over how much he loves me. And for once, I remain completely in the moment, wanting to feel every single thing he's doing and saying to me. When he finally tosses the wrapper aside and readies himself against me, he looks down at me and smiles, then strokes the side of my face with his fingertips.

"Tell me you love me," he says.

I hold his gaze with unwavering confidence, wanting him to feel the honesty in my words. "I love you, Holder. *So* much. And just so you know . . . so did Hope."

His eyebrows draw apart and he lets out a quick rush of air as if he's been holding it in for thirteen years, waiting for those exact words. "I wish you could feel what that just did to me." He immediately covers my mouth with his and the familiar, sweet mixture of him seeps into my mouth at the same moment he pushes inside me, filling me with so much more than just himself. He fills me with his honesty, his love for me, and for a moment . . . he fills me with a piece of our forevers. I grasp his shoulders and move with him, feeling everything. Every single beautiful thing.

I roll over and Holder is sitting up next to me on the bed, looking down at his phone. He shifts his focus to me when I stretch, then bends down to kiss me, but I immediately turn my head.

"Morning breath," I mumble, crawling out of bed. Holder laughs, then returns his attention to his phone. I somehow made it back into my T-shirt overnight, but I'm not even sure when that happened. I take it off and slip into the bathroom to shower. When I'm finished, I walk back into the room and he's packing up our things.

"What are you doing?" I ask, watching him fold my shirt and place it back into the bag. He looks up at me briefly, then back down to the clothes spread out on the bed.

"We can't stay here forever, Sky. We need to figure out what you want to do."

I take a few steps toward him, my heart speeding up in my chest. "But . . . but I don't know yet. I don't even have anywhere to go."

He hears the panic in my voice and walks around the bed, slipping his arms around me. "You have me, Sky. Calm down. We can go back to my house and figure this out. Besides, we're both still in school. We can't just stop going and we definitely can't live in a hotel forever."

The thought of going back to that town, just two miles

321

from Karen, makes me uneasy. I'm afraid being so close to her will incite me to confront her, and I'm not ready to do that yet. I just want one more day. I want to see my old house again for one last time in hopes that it will spark more memories. I don't want to rely on Karen to have to tell me the truth. I want to figure out as much as I can on my own.

"One more day," I say. "Please, let's just stay one more day, then we'll go. I need to try to figure this out and in order to do that, I need to go there one more time."

Holder puts space between us and he eyes me, shaking his head. "No way," he says firmly. "I'm not putting you through that again. You're not going back."

I place my hands on his cheeks reassuringly. "I need to, Holder. I swear I won't get out of the car this time. I swear. But I need to see the house again before we go. I remembered so much while I was there. I just want a few more memories before you take me back and I have to decide what to do."

He sighs and paces the floor, not wanting to agree to my desperate plea.

"Please," I say, knowing he won't be able to say no if I continue to beg. He slowly turns to the bed and picks the bags of clothes up, tossing them toward the closet.

"Fine. I told you I would do whatever it was you felt you needed to do. But I'm not hanging all of those clothes back up," he says, pointing to the bags by the closet.

I laugh and rush to him, throwing my arms around his neck. "You're the best, most understanding boyfriend in the whole wide world."

He sighs and returns my hug. "No, I'm not," he says, pressing his lips to the side of my head. "I'm the most *whipped* boyfriend in the whole wide world."

Out of all the minutes in the day, we *would* pick the same ten minutes to sit across the street from my house that my father picks to pull up into the driveway. As soon as my father's car comes to a stop in front of the garage, Holder lifts his hand to his ignition.

I reach over and place my trembling hand on his. "Don't leave," I say. "I need to see what he looks like."

Holder sighs and forces his head into the back of his seat, knowing full well that we should leave, but also knowing there's no way I'll let him.

I quit looking at Holder and look back at the police cruiser parked in the driveway across the street from us. The door opens and a man steps out, decked out in a uniform. His back is to us and he's holding a cell phone up to his ear. He's in the middle of a conversation, so he pauses in the yard and continues talking into the phone without heading inside. Looking at him, I don't have any reaction at all. I don't feel a single thing until the moment he turns around and I see his face.

"Oh, my God," I whisper aloud. Holder looks at me questioningly and I just shake my head. "It's nothing," I say. "He just looks . . . familiar. I haven't had an image of him in my head at all but if I was to see him walking down the street, I would know him."

We both continue to watch him. Holder's hands are

323

gripping the steering wheel and his knuckles are white. I look down at my own hands and realize I'm gripping the seatbelt in the same fashion.

My father finally pulls the phone from his ear and places it into his pocket. He begins walking in our direction and Holder's hands immediately fall back to the ignition. I gasp quietly, hoping he doesn't somehow know we're watching him. We both realize at the same time that my father is just headed to the mailbox at the end of the driveway, and we immediately relax.

"Have you had enough?" Holder says through gritted teeth. "Because I can't stay here another second without jumping out of this car and beating his ass."

"Almost," I say, not wanting him to do anything stupid, but also not wanting to leave just yet. I watch as my father sorts through the mail, walking back toward the house, and for the first time it hits me.

What if he remarried?

What if he has other children?

What if he's doing this to someone else?

My palms begin to sweat against the slick material of the seatbelt, so I release it and wipe them across my jeans. My hands begin to tremble even more than before. I suddenly can't think of anything other than the fact that I can't let him get away with this. I can't let him walk away, knowing he might be doing this to someone else. I need to know. I owe it to myself and to every single child my father comes in contact with to ensure he's not the evil monster that's painted in my memories. In order to know for sure, I know I need to see him. I need to speak to him. I need to know why he did what he did to me.

When my father unlocks the front door and disappears inside, Holder lets out a huge breath.

"Now?" he says, turning toward me.

I know beyond a doubt he would tackle me right now if he expected me to do what I'm about to do. Just so I don't give off any clues, I force a smile and nod. "Yeah, we can go now."

He places his hand back on the ignition. At the same time he turns his wrist to crank it, I release my seatbelt, swing open the door, and run. I run across the street and across my father's front yard, all the way to the porch. I never even hear Holder coming up behind me. He doesn't make a noise as he wraps his arms around me and physically lifts me off my feet, carrying me back down the steps. He's still carrying me and I'm kicking him, trying to pry his arms from around my stomach.

"What the hell do you think you're *doing*?" He doesn't put me down, he just continues to dominate my strength while he carries me across the yard.

"Let go of me right now, Holder, or I'll scream! I swear to God, I'll scream!"

With that threat, he spins me around to face him and he shakes my shoulders, glaring at me with utter disappointment. "Don't *do* this, Sky. You don't need to face him again, not after what he's done. I want you to give yourself more time."

I look up at him with an ache in my heart that I'm sure is clearly seen in my eyes. "I have to know if he's doing this to anyone else. I need to know if he has more kids. I can't just let it go, knowing what he's capable of. I have to see him. I have to talk to him. I need to know that he's not that man anymore before I can allow myself to get back in that car and just drive away."

He shakes his head. "Don't do this. Not yet. We can make a few phone calls. We'll find out whatever we can online about him first. Please, Sky." He slides his hands from my shoulders to my arms and urges me toward his car. I hesitate, still adamant that I need to see him face to face. Nothing I find out about him online will tell me what I can gain from just hearing his voice or looking him in the eyes.

"Is there a problem here?"

Holder and I both snap our heads in the direction of the voice. My father is standing at the base of the porch steps. He's eyeing Holder, who still has a firm grip on my arms. "Young lady, is this man hurting you?"

The sound of his voice alone makes my knees buckle. Holder can feel me weakening, so he pulls me against his chest. "Let's go," he whispers, wrapping his arm around me and ushering me forward, back toward his car.

"Don't move!"

I freeze, but Holder continues to try to push me forward with more urgency.

"Turn around!" My father's voice is more demanding this time. Holder pauses right along with me now, both of us knowing the ramifications of ignoring the directions of a cop.

"Play it off," Holder says into my ear. "He might not recognize you."

I nod and inhale a deep breath, then we both turn around slowly. My father is several feet away from the house now, closing in on us. He's eyeing me hard, walking toward me with his hand on his holster. I dart my eyes to the

ground, because his face is full of recognition and it terrifies me. He stops several feet from us and pauses. Holder
tightens his grip around me and I continue to stare at the
ground, too scared to even breathe.

"*Princess?*"

Monday, October 29, 2012
4:35 p.m.

"Don't you fucking touch her!"

Holder is yelling and there's pressure under my arms. His voice is close, so I know he's holding me. I drop my hands to my sides and feel grass between my fingers.

"Baby, open your eyes. Please." Holder's hand is caressing the side of my face. I slowly open my eyes and look up. He's looking down at me, my father hovering right behind him. "It's okay, you just passed out. I need you to stand up. We need to leave."

He pulls me to my feet and keeps his arm around my waist, practically doing the standing for me.

My father is right in front of me now, staring. "It *is* you," he says. He glances at Holder, then back to me. "Hope? Do you remember me?" His eyes are full of tears.

Mine aren't.

"Let's go," Holder says again. I resist his pull and step out of his grasp. I look back at my father . . . at a man who is somehow exhibiting emotions as if he once must have loved me. He's full of shit.

"Do you?" he says again, taking another step closer. Holder inches me back with each step closer my father gets. "Hope, do you remember me?"

"How could I *forget* you?"

The irony is, I *did* forget him. Completely. I forgot all

about him and the things he did to me and the life I had here. But I don't want him to know that. I want him to know that I remember him, and every single thing he ever did to me.

"It's you," he says, fidgeting his hand down at his side. "You're alive. You're okay." He pulls out his radio, I'm assuming in an attempt to call in the report. Before his finger can even press the button, Holder reaches out and knocks the radio out of his hand. It falls to the ground and my father bends down and grabs it, then takes a defensive step back, his hand resting on his holster again.

"I wouldn't let anyone know she's here if I were you," Holder says. "I doubt you would want the fact that you're a fucking pervert to be front-page news."

All the color immediately washes from my father's face and he looks back at me with fear in his eyes. *"What?"* He's looking at me in disbelief. "Hope, whoever took you . . . they lied to you. They told you things about me that weren't true." He's closer now and his eyes are desperate and pleading. "Who took you, Hope? Who was it?"

I take a confident step toward him. "I remember everything you did to me. And if you just give me what I'm here for, I swear I'll walk away and you'll never hear from me again."

He continues to shake his head, disbelieving the fact that his daughter is standing right in front of him. I'm sure he's also trying to process the fact that his whole life is now in jeopardy. His career, his reputation, his freedom. If it were possible, his face grows even paler when he realizes that he can't deny it any longer. He knows I know.

"What is it you want?"

I look toward the house, then back to him again. "Answers," I say. "And I want anything you have that belonged to my mother."

Holder has a death grip on my waist again. I reach down and grip his hand with mine, just needing the reassurance that I'm not alone right now. My confidence is quickly fading with each moment spent in my father's presence. Everything about him, from his voice to his facial expressions to his movements, makes my stomach ache.

My father glances at Holder briefly, then turns to look at me again. "We can talk inside," he says quietly, his eyes darting around to the houses surrounding us. The fact that he appears nervous now only proves that he's weighed his options and he doesn't have very many to choose from. He nudges his head toward the front door and begins making his way up the steps.

"Leave your gun," Holder says.

My father pauses, but doesn't turn around. He slowly reaches to his side and removes his gun. He places it gently on the steps of the porch, then begins to ascend the stairs.

"Both of them," Holder says.

My father pauses again before reaching the door. He bends down to his ankle and lifts his pant leg, then removes that gun as well. Once both guns are out of his reach, he walks inside, leaving the door open for us. Before I step inside, Holder spins me around to face him.

"I'm staying right here with the door open. I don't trust him. Don't go any farther than the living room."

I nod and he kisses me quick and hard, then releases me. I step into the living room and my father is sitting on his couch, his hands clasped in front of him. He's staring down at the floor. I walk to the seat nearest me and sit on the edge of it, refusing to relax into it. Being in this house and in his presence is causing my mind to clutter and my chest to tighten. I take several slow breaths, attempting to calm my fear.

I use the moment of silence between us to find something in his features that resembles mine. The color of his hair, maybe? He's much taller than me and his eyes, when he's able to look at me, are dark green, unlike mine. Other than the caramel color of his hair, I look nothing like him. I smile at the fact that I look nothing like him.

My father lifts his eyes to mine and he sighs, shifting uncomfortably. "Before you say anything," he says. "You need to know that I loved you and I've regretted what I did every second of my life."

I don't verbally respond to that statement, but I have to physically restrain myself from reacting to his bullshit. He could spend the rest of his life apologizing and it would never be enough to erase even one of the nights my doorknob turned.

"I want to know why you did it," I say with a shaky voice. I hate that I sound so pathetically weak right now. I sound like the little girl who used to beg him to stop. I'm not that little girl anymore and I sure as hell don't want to appear weak in front of him.

He leans back in his seat and rubs his hands over his eyes. "I don't know," he says, exasperated. "After your mother died, I started drinking heavily again. It wasn't until a year later that I got so drunk one night that I woke up the next morning and knew I had done something terrible. I was hoping it was just a horrible dream, but when I went to wake you up that morning you were . . . different. You weren't the same happy little girl you used to be. Overnight, you somehow became someone who was terrified of me. I hated myself. I'm not even sure what I did to you because I was too drunk to remember. But I knew it was something awful and I am so, so sorry. It never happened again and I did everything I could to make it up to you. I bought you presents all the time and gave you whatever you wanted. I didn't want you to remember that night."

I grip my knees in an attempt not to leap across the living room and strangle him. The fact that he's trying to play it off as happening one time makes me hate him even more than before, if that's even possible. He's treating it like it was an accident. Like he broke a coffee mug or had a fucking fender bender.

"It was night . . . after night . . . after night," I say. I'm having to muster up every ounce of control I can find to not scream at the top of my lungs. "I was scared to go to bed and scared to wake up and scared to take a bath and scared to speak to you. I wasn't a little girl afraid of monsters in her closet or under her bed. I was terrified of the monster that was supposed to love me! You were supposed to be *protecting* me from the people like you!"

Holder is kneeling at my side now, gripping my arm as I scream at the man across the room. My whole body is shaking and I lean into Holder, needing to feel his calmness. He rubs my arm and kisses my shoulder, letting me get out the things I need to say without once trying to stop me.

My father sinks back into his seat and tears begin flowing from his eyes. He doesn't defend himself, because he knows I'm right. He has nothing at all to say to me. He just cries into his hands, feeling sorry that he's finally being confronted, and not at all sorry for what he actually did.

"Do you have any other children?" I ask, glaring at the eyes so full of shame that they can't even make contact with mine. He drops his head and presses a palm to his forehead, but fails to answer me. "*Do* you?" I yell. I need to know that he hasn't done this to anyone else. That he's not *still* doing it.

He shakes his head. "No. I never remarried after your mother." His voice is defeated and from the looks of him, so is he.

"Am I the only one you did this to?"

He keeps his eyes trained to the floor, continuing to avoid my line of questions with long pauses. "You owe me the truth," I say, steadily. "Did you do this to anyone else before you did it to me?"

I can sense him closing up. The hardness in his eyes makes it evident that he has no intention of revealing any more truths. I drop my head into my hands, not knowing what to do next. It feels so wrong leaving him to live his life like he is, but I'm also terrified of what might happen if I report him. I'm scared of how much my life will change. I'm scared that no one will believe me, since it was so many years ago. But what terrifies me more than any of that is the fear that I love him too much to want to ruin the rest of his life. Being in his presence not only reminds me of all the horrible things he did to me, it also reminds me of the father he once was underneath all of that. Being inside this house is causing a hurricane of emotions to build within me. I look at the table in the kitchen and begin to recall good memories of conversations we had sitting there. I look at the back door and remember us running outside to go watch the train pass by in the field behind our house. Everything about my surroundings is filling me with conflicting memories, and I don't like loving him just as much as I hate him.

I wipe tears from my eyes and look back at him. He's staring silently down at the floor and as much as I try not to, I see glimpses of my daddy. I see the man who loved me like he used to love me . . . long before I became terrified of the doorknob turning.

Fourteen years earlier

"Shh," she says, brushing the hair behind my ears. We're both lying on my bed and she's behind me, snuggling me against her chest. I've been up sick all night. I don't like being sick, but I love the way my mommy takes care of me when I am.

I close my eyes and try to fall asleep so I'll feel better. I'm almost asleep when I hear my doorknob turn, so I open my eyes. My daddy walks in and smiles down at my mommy and me. He stops smiling when he sees me, though, because he can tell I don't feel good. My daddy doesn't like it when I feel sick because he loves me and it makes him sad.

He sits down on his knees next to me and touches my face with his hand. "How's my baby girl feeling?" he says.

"I don't feel good, Daddy," I whisper. He frowns when I say that. I should have just told him I felt good so he wouldn't frown.

He looks up at my mommy, lying in bed behind me, and he smiles at her. He touches her face just like he touched mine. "How's my other girl?"

I can feel her touch his hand when he talks to her. "Tired," she says. "I've been up all night with her."

He stands up and pulls her hand until she stands up, too. I watch him wrap his arms around her and hug her, then he kisses her on the cheek. "I'll take it from here," he says, running his hand down her hair. "You go get some rest, okay?"

My mommy nods and kisses him again, then walks out of the room. My daddy walks around the bed and he lies in the same spot my mommy was in. He wraps his arms around me just like she did, and he starts singing me his favorite song. He says it's his favorite song, because it's about me.

> "I've lost a lot in my long life.
> Yes, I've seen pain and I've seen strife.
> But I'll never give up; I'll never let go.
> Because I'll always have my ray of hope."

I smile, even though I don't feel good. My daddy keeps singing to me until I close my eyes and fall asleep.

It's the first memory I've had before all of the bad stuff took over. My only memory from before my mother died. I still don't remember what she looked like because the memory was more of a blur, but I remember how I felt. I loved them. *Both* of them.

My father looks up at me now, his face completely awash in sorrow. I have no sympathy for him whatsoever because . . . where was *my* sympathy? I do know that he's in a vulnerable position right now and if I can use that to my advantage in order to pull the truth from him, then that's what I'm going to do.

I stand up and Holder tries to take my arm, so I look down at him and shake my head. "It's okay," I assure him. He nods and reluctantly releases me, allowing me to walk toward my father. When I reach him, I kneel down on the floor in front of him, looking up into eyes full of regret. Being this close to him is causing my body to tense and the anger in my heart to build, but I know I have to do this if I want him to give me the answers I need. He needs to believe I'm sympathizing with him.

"I was sick," I say, calmly. "My mother and I . . . we were in my bed and you came home from work. She had been up with me all night and she was tired, so you told her to go get some rest."

A tear rolls down my father's cheek and he nods, but barely.

"You held me that night like a father is supposed to hold his daughter. And you sang to me. I remember you used to sing a song to me about your ray of hope." I wipe the tears out of my eyes and keep looking up at him. "Before my mother died . . . before you had to deal with that heartache . . . you didn't always do those things to me, did you?"

He shakes his head and touches my face with his hand. "No, Hope. I loved you so much. I still do. I loved you and your mother more than life itself, but when she died . . . the best parts of me died right along with her."

I fist my hands, recoiling slightly at the feel of his fingertips on my cheek. I push through, though, and somehow keep myself calm. "I'm sorry you had to go through that," I say firmly. And I *am* sorry for him. I remember how much he loved my mother, and regardless of how he dealt with his grief, I can find it in me to wish he never had to experience her loss.

"I know you loved her. I remember. But knowing that doesn't make it any easier to find it in my heart to forgive you for what you did. I don't know why whatever is inside of you is so different from what's inside other people . . . to the point that you would allow yourself to do what you did to me. But despite the things you did to me, I know you love me. And as hard as it is to admit . . . I once loved you, too. I loved all the good parts of you."

I stand up and take a step back, still looking into his eyes. "I know you aren't all bad. I *know* that. But if you love me like you say you do . . . if you loved my mother at *all* . . . then you'll do whatever you can to help me heal. You owe me that much. All I want is for you to be honest so I can leave here with some semblance of peace. That's all I'm here for, okay? I just want peace."

He's sobbing now, nodding his head into his hands. I walk back to the couch and Holder wraps his arm tightly around me, still kneeling next to me. Tremors are still wracking my body, so I wrap my arms around myself. Holder can feel what this is doing to me, so he slides his fingers down my arm until he finds my pinky, then wraps his around it. It's an extremely small gesture, but he couldn't have done anything more perfect to fill me with the sense of security that I need from him right now.

My father sighs heavily, then drops his hands. "When I first started drinking . . . it was only once. I did something to my little sister . . . but it was only one time." He looks back up at me and his eyes are still full of shame. "It was years before I met your mother."

My heart breaks at his brutal honesty, but it breaks even more that he somehow thinks it's okay that it only happened once. I swallow the lump in my throat and continue my questions. "What about *after* me? Have you done it to anyone else since I was taken?"

His eyes dart back to the floor and the guilt in his demeanor is like a punch straight to my gut. I gasp, holding back the tears. "Who? How many?"

He shakes his head slightly. "There was just one more. I stopped drinking a few years ago and haven't touched anyone since." He looks back up at me, his eyes desperate and hopeful. "I swear. There were only three and they were at the lowest points of my life. When I'm sober, I'm able to control my urges. That's why I don't drink anymore."

"Who was she?" I ask, wanting him to have to face the truth for just a few more minutes before I walk out of his life forever.

He nudges his head to the right. "She lived in the house next door. They moved when she was around ten, so I don't know what happened to her. It was years ago, Hope. I haven't done it in years and that's the truth. I swear."

My heart suddenly weighs a thousand pounds. The grip around my arm is gone and I look up to see Holder falling apart right before my eyes.

His face contorts into an unbearable amount of agony and he turns away from me, pulling his hands through his hair. "Les," he whispers painfully. "Oh, God, no." He presses his head into the doorframe, tightly gripping the back of his neck with both hands. I immediately stand and walk to him, placing my hands on his shoulders, fearing that he's about to explode. He begins to shake and he's crying, not even making a sound. I don't know what to say or what to do. He just keeps saying "no" over and over, shaking his head. My heart is breaking for him, but I have no clue how to help him right now. I understand what he means by thinking everything he says to me is the wrong thing, because there's absolutely nothing I could say to him right now that could help. Instead, I press my head against him and he turns slightly, cradling me in his arm.

The way his chest is heaving, I can feel him trying to keep his anger at bay. His breaths begin to come in sharp spurts as he attempts to calm himself. I grip him tighter, hoping to be able to keep him from unleashing his anger. As much as I want him to . . . as much as I want him to physically retaliate against my father for what he did to Les and me, I fear that in this moment, Holder is full of too much hate to find it in himself to stop.

He releases his hold and brings his hands up to my

shoulders, pushing me away from him. The look in his eyes is so dark; it immediately sends me into defense mode. I step between him and my father, not knowing what else I can do to keep him from attacking, but it's as though I'm not even here. When Holder looks at me, he looks straight through me. I can hear my father stand up behind me and I watch as Holder's eyes follow him. I spin around, prepared to tell my father to get the hell out of the living room, when Holder grips my arms and shoves me out of the way.

I trip and fall to the floor, watching in slow motion as my father reaches behind the couch and spins around, holding a gun in his hand, pointing it directly at Holder. I can't speak. I can't scream. I can't move. I can't even close my eyes. I'm forced to watch.

My father pulls his radio to his mouth, holding the gun firmly in his hand with a lifeless expression. He presses the button and never takes his eyes off Holder while he speaks into it. "Officer down at thirty-five twenty-two Oak Street."

My eyes immediately dart to Holder, then back to my father. The radio drops from his hands and onto the floor in front of me. I pull myself up, still unable to scream. My father's defeated eyes fall on mine as he slowly turns the gun and points it at himself. "I'm so sorry, Princess."

The sound explodes, filling the entire room. It's so loud. I squeeze my eyes shut and cover my ears, not sure where the sound is even coming from. It's a high-pitched noise, like a scream. It sounds like a girl screaming.

It's me.

I'm screaming.

I open my eyes and see my father's lifeless body just feet in front of me. Holder's hand clamps over my mouth and he lifts me up, pulling me out the front door. He's not even trying to carry me. My heels are dragging in the grass and he's holding on to my mouth with one hand and my waist with his other arm. When we reach the car, he keeps his hand clamped tight, muffling my scream. He's looking around frantically, making sure no one is witnessing whatever chaos this is going on right now. My eyes are wide and I'm shaking my head out of denial, expecting the last minute of my life to just go away if I refuse to believe it.

"Stop. I need you to stop screaming. Right now."

I nod vigorously, somehow silencing the involuntary sound coming from my mouth. I'm trying to breathe and I can hear the air being sucked in and out of my nose in quick spurts. My chest is heaving and when I notice the blood splattered across the side of Holder's face, I try not to scream again.

"Do you hear that?" Holder says. "Those are sirens, Sky. They'll be here in less than a minute. I'm removing my hand and I need you to get in the car and be as calm as you can because we need to get out of here."

I nod again and he removes his hand from my mouth, then shoves me into the car. He runs around to his side and quickly climbs in, then cranks the car and pulls onto the road. We round the corner just as two police cars turn the corner at the opposite end of the road behind us. We drive away and I drop my head between my knees, attempting to catch a breath. I don't even think about what just happened. I can't. It didn't happen. It couldn't have. I focus on the fact that this is all a horrible nightmare, and I just breathe. I breathe just to make sure I'm still alive, because this sure as hell doesn't feel like life.

We both move through the hotel room door like zombies.
I don't even remember getting from the car into the hotel.
When he reaches the bed, Holder sits and removes his
shoes. I've only made it a few feet, paused where the entryway meets the room. My hands are at my sides and my head
is tilted. I'm staring at the window across the room. The
curtain panels are open, revealing nothing but a gloomy
view of the brick building just feet away from the hotel. Just
a solid wall of brick with no visible windows or doors. Just
brick.

Looking out the window at the brick wall is how I feel
when I view my own life. I try to look to the future, but I
can't see past this moment. I have no idea what's going to
happen, who I'll live with, what will happen to Karen, if I'll
report what just happened. I can't even venture a guess. It's
nothing but a solid wall between this moment and the next,
without so much as a clue sprawled across it in spray paint.

For the past thirteen years, my life has been nothing but
a brick wall separating the first few years from the rest. A
solid block, separating my life as Sky from my life as Hope.
I've heard about people somehow blocking out traumatic
memories, but I always thought that maybe it was more of
a choice. I literally, for the past thirteen years, have not had
a single clue who I used to be. I know I was young when I

was taken from that life, but even then I would assume I would have a few memories. I guess the moment I pulled away with Karen, I somehow made a conscious decision, at that young age, to never recall those memories. Once Karen began telling me stories of my "adoption," it must have been easier for my mind to grasp the harmless lies than to remember my ugly truth.

I know I couldn't explain at the time what my father was doing to me, because I wasn't sure. All I knew was that I hated it. When you aren't sure what it is you hate or why you even hate it, it's hard to hold on to the details . . . you just hold on to the feelings. I know I've never really been all that curious to delve up information about my past. I've never really been that curious to find out who my father was or why he "put me up for adoption." Now I know it's because somewhere in my mind, I still harbored hatred and fear for that man, so it was just easier to erect the brick wall and never look back.

I still do harbor hatred and fear for him, and he can't even touch me anymore. I still hate him, and I'm still scared to death of him, and I'm still devastated that he's dead. I hate him for instilling awful things in my memory and somehow making me grieve for him in the midst of all the awful. I don't want to grieve over his loss. I want to rejoice in it, but it's just not in me.

My jacket is being removed. I look away from the brick wall taunting me from outside the window and turn my head around to see Holder standing behind me. He lays my jacket across a chair, then takes off my blood-splattered shirt. A raw sadness consumes me, realizing I'm genetically linked to the lifeless blood now covering my clothes and face. Holder walks around to my front and reaches down to the button on my jeans and unbuttons them.

He's in his boxer shorts. I never even noticed he took off his clothes. My eyes travel up to his face and he's got specks of blood on his right cheek, the one that was exposed to the cowardliness of my father. His eyes are heavy, keeping them focused on my pants as he slides them down my legs.

"I need you to step out of them, babe," he says softly when he reaches my feet. I grasp his shoulders with my hands and take one foot out of my jeans, then the other. I keep my hands on his shoulders and my eyes trained on the blood splattered in his hair. I mechanically reach over and slip my fingers over a strand of his hair, then pull my hand up to inspect it. I slide the blood around between my fingertips, but it's thick. It's thicker than blood should be.

That's because it's not only my father's *blood* that's all over us.

I begin wiping my fingers across my stomach, frantically trying to get it off me, but I'm just smearing it everywhere. My throat closes up and I can't scream. It's like the dreams I've had where something is so terrifying, I lose any ability to make a sound. Holder looks up and I want to scream and yell and cry, but the only thing I can do is widen my eyes and shake my head and continue to wipe my hands across my body. When he sees me panicking, he stands straight up and lifts me into his arms, then swiftly carries me to the shower. He sets me down at the opposite end from the showerhead, then steps in with me and turns the water on. He closes the shower curtain once the water is warm, then he turns to face me and grabs my wrists that are still attempting to wipe the redness away. He pulls me to him and turns us both to where I'm standing under the warm stream of water. When the water splashes me in the eyes, I gasp and suck in a huge breath of air.

He reaches down to the side of the tub and grabs the bar of soap, tearing off the soaked paper packaging. He leans out of the shower and pulls back in, holding a washcloth. My whole body is shaking now, even though the water is warm. He rubs soap and water into the washcloth, then presses it to my cheek.

"Shh," he whispers, staring into my panic-stricken eyes. "I'm getting it off you, okay?"

He begins gently wiping my face and I squeeze my eyes shut and nod. I keep my eyes closed because I don't want to see the blood-tinted washcloth when he pulls it away from my face. I wrap my arms around myself and remain as still as possible under his hand, aside from the tremors still wracking my body. It takes him several minutes of wiping the blood away from my face and arms and stomach. Once he finishes that task, he reaches behind my head and removes my ponytail holder.

"Look at me, Sky." I open my eyes and he places his fingers lightly on my shoulder. "I'm going to take off your bra now, okay? I need to wash your hair and I don't want to get anything on it."

Get anything on it?

When I realize he's referring to what's more than likely embedded throughout my hair, I begin to panic again and pull the straps of my bra down, then just pull the bra over my head.

"Get it out," I say quietly and quickly, leaning my head back into the water, attempting to saturate my hair by running my fingers through it under the stream. "Just get it *off* me." My voice is more panicky now.

He grabs my wrists again and pulls them away from my hair, then wraps them around his waist.

"I'll get it. Hold on to me and try to relax. I'll do it."

I press my head against his chest and tighten my hold around him. I can smell the shampoo as he pours it into his hands and brings the liquid to my hair, spreading it around with his fingertips. He scoots us a step closer until the water touches my head, which is pressed into his shoulder. He massages and scrubs my hair, rinsing it repeatedly. I don't even ask why he keeps rinsing it; I just let him rinse it as many times as he needs to.

Once he's finished, he turns us around in the shower until he's under the stream of water and he runs the shampoo through his own hair. I release my hold from around his waist and back away from him, not wanting to feel like there's anything getting on me again. I look down at my stomach and hands and don't see any traces of my father left on me. I look back up at Holder and he's scrubbing his face and neck with a fresh washcloth. I stand there, watching him calmly wash away what happened to us no less than an hour ago.

When he's finished, he opens his eyes and looks down at me with regret. "Sky, I need you to make sure I got it all, okay? I need you to wipe away anything I missed."

He's talking to me so calmly, like he's trying not to break me. It's his voice that makes me realize that's exactly what he's trying to avoid. He's afraid I'm about to break, or crack, or flip out.

I'm scared he might be right, so I take the washcloth

out of his hands and force myself to be strong and inspect him. There's still a small area of blood over his right ear, so I reach the washcloth up and wipe it away. I pull the washcloth back and look down at the last speck of blood left on the two of us, then I run it under the stream of water and watch as it washes away.

"It's all gone," I whisper. I'm not even sure I'm referring to the blood.

Holder takes the washcloth out of my hand and tosses it onto the edge of the tub. I look up at him, and his eyes are redder than before and I can't tell if he's crying, because the water is running down his face in the same pattern that tears would be if they were even there. It's then, when all of the physical remnants of my past are washed away, that I'm reminded of Lesslie.

My heart breaks all over again, this time for Holder. A sob breaks out of me and I slap my hand over my mouth, but my shoulders continue to shake. He pulls me to his chest and presses his lips to my hair.

"Holder, I'm so sorry. Oh, my God, I'm so sorry." I'm crying and holding on to him, wishing his hopelessness were as easy to wash away as the blood. He's holding me so tightly, I can barely breathe. But he needs this. He needs me to feel his pain right now, just like I need for him to feel mine.

I take every single word my father said today and attempt to cry them out of me. I don't want to remember his face. I don't want to remember his voice. I don't want to remember how much I hate him and I especially don't want to remember how much I loved him. There's nothing like the guilt you feel when there's room in your heart to love evil.

Holder moves one of his hands to the back of my head

and pulls my face against his shoulder. His cheek presses against the top of my head and I can hear him crying now. It's quiet and he's trying so hard to hold it in. He's in so much pain because of what my father did to Lesslie, and I can't help but place some of that blame on myself. If I had been around, he never would have touched Lesslie and she never would have suffered. If I had never climbed into that car with Karen, Lesslie might still be alive today.

I curl my hands up behind Holder's arms and grip his shoulders. I lift my cheek and turn my mouth toward his neck, kissing him softly. "I'm so sorry. He never would have touched her if I . . ."

Holder grips my arms and pushes me away from him with such force, my eyes widen and I flinch when he speaks. "Don't you dare say that." He releases his hold and swiftly brings his hands to my face, gripping me tightly. "I don't ever want you to apologize for a single thing that man did. Do you hear me? It's not your fault, Sky. Swear to me you will never let a thought like that consume you ever again." His eyes are desperate and full of tears.

I nod. "I swear," I say weakly.

He never looks away, searching my eyes for truth. His reaction has left my heart pounding, shocked at how quick he was to dismiss any fault I may have had. I wish he was just as quick to dismiss his own faults, but he isn't.

I can't take the look in his eyes, so I throw my arms around his neck and hug him. He tightens his grip around me and holds me with pained desperation. The truth about Lesslie and the reality of what we just witnessed hits us both, and we cling to each other with everything we have. He's finished trying to be strong for me. The love he had for Lesslie and the anger he's feeling over what happened to her are pouring out of him.

I know Lesslie would need him to feel her heartache, so I don't even try to comfort him with words. We both cry for her now, because she had no one to cry for her then. I kiss the side of his head, my hands gripping his neck. Each time my lips touch him, he holds me just a little bit tighter. His mouth grazes my shoulder and soon we're both attempting to kiss away every ounce of the heartache that neither one of us deserves. His lips become adamant as he kisses my neck harder and faster, desperately trying to find an escape. He pulls back and looks into my eyes, his shoulders rising and falling with every breath he's struggling to find.

In one swift movement, he crashes his lips to mine with an intense urgency, gripping my hair and my back with his trembling hands. He pushes my back against the shower wall as he slides his hands down behind my thighs. I can feel the despair pouring out of him as he lifts me up and wraps my legs around his waist. He wants his pain to go away, and he needs me to help him. Just like I needed him last night.

I wrap my arms around his neck, pulling him against me, allowing him to consume me for a break from his heartache. I let him, because I need a break just as badly as he does right now. I want to forget about everything else.

I don't want this to be our life tonight.

With his body pressing me into the wall of the shower, he uses his hands to grip the sides of my face, holding me still as our mouths anxiously search each other's for any semblance of relief from our reality. I'm grasping his upper back with my arms as his mouth moves frenziedly down my neck.

"Tell me this is okay," he says breathlessly against my skin. He lifts his face back to mine, nervously searching my eyes as he speaks. "Tell me it's okay to want to be inside you right now . . . because after everything we've been through today, it feels wrong to need you like I do."

I grip his hair and pull him closer, covering his mouth with mine, kissing him with such conviction that my words aren't even needed. He groans and separates me from the shower wall, then walks out of the bathroom to the bed with me still wrapped around him. He's not being gentle at all with the way he rips off the last two items of clothing between us and ravishes my mouth with his, but I honestly don't know if my heart could take gentle right now.

He's standing at the edge of the bed leaning over me, his mouth meshed to mine. He breaks apart momentarily to put on a condom, then he grabs my waist and pulls me to the edge of the bed with him. He lifts my leg behind the knee and brings it up to his side, then slides his hand underneath my arm and grips my shoulder. The moment his eyes fall back to mine, he pushes himself into me without hesitation. I gasp from the sudden force of him, shocked by the intense pleasure that takes over the momentary flash of pain. I wrap my arms around him and move with him as he grips my leg tighter, then covers my mouth with his. I close my eyes and let my head sink deeper into the mattress as we use our love to temporarily ease the anguish.

His hands move to my waist and he pulls me against him, digging his fingers deeper into my hips with each frantic, rhythmic movement against me. I grab hold of his arms and relax my body, allowing him to guide me in whatever way can help him right now. His mouth breaks away and he opens his eyes at the same time I open mine. His eyes are still fresh with tears, so I let go of him and bring my hands to his face, attempting to soothe his pained features with my touch. He continues looking at me, but he turns his head and kisses the inside of my palm, then drops himself on top of me, stopping suddenly.

We're both panting for air and I can feel him inside me, still needing me. He keeps his eyes locked with mine as he slides his arms underneath my back and pulls me to him, lifting us both up. We never separate as he turns us around and slides himself down to the floor with his back against the bed, me straddling his lap. He slowly pulls me in for a kiss. A gentle kiss this time.

The way he's holding me against him protectively now, trailing kisses along my lips and jaw—it's almost as if he's a different Holder than the one I had just thirty seconds ago, yet still wholly passionate. One minute he's frantic and heated . . . the next minute he's gentle and coaxing. I'm beginning to appreciate and love the unexpectedness in him.

I can feel him wanting me to take control now, but I'm nervous. I'm not sure that I even know how. He senses my unease and he moves his hands to my waist, slowly guiding me, barely moving me on top of him. He's watching me earnestly, making sure I'm still here with him.

I *am*. I'm so completely here with him right now I can think of nothing else.

He brings one of his hands to my face, still guiding me with his other hand on my waist. "You know how I feel about you," he says. "You know how much I love you. You know I would do whatever I could to take away your pain, right?"

I nod, because I do know. And looking into his eyes

right now, seeing the raw honesty in them, I know he's felt this way about me long before this moment.

"I need that from you so fucking bad right now, Sky. I need to know you love me like that."

Everything about him, from his voice to the look on his face, becomes tortured. I would do whatever it took to take that away from him. I lace our fingers together and cover both our hearts with our hands, working up the courage to show him how incredibly much I love him. I stare him straight in the eyes as I lift up slightly, then slowly lower myself back down on top of him.

He groans heavily, then closes his eyes and leans his head back, letting it fall against the mattress behind him.

"Open your eyes," I whisper. "I want you to watch me."

He raises his head, looking at me through hooded eyes. I continue to slowly take control, wanting nothing more than for him to hear and feel and see just how much he means to me. Being in control is a completely different sensation, but it's a good one. The way he's watching me makes me feel needed like no one's ever been able to make me feel. In a way, he makes me feel *necessary*. Like my existence alone is necessary for his survival.

"Don't look away again," I say, easing myself up. When I lower myself back onto him, his head sways slightly from the intensity of the sensation and a moan escapes my throat, but he keeps his tortured eyes locked firmly on mine. I'm no longer in need of his guidance, and my body becomes a rhythmic reflection of his.

"The first time you kissed me?" I say. "That moment when your lips touched mine? You stole a piece of my heart that night." I continue my rhythm as he watches me fervently. "The first time you told me you lived me because you weren't ready to tell me you loved me yet?" I press my hand harder against his chest and move myself in closer to him, wanting him to feel every part of me. "Those words stole another piece of my heart."

He opens his hand that I have pressed over my heart until his palm is flat against my skin. I do the same to him. "The night I found out I was Hope? I told you I wanted to be alone in my room. When I woke up and saw you in my bed I wanted to cry, Holder. I wanted to cry because I needed you there with me so bad. I knew in that moment that I was in love with you. I was in love with the way you loved me. When you wrapped your arms around me and held me, I knew that no matter what happened with my life, you were my home. You stole the biggest piece of my heart that night."

I lower my mouth to his and kiss him softly. He closes his eyes and begins to ease his head against the bed again. "Keep them open," I whisper, pulling away from his lips. He opens them, regarding me with an intensity that penetrates straight to my core. "I want you to keep them open . . . because I need you to watch me give you the very last piece of my heart."

He releases a vast breath and it's almost as if I can see the pain literally escaping him. His hands tighten around mine as the look in his eyes instantly changes from an intense hopelessness to a fiery need. He begins moving with me as we hold each other's gaze. The two of us gradually become one as we silently express with our bodies and our hands and our eyes what our words are unable to convey.

We remain in a connected cadence until the very last

moment, when his eyes grow heavy. He drops his head back, consumed by the shudders that are taking over his release. When his heart rate begins to calm against my palm and he's able to connect with my eyes again, he pulls his hands from mine and grips the back of my head, kissing me with an unforgiving passion. He leans forward as he lowers my back to the floor, trading dominance with me, kissing me with abandon.

We spend the rest of the night taking turns expressing how we feel without uttering a single word. By the time we finally reach the point of exhaustion, wrapped up in each other's arms, I begin to fall asleep in a wave of disbelief. We have just wholly fallen into each other, heart and soul. I never thought I would ever be able to trust a man enough to share my heart, much less hand it over completely.

Holder isn't next to me when I roll over and feel for him. I sit up on the bed and it's dark outside, so I reach over and turn on the lamp. His shoes aren't where they were when he took them off, so I pull on my clothes and make my way outside to find him.

I walk past the courtyard, not spotting him sitting in any of the cabanas. Just as I'm about to turn around and head back, I see him lying on the concrete next to the pool with his hands locked behind his head, looking up at the stars. He looks incredibly peaceful right now, so I choose to walk back to one of the cabanas and leave him undisturbed.

I curl up into the seat and pull my arms into my sweater, leaning my head back as I watch him. There's a full moon out, so everything about him is illuminated in a soft bask of light, making him appear almost angelic. He's lost in the sky with a look of serenity across his face, making me grateful that he's able to find enough peace within himself to get through today. I know how much Lesslie meant to him and I know what his heart is going through today. I know exactly what he's feeling, because our pain is shared now. Whatever he goes through, I feel. Whatever I go through, he feels. It's what happens when two people become one: they no longer share only love. They also share all of the pain, heartache, sorrow, and grief.

Despite the calamity that is my life right now, there's a warm sense of comfort surrounding me after being with him tonight. No matter what happens, I know for a fact that Holder will see me through every second of it, maybe even carrying me through at times. He's proven to me that I'll never feel completely hopeless again, so long as he's in my life.

"Come lie with me," he says, never taking his eyes off the sky above him. I smile and ease out of my seat, then walk toward him. When I reach him, he removes his jacket and places it over me as I ease down onto the cold concrete and curl up against his chest. He strokes my hair as we both stare up at the sky, silently regarding the stars.

Pieces of a memory begin to flash in my mind and I close my eyes, actually wanting to recall it this time. It feels like a happy one, and I'll take as many of those as I can get. I hug him tightly and allow myself to fall openly into the memory.

Thirteen years earlier

"Why don't you have a TV?" I ask her. I've been with her for lots of days now. She's really nice and I like it here, but I miss watching TV. Not as bad as I miss Dean and Lesslie, though.

"I don't have a TV because people have become dependent on technology and it makes them lazy," Karen says. I don't know what she means, but I pretend I do. I really like it at her house and I don't want to say anything that will make her want to take me back home to my daddy yet. I'm not ready to go back.

"Hope, do you remember a few days ago I told you I had something really important to talk to you about?"

I don't really remember, but I nod my head and pretend I do. She scoots her chair closer to mine at the table to get closer to me. "I want you to pay attention to me, okay? This is very important."

I nod my head. I hope she's not telling me she's taking me home now. I'm not ready to go home. I do miss Dean and Lesslie, but I really don't want to go back home with my daddy.

"Do you know what adoption means?" she asks.

I shake my head because I've never heard of that word.

"Adoption is when someone loves a child so much, that they want them to be their son or daughter. So they adopt them in order to become their mommy or daddy." She takes

my hand and squeezes it. "I love you so much that I'm going to adopt you so you can be my daughter."

I smile at her, but I really don't understand what she means. "Are you coming to live with me and my daddy?"

She shakes her head. "No, sweetie. Your daddy loves you very, very much, but he can't take care of you anymore. He needs for me to take care of you now, because he wants to make sure you're happy. So now, instead of living with your daddy, you're going to live with me and I'll get to be your mommy."

It feels like I want to cry, but I don't know why. I like Karen a lot, but I love my daddy, too. I like her house and I like her cooking and I like my room. I really want to stay here really bad, but I can't smile because my tummy hurts. It started hurting when she said my daddy couldn't take care of me anymore. I wonder if I made him mad. I don't ask if I made him mad, though. I'm scared if she thinks I still want to live with my daddy, that she'll take me back to live with him. I do love him, but I'm too scared to go back and live with him.

"Are you excited about me adopting you? Do you want to live with me?"

I do want to live with her but I feel sad because it took us lots of minutes or hours to drive here. That means we're far away from Dean and Lesslie.

"What about my friends? Will I get to see my friends again?"

Karen moves her head to the side and smiles at me, then tucks my hair behind my ear. "Sweetie, you're going to make a lot of new friends."

I smile back at her, but my tummy hurts. I don't want

new friends. I want Dean and Lesslie. I miss them. I can feel my eyes burning and I try not to cry. I don't want her to think I'm not happy about her adopting me, because I am.

Karen reaches down and hugs me. "Sweetie, don't worry. You'll see your friends again someday. But right now we can't go back, so we'll make new friends here, okay?"

I nod and she kisses me on top of the head while I look down at the bracelet on my hand. I touch the heart on it with my fingers and hope that Lesslie knows where I am. I hope they know I'm okay, because I don't want them to worry about me.

"There's one more thing," she says. "You're going to love it."

Karen leans back in her seat and pulls a piece of paper and a pencil to the spot in front of her. "The best part of being adopted is that you get to pick your very own name. Did you know that?"

I shake my head. I didn't know people got to pick their own names.

"Before we pick your name, we need to know what names we can't use. We can't use the name you had before, and we can't use nicknames. Do you have any nicknames? Anything your daddy calls you?"

I nod my head, but I don't say it.

"What does he call you?"

I look down at my hands and clear my throat. "Princess," I say quietly. "But I don't like that nickname."

She looks sad when I say that. "Well then, we will never call you Princess again, okay?"

I nod. I'm happy she doesn't like that name, either.

"I want you to tell me some things that make you happy.

Beautiful things and things you love. Maybe we can pick you a name from those."

I don't even need her to write them down, because there's only one thing I feel that way about. "I love the sky," I say, thinking about what Dean told me to remember forever.

"Sky," she says, smiling. "I love that name. I think it's perfect. Now let's think of one more name, because everyone needs two names. What else do you love?"

I close my eyes and try to think of something else, but I can't. The sky is the only thing I love that's beautiful and makes me happy when I think about it. I open my eyes back up and look at her. "What do you love, Karen?"

She smiles and puts her chin in her hand, resting her elbow on the table. "I love lots of things. I love pizza the most. Can we call you Sky Pizza?"

I giggle and shake my head. "That's a silly name."

"Okay, let me think," she says. "What about teddy bears? Can we call you Teddy Bear Sky?"

I laugh and shake my head again.

She pulls her chin out of her hand and leans toward me. "Do you want to know what I really love?"

"Yeah," I say.

"I love herbs. Herbs are healing plants and I love growing them to find ways to help people feel better. Someday I want to own my own herbal business. Maybe for good luck, we could pick out the name of an herb. There are hundreds of them and some of them are really pretty names." She stands up and walks to the living room and grabs a book, then brings it back to the table. She opens it up and points to one of the pages. "What about thyme?" she says with a wink.

I laugh and shake my head.

"How about . . . calendula?"

I shake my head again. "I can't even say that word."

She crinkles up her nose. "Good point. I guess you need to be able to say your own name." She looks down at the page again and reads a few more out loud, but I don't like them. She turns the page one more time and says, "What about Linden? It's more of a tree than an herb, but its leaves are shaped like a heart. Do you like hearts?"

I nod. "Linden," I say. "I like that name."

She smiles and closes the book, then leans down closer to me. "Well then, Linden Sky Davis it is. And just so you know, you now have the most beautiful name in the world. Let's not think about your old names ever again, okay? Promise me from now on we'll only think about your beautiful new name and your beautiful new life."

"I promise," I say. And I do promise. I don't want to think about my old names or my old room or all the things that my daddy did to me when I was his princess. I love my new name. I love my new room where I don't have to worry if the doorknob is going to turn.

I reach up and hug her and she hugs me back. It makes me smile, because it feels just like the way I thought it would feel every time I wished my mommy was alive to hug me.

I reach my hand up to my face and wipe away a tear. I'm not even sure why my tears are falling right now; the memory wasn't really a sad one. I think it's the fact that it's one of the first moments I ever started to love Karen. Thinking about how much I love her makes me hurt because of what she did. It hurts because I feel like I don't even know her. I feel like there's a side to her that I never even knew existed.

That's not what scares me the most, though. What scares me the most is that I'm afraid the only side of her I *do* know . . . doesn't really exist at *all*.

"Can I ask you something?" Holder says, breaking the silence.

I nod against his chest, wiping the last tear from my cheek. He wraps both of his arms around me in an attempt to keep me warm when he feels me shiver against his chest. He rubs my shoulder with his hand and kisses my head.

"Do you think you'll be okay, Sky?"

It's not an uncommon question. It's a very simple, straightforward question, yet it's the hardest question I think I've ever had to answer.

I shrug. "I don't know," I reply honestly. I want to think I'll be okay, especially knowing Holder will be by my side. But to be honest, I really don't know if I will be.

"What scares you?"

"Everything," I reply quickly. "I'm terrified of my past. I'm terrified of the memories that flood my mind every time I close my eyes. I'm terrified of what I saw happen today and how it'll affect me the nights that you aren't there to divert my thoughts. I'm terrified that I don't have the emotional capacity to deal with what may happen to Karen. I'm scared of the thought that I have no idea who she even is anymore." I lift my head off his chest and look him in the eyes. "But do you know what scares me the most?"

He runs his hand over my hair and keeps his eyes on mine; wanting me to know that he's listening. "What?" he asks, his voice full of genuine concern.

"I'm scared of how disconnected I feel from Hope. I know we're the same person, but I feel like what happened to her didn't really happen to me. I feel like I abandoned her. Like I left her there, crying against that house, terrified for all of eternity, while I just got into that car and rode away. Now I'm two completely separate people. I'm this little girl, eternally scared to death . . . but I'm also the girl who abandoned her. I feel so guilty for putting up this wall between both lives and I'm scared neither of those lives or those girls will ever feel whole again."

I bury my head in his chest, knowing I'm more than likely not making any sense. He kisses the top of my head and I look back up at the sky, wondering if I'll ever be able to feel normal again. It was so much easier not knowing the truth.

"After my parents divorced," he says, "my mother was worried about us, so she put me and Les in therapy. It only lasted for about six months . . . but I remember always being so hard on myself, thinking I was the reason for their divorce. I felt like what I failed to do the day you were taken put a lot of stress on them. I know now that most of what I blamed myself for back then was out of my control. But there was something my therapist did once that sort of helped me. It felt really awkward at the time, but every now and then I catch myself still doing it in certain situations. He had me visualize myself in the past, and he would have me talk to the younger version of myself and say everything I needed to say." He pulls my face up so that I'm looking at him. "I think you should try that. I know it sounds lame, but really. It might help you. I think you need to go back and tell Hope everything you wish you could have told her the day you left her."

I rest my chin on his chest. "What do you mean? Like I should visualize myself talking to her?"

"Exactly," he says. "Just try it. Close your eyes."

I close them. I'm not sure what it is I'm doing, but I do it anyway.

"Are they closed?"

"Yes." I lay my hand over his heart and press the side of my head into his chest. "I'm not sure what to do, though."

"Just envision yourself as you are now. Envision yourself driving up to your father's house and parking across the street. But visualize the house how it was back then," he says. "Picture it how it was when you were Hope. Can you remember the house being white?"

I squeeze my eyes shut even harder, vaguely recalling the white house from somewhere deep within my mind. "Yes."

"Good. Now you need to go find her. Talk to her. Tell her how strong she is. Tell her how beautiful she is. Tell her everything she needs to hear from you, Sky. Everything you wish you could have told *yourself* that day."

I clear my mind and go with his suggestion. I envision myself as I am now and what would be happening if I actually drove up to that house. I would more than likely be wearing my sundress with my hair pulled back into a ponytail since it's so hot. It's almost as if I can feel the sun beating down through the windshield, warming my skin again.

I make myself step out of my car and walk across the street, even though I'm reluctant to head toward that house. My heart immediately speeds up. I'm not sure that I *want* to see her, but I do what Holder suggests and I keep walking forward. As soon as the side of the house is in view, she's there. Hope is sitting in the grass with her arms folded over her knees. She's crying into them and it completely shatters my heart.

I slowly walk up to her and pause, then tentatively lower myself to the ground, unable to take my eyes off this fragile little girl. When I'm situated on the grass directly in front of her, she lifts her head from her folded arms and looks up at me. When she does, my soul crumbles because the look in her dark brown eyes is lifeless. There's no happiness there at all. I try to smile at her, though, because I don't want her to see how much her pain is hurting me.

I stretch my hand out to her, but stop a few inches before I reach her. Her sad brown eyes drop to my fingers and she stares at them. My hands are shaking now and she can see that. Maybe the fact that she can see that I'm also scared helps me gain her trust, because she lifts her head even higher, then unfolds her arms and places her tiny hand in mine.

I'm looking down at the hand of my childhood, holding on to the hand of my present, but all I want to do is hold more than just her hand. I want to grab all of her pain and fear, too, and take it from her.

Remembering the things Holder said I should tell her, I look down at her and clear my throat, squeezing her hand tightly in mine.

"Hope." She continues to look at me patiently while I dig deep for the courage to speak to her . . . to tell her everything she needs to know. "Do you know that you're one of the bravest little girls I've ever met?"

She shakes her head and looks down at the grass. "No, I'm not," she says quietly, convinced in her belief.

I reach out and take her other hand in mine and look her directly in the eyes. "Yes, you are. You're *incredibly* brave. And you're going to make it through this because you have a very strong heart. A heart that is capable of loving so much about life and people in a way you never dreamt a heart could love. And you're beautiful." I press my hand to her heart. "In here. Your heart is so beautiful and someday someone is going to love that heart like it deserves to be loved."

She pulls one of her hands back and wipes her eyes with it. "How do you know all that?"

I lean forward and wrap my arms around her completely. She returns my embrace by putting her arms around me and letting me hold her. I lean my head down and whisper in her ear. "I know, because I've been through exactly what you're going through. I know how bad it hurts your heart that your daddy does this to you, because he did it to me, too. I know how much you hate him for it, but I also know

367

how much you love him because he's your daddy. And it's okay, Hope. It's okay to love the good parts of him, because he's not all bad. It's also okay to hate those bad parts of him that make you so sad. It's okay to feel *whatever* you need to feel. Just promise me that you will never, ever feel guilty. Promise me that you will never blame yourself. It's not your fault. You're just a little girl and it's not your fault that your life is so much harder than it should be. And as much as you'll want to forget these things ever happened to you and as much as you'll want to forget this part of your life existed, I need for you to remember."

I can feel her arms trembling against me now and she's quietly crying against my chest. Her tears force the release of my own tears. "I want you to remember who you are, despite the bad things that are happening to you. Because those bad things aren't *you*. They are just things that *happen* to you. You need to accept that who you are, and the things that happen to you, are not one and the same."

I gently lift her head off my chest and look into her brown, tearful eyes. "Promise me that no matter what, you will never be ashamed of who you are, no matter how bad you want to be. And this might not make sense to you right now, but I want you to promise me that you will never let the things your daddy does to you define and separate you from who you are. Promise me that you will never lose Hope."

She nods her head as I wipe her tears away with my thumbs. "I promise," she says. She smiles up at me and for the first time since seeing her big brown eyes, there's a trace of life in them. I pull her onto my lap and she wraps her arms around my neck as I hold her and rock her, both of us crying in each other's arms.

"Hope, I promise that from this point forward, I will never, ever let you go. I'm going to hold you and carry you with me in my heart forever. You'll never have to be alone again."

I'm crying into Hope's hair, but when I open my eyes I'm crying into Holder's arms. "Did you talk to her?" he asks.

I nod my head. "Yes." I'm not even trying to choke back the tears. "I told her everything."

Holder begins to sit up, so I move up with him. He turns toward me and takes my face in his hands. "No, Sky. You didn't tell *her* everything . . . you told *you* everything. Those things happened to *you*, not to someone else. They happened to Hope. They happened to Sky. They happened to the best friend that I loved all those years ago, and they happened to the best friend I love who's looking back at me right now." He presses his lips to mine and kisses me, then pulls away. It's not until I look back at him that I notice he's crying with me. "You need to be proud of the fact that you survived everything you went through as a child. Don't separate yourself from that life. Embrace it, because I'm so fucking proud of you. Every smile I see on your face just blows me away, because I know the courage and strength it took when you were just a little girl to ensure that part of you remained. And your laugh? My *God*, Sky. Think about how much courage it took you to laugh again after everything that happened to you. And your heart . . ." he says, shaking his head disbelievingly. "How your heart can possibly find a way to love and trust a man again proves that I've fallen in love with the bravest woman I've ever known. I know how much courage it took for you to allow me in after what your father did to you. And I swear I will spend every last breath thanking you for allowing yourself to love me. Thank you *so* much for loving me, Linden Sky Hope."

He pronounces each of my names slowly, not even attempting to wipe away my tears because there are too many. I throw my arms around his neck and let him hold me. All seventeen years of me.

The sun is so bright; it's beaming through the blanket I've pulled over my eyes. It's not the sun that woke me up, though. It was the sound of Holder's voice.

"Look, you have no idea what she's been through the past two days," Holder says. He's trying to speak softly, either in an attempt not to wake me, or in an attempt for me not to hear his conversation. I don't hear anyone speak in return, so he must be on the phone. Who the hell is he talking to, though?

"I understand your need to defend her. Believe me, I do. But you both need to know that she's not walking into that house alone."

There's a long pause before he sighs heavily into the phone. "I need to make sure she eats something, so give us some time. Yes, I promise. I'm waking her up as soon as I hang up. We'll leave within the hour."

He doesn't say good-bye, but I hear the phone drop onto the table. Within seconds, the bed dips and he's sliding an arm around me. "Wake up," he says into my ear.

I don't move. "I am awake," I say from underneath the covers. I feel his head press into my shoulder.

"So you heard that?" he asks, his voice low.

"Who was it?"

He shifts on the bed and pulls the covers off of my head.

"Jack. He claims Karen confessed everything to him last night. He's worried about her. He needs you to talk to her."

My heart stops midbeat. "She confessed?" I ask warily, sitting up in the bed.

He nods. "We didn't go into details, but he seems to know what's going on. I did tell him about your father, though . . . only because Karen wanted to know if you saw him. When I woke up today it was on the news. They ruled it a suicide, based on the fact that he called it in himself. They aren't even opening it for investigation." He holds my hand and caresses it with his thumb. "Sky, Jack sounds desperate for you to come back. I think he's right . . . we need to go back and finish this. You won't be alone. I'll be there and Jack will be there. And from the sound of it, Karen is cooperating. I know it's hard but we don't have a choice."

He's talking to me like I need to be convinced, when really I'm ready. I need to see her face to face in order to get the last of my questions answered. I throw the covers off me completely and scoot off the bed, then stand up and stretch. "I need to brush my teeth and change first. Then we can go." I walk to the bathroom and don't turn around, but I can feel the pride rolling off him. He's proud of me.

Holder hands me his cell phone once we're on the road. "Here. Breckin and Six are both worried about you. Karen got their numbers out of your cell phone and has been calling them all weekend, trying to find you."

"Did you talk to either of them?"

He nods. "I spoke with Breckin this morning, right before Jack called. I told him you and your mother got into a fight and you just wanted to get away for a few days. He's fine with that explanation."

"What about Six?"

He glances at me and gives me a half smile. "Six you might need to contact. I've been talking to her through email. I tried to appease her with the same story I told Breckin, but she wasn't buying it. She said you and Karen don't fight and I need to tell her the truth before she flies back to Texas and kicks my ass."

I wince, knowing Six must be worried sick about me. I haven't texted her in days, so I decide to put off calling Breckin and shoot Six an email, instead.

"How do you email someone?" I ask. Holder laughs and takes his phone, pressing a few buttons. He hands it back to me and points to the screen.

"Just type what you need to say in there, then hand it back to me and I'll send it."

I type out a short email, telling her that I found out a few things about my past and I needed to get away for a few days. I assure her that I'll call her to explain everything in the next few days, but I'm really not sure that I'll actually tell her the truth. At this point, I'm not sure I want anyone to know about my situation. Not until I have all the answers.

Holder sends the email, then takes my hand and laces his fingers through mine. I focus my gaze out the window and stare up at the sky.

"You hungry?" he asks, after driving in complete silence for over an hour. I shake my head. I'm too nervous to eat anything, knowing I'm about to face Karen. I'm too nervous to even hold a normal conversation. I'm too nervous to

Colleen Hoover

do anything but stare out the window and wonder where I'll be when I wake up tomorrow.

"You need to eat, Sky. You've barely eaten anything in three days and with your tendency to pass out, I don't think food would be a bad idea right now."

He won't give up until I eat, so I just relent. "Fine," I mumble.

He ends up choosing a roadside Mexican restaurant after I fail to make a choice about where to eat. I order something off the lunch menu, just to appease him. I more than likely won't be able to eat anything.

"You want to play Dinner Quest?" he says, dipping a tortilla chip into his salsa.

I shrug. I really don't want to face what I'll be doing in five hours, so maybe this will help get my mind off things. "I guess. On one condition, though. I don't want to talk about anything that has anything to do with the first few years of my life, the last three days, or the next twenty-four hours."

He smiles, seemingly relieved. Maybe he doesn't want to think about any of it, either.

"Ladies first," he says.

"Then put down that chip," I say, eyeing the food he's about to put in his mouth.

His eyes drop to the chip and he frowns playfully. "Make it a quick question then, because I'm starving."

I take advantage of my turn by downing a drink of my soda, then taking a bite of the chip that I just took out of his hands. "Why do you love running so much?" I ask.

"I'm not sure," he says, sinking back into his seat. "I started running when I was thirteen. It started out as a way

374

to get away from Les and her annoying friends. Sometimes I would just need out of the house. The squealing and cackling of thirteen-year-old girls can be extremely painful. I liked the silence that came with running. If you haven't noticed, I'm sort of a thinker, so it helps me to clear my head."

I laugh. "I've noticed," I say. "Have you always been like that?"

He grins and shakes his head. "That's two questions. My turn." He takes the chip that I was about to eat out of my hand and he pops it into his mouth, then takes a drink of his soda. "Why didn't you ever show up for track tryouts?"

I cock my eyebrow and laugh. "That's an odd question to ask now. That was two months ago."

He shakes his head and points a chip at me. "No judging when it comes to my choice in questions."

"Fine." I laugh. "I don't know, really. School just wasn't what I thought it would be. I didn't expect the other girls to be so mean. None of them even spoke to me unless it was to inform me of what a slut I was. Breckin was the only person in that whole school who made any effort."

"That's not true," Holder says. "You're forgetting about Shayla."

I laugh. "You mean Shayna?"

"Whatever," he says, shaking his head. "Your go." He quickly shoves another chip in his mouth and grins at me.

"Why did your parents divorce?"

He gives me a tight-lipped smile and drums his fingers lightly on the table, then shrugs his shoulders. "I guess it was time for them to," he says indifferently.

"It was time?" I ask, confused by his vague answer. "Is there an expiration date on marriages nowadays?"

He shrugs. "For some people, yes."

I'm interested in his thought process now. I'm hoping he doesn't move on to his turn now that my question has been asked, because I really want to know his views on this. Not that I'm planning on getting married anytime soon. But he is the guy I'm in love with, so it wouldn't hurt to know his stance so I'm not as shocked years down the road.

"Why do you think their marriage had a time limit?" I ask.

"All marriages have a time limit if you enter them for the wrong reasons. Marriage doesn't get easier . . . it only gets harder. If you marry someone hoping it will improve things, you might as well set your timer the second you say, 'I do.'"

"What wrong reasons did they have to get married?"

"Me and Les," he says flatly. "They knew each other less than a month when my mother got pregnant. My dad married her, thinking it was the right thing to do, when maybe the right thing to do was to never knock her up in the first place."

"Accidents happen," I say.

"I know. Which is why they're now divorced."

I shake my head, sad that he's so casual about his parents' lack of love for each other. I guess it's been eight years, though. The ten-year-old Holder may not have been so casual about the divorce as it was actually occurring. "But you don't think divorce is inevitable for every marriage?"

He folds his arms across the table and leans forward, narrowing his eyes. "Sky, if you're wondering if I have commitment issues, the answer is no. Someday in the far, far, far away future . . . like postcollege future . . . when I propose to you . . . which I *will* be doing one day because you aren't getting rid of me . . . I won't be marrying you with the hope that our marriage will work out. When you become mine, it'll be a forever thing. I've told you before that the only thing that matters to me with you are the forevers, and I mean that."

I smile at him, somehow a little bit more in love with him than I was thirty seconds ago. "Wow. You didn't need much time to think *those* words out."

He shakes his head. "That's because I've been thinking about forever with you since the second I saw you in the grocery store."

Our food couldn't have arrived at a more perfect time, because I have no idea how to respond to that. I pick up my fork to take a bite but he reaches across the table and snatches it out of my hand.

"No cheating," he says. "We're not finished and I'm about to get really personal with my question." He takes a bite of his food and chews it slowly as I wait for him to ask me his "really personal" question. After he takes a drink, he takes another bite of food and grins at me, purposely dragging out his turn so he can eat.

"Ask me a damn question," I say with feigned irritation.

He laughs and wipes his mouth with his napkin, then leans forward. "Are you on birth control?" he asks in a hushed voice.

His question makes me laugh, because it really isn't all that personal when you're asking the girl you're having sex with. "No, I'm not," I admit. "I never really had a reason to be on it before you came barging into my life."

"Well, I want you on it," he says decisively. "Make an appointment this week."

I balk at his rudeness. "You could ask me a little more politely, you know."

He arches an eyebrow as he takes a sip of his drink, then places it calmly back down on the table in front of him. "My bad." He smiles and flashes his dimples at me. "Let me rephrase my words, then," he says, lowering his voice to a husky whisper. "I plan on making love to you, Sky. *A lot.* Pretty much any chance we get, because I rather enjoyed you this weekend, despite the circumstances surrounding it all. So in order for me to continue to make love to you, I would very much appreciate it if you would make alternative contraceptive arrangements so that we don't find ourselves in a pregnancy-induced marriage with an expiration date on it. Do you think you could do that for me? So that we can continue to have lots and lots and lots of sex?"

I keep my eyes locked on his as I slide my empty glass to the waitress, who is now staring at Holder with her jaw wide open. I keep a straight face when I reply.

"That's much better," I say. "And yes. I believe I can arrange that."

He nods once, then slides his glass next to mine, glancing up at the waitress. She finally snaps out of her trance and quickly refills our glasses, then walks away. As soon as she's gone, I glare at Holder and shake my head. "You're evil, Dean Holder." I laugh.

"What?" he says innocently.

"It should be illegal for the words 'make love' and 'sex' to flow past your lips when in the presence of any female besides the one who actually gets to experience you. I don't think you realize what you do to women."

He shakes his head and attempts to brush off my comment.

"I'm serious, Holder. Without trying to explode your ego, you should know that you're incredibly appealing to pretty much any female with a pulse. I mean, think about it. I can't even count the number of guys I've met in my life, yet somehow you're the only one I've ever been attracted to? Explain that one."

He laughs. "That's an easy one."

"How so?"

"Because," he says, looking at me pointedly. "You already loved me before you saw me in the grocery store that day. Just because you blocked the memory of me out of your mind doesn't mean you blocked the memory of me out of your heart." He brings a forkful of food to his mouth, but pauses before he takes a bite. "Maybe you're right, though. It could have just been the fact that you wanted to lick my dimples," he says, shoving the forkful into his mouth.

"It was definitely the dimples," I say, smiling. I can't count the number of times he's made me smile in the half hour we've been here, and I've somehow eaten half of the food on my plate. His presence alone works wonders for a wounded soul.

Tuesday, October 30, 2012
7:20 p.m.

We're a block from Karen's house when I ask him to pull over. The anticipation during the drive over here was torture enough, but actually arriving is absolutely terrifying. I have no idea what to say to her or how I'm supposed to react when I walk through the front door.

Holder pulls over to the side of the road and puts the car in park. He looks over at me with concern in his eyes. "You need a chapter break?" he asks.

I nod, inhaling a deep breath. He reaches across the seat and grabs my hand. "What is it that scares you the most about seeing her?"

I shift in my seat to face him. "I'm scared that no matter what she says to me today, I'll never be able to forgive her. I know that my life turned out better with her than it would have if I had stayed with my father, but she had no way of knowing that when she stole me from him. The fact that I know what she's capable of makes it impossible for me to forgive her. If I couldn't forgive my father for what he did to me . . . then I feel like I shouldn't forgive her, either."

He brushes his thumb across the top of my hand. "Maybe you'll never forgive her for what she did, but you *can* appreciate the life she gave you after she did it. She's been a good mom to you, Sky. Remember that when you talk to her today, okay?"

I expel a nervous breath. "That's the part I can't get over," I say. "The fact that she *has* been a good mom and I love her for it. I love her so much and I'm scared to death that after today, I won't have her anymore."

Holder pulls me to him and hugs me. "I'm scared for you, too, babe," he says, unwilling to pretend everything will be okay when it can't. It's the fear of the unknown that we're both wrapped up in. Neither of us has any idea what path my life will take after I walk through that front door, and if it's a path we'll even be able to take together.

I pull apart from him and place my hands on my knees, working up courage to get this over with. "I'm ready," I say. He nods, then pulls his car back onto the road and rounds the corner, coming to a stop in my driveway. Seeing my home causes my hands to tremble even more than they were before. Holder opens the driver's-side door when Jack walks outside and he turns to face me.

"Stay here," he says. "I want to talk to Jack first." Holder gets out of the car and shuts the door behind him. I stay put like he asked me to because I'm honestly in no hurry to get out of this car. I watch as Holder and Jack speak for several minutes. The fact that Jack is here, still supporting her, makes me wonder if Karen actually told him the truth about what she did. I doubt he would be here if he knew the truth.

Holder walks back to the car, this time to the passenger door where I'm seated. He opens the door and kneels down next to me. He brushes his hand across my cheek and strokes my face with the back of his fingertips. "Are you ready?" he asks.

I feel my head nodding, but I don't feel in control of

the movement. I see my feet stepping out of the car and my hand reaching into Holder's, but I don't know how I'm moving when I'm consciously trying to keep myself seated in the car. I'm not ready to go in, but I'm walking away from the car in Holder's arms toward the house, anyway. When I reach Jack, he reaches out to hug me. As soon as his familiar arms wrap around me, I catch back up to myself and take a deep breath.

"Thank you for coming back," he says. "She needs this chance to explain everything. Promise me you'll give that to her."

I pull away from him and look him in the eyes. "Do you know what she did, Jack? Did she tell you?"

He nods painfully. "I know and I know it's hard for you. But you need to let her tell you her side."

He turns toward the house and keeps his arm around my shoulders. Holder takes my hand and they both walk me to the front door like I'm a fragile child.

I'm *not* a fragile child.

I pause on the steps and turn to face them. "I need to talk to her alone."

I know I thought I wanted Holder with me, but I need to be strong for myself. I love the way he protects me, but this is the hardest thing I've ever had to do and I want to be able to say I did it myself. If I can face this on my own, I know I'll have the courage to face anything.

Neither of them objects, which fills me with appreciation for them, knowing they both have faith in me. Holder squeezes my hand and urges me forward with confidence in his eyes. "I'll be right here," he says.

I take a deep breath, then open the front door.

I step into the living room and Karen stops pacing the floor and spins around, taking in the sight of me. As soon as we make eye contact, she loses control and rushes toward me. I don't know what look I expected to see on her face when I walked through this door, but it certainly wasn't a look of relief.

"You're okay," she says, throwing her arms around my neck. She presses her hand to the back of my head and pulls me against her as she cries. "I'm so sorry, Sky. I'm so, so sorry you found out before I could tell you." She's trying hard to speak, but the sobs have taken over full force. Seeing her in this much pain tears at my heart. Knowing she's been lying to me doesn't immediately refute the thirteen years I've loved her, so seeing her in pain only causes me pain in return.

She takes my face in her hands and looks me in the eyes. "I swear to you I was going to tell you everything the moment you turned eighteen. I hate that you had to find it all out on your own. I did everything I could to prevent that from happening."

I grab her hands and remove them from my face, then step around her. "I have no idea how to respond to anything you're saying right now, Mom." I spin around and look her in the eyes. "I have so many questions but I'm too scared to ask them. If you answer them, how do I know you'll be telling me the truth? How do I know you won't lie to me like you've been lying to me for the last thirteen years?"

Karen walks to the kitchen and picks up a napkin to wipe her eyes. She inhales a few shaky breaths, attempting to regain control of herself. "Come sit with me, sweetie," she says, walking past me toward the couch. I remain standing while I watch her take a seat on the edge of the cushion. She glances up at me, her entire face awash with heartache. "Please," she says. "I know you don't trust me and you have every right not to trust me for what I did. But if you can find it in your heart to recognize the fact that I love you more than life itself, you'll give me this chance to explain."

Her eyes speak nothing but truth. For that, I walk to the couch and take a seat across from her. She takes a deep breath, then exhales, controlling herself long enough to begin with her explanation.

"In order for me to explain the truth about what happened with you . . . I first need to explain the truth about what happened to me." She pauses for a few minutes, attempting not to break down again. I can see in her eyes that whatever she's about to say is almost unbearable for her. I want to go to her and hug her, but I can't. As much as I love her, I just can't console her.

"I had a wonderful mom, Sky. You would have loved her so much. Her name was Dawn and she loved my brother and me with everything she had. My brother, John, was ten years older than me, so we never had to experience the sibling rivalry growing up. My father passed away when I was nine, so John was like the father figure in my life rather than a sibling. He was my protector. He was such a good brother and she was such a good mother. Unfortunately, when I turned thirteen, the fact that John was like a father to me became his reality the day my mother died.

"John was only twenty-three and was fresh out of college at the time. I didn't have any other family willing to take me in, so he did what he had to do. At first, things were okay. I missed my mother more than I should have and, to be honest, John was having a hard time dealing with everything laid out in front of him. He had just started his new job, fresh out of college, and things were tough for him. For both of us. By the time I turned fourteen, the stressors of his new job were really getting to him at this point. He began drinking and I began rebelling, staying out later than I should have on several occasions.

"One night when I came home, he was so angry with me. Our argument soon turned into a physical fight and he hit me several times. He had never physically hurt me before and it terrified me. I ran to my room and he came in several minutes later to apologize. His behavior the previous few months as a result of his alcohol abuse already had me scared of him. Now, coupled with the fact that it had caused him to physically hurt me . . . I was terrified of him."

Karen shifts in her seat and reaches down to sip from a glass of water. I watch her hand as she brings the glass to her mouth and her fingers are trembling.

"He tried to apologize but I refused to listen. My stubbornness pissed him off even more, so he pushed me back on the bed and started screaming at me. He went on and on, telling me that I had ruined his life. He said I needed to be thanking him for everything he was doing for me . . . that I owed him for having to work so hard to take care of me."

Karen clears her throat and new tears form in her eyes as she struggles to continue with the painful truth of her past. She brings her eyes to meet mine and I can tell that the words on the tip of her tongue are almost too hard for her to release.

"Sky . . ." she says achingly. "My brother raped me that

night. Not only did he do it that night, but it continued almost every night after that for two solid years."

I bring my hands to my mouth and gasp. The blood rushes from my head, but it feels as though it rushes from the rest of my body as well. I feel completely empty hearing her words, because I'm terrified to hear what I think she's about to tell me. The look in her eyes is even emptier than how I'm feeling right now. Rather than wait for her to tell me, I just come out and ask her.

"Mom . . . is John . . . he was my father, wasn't he?"

She quickly nods her head as tears drop from her eyes. "Yes, sweetie. He was. I'm so sorry."

My whole body jerks with the sob that breaks free and Karen's arms are around me as soon as the first tears escape my eyes. I throw my arms around her and grasp her shirt. "I'm so sorry he did that to you," I cry. Karen sits next to me on the couch and we hold each other while we cry over the things that were done to us at the hands of a man we both loved with all of our heart.

"There's more," she says. "I want to tell you everything, okay?"

I nod as she pulls herself away from me and takes my hands in hers.

"When I turned sixteen, I told a friend of mine what he was doing to me. She told her mother, who then reported it. By that time, John had been in the police force for three years and was making a name for himself. When he was questioned about the report, he claimed I was making it up because he wouldn't allow me to see my boyfriend. He was eventually cleared and the case was dismissed, but I knew I could never go back to live with him. I lived with a few friends until I graduated high school two years later. I never spoke to him again.

"Six years had passed before I saw him again. I was twenty-one and in college by that time. I was at a grocery store and was on the next aisle when I heard his voice. I froze, unable to breathe as I listened to his conversation. I would have been able to recognize his voice anywhere. There's something about a voice that terrifies you that you'll never be able to forget, no matter what.

"But that day, it wasn't his voice that had me paralyzed . . . it was yours. I heard him talking to a little girl and I was immediately taken back to all those nights he hurt me. I was sick to my stomach, knowing what he was capable of. I followed at a distance, watching the two of you interact. He walked a few feet away from the shopping cart at one point and I caught your eye. You looked at me for a long time and you were the most beautiful little girl I'd ever seen. But you were also the most broken little girl I'd ever seen. I knew the second I looked into your eyes that he was doing to you exactly what he had done to me. I could see the hopelessness and fear in your eyes when you looked back at me.

"I spent the next several days attempting to find out everything I could about you and your relationship to him. I learned about what happened to your mother, and that he was raising you alone. I finally got the courage to phone in an anonymous report, hoping he would finally get what he deserved. I learned a week later that after interviewing you, the case was immediately dismissed by Child Protective Services. I'm not sure if the fact that he was high up in law enforcement had anything to do with the dismissal, but I'm almost positive it did. Regardless, that was twice that he had gotten away with it. I couldn't bear the thought of allowing you to stay with him, knowing what was happening to you. I'm sure there were other ways I could have handled it, but I was young and scared to death for you. I didn't know what else to do because the law had already failed us both.

"A few days later I had made up my mind. If no one else was going to help you get away from him . . . then I was. The day when I pulled up to your house I'll never forget that broken little girl crying into her arms, sitting alone in the grass. When I called your name and you came to me, then climbed into the car with me . . . we drove away and I never looked back."

Karen squeezes my hands between hers and looks at me hard. "Sky, I swear with all of my heart that all I ever wanted to do was protect you from him. I did everything I could to keep him from finding you. To keep you from finding *him*. We never spoke about him again and I did my best to help you move past what happened to you so you could have a normal life. I knew that I couldn't get away with hiding you forever. I knew there would come a day that I would have to face what I did . . . but none of that mattered to me. None of that matters to me still. I just wanted you safe until you were old enough, so that you would never be sent back to him.

"The day before I took you, I went to your house and no one was there. I went inside because I wanted to find some things that might comfort you once you were safe with me. Something like a favorite blanket or a teddy bear. Once I was actually inside your bedroom, I realized that anything in that house couldn't possibly bring you comfort. If you were anything like me, everything that had a connection to him reminded you of what he had done to you. So I didn't take anything, because I didn't want you to remember what he had done to you."

She stands up and quietly walks out of the room, then returns moments later with a small wooden box. She places it into my hands. "I couldn't leave without these. I knew that when the day came for me to tell you the truth, that you would want to know all about your mother, too. I couldn't find much, but what I did find I kept for you."

Tears fill my eyes as I run my fingers over the wooden box that holds the only memories of a woman I never thought I would have a chance to remember. I don't open it. I can't. I need to open it alone.

Karen tucks my hair behind my ear and I look back up at her. "I know what I did was wrong, but I don't regret it. If I had to do it again just to know you would be safe, I wouldn't think twice about it. I also know that you probably hate me for lying to you. I'm okay with that, Sky, because I love you enough for the both of us. Never feel guilty for how you feel about what I've done to you. I've had this conversation and this moment planned out for thirteen years, so I'm prepared for whatever you decide to do and whatever decision you make. I want you to do what's best for you. I'll call the police right now if that's what you want me to do. I'll be more than willing to tell them everything I just told you if it would help you find peace. If you need me to wait until your actual eighteenth birthday so you can continue to live in this house until then, I will. I'll turn myself in the second you're legally allowed to take care of yourself, and I'll never question your request. But whatever you choose,

Sky. Whatever you decide to do, don't worry about me. Knowing you're safe now is everything I could ever ask for. Whatever comes next for me is worth every second of the thirteen years I've had with you."

I look back down at the box and continue to cry, not having a clue what to do. I don't know what's right or what's wrong or if right *is* wrong in this situation. I know that I can't answer her right now. I feel like with everything she's just told me, all that I thought I knew about justice and fairness has just slapped me in the face.

I look back up at her and shake my head. "I don't know," I whisper. "I don't know what I want to happen." I *don't* know what I want, but I know what I need. I need a chapter break.

I stand up and she remains seated, watching me as I walk to the door. I can't look her in the eyes as I open the front door. "I need to think for a while," I say quietly, making my way outside. As soon as the front door closes behind me, Holder's arms wrap around me. I cradle the wooden box in one hand and wrap my other arm around his neck, burying my head into his shoulder. I cry into his shirt, not knowing how to begin processing everything I've just learned. "The sky," I say. "I need to look at the sky."

He doesn't ask any questions. He knows exactly what I'm referring to, so he grabs my hand and leads me to the car. Jack slips back into the house as Holder and I pull out of the driveway.

Holder never asks me what Karen said while I was inside the house with her. He knows that I'll tell him when I can, but right now in this moment, I don't think I can. Not until I know what I want to do.

He pulls the car over when we get to the airport, but pulls up significantly farther than where we normally park. When we walk down to the fence, I'm surprised to see an unlocked gate. Holder lifts the latch and swings it open, motioning for me to walk through.

"There's a gate?" I ask, confused. "Why do we always climb the fence?"

He shoots me a sly grin. "You were in a dress the two times we've been here. Where's the fun in walking through a gate?"

Somehow, and I don't know how, I find it in me to laugh. I walk through the gate and he closes it behind me, but remains on the other side of it. I pause and reach my hand out to him. "I want you to come with me," I say.

"Are you sure? I figured you'd want to think alone tonight."

I shake my head. "I like being next to you out here. It wouldn't feel right if I was alone."

He opens the gate and takes my hand in his. We walk down to the runway and claim our usual spots under the stars. I lay the wooden box next to me, still not sure that I have the courage to open it. I'm not really sure of anything right now. I lie still for over half an hour, silently thinking about my life . . . about Karen's life . . . about Lesslie's life . . . and I feel like the decision I'm having to make needs to be one for all three of us.

"Karen is my aunt," I say aloud. "My biological aunt." I don't know if I'm saying it out loud for Holder's benefit or if I just want to say it out loud for myself.

Holder wraps his pinky around mine and turns his head to look at me. "Your dad's sister?" he asks, hesitantly. I nod and he closes his eyes, understanding what that means for Karen's past. "That's why she took you," he says knowingly. He says it like it makes complete sense. "She knew what he was doing to you."

I confirm his statement with a nod. "She wants me to decide, Holder. She wants me to choose what happens next. The problem is, I don't know what choice is the right one."

He takes my entire hand in his now, intertwining our fingers. "That's because none of them are the right choice," he says. "Sometimes you have to choose between a bunch of wrong choices and no right ones. You just have to choose which wrong choice feels the least wrong."

Making Karen pay for something she did out of complete selflessness is without a doubt the *worst* wrong choice. I know it in my heart, but it's still a struggle to accept that what she did is something that should have no consequences. I know she didn't know it at the time, but the fact that Karen took me away from my father only led to what happened to Lesslie. It's hard to ignore that Karen's taking me indirectly led to what happened to my best friend—to the only other girl in Holder's life whom he feels he let down.

"I need to ask you something," I say to him. He silently waits for me to speak, so I sit up and look down at him. "I don't want you to interrupt me, okay? Just let me get this out."

He touches my hand and nods, so I continue. "I know that Karen did what she did because she was only trying to save me. The decision she made was made out of love . . . not hate. But I'm scared that if I don't say anything . . . if we keep it to ourselves . . . that it will affect *you*. Because I know that what my father did to Les was only done because I wasn't there, taking her place. And I know there was no way Karen could have foreseen what he would do. I know she tried to do the right thing by reporting him before she became so desperate. But what happens to us? To you and me, when we try to go back to how things were before? I'm scared you'll hate Karen forever . . . or that you'll eventually begin to resent me for whatever choice I make tonight. And I'm not saying I don't want you to feel whatever it is you need to feel. If you need to hate Karen for what happened to Les, I understand. I guess I just need to know that whatever I choose . . . I need to know . . ."

I attempt to find the most eloquent way to say it, but I can't. Sometimes the simplest questions are the hardest to ask. I squeeze his hand and look him in the eyes. "Holder . . . will you be okay?"

His expression is unreadable as he watches me. He laces his fingers through mine and turns his attention back to the sky above us.

"All this time," he says quietly. "For the past year I've done nothing but hate and resent Les for what she did. I hated her because we led the exact same life. We had the exact same parents who went through the exact same divorce. We had the exact same best friend who was ripped from our lives. We shared the exact same grief over what happened to you, Sky. We moved to the same town in the same house with the same mom and the same school. The things that happened in her life were the exact same things that happened in mine. But she always took it so much harder. Sometimes at night I would hear her crying. I would always go lie with her and hold her, but there were so many times I just wanted to scream at her for being so much weaker than me.

"Then that night . . . when I found out what she did . . . I hated her. I hated her for giving up so easily. I hated that she thought her life was so much harder than mine, when they were the exact same."

He sits up and turns to face me, taking both of my hands in his. "I know the truth now. I know that her life was a *million* times harder than mine. And the fact that she still smiled and laughed every single day, but I never had a single clue what kind of shit she had been through . . . I finally see how brave she really was. And it wasn't her fault that she didn't know how to deal with it all. I wish that she had asked for help or told someone what happened, but everyone deals with these things differently, especially when you think you're all alone. You were able to block it out and that's how you coped. I think she tried to do that, but she was a lot older when it happened to her so it made it impossible. Instead of blocking it out and never thinking about it again, I know she did the exact opposite. I know that it consumed every part of her life until she just couldn't take it anymore.

"And you can't say that Karen's choice had any direct

link to what your father did to Les. If Karen had never taken you away from him, he more than likely would have still done those things to Les whether you were there or not. It's who he was. It's what he did. So if you're asking me if I blame Karen, the answer is no. The only thing I wish Karen would have done differently . . . is I wish she could have taken Les, too."

He wraps his arms around me and brings his mouth to my ear. "Whatever you decide. Whatever you feel will make your heart heal faster . . . that's what I want for you. That's what Les wants for you, too."

I hug him back and bury my head against his shoulder. "Thank you, Holder."

He holds me silently while I think about the decision that isn't even much of a decision anymore. After a while, I pull away from him and lift the box into my lap. I run my fingers across the top of it and hesitate before touching the latch. I press on it and slowly lift the lid as I close my eyes, hesitant to see what's inside it. I take a deep breath once the lid is lifted, then I open my eyes and peer down into the eyes of my mother. I pick the picture up between my trembling fingers, looking at a woman who could be no one else but the person who created me. From my mouth to my eyes to my cheekbones, I'm her. Every part of me is her.

I set the picture down and pick up the one beneath it. This one causes even more emotions to resurface, because it's a picture of both of us. I can't be older than two and I'm sitting in her lap with my arms wrapped around her neck. She's kissing me on the cheek and I'm staring at the camera with a smile bigger than life. Tears fall onto the picture in my hands, so I wipe them off and place the pictures in

Holder's hands. I need for him to see what I so desperately had to go back to my father's house for.

There's one more item in the box. I pick it up and lace the necklace through my fingers. It's a silver locket in the shape of a star. I snap it open and look at the picture of myself as an infant. Inscribed inside the locket on the side opposite the photo it says, "My ray of Hope."

I unclasp the necklace and bring it to the back of my neck. Holder reaches up and takes both clasps while I pull my hair up. He fastens it and I let my hair down, then he kisses the side of my head.

"She's beautiful. Just like her daughter." He hands the pictures back to me and kisses me gently. He looks down at my locket and opens it, then stares at it for several moments, smiling. He snaps it shut and looks back into my eyes. "Are you ready?"

I place the pictures back inside the box and shut the lid, then look back up at him confidently and nod. "I am."

Holder walks inside with me this time. Karen and Jack are on the couch and he has his arm around her, holding her hand. She looks up at me when I walk through the door and Jack stands up, preparing to give us privacy once again. "It's okay," I say to him. "You don't have to leave. This won't take long."

My words concern him, but he doesn't say anything in response. He walks a few feet away from Karen so that I can sit next to her on the couch. I place the box on the table in front of her, then take my seat. I turn toward her, knowing that she has no idea what her future holds for her. Despite the fact that she has no idea what choice I've made and what's going to happen to her, she still smiles at me reassuringly. She wants me to know that she's okay with whatever I chose.

I take her hands in mine and I look her directly in the eyes. I want her to feel and believe what I'm about to say to her, because I don't want there to be anything but truth between us.

"Mom," I say, regarding her with as much confidence as I can. "When you took me from my father, you knew the potential consequences of your decision, but you did it anyway. You risked your entire life just to save mine, and I could never ask for you to suffer because of that choice.

Giving up your life for me is more than I could ever ask of you. I'm not about to judge you for what you did. The only appropriate thing for me to do at this point . . . is to thank you. So, thank you. Thank you so much for saving my life, Mom."

Her tears are now falling even harder than my own. We wrap our arms around each other and we cry. We cry mother to daughter. We cry aunt to niece. We cry victim to victim. We cry survivor to survivor.

I can't begin to imagine the life that Karen has led the past thirteen years. Every choice she made was for my benefit alone. She had assumed once I turned eighteen, that she would confess what she did and would turn herself in to face the consequences. Knowing that she loves me enough that she would be willing to give her whole life up for me almost makes me feel unworthy, now that I know that two people in this world love me in that way. It's almost too much to accept.

It turns out Karen really does want to take the next step with Jack, but she was hesitant because she knew she would break his heart once he found out the truth. What she wasn't expecting is that Jack loves her unconditionally . . . the same way she loves me. Hearing her confess her past and the choices she had to make only made him more certain about his love for her. I'm guessing that his things will be completely moved in by next weekend.

Karen spends the evening patiently answering all of my questions. My main question was that I didn't understand how I could have a legal name and the documents to back it up. Karen laughed at that question and explained that, with enough money and the right connections, I was conveniently "adopted" from out of the country and obtained my citizenship when I was seven. I don't even ask her for the details, because I'm scared to know.

Another question I needed the answer to was the most obvious one . . . could we get a TV now. Turns out she doesn't despise technology nearly as much as she had to let on over the years. I have a feeling we'll be doing some shopping in the electronics department tomorrow.

Holder and I explained to Karen how he came to find out who I was. At first, she couldn't understand how we could have had such a strong connection at that young an age . . . strong enough for him to remember me. But after seeing us interact for a while longer, I think she's convinced that our connection is real now. Unfortunately, I can also see the concern in her eyes every time he leans in to kiss me or puts his hand on my leg. She is, after all, my mother.

After several hours pass and we've all reached the most peaceful point we can possibly reach after the weekend we've had, we call it a night. Holder and Jack tell us both good-bye and Holder assures Karen that he'll never again send me another ego-deflating text. He winks at me over her shoulder when he says it, though.

Karen hugs me more than I've ever been hugged in a single day. After her final hug for the night, I go to my room and crawl into my bed. I pull the covers up over me and lock my hands together behind my head, looking up at the stars on my ceiling. I contemplated tearing them down, thinking they would only serve to bring about more negative memories. I didn't remove them, though. I'm leaving them because now when I look at them, they remind me of Hope. They remind me of *me*, and everything I've had to overcome to get to this point in my life. And while I could sit here and feel sorry for myself, wondering why all of this happened to me . . . I'm not going to do it. I'm not going to wish for a perfect life. The things that knock you down in life are tests, forcing you to make a choice between giving in and remaining on the ground or wiping the dirt off and standing up even taller than you did *before* you were knocked down. I'm choosing to stand up taller. I'll probably get knocked down a few more times before this life is through with me, but I can guarantee you I'll never stay on the ground.

There's a light tap on my bedroom window right before it rises. I smile and scoot over to my side of the bed, waiting for him to join me.

"I don't get a greeting at the window tonight?" he says in a hushed voice, lowering the window behind him. He walks to his side of my bed and lifts the covers, then scoots in beside me.

"You're freezing," I say, snuggling into his arms. "Did you walk here?"

He shakes his head and squeezes me, then kisses my forehead. "No, I ran here." He slides one of his hands down to my butt. "It's been over a week since either of us has exercised. Your ass is starting to get really huge."

I laugh and hit him on the arm. "Try to remember, the insults are only funny in text form."

"Speaking of . . . does this mean you get your phone back?"

I shrug. "I don't really want that phone back. I'm hoping my whipped boyfriend will get me an iPhone for Christmas."

He laughs and rolls on top of me, meshing his ice-cold lips with mine. The contrasting temperatures of our mouths are enough to make him groan. He kisses me until his entire body is well above room temperature again. "You know what?" He pulls up on his elbows and peers down at me with his adorable, dimpled grin.

"What?"

His voice drops into that lyrical, godlike octave again. "We've never had sex in your bed."

I contemplate his thought for half a second, then shake my head and roll him onto his back. "And it will remain that way as long my mother is down the hall."

He laughs and grabs me by the waist and pulls me on top of him. I lay my head on his chest and he wraps his arms tightly around me.

"Sky?"

"Holder?" I mimic.

"I want you to know something," he says. "And I'm not saying this as your boyfriend or even as your friend. I'm saying this because it needs to be said by someone." He stops stroking my arm and he stills his hand on the center of my back. "I'm so proud of you."

I squeeze my eyes shut and swallow his words, sending them straight to my heart. He moves his lips to my hair and kisses me for either the first time or the twentieth time or the millionth time, but who's counting?

I hug him tighter and exhale. "Thank you." I lift my head up and rest my chin on his chest, looking up at him while he smiles back at me. "And it's not what you just said that I'm thanking you for, Holder. I need to thank you for everything. Thank you for giving me the courage to always ask the questions, even when I didn't want the answers. Thank you for loving me like you love me. Thank you for showing me that we don't always have to be strong to be there for each other—that it's okay to be weak, so long as we're *there*. And thank you for finally finding me after all these years." I trail my fingers across his chest until they reach his arm. I run them across each letter of his tattoo, then lean forward and press my lips to it and kiss it. "But mostly, thank you for losing me all those years ago . . . because my life wouldn't be the same if you had never walked away."

My body rises and falls against his huge intake of breath. He cups my face in his hands and he attempts to smile, but it doesn't reach his pain-filled eyes. "Out of all the times I imagined what it would be like if I ever found you . . . I never thought it would end with you thanking me for losing you."

"End?" I ask, disliking the term he chose. I lift up and kiss him briefly on the lips and pull back. "I hope this isn't our end."

"Hell no, this isn't our end," he says. He tucks a stray lock of hair behind my ear and keeps his hand there. "And I wish I could say we were about to live happily ever after, but I can't. We both still have so much to work through. With everything that's happened between you, me, your mother, your dad, and what I know happened to Les . . . there will be days that I don't think we'll know how to survive. But we will. We will, because we have each other. So, I'm not worried about us, babe. I'm not worried about us at all."

I kiss him on his dimple and smile. "I'm not worried about us either. And for the record, I don't believe in happily-ever-afters."

He laughs. "Good, because you're not really getting one. All you're getting is me."

"That's all I need," I say. "Well . . . I need the lamp. And the ashtray. And the remote control. And the paddle-ball game. And you, Dean Holder. But that's *all* I need."

Thirteen years earlier

"What's he doing out there?" I ask Lesslie, looking out the living room window at Dean. He's on his back in their driveway, looking up at the sky.

"He's stargazing," she says. "He does it all the time."

I turn around and look at her. "What's stargazing?"

She shrugs her shoulders. "I dunno. That's just what he calls it when he stares at the sky for a long time."

I look out the window again and watch him for a little longer. I don't know what stargazing is, but it sounds like something I would like. I love the stars. I know my mom loved them, too, because she put them all over my room. "I want to do it," I say. "Can we go do it, too?" I look back at her but she's taking off her shoes.

"I don't want to go. You can go and I'll help my mom get our popcorn and movie ready."

I like the days I get to have sleepovers with Lesslie. I like any days I don't have to be at home. I slide off the couch and walk to the front door to slip my shoes on, then walk outside and go lie next to Dean in the driveway. He doesn't even look at me when I lie down next to him. He just keeps looking up at the sky, so I do the same thing.

The stars are really bright tonight. I've never looked up at them like this before. They're so much prettier than the stars on my ceiling. "Wow. It's so beautiful."

"I know, Hope," he says. "I know."

It's quiet for a long time. I don't know if we watch the stars for lots of minutes or hours, but we keep watching them and we don't talk. Dean doesn't really talk a whole bunch. He's a lot quieter than Lesslie.

"Hope? Will you promise me something?"

I turn my head and look at him, but he's still looking up at the stars. I've never promised anyone anything before except my daddy. I had to promise him I wouldn't tell anyone how he makes me thank him and I haven't broken his promise, even though sometimes I wish I could. If I ever did break my daddy's promise, I would tell Dean because I know he would never tell anyone.

"Yes," I say to him.

He turns his head and looks at me, but his eyes look sad. "You know sometimes when your daddy makes you cry?"

I nod my head and try not to cry just thinking about it. I don't know how Dean knows that my daddy is always the reason why I'm crying, but he does.

"Will you promise me that when he makes you sad, you'll think about the sky?"

I don't know why he wants me to promise him that but I nod anyway. "But why?"

"Because." He turns his face back up to the stars. "The sky is always beautiful. Even when it's dark or rainy or cloudy, it's still beautiful to look at. It's my favorite thing because I know if I ever get lost or lonely or scared, I just have to look up and it'll be there no matter what . . . and I know it'll always be beautiful. It's what you can think about when your daddy is making you sad, so you don't have to think about him."

I smile, even though what we're talking about is making me sad. *I just keep looking up at the sky like Dean is, thinking about what he said. It makes my heart feel happy to have somewhere to go now when I don't want to be where I am. Now when I'm scared, I'll just think about the sky and maybe it'll help me smile, because I know it'll always be beautiful no matter what.*

"I promise," I whisper.

"Good," he says. He reaches his hand out and wraps his pinky around mine.

Acknowledgments

WHEN I WROTE MY first two novels, I didn't use beta readers or bloggers. (By ignorance, not choice.) I didn't even know what an ARC was.

Oh, how I wish I had.

Thank you to ALL bloggers who work so hard to share your love for reading. You are definitely the lifeline for authors, and we thank you for everything you do.

A very special thank you to Maryse, Tammara Webber, Jenny and Gitte with Totallybookedblog.com, Tina Reber, Tracey Garvis-Graves, Abbi Glines, Karly Blakemore-Mowle, Autumn with Autumnreview.com, Madison with Madisonsays.com, Molly Harper with Toughcriticbookreviews.com, Rebecca Donovan, Nichole Chase, Angie Stanton, Sarah Ross, Lisa Kane, Gloria Green, Cheri Lambert, Trisha Rai, Katy Perez, Stephanie Cohen, and Tonya Killian for taking the time to give me such detailed, incredibly helpful feedback. I know I annoyed the living hell out of most of you for the entire month of December, so thank you for putting up with my many, many, many "updated" files.

And ERMAGHERD! I can't thank you enough, Sarah Augustus Hansen. Not only for making me the most beautiful cover ever, but for granting my requests for millions of changes, only to end up going with your original suggestion. Your patience with me knows no bounds. For that, I'm declaring Holder yours. Okay.

For my husband, who insists he be listed in the acknowledgments of this book for suggesting that one word which helped me finish that one sentence in that one paragraph in that one scene. Without that word (it was *floodgates*, people) I don't think this book would have been completed. He requested I say that. But in a way he's right. Without the one word he suggested, the book more than likely would have moved along just fine. But without his support, enthusiasm, and encouragement, I could have never written a single word at all.

For my family (namely Lin, because she needs me more than anyone else). I don't really remember what everyone looks like and I'm having a hard time recalling most of your names, but now that this book is complete I vow to answer your phone calls, respond to your texts, look you in the eyes when you speak to me (rather than gazing off into the land of fiction), come to bed before four in the morning, and never, ever check an email while I'm on the phone with you again. Until I start writing my next book, anyway.

And for the three best children in the whole wide world. I miss the living hell out of y'all. And yes, boys . . . Mommy just cussed. *Again.*

About the Author

COLLEEN HOOVER is the *New York Times* bestselling author of three novels: *Slammed*, *Point of Retreat*, and *Hopeless*. She lives in Texas with her husband and their three boys. To read more about this author, visit her website at www.colleenhoover.com.

If you or someone you know needs assistance/information regarding sexual abuse, please contact www.rainn.org or call 1-800-656-HOPE.

For your local suicide hotline number, please visit www.suicidehotlines.com, http://www.suicidepreventionlifeline.com or call 800-273-TALK.

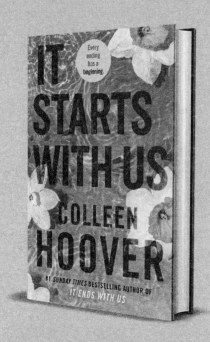
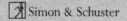